TRUTH or DARE

ALSO BY
JAYNE ANN KRENTZ

Light in Shadow
Summer in Eclipse Bay
Smoke in Mirrors
Dawn in Eclipse Bay
Lost & Found
Eclipse Bay
Soft Focus
Eye of the Beholder
Flash
Sharp Edges
Deep Waters
Absolutely, Positively
Trust Me
Grand Passion
Hidden Talents
Wildest Heart
Family Man
Perfect Partners
Sweet Fortune
Silver Linings
The Golden Chance

BY JAYNE ANN KRENTZ
WRITING AS JAYNE CASTLE

Harmony
After Dark
Amaryllis
Zinnia
Orchid

A
Whispering
Springs
Novel

TRUTH or DARE

Jayne Ann Krentz

Doubleday Large Print Home Library Edition

G. P. PUTNAM'S SONS

New York

This Large Print Edition, prepared especially for Doubleday Large Print Home Library, contains the complete, unabridged text of the original Publisher's Edition.

G. P. Putnam's Sons
Publishers Since 1838
a member of
Penguin Group (USA) Inc.
375 Hudson Street
New York, NY 10014

Published simultaneously in Canada

ISBN 0-7394-4038-1

Printed in the United States of America

To my brother, James Castle, with much love.
Thanks so much for the help with the GFI-PI!

TRUTH or DARE

1

He hated cases that ended the way this one was going to end. Ethan Truax closed the file folder and placed his hands on the small round table. He regarded the man sitting in the undersized hotel room chair across from him.

"You're sure these numbers are solid?" he asked neutrally.

"Absolutely." Dexter Morrow smiled his reassuring investment adviser's smile. It did nothing to conceal the calculating expression in his eyes. "I took them straight off Katherine's personal laptop last night after she went to sleep."

"You did say that you were close to the boss."

Morrow chuckled. It was the kind of man-to-man laugh that you heard in locker rooms and bars. "*Real* close. I can tell you from personal experience that she's almost as good in bed as she is at running her company."

Ethan managed to keep his face expressionless but it was not easy. He was here to get the job done for the client, not to defend her honor.

Outside the window the Arizona sun shone down on the hotel's blue-tiled pool and lounge area. It was warm and bright, the kind of day that made the state famous. But in here there was a chill in the air, and it was not coming from the air conditioner.

Morrow casually cocked one ankle on his knee. The collar of his pricey, cream-colored polo shirt was edged with a thin black stripe. The shirt complemented the designer-label trousers and Euro-leather loafers. A gold Swiss watch gleamed on his wrist.

Dexter Morrow had it made. He worked in a plush office, played golf in the middle of the week and entertained his clients in expensive places such as the Desert View

Country Club. He was a winner here in Whispering Springs.

Ethan was about to take it all away from him.

"All right," Ethan said quietly, more than ready for the endgame. "We've got a deal."

Morrow glanced at the aluminum-sided suitcase that sat on the floor beside Ethan's chair. "You brought the cash?"

"Small bills, as agreed." Ethan reached down, grasped the handle of the suitcase and shoved it across the carpet toward Morrow.

In a world where money could be transferred around the globe in the blink of an eye with computers, hard cash in a suitcase was still the transfer method of choice for those who did not want to leave any electronic tracks for the Feds or the SEC to uncover.

Morrow picked up the suitcase and hoisted it onto the table. Ethan could tell that he was trying to appear cool but he was not doing a very good job of it. Morrow's fingers shook a little when he unsnapped the locks. The guy was excited.

Morrow raised the lid and looked at the stacks of neatly banded bills. Near-feverish anticipation radiated from him in heavy waves that in another man might have been mistaken for a sick lust.

"You want to count it?" Ethan asked softly.

"That would take too long. I've got to get back to the office. I don't want anyone to start asking questions." Morrow reached into the suitcase. "I'll just do a random check."

Ethan got to his feet and put some distance between himself and the table. You never knew how a man would react when he realized he'd been cornered.

Morrow riffled through a stack of crisply cut blank paper bundled beneath the single real twenty-dollar bill. For a couple of seconds he did not appear to understand what had happened. Then comprehension struck. His tanned face flushed a dark red. He swung around to face Ethan.

"What the hell is going on here?" he snarled.

The bathroom door opened. Katherine Compton walked out.

"I was just about to ask you the same question, Dex," she said. Her voice was flat with controlled anger. Her handsome features were tight and drawn. "But that would be a waste of time, wouldn't it? I already know the answer. You just tried to sell those confidential bid figures to Mr. Truax."

Something that might have been panic flickered across Morrow's face. "He said his name was Williams."

"It's Truax," Ethan said. "Ethan Truax of Truax Investigations."

Morrow's hands clenched and unclenched at his sides. He appeared to be having difficulty connecting the dots. "You're a private investigator?"

"Yes," Ethan said.

He was a little surprised by Morrow's stunned expression. The guy had a history of scams like this one. You'd think he'd be accustomed to having things go wrong once in a while. It wasn't like he was in any real jeopardy here, and he had to know that. Employers almost never prosecuted in these situations. They didn't want the negative publicity.

"I hired Ethan last week when I started to get suspicious of you, Dex," Katherine said.

Morrow spread his hands in a pleading gesture. "Darling, you don't understand."

"Unfortunately, I do," she said. "I understand everything. You certainly made a fool out of me for a while, but it's over."

Morrow glanced briefly at Ethan. Rage darkened his face. He turned back to Katherine. "You've got it all wrong. You're making a huge mistake here."

"No," Katherine said.

"Listen to me. I knew there was a leak and I knew that it was very close to you. I was trying to identify the bastard who was screwing you."

"You were the bastard who was screwing me," Katherine said.

"That's not true. I love you. I was trying to protect you. When Truax put out feelers letting me know that he was in the market for those bid figures, I thought I'd finally gotten a lead on who was behind the inside leaks. I'm here because I wanted to set him up so that I could get him to spill some information. I was playing him."

"Don't worry," Katherine said. "I'm not going to file charges. A court case would hurt the company. We're all about trust and long-term business relationships at Compton Investments." She smiled thinly. "But then, you already know that, don't you, Dex? After all, you've worked for me for nearly a year."

"Katherine, you've got this all wrong."

"You can go now," she said. "A security

guard will meet you at the office. He'll stay with you while you clean out your desk, and then he'll take your keys and escort you out of the building. You know the drill. Standard procedure in situations like this. No one will be told why you were let go. I'm sure that everyone in the firm is aware that you and I were involved. The assumption will be made that we ended our personal relationship. Whenever that sort of thing happens, it is always the lower-ranking executive who leaves the firm, isn't it?"

"Katherine, you can't do this to us."

"I'm not doing it to *us*. I'm doing it to you. Speaking of keys, I'll take back the one to my front door that I gave you a few months ago. You won't be needing it anymore." She held out her hand, palm up.

"I'm telling you, you're making a mistake." Morrow sounded hoarse now.

"No, I'm correcting the one I made when I got involved with you. My key, please." Her tone sharpened without warning. "Now."

Morrow actually flinched. Ethan was impressed by the speed with which he got the gold key chain out of his pocket.

Morrow fumbled the key off the ring and tossed it to Katherine.

"I'll have the locks changed, just to be on the safe side, of course." Katherine dropped the key into her purse. "This morning after you left I packed up the things you've been keeping at my place for the past few months. The spare shirts and the razor and such. I dropped them off at your condo."

Morrow's face worked furiously. He looked at Ethan. "This is your fault, you son of a bitch. You'll regret it, I promise you that much."

Ethan took the tiny digital recorder out of his pocket. They all looked at it. Without a word he switched it off.

Morrow's jaw locked when he understood that the threat had been recorded. Without saying another word, he picked up his briefcase, his grip so fierce it squeezed the blood out of his knuckles.

He went to the door, opened it and let himself out of the hotel room.

There was a short silence. The room seemed to exhale deeply on a long sigh.

Katherine did not take her gaze off the door. "Do you think he meant that threat he made to you, Ethan?"

"Don't worry about it." Ethan went to the table, picked up the packet of phony twenties and tossed it back into the suitcase. "Guys like Morrow prefer not to take the risk of getting physical. When they get caught, they disappear as fast as possible. He'll be out of town by this time tomorrow. Day after at the latest. In a couple of weeks he'll be set up somewhere else, working on his next scam."

She grimaced. "I'm not doing the world any favors by letting him go without bringing charges, am I?"

"Not your job to do the world a favor," he said without inflection. "You've got a responsibility to your company and your clients. It's a tough call."

"No," she said without hesitation, "it's not. The company comes first. We're in the middle of some extremely delicate negotiations. Between the three branches of Compton Investments here in Whispering Springs and in the Phoenix area, I've got over fifty employees and hundreds of clients who will be directly affected by this deal. I've got an obligation to all of them."

Spoken like the real CEO she is, he thought.

Katherine shook her head, looking weary now that it was all over. "I never thought I'd ever get taken in like that by a man, you know. I was always so sure of myself and my instincts. So sure that I could spot a phony."

"You did spot Morrow." He closed the lid of the case and snapped it shut. "That's why you picked up the phone and called me, remember?"

She was startled by that observation. After contemplating it for a moment, she nodded once, acknowledging the truth of the statement.

"Yes, I did call you, didn't I?" She walked resolutely toward the door. "Thank you for reminding me of that salient fact, Mr. Truax. In all the excitement, I had forgotten that I was the one who finally realized that there was something a little too good to be true about Dexter Morrow."

Ethan followed her out into the hall and closed the door. "Your instincts were working just fine."

"I was actually thinking of marrying him, you know."

Ethan nodded.

"It would have been my second marriage," she added.

Ethan nodded again. He stopped in front of the elevators and pressed the call button.

"My first husband married me because he wanted to get his hands on my father's company," Katherine continued. "When he realized that I was the heir apparent and that I intended to run Compton myself, he filed for divorce."

Ethan prayed to the hotel gods in the vain hope that the elevator doors would open quickly. He understood the client's need to talk after it was all over. He usually made it a point to listen patiently. He considered the debriefing part of the job. But today he just wanted to be done. A bone-deep weariness was creeping through him.

The adrenaline rush that generally accompanied the satisfactory resolution of a case had not hit him back there in the hotel room. Maybe that was because he had not been sleeping well lately.

He knew the reason for the insomnia. It was November. November was a bad time. If the past two years were anything to go by, he would not sleep well again until December.

Mercifully, the elevator doors opened. Katherine moved inside ahead of him.

"Have you ever been married?" she asked.

"Oh, yeah," Ethan said.

Her brow climbed. "Divorced?"

"Three times."

She frowned. He was not surprised. One or two divorces were acceptable in this sophisticated day and age. There were excuses that could be made. Three, however, raised questions concerning possible innate character flaws.

"Are you married now?" Katherine asked.

He thought about Zoe waiting for him at home. He summoned up the image of her sitting across from him at breakfast that morning, vibrant and vivid in an amethyst-colored pantsuit. He remembered how the morning sun streaming through the window had touched off sparks in her dark auburn hair and how she had looked at him with her mysterious, smoky eyes. His woman; his wife.

The mental picture was a talisman that he carried against the dark forces of November that swirled around him. But part of him dreaded the future because he was pretty sure that sooner or later those forces would triumph and drive Zoe away from him.

He punched the lobby button.

"Sort of," he said.

2

It had been a good day. She had not encountered any screaming walls.

For the vast majority of interior designers, "screaming walls" implied an unfortunate choice of paint color or a really bad window treatment. But for a *psychic* designer who happened to be acutely sensitive to the invisible aura left in rooms that had been scenes of violence or strong passions, the term "screaming walls" could be interpreted quite literally.

She had not set out in life with the intent of becoming an interior designer, Zoe reflected as she poured two glasses of wine. Her original plan had been to pursue a career as an art curator. But the murder of her first husband had changed everything.

She was the first to admit that she had lost control for a time following Preston's death. What could she say? She had been a desperate woman. The cops had concluded that Preston had been shot by a transient burglar. The instant she had stepped into the cottage where the murder occurred she knew that was not what had happened. The walls had screamed bloody murder.

In her passion to see justice done, she had made the near-fatal mistake of telling everyone who would listen that Preston had been killed by someone close to him. In a desperate attempt to convince her scheming in-laws that one of them was to blame, she had told them that she could sense the terrible rage that the murderer had felt clinging to the walls of the cottage.

Big mistake.

Her wild claims of psychic talents had given her in-laws the excuse they needed to have her committed against her will to a very private, very exclusive psychiatric hospital. She knew that she was not insane when she had entered the place, but the ordeal of her stay there had very nearly turned the phony diagnosis into a reality. To this day, she still had nightmares in which she walked the halls of Candle Lake Manor.

Zoe put the two glasses of wine on a tray together with a plate of cheese and crackers. She picked up the tray and carried it out into the living room of her small apartment.

Ethan was on the sofa, leaning forward slightly, legs apart, elbows resting on his thighs. He wore a black crew-neck tee shirt and khaki pants. He held the remote loosely in one hand, absently clicking through the early evening news programs.

She remembered her first impression of him that memorable day six weeks before in October when she had walked into his second-floor office on Cobalt Street. The interior designer in her had taken one look at him and concluded that he had a lot in common with his furniture: well-used and a little worn around the edges but definitely heirloom quality because of the solid, old-fashioned construction.

This was the kind of man who finished what he started; the kind who did not quit until the job was done. You'd have to kill him to stop him, and she did not think that would be easy.

The strong, solid, reliable part was okay, she had decided. What had worried her at the beginning were his eyes. They were amber-brown, enigmatic and intelligent; the eyes of a top-of-the-food-chain predator.

Their quickie Las Vegas wedding had been intended only as a short-term strategy to protect her from her wealthy relatives, who had a strong financial motive for seeing her dead. The decision to give the marriage a real try had come later, after all the excitement of nearly getting murdered had faded.

They had agreed to take things slowly; after all, they were well aware that each of them had brought a lot of baggage into this arrangement. It was a good bet that any reputable counselor or therapist would have advised against the marriage, and not just because it had been carried out in such haste.

Zoe wouldn't have blamed the professionals. The odds against a successful, stable relationship between an escapee from a psychiatric hospital and a man who had been married and divorced three times had to be somewhere in the vicinity of astronomically bad.

Added to those negatives was Ethan's opinion of psychics. It had been formed in the wake of his brother's murder, when a charlatan who claimed to see visions had convinced Ethan's sister-in-law, Bonnie, that her husband was still alive. The emotional pain caused by the phony had been nothing short of devastating. Ethan's vengeful fury had been white-hot. Bonnie had confided to Zoe that she was amazed that the fraudulent psychic had survived Ethan's wrath.

And just to top it off, Ethan had once had a very bad experience with an interior designer.

But in spite of all the reasons why the marriage was probably doomed at the outset, Zoe thought, she and Ethan had decided to fling caution to the wind and take their chances. Probably because both of them had had a lot of experience with taking risks.

Up until the first of November she had convinced herself that they were going to win the big cosmic bet—they were going to make it. She had even invested in a new set of vibrant, chili-red dishes.

For the first couple of weeks of their odd

marriage, they had shifted naturally and easily into a pattern that she would have described as "domestic" were it not for the fact that it was difficult to use that word when talking about Ethan. He was a lot of things, including smart, sexy and strong-willed, but he definitely did not invoke the sort of warm, cozy images implied by the term "domestic."

Although she had kept her apartment at Casa de Oro, the two of them had spent every night together, usually out at Nightwinds, Ethan's pink monstrosity of a home. All the building blocks of a solid, stable relationship appeared to be coming together. They were learning to work around each other in the kitchen. They had discovered that they were both early risers. Neither of them left their clothes on the floor. They both showered daily. What more could you ask for at the start of a marriage?

But things had changed with the advent of November. She sensed that Ethan was pulling back, putting some distance between them. He seemed restless and moody. She knew he wasn't sleeping well. The silences between them were no longer comfortable or companionable and there were more of them. He avoided her attempts to get him to talk about whatever it was that was bothering him.

It was as if they were involved in an affair rather than a marriage, she thought; an affair that was headed for the rocks.

Maybe it had been a mistake to start remodeling Nightwinds so soon. The decision to repaint had forced them to vacate the big house with its multiple bathrooms and large living spaces and move into her tiny apartment. Here there was only one bath and no place where either of them could go to be alone for a while.

She told herself that housing Ethan in this small, cramped space was akin to keeping a lion in a cage at the zoo. You had to expect that there would be some issues.

"How did Katherine Compton handle the final scene this afternoon?" she asked, setting the tray down on the coffee table.

"She wasn't happy about having her suspicions confirmed, but she was pretty cool about it." Ethan clicked off the TV and set the remote down next to the tray. He picked up one of the glasses. "The hardest part for her is dealing with the fact that she allowed Dexter Morrow to get past her defenses. She told me that she felt like she'd been a fool."

Zoe curled herself into the corner of the sofa and rested one arm along the back. "I can understand that. What did you say to her?"

He shrugged. "I reminded her that she was the one who called me and asked me to investigate Morrow. Whatever else she is, Katherine Compton is no fool. It may have taken her a while to face the problem, but in the end she took care of it like the gutsy executive she is. She'll be okay."

"What about you?"

He had been about to take a swallow of wine but he paused, the glass a few inches from his mouth. "What about me?"

"This case seems to have gone very well. You said yourself that it was fairly routine."

"It was." He drank some wine and lowered the glass. "Morrow was greedy. When he started to smell the cash I was offering, he got careless."

"If it was all so cut and dried, why is it bothering you so much?"

For a few seconds she thought that he was not going to answer her.

"Damned if I know," he said finally.

She smiled slightly. "You know what I think?"

"No, but you're going to tell me, aren't you?"

"Of course. I consider it my duty as your wife, and you know how strongly I feel about the importance of communication in a marriage."

"Uh-huh."

"I think that, at heart, you're a romantic," she said gently.

He winced. "Bullshit."

"You had problems with this case because you knew that, in the end, your client was going to get hurt."

"Clients get bad news from me all the time. Katherine wasn't the first and she won't be the last."

"I know, but that doesn't mean that you like that part of the job or that you find it easy."

He took another swallow of wine and settled into the opposite corner of the sofa. "You think maybe I'm in the wrong line of work?"

She nearly dropped the cracker she had just picked up off the plate. Her first thought was that he was joking. Then she saw his eyes.

"No," she said. "I think you're doing the kind of work that you were born to do, the only kind that you can do."

"Yeah?"

"Yours is a calling, Ethan."

In spite of his obviously grim mood, his mouth twitched a little at the corner. "That's got to be the one and only time in the entire history of the world that anyone referred to the private investigation business as a calling."

"In your case it's the simple truth. Tell me about what happened in that hotel room today."

He ate a cracker with some cheese, took another swallow of wine and then started to talk. She listened while he described how he had lured Dexter Morrow to the room and how Katherine Compton had insisted on hiding in the bathroom against his recommendation.

"My biggest concern was that Morrow would want to use the facilities before I got him to implicate himself," Ethan said. "But I understood why she needed to be there so I agreed to let her wait in the bathroom. Luckily everything went smoothly. Like I said, Morrow was greedy. He didn't want to waste any time. But I sure as hell didn't offer him a beer or a bottle of water."

"Good thinking."

"Thanks. I was pretty proud of that bit of strategy, myself."

He talked some more, eventually following her into the kitchen to finish his story. He lounged in the doorway, drinking his wine and watching while she put the finishing touches on the vegetable curry she had prepared.

Like a real husband. The thought lifted her spirits.

There was one aspect of the tale that worried her.

"You're sure that Morrow won't be a problem?" she asked while she scooped the rice out of the rice maker and piled it into one of the new chili-red bowls. "He must blame you for ruining his cushy setup there at Compton."

"I told Katherine that guys like Morrow don't hang around once the con goes sour, and that's the truth. He'll cut his losses and take off."

Ethan sat down at the table. He examined the array of little side dishes containing curry condiments with what appeared to be real enthusiasm. Her spirits rose a little higher. Ethan's sister-in-law, Bonnie, swore by the old saying that the way to a man's heart was through his stomach. Maybe she was right.

Zoe put the platter of fragrant curry and the bowl of rice on the table. "Do you think

Morrow felt anything at all for Katherine Compton?"

"Whatever it was, it wasn't strong enough to prevent him from betraying her for a couple hundred thousand bucks."

"Obviously." She got the salad out of the refrigerator, set it on the table and sat down across from him. "What a shame that Katherine was genuinely in love with Morrow."

"She wasn't blindly in love." Ethan picked up the half-finished bottle of wine and refilled their glasses. "When she realized what was going on, she did what she had to do."

"Guess that's why she's a successful CEO of her own company."

"Guess so." Ethan ladled curry over the small mountain of rice he had put on his plate and helped himself to peanuts, raisins and chutney from the little dishes. "She also has the distinction of being my first major business client here in Whispering Springs, for which I am profoundly grateful."

"Correction, I was your first major business client." She glowered. "I'm crushed that you could forget a thing like that."

"You were my first *private* client. Big difference."

"You're sure?"

"I'm sure. And believe me, I have not forgotten anything about your case."

"Probably hard to forget a case when you end up marrying the client," she said.

"This is true."

She did not know where to go with that. It occurred to her that this was the second time within the hour that she had found a way to slip a reference to their marital status into the conversation. The first had occurred out in the other room, when she had made it clear that she felt it was her duty as his wife to give him her opinion, and now this unsubtle comment about marrying his first client.

Ethan got a reflective expression. "This feels weird."

She froze. "The curry?"

"Not the curry. The curry is great. I meant that it feels weird to talk about a case after it's all over the way I'm doing this evening."

She tensed, vaguely defensive. "You don't have to talk about it if you don't want to."

"No, it's okay. I'm just not used to it, that's all."

She relaxed slightly. "Ethan, it's what married people do."

"Yeah?" He gave her a wry smile. "I never did it with any of my former wives."

"Why not?"

"Probably because none of them was interested. Let's face it, most of the stuff a PI does sounds pretty boring when you try to explain it to someone else. Ninety percent of my job is handled on the phone and the computer."

"But it's not boring to you, right?" she asked.

"No. But then, it's what I do."

"If it doesn't bore you," she said patiently, "it doesn't bore me."

"You're sure?"

"Positive."

"Okay, so much for my day." Ethan forked up a bite of curry. "How was yours?"

"Not nearly so exciting. I spent the morning in my library at the Designers' Dream Home. I think it's finally coming together."

The invitation to participate in the annual Designers' Dream Home project had been a coup for her and her one-person interior design firm, Enhanced Interiors. A committee had selected a newly completed, high-end Whispering Springs residence to be the model home. The same committee had chosen a handful of local designers to finish the project. She had been one of the lucky few.

Each designer had been assigned a room and asked to create a dream space. She had gotten the library.

The project had chewed up far more of her time than she had anticipated, but she told herself it would be worth it. In addition to being a profitable fund-raiser for Whispering Springs charities, the Designers' Dream Home focused invaluable attention on those designers selected to work on it. When it was completed there would be media coverage and public tours. The various rooms and their creators were slated to be photographed for a major southwestern lifestyle magazine.

"Lindsey Voyle give you any more trouble?" Ethan asked.

Lindsey Voyle, an interior designer who had recently opened a business in town, was the only fly in the show house project ointment, in Zoe's opinion. Their professional styles were one hundred and eighty degrees apart, but that was not the real problem. The chief issue was that, from the moment they had been introduced, Lindsey Voyle had exuded an inexplicable, thinly veiled hostility toward her.

She wrinkled her nose, aware that Ethan

found the rivalry between Lindsey and her amusing.

"Lindsey was at the show house when I went there today." She reached for the bowl of mango chutney. "She had the nerve to give me advice on my feng shui technique. She said that I had created a bad energy flow by my use of too much intense color."

"Bad energy flow, huh? Sounds scary."

She reminded herself that Ethan also found the concept of designing proper energy flows in a room or a workspace extremely humorous.

"Lindsey claims that she took a workshop from a feng shui master in LA and knows all of the basic principles," Zoe said.

"What did you tell her?"

"Not what I felt like telling her, that's for sure. I just said that my design style wasn't pure feng shui. I explained that I use elements of several different design philosophies—some ancient, some new—to create positive energy flow in a space." Zoe spooned more chutney on her curry. "I made it clear that I rely on my own sense of a space for ideas and inspiration, not the rules of a particular school of design."

Ethan raised his brows. "You told her that

you believe you're psychic when it comes to getting a feel for a room?"

"Of course not. She already thinks that I'm a half-baked professional with no real sense of color or style. I didn't want her to spread the word that I'm a complete flake."

He nodded. "Probably be bad for business."

"There's a fine line between being known as a fashionable designer who uses the principles of feng shui and getting a reputation as a phony who is into the woo-woo thing."

"I can see that."

"Forget Lindsey Voyle. The less said about her the better. The sort of good news today is that I got a phone call from Tabitha Pine."

"Speaking of complete flakes," Ethan said around a mouthful of salad.

She frowned. "There is nothing flaky about teaching meditation techniques. A lot of people find them very useful for stress reduction. There's scientific evidence that meditation can lower blood pressure and anxiety levels."

"I'll stick with my own tried-and-true method of stress reduction."

"What's that?"

"Sex."

"Regardless of your opinion of meditation as a stress-reducing therapy, it so happens that teaching the techniques can be quite profitable. Tabitha Pine recently bought a very large, very high-end estate just outside of town. She wants the interior completely redone with the goal of maximizing the flow of positive energy."

"Right up your alley. Congratulations. I can see it now, Zoe Truax, the designer of choice for gurus everywhere. Pine sounds like an ideal client."

"Not quite." Zoe sighed. "Not yet, at any rate. Turns out she wants to see proposals from me and someone else before she chooses her designer."

"I'm getting a bad feeling about this."

"Guess who else was asked to draw up a proposal?"

"Lindsey Voyle?"

"Yep."

"Oh, man, this could get ugly," Ethan said. "We could be looking at dueling designers meeting at high noon in the middle of Fountain Square for a showdown. What will it be? Measuring tapes at twenty paces? Fabric swatches at ten?"

"I'm glad you find this entertaining."

He chuckled. "Honey, my money is on you. When it comes to designing positive energy flow, nobody does it better."

"I do not want any wisecracks from you, Truax. Just because you don't buy into the concept of enlightened interior design, that doesn't mean that the people who do buy into it are complete wack jobs."

Ethan managed to look deeply offended. "I would never call the folks who pay you actual money to rebalance the psychic energy in their homes wack jobs."

"What would you call them?"

"Clients," he said smoothly.

She gave him an approving nod. "Right answer."

"I learn fast." He turned serious. "But are you sure you really want to do Tabitha Pine's house? Given this guru gig of hers, she probably has some strong opinions about energy flows. Could be frustrating to work with her."

"I enjoy clients who have definite notions about what they like and dislike. Their ideas sometimes make me see things in a different light. It's always challenging to design for strong-minded people, and I learn something when I do it."

"I have plenty of strong opinions about what you've got planned for Nightwinds, but you never call my ideas challenging. Mostly we argue about them."

She thought about their latest discussion regarding Nightwinds. The old mansion was an over-the-top, flaming-pink, Hollywood-esque version of a Mediterranean-style villa. Ethan had more or less inherited it from his uncle because no realtor in Whispering Springs had been able to sell it.

"Not true." She gave him her most polished, professional smile, the one she reserved for difficult clients who needed extreme guidance. "As a client, you are always a challenge."

"But?"

"But if I let you have your way you'd have nothing but plain white walls and recliners in every room at Nightwinds."

"That is a gross exaggeration." A gotcha gleam lit his eyes. "I don't need recliners in the bathrooms."

"Are you sure?"

He hesitated, dark brows tightening a little as he contemplated the question. "Well, now that you mention it . . ."

She held up a hand, palm out. "Don't go there, Truax."

He shrugged. "Probably wouldn't fit, anyway."

"Probably not."

She watched him work his way through the curry and salad and decided that some of the tension in him had eased. But she could still sense the dark currents shifting under the surface. Whatever was going on with Ethan, she was pretty sure that it involved something deeper and more disturbing than the less-than-happy ending of the Dexter Morrow case.

She heard the muted hum of Ethan's electric shaver when she went past the bathroom door. Earlier she had heard the shower running. She stopped in the middle of the hall and stood thinking for a long moment.

Then she made up her mind. Tightening the sash of her robe, she opened the door. Warm, steamy air enveloped her. Ethan stood in front of the mirror, a towel wrapped negligently around his waist. She had a sudden urge to run her palms along the sleekly muscled contours of his back.

He looked at her through the fog that cloaked the mirror. She caught her breath when she saw that the brooding, enigmatic shadows had returned to his tiger eyes.

"You don't have to shave before you come to bed anymore," she said, trying to keep her tone light. "We're married now, remember?"

Okay, was that the third or fourth time she'd managed to use the *M* word this evening? She had lost count.

He switched off the razor and set it very deliberately on the counter. "I remember."

She could have sworn that the temperature in the small, intimate room rose several degrees. She was suddenly transported into the tropics. A sultry, sensual awareness tingled through her.

Given his odd mood, she thought, maybe opening the bathroom door had not been such a good idea.

But it was too late to change her mind. Ethan was moving through the steamy mist, closing in on her with that supple, controlled energy that was so much a part of him.

When he reached her, he caught her face between his hands, fingers sinking into her hair. His mouth closed over hers. The fierce, hot urgency emanating from him made her tremble in response.

His kiss was compelling and demanding. It transformed the tingles of awareness into snapping, arcing, sizzling electrical impulses. Every nerve in her body lit up. She hoped she was not actually glowing.

Ethan worked the kiss, tasting her, wooing her, summoning the response he wanted—no, *needed*—from her. His powerful hands moved down to her waist. He unknotted the sash that bound her robe and slipped the garment off her shoulders. It fell to the floor, pooling at her feet. Her nightgown was next.

When she was naked, he wrapped his arms around her and pulled her close, holding her so tightly she could scarcely move. Excitement flooded through her veins.

With a soft little murmur of pleasure and anticipation, she clung to him, her fingers biting into his sleekly muscled shoulders. Her breasts were crushed into the curling hair of his chest.

The towel that had encircled his waist disappeared. She felt his erection, heavy and hard, pushing against her bare thigh. In spite of the gathering storm of passion, a flutter of unease drifted, ghost-like, through her.

There was something a little off here.

Although Ethan's mood had lightened for a time during dinner and afterward, the bleak, edgy quality was back. He was channeling that dark energy, either consciously or unconsciously, into raw, sexual hunger.

This was not the first time he had made love to her while in the grip of this dangerous mood during the past several days. What had he said at dinner? Something about sex being his stress-reduction technique of choice.

Perhaps "dangerous" was not quite the right word to describe the blaze she sensed burning in him. She certainly did not fear for her own personal safety. Ethan would never hurt her. But she knew that he was using sex as a temporary antidote for some poison that was attacking his spirit.

What really worried her was that she was quite sure that a few good orgasms were not going to effect a permanent cure for whatever it was that ailed him.

His hands closed around her waist, lifting her off her feet. She assumed that he was going to carry her out of the tropics and into the bedroom. Instead he swung her around and set her down on the counter next to the sink.

She drew a startled breath when the cool tiles made contact with her bare buttocks, but before she could grasp the fact that she and Ethan were not headed for the bed, he had moved between her legs.

She could feel his desire beating at her, a hot desert wind.

"The shower and the shave were supposed to slow me down." He touched her clitoris, stroking slowly. "You shouldn't have interrupted."

"It's okay." She was already damp. Reaching down she took him in her fingers. "You don't have to go slow. Not every time. Sometimes fast is good."

"For me, maybe, not for you. I want it to be good for you."

"Ethan, it's okay." She drew him closer, brushing the broad head of his heavily engorged penis against the damp opening of her body, doing everything she could to tempt him. "You don't have to always be in control. Not with me."

He groaned. Every muscle in his body tightened.

"Zoe."

He gripped her thighs and pushed himself into her, driving deep and hard. She wrapped her legs around his waist and held him tightly while he hurtled toward his climax and whatever brief peace it would give him.

3

Arcadia Ames came awake riding a rush of nerve-screaming adrenaline. She opened her eyes, listening intently, shivering with reaction. Heart pounding, she tried to breathe slowly but it was impossible. She needed air.

Nothing moved in the darkness of her bedroom. There was enough moonlight to show her that the corners were empty. No one stood over her bed. No menacing figure loomed in the doorway. There was no telltale brush of footsteps from the living room or the kitchen.

All the available evidence reported by her eyes and ears assured her that the sophisticated security system Harry had installed had not been tripped. She was alone in the condominium.

But the sensation of being watched was so strong that she could not ignore it. Frustration and dread mingled inside her.

What was wrong with her lately? She'd had this weird feeling several times in the past couple of days, and tonight it was really bad. Maybe those months she had spent in Candle Lake Manor Psychiatric Hospital had affected her more than she had realized.

She had deliberately had herself committed to the loony bin as one step in a master plan she had devised to hide from her husband. Grant had wanted her dead. She had figured that he would never think to look for her in a private asylum.

But Candle Lake Manor had proven to be a disastrous choice. It had been run by a corrupt administrator who had allowed the thug-like orderlies to have the run of the place after hours.

Much of the late-night activity was relatively harmless. Some of the orderlies had sold drugs from the hospital's supply room. Others had zoned out on the stolen meds. Most had just napped. But a few of the brutes had amused themselves raping the helpless, doped-up female patients.

The only good thing that had come out of her time at Candle Lake was her friendship with Zoe. The two of them had plotted their escape together. They had been forced to carry it out ahead of schedule because one night two of the vicious orderlies had come for Arcadia. She shivered at the memory of the attempted rape. If Zoe hadn't heard the men taking her down the hall to the examination room that night . . .

No. Don't go there. There was no reason to fear anyone at Candle Lake Manor. Ethan had pretty much wiped the hospital off the map last month.

The only thing she had to fear was Grant.

The bastard was supposed to be dead, but she knew him too well to believe in that very convenient skiing accident in Switzerland. His body had never been found, supposedly buried under untold tons of snow. But her intuition told her that he had faked his own death and was now living under an assumed name somewhere.

Just as she was doing.

Very slowly she extended one arm, reached down and found the pistol that she always kept beneath the bed at night whenever Harry was away. The feel of the grip in her hand was somewhat reassuring. After the escape from Candle Lake, she and Zoe had each taken steps to acquire a greater sense of security. Zoe had signed up for self-defense lessons.

Knowing that Grant might someday decide to return from the grave, Arcadia had opted to buy a gun and had learned how to use it.

Pistol in hand, she slid her legs out from under the white sheets, got to her feet and went to the doorway to look down the hall. The light that was always on in the living room cast a gentle glow across the white carpet and the pale furnishings. None of the familiar shadows shifted.

She went forward cautiously, the silver-gray silk nightgown drifting around her ankles. When she reached the bank of electrical switches, she flipped all of them at once, illuminating every room of the condo, including the closets.

Methodically she checked every lock and every alarm on every window and the front door. When she was certain that all was secure, she turned off the lights again and went to stand at the window. She had deliberately chosen a condo on the second floor, not only because she thought it would be harder for someone to crawl through a window, but also because it gave her a better view of the pool and garden in the center of the complex.

She looked out into the desert night. In common with Sedona and several other Arizona communities, Whispering Springs did not have a lot of streetlights. Officially the idea was that heavy illumination of the residential and commercial neighborhoods interfered with the citizens' and tourists' enjoyment of the glorious nighttime skies. Arcadia suspected that was an excuse. She had a hunch that the local governments liked the notion of saving money on electricity bills. The good people of Arizona were not real keen on taxes.

The homeowners' association to which she belonged had put in some low-level lamps along the walkways and around the fence that enclosed the pool. The glow from the weak bulbs did not extend far. When she looked down she saw a lot of shadows.

She watched for a long time, but with the exception of a prowling cat, nothing moved.

The phone warbled, startling her. She was annoyed to feel her pulse kick up again. Irritated by her own reaction, she walked across the room and hesitated before she willed herself to pick up the instrument. Damnit, she would not allow her nerves to control her.

"Hello?"

"You okay?" Harry Stagg asked without preamble.

She was surprised by the monumental relief she felt at the sound of his voice. She released the breath she had not realized she had been holding.

The muffled beat of heavy rock music played somewhere in the background on Harry's end of the connection. She almost smiled. Harry was not a big fan of rock. Like her, he was a jazz aficionado.

"I'm fine," she said. She allowed herself to relax against the back of one of the pair of white leather chairs that sat in front of the coffee table.

"You don't sound fine," Harry said. "You sound tense. Did I wake you? Thought you'd still be up."

They were both night people. It was one of the many things they had in common. She did not want to explain that she had not been sleeping well since he had left and that she had tried to make up for it tonight by going to bed earlier than usual.

"No. I was awake." She put the pistol down on the table and carried the phone back to the window. "How's the job going?"

Harry Stagg was unlike any other man she had ever met; a far cry from the sleek, wealthy, powerful financiers and investors who had populated the world in which she had once moved. The exact opposite of Grant.

She had met him last month when Ethan imported him from California to protect her while he and Zoe dealt with the threat from Zoe's in-laws.

Physically Harry bore a striking resemblance to a living skeleton. When he smiled he looked like a Halloween decoration. But in the few weeks they had known each other she had come to believe that they were soul mates.

Harry's card declared that he was a security consultant. From what she could tell, that term covered a great deal of territory. But she knew that in this instance it was a euphemism for bodyguard. Last week he had left to take a short-term position looking after the teenage daughter of a Texas businessman. The young woman was a senior in high school. She had been packed off to the West Coast to tour various California college campuses. The stated objective was to gather information that would assist her in deciding which institution of higher learning she wanted to attend. But according to Harry her primary interests thus far had been shopping and star-gazing.

"Routine," Harry said. "The kid bought three more pairs of shoes today along with a couple of purses and a skimpy little shirt that shows off the ring in her belly button. She also picked up some jeans that are so tight I think she's gonna have to paint them on with a brush."

"You shouldn't be noticing things like that, Harry. You're a professional, remember?"

"Professionals are paid to notice every detail. After seeing her in that dinky little shirt, I'm pretty sure she's had a boob job."

"At her age?"

"I get the impression that kids her age in her income bracket put boob jobs in the same category as getting their teeth straightened."

"Has she actually spent any time on a college campus?"

"We managed a solid fifteen minutes at Pomona and maybe half an hour at USC today."

"Good schools. Does she have the grades and SAT scores for them?"

"Don't know about that, but her daddy's got enough cash to buy her way into any school she fancies."

The rock music boomed louder in the background.

"Where are you?" she asked.

"Some kind of teenage club. I'll be lucky if I don't need hearing aids after this gig."

"How much longer is it going to last?"

"The job or the music?"

She smiled slightly. "The job."

"Well, I gotta tell you, my heart nearly failed me this morning when she announced that she wanted to extend her stay to the end of the month. But luckily her daddy phoned and told her that she had to go back to Texas in ten days."

"Do you have to fly back with her?"

"No. Daddy's sending one of the people from his regular agency to pick her up here and escort her to Dallas. The only reason he hired me was because he wanted someone who knew the local scene while she was in Southern California."

"So you'll be home in ten days?"

There was a lengthy pause. For a few seconds she thought his phone had cut out. Then she realized that she could still hear the hard rock in the background.

"Harry?"

"I'm here," he said in an oddly neutral tone of voice.

"Thought I'd lost you. Did something happen? Do you have to get off the phone?"

"No. Just realized I hadn't thought of Whispering Springs as home, that's all."

"Oh." She did not know what to say. The truth was that, although she had lived there for a little more than a year, she had only recently begun to think of Whispering Springs as home, herself. She was not sure quite when that had happened. Sometime after she had met Harry, she thought.

But whatever this place was to her, it was not Harry's home, she reminded herself. His address was in San Diego. She should not forget significant facts like that.

"Yeah," he said, no longer sounding the least bit neutral.

It occurred to her that she had just lost the thread of the conversation. "Yeah, what?"

"Yeah, I'll be home in ten days, right after I put the kid on the plane," Harry said calmly.

The certainty in his voice worked like a dose of some magic antidepressant medication.

"Sounds good," she said.

Relief and a sense of happiness replaced the adrenaline that had awakened her earlier.

When she ended the call a short time later she felt steadier, calmer.

No longer afraid of the dark.

4

Ethan moved stealthily but she was awake and she felt him leave the bed.

She gave him a few seconds just to be sure he wasn't headed for the bathroom. A person could have a legitimate reason for going in that direction in the middle of the night, she reminded herself. She would not get mad unless he started to get dressed.

She opened her eyes and watched him make his way across the small bedroom to the closet. He opened the door and reached inside. When his hand reappeared she saw that he had a pair of trousers in it.

"You know, you could have made a good

living as a cat burglar." She sat up in the middle of the bed and wrapped her arms around her knees. "You're pretty good at sneaking out of a lady's bedroom."

He went still for an instant and then stepped into the pants. "Sorry. Didn't mean to wake you."

"Yes, I could see that."

"Zoe—"

"Are you going to tell me what's going on here, Ethan?"

"I couldn't sleep." He pulled a fresh black tee shirt over his head. "Figured you wouldn't want me pacing your living room until dawn so I thought I'd take a walk outside."

"A walk outside."

"Yeah."

"In the middle of the night?"

"Figured some fresh air might help."

"Bull." She flung the sheet aside and bounded to her feet. "You were going to walk out on me, weren't you?"

"What the hell are you talking about?"

"You were going to walk out on me in the middle of the night." Belatedly she realized she was waving her hands. She hated when that happened. She folded them very tightly beneath her breasts instead, hugging her pain and outrage close. "I can't believe it. I expected better than that from you, Ethan Truax."

"Let's get something straight here." He zipped up his trousers with a swift, economical motion. "I wasn't walking out. I was going for a walk. Big difference."

"I don't believe that for a moment. You've been acting weird for the past couple of weeks and I think it's because you've changed your mind about wanting to be married." Tears burned in her eyes. "You've changed your mind and you haven't got the guts to tell me, do you?"

"That's not true."

"You don't want to be married. Is that it? You'd rather be involved in an affair. You want to be free to walk away when things get boring. Admit it."

"Damnit, stop putting words in my mouth." He closed the gap between them in two long strides and gripped her forearms. "I'm not looking for a way out of this marriage."

"No?"

"No."

She raised her chin. "Then why are you acting like a man who's hunting for the nearest exit?"

"I don't want out," he said roughly. "But it might be better if I moved back into Nightwinds for a while."

"I *knew* it."

"No, you don't know anything. You just think you do. This has got nothing to do with you or our marriage."

"That's a lie. Whatever is going on here is causing some serious damage to this relationship."

"Zoe, I'm not good company right now."

She unfolded her arms and put her hands on his shoulders. "We're not dating, we're married, remember? That means that you don't have to worry about whether or not you're good company."

"Yeah?" He sounded grimly amused. "That hasn't been my experience, and I've had plenty of it."

"We will *not* go into your previous marital experience. It was all warped."

"Warped, huh? I wondered what was wrong."

"You put up with my bad dreams." She gave him a small shake that did not move him a fraction of an inch. "I put up with you when you're not good company. That's how it works."

"Zoe—"

"Tell me what's going on with you. I know there's something wrong. Talk to me, Truax."

He released her and took a step back. "I get a little restless this time of year, that's all."

"What is it? The weather?" That did not seem likely. Granted, it was November, but this was Arizona. The weather had been Chamber of Commerce perfect for the past few weeks. "Do the shorter days bother you? Have you got that seasonal thing with the light syndrome?"

"No. It's not the weather or the hours of daylight." He looked at her from the other side of a wedge of moonlight. "It's something that has happened to me for the past couple of years in November. This is the month that Drew was kidnapped and murdered."

"The anniversary of your brother's death." She suddenly understood. Relief mingled with an upwelling of sympathy. Hurrying toward him, she put her arms around him. "Of course. I should have realized. I got very depressed for a few days in August this year. I couldn't figure out why until I remembered that it was very close to the date that Preston died."

Her husband's murder had precipitated a series of devastating events that had included the nightmare of her involuntary commitment to Candle Lake Manor Psychiatric Hospital. August would always bring back the bad memories. November would no doubt forever be bad for Ethan.

Ethan folded her close. "Bonnie and the boys go through the same thing each year."

She thought about the meals they had shared with his sister-in-law and nephews in the past few weeks. There had been a certain tension in the air, she realized.

"Bonnie seemed a little quiet for a while at the beginning of the month. I noticed that Jeff and Theo have been squabbling more than usual, too," she said.

"Bonnie and Theo got through it much easier this year but Jeff is still having problems." He rubbed the back of his neck. "I guess I am, too."

"When does the bad time usually end for you?"

"At the end of the month." He hesitated a fraction of a beat before adding, "Right after the date of Simon Wendover's boating accident. He died two years after Drew, almost to the day."

"I see."

She knew that Simon Wendover was the man who had been responsible for the murder of Drew Truax. Ethan had tracked him down and gathered evidence against him. But in the end the wheels of justice had not only ground slowly, they had ground very poorly. Wendover had walked out of the courtroom a free man.

He had not enjoyed his freedom for long, however. A month after the trial ended, Wendover died in a boating accident.

She stood with Ethan in the moonlight, hugging him until she felt some of the tension go out of him. Then she took his hand.

"Come on." She led him out of the bedroom. "Let's go into the kitchen and get you some warm milk."

"That's what I give you after one of your nightmares."

"It works, doesn't it?"

"I think maybe I'd do better with a shot of something stronger."

She smiled. "Whatever."

He followed her into the kitchen. She got the brandy down from the cupboard and poured some into a glass. They sat together at the table while he drank it.

When he finished the brandy they went back to the darkened bedroom. Ethan took off his clothes for the second time that night.

Zoe yawned and crawled into the rumpled bed. "If you can't sleep, go out into the living room and read or something. But promise me you won't sneak out for a late-night walk alone."

"All right," he said.

He got into bed beside her and tucked her into the curve of his body. She felt him relax heavily against her.

After a while he slept.

She did not. Instead she lay awake for a long time thinking about what Ethan had said. She was pretty sure that what he had told her was the truth, as far as it went. He had not lied to her. She knew what lies sounded like. She had told a lot of them, herself, in the months after the escape from Candle Lake Manor, when she had been forced to assume a new identity.

No, Ethan had not lied tonight. But he had not told her the whole truth, either. She wondered what it was that he had left out and why he had felt compelled to do so.

5

Shelley Russell shook the photos out of the envelope and put them on the desk. "Will these do?"

The big man reached out and scooped up the pictures. She was proud of the shots. It had taken her three days in Whispering Springs to get all of them, but she thought John Branch and his secretive employer would be satisfied.

She studied Branch while he flipped through the stack of glossies. She was eighty-two years old and he was in his early thirties, but that didn't mean she couldn't enjoy a few interesting fantasies. And Branch was definitely a walking fantasy if you liked the macho, clean-cut, military type.

She'd always had a weakness for a man in uniform. Hell, she'd married two of them. Buried one and divorced the other.

Branch was iron-jawed, cold-eyed and good-looking, with the kind of cheekbones that would have done a Viking proud. He could have modeled for a recruitment poster for some elite military unit. She wouldn't be surprised to learn that he'd been Special Forces at some time in the past.

Branch clearly took his workouts seriously. He rippled and bulged in all the right places. This was her second meeting with him. He was dressed very much as he had been the first time. His jeans were so snug around his bulging thighs it was a wonder the seams hadn't split. His gray, short-sleeved pullover was stretched so tightly across his chest she could see every well-defined muscle.

But even if she had been forty or fifty years younger, she didn't think she would have allowed herself to do more than fantasize about John Branch. After what seemed a lifetime in the investigation business, she knew better than to get personally involved with a client. But it wasn't professional ethics that would have stopped her. She'd broken the rules and slept with a few clients over the years and the sky had not fallen.

But John Branch was different. She was starting to think that there was something slightly screwy with his wiring. The man had more than a military bearing; he possessed a robotic quality that was downright spooky.

"These are excellent shots, Ms. Russell," Branch said. Each word was enunciated with clipped, military-style precision. "You do good surveillance work."

"I'm glad you're satisfied." Her chair squeaked when she leaned back. It had squeaked like that for at least twenty years. One of these days she would have to oil it. "You're sure that's the woman you're looking for?"

"The subject has obviously changed her hair color and is dressing in a different style, but some things can't be altered. Looks like she fits the physical description I gave you."

"I got real close to her on several occasions. Definitely the same height, build and eyes. Maybe a little thinner is all."

"I'll show these to my boss. He'll make the final ID." Branch put the photos down one by one on the desk, arranging them in a neat, orderly line. "Were you able to identify everyone who is closely associated with her?"

"Yes." She handed Branch the two pages of notes that she had written up on her laptop. "They're all there in that group shot taken outside the pizza parlor. The two women on the right are Bonnie Truax and Zoe Truax. Zoe is the former Sara Cleland. She used the name Zoe Luce for most of last year and then married a man named Ethan Truax."

Branch looked up sharply. "Why the different ID?"

"Apparently she was trying to conceal the fact that she had spent some time in a psychiatric hospital."

Branch frowned. "What about the young boys?"

"They belong to Bonnie. Their father is dead, murdered about three years ago in LA."

Branch concentrated on the two men in the shot. "Who's the bald guy in denim, the one who looks like he rides with a biker gang?"

"His name is Singleton Cobb." She was amused by Branch's assessment of Cobb.

"Appearances can be deceiving, as they say. He operates an antiquarian bookshop there in Whispering Springs. Deals in old and rare volumes."

Branch moved his head a couple of times; an android trying to assimilate data that did not compute. "Doesn't look like a book dealer."

"No," she agreed.

"Got anything else on him?"

"You didn't give me enough time to do an in-depth background check on any of those people," she reminded him. "You said your boss was in a hurry for the ID on the woman."

Branch tapped the photo. "Think this Cobb is personally involved with the subject?"

She shrugged. "Just a friend, as far as I could tell. Want me to dig around some more?"

"Not at this point. I'll see if my boss needs more info on him." Branch switched his attention to the next man in the picture. "What about him?"

"Ethan Truax. The husband of Zoe. He's a private investigator. Has a small office in Whispering Springs."

"An investigator?" Branch hardened all

over. Muscles swelled in his upper arms. His neck got thicker. "My boss will want to know what the subject is doing with a PI for a friend."

"She's not doing anything in particular with him as far as I could tell. Certainly not in a professional capacity. Like Cobb, Truax appears to be an acquaintance. He's definitely not intimately involved with the, uh, subject."

Branch contemplated Truax for a while longer before pointing to the next photo. "The subject owns this shop?"

"Gallery Euphoria, yes. It's located in an upscale shopping arcade called Fountain Square in Whispering Springs. Features high-end gifts. Handmade jewelry, ceramics, artwork, that kind of thing."

"A real change of pace for the subject," Branch mused. "She used to be a financial trader."

"Mr. Branch, are you absolutely certain this is the woman your agency is looking for? I agree that she fits the physical description you gave me, but I've got to tell you that nothing else matches. I did a more thorough background check on her. Arcadia Ames appears to be a completely different person."

"She bought herself a new ID. Maybe a

couple of them. Not that hard to do these days."

"I know," Shelley said patiently. "But if that is the case, she got a very, very good package. I've been in this business a long time and I've never seen anything this complete. I tracked her all the way back through college, high school and grade school. I can tell you when she got her childhood vaccinations. That sort of detail is not typical of most fake identities."

"She made a fortune laundering money for terrorists and drug dealers," Branch said softly. "She can afford the best."

"I just want to be absolutely certain that this is the person your boss is looking for, that's all. This isn't the kind of situation where you folks want to make a mistake."

"Don't worry, Ms. Russell. My boss won't make a move without being absolutely certain."

"What happens next?"

"I'm not allowed to give out that kind of information."

"Never hurts to ask. I'm a little curious, that's all. Not often the Feds come to a one-person operation like mine for assistance." She paused a beat. "Not that I don't appreciate the business."

Branch's blond brows came together in a serious line. She knew that he was debating how much to tell her. The Feds always hated to answer questions from civilians. They preferred to work on a need-to-know basis.

"Whispering Springs is a relatively small town," Branch said finally. "My boss didn't want to risk sending in a team to do the initial surveillance and verification. Figured the subject might notice pros. He decided a low-profile investigator who knew how to do things the old-fashioned way would be less obvious."

She pretended to be oblivious to the small insults. She *was* a pro, damnit. She'd been an investigator since long before Branch was born. But he was right about one thing. She was about as low-profile as they came.

"There's a good-sized private firm in Whispering Springs," she said. "Radnor Security Systems. Why didn't your boss give them a call?"

"Similar reasons." Branch got to his feet and started to gather up the photos. "In a small, close-knit community it's never a good idea to use local talent for this kind of thing. Everyone knows everyone else. Too much chance that someone will talk. First thing you know, the subject gets wind that she's being watched and does another vanishing act."

"Your boss sounds like the careful type."

"He is."

She was about to try another question or two about his boss, aware that she was pushing the envelope, but she was interrupted by a soft, insistent *ping, ping, ping.*

Branch frowned. "What's that?"

"My watch. Sorry." Irritated, she pushed the tiny button to silence the alarm. "Time for my pills. When you get to be my age, you wish you'd bought shares in the pharmaceutical companies."

He nodded once, apparently satisfied.

She watched him square the edges of the photos and insert them neatly back into the envelope. There was something unsettling about the way he performed the small action, as if he were folding a parachute or cleaning a rifle. Making sure everything was shipshape and battle-ready. You'd think that his life might depend on how perfectly he angled the corners of those photos.

"Order" and "precision" were obviously words to live by as far as John Branch was concerned.

"We appreciate your assistance, Ms. Russell. Your government thanks you." Branch tucked the envelope of photos and the file folder she had given him under his arm. "Do I owe you anything else?"

"No. The advance you gave me covered my time and the cost of the photos." She hadn't charged him for the duplicate set that she had ordered for her office file. Her contribution toward reigning in the national debt, she told herself.

Branch inclined his head once, turned on his heel and walked out of her office.

When the door closed behind him she got to her feet, went to the window and watched him get into an unmarked white van.

Branch managed to make the simple act of exiting from the parking lot and merging with the Phoenix traffic look like a carefully calculated military maneuver.

She stood there for a while, thinking, until her watch pinged again.

With a sigh, she went into the bathroom that doubled as a storage closet, opened the drawer beside the sink and took out the large, seven-day pill organizer. The long plastic box was divided into a series of squares, one for each day of the week. Each daily square was, in turn, subdivided into four smaller openings labeled *Morning*, *Noon*, *Evening* and *Night*. Each opening was filled with pills, a lot of them. She had prescriptions for everything from arthritis and mild incontinence to heart and blood pressure problems.

So many pills, she thought, but none of them gave her the one thing she missed the most these days: a good night's sleep.

When she finished swallowing the meds, she went back out into her office, sat down at her desk and pulled out the little notebook she had used to jot down her initial observations of John Branch and his mysterious employer.

She studied the one word she had written and underlined twice after Branch had showed her his ID. *Feds*.

6

I'm not concerned about her two female friends," Grant Loring said into the pay phone. "From what you've told me, neither of them sounds like a potential problem."

"Yes, sir, I agree," John Branch said on the other end of the line.

Grant had to listen closely to catch the words. The dull roar of background noise in the huge mall made it difficult to hear clearly.

It was ridiculous having to conduct business on a pay phone in a shopping mall, he thought. It was also tiresome and inefficient. Over the course of the past few days he'd spent an inordinate amount of extremely valuable time in cabs coming or going from malls and sprawling Scottsdale resorts in order to make use of anonymous phones.

The communications difficulties were only part of the problem. He'd had to tell Branch to leave the copies of the photos and the file taped to the bottom of a toilet in a men's room because he couldn't risk having the data sent via computer. He was forced to use cash for everything, which was also a real pain in the ass. The most annoying aspect of the situation was that he was obliged to rely on third-rate personnel such as the elderly private investigator for data collection.

But he knew only too well that in an age when phones could be monitored from thousands of miles away and credit card transactions could be easily traced on the Internet, the low-tech approach was the only way to go if he hoped to avoid drawing the attention of some old and ruthless enemies.

Two years ago he'd lived his business life on-line and it had nearly gotten him killed.

He waited until a gaggle of boisterous teenagers had moved past the entrance to the phone lobby before he resumed the conversation.

"Like I said, we don't have to worry about

the two females. According to Russell's report, one of them is a certified nutcase with a history of having been committed to a psychiatric hospital, and the other one is a single mother who works part-time in a library."

"Yes, sir," Branch said.

"If Arcadia Ames were to simply disappear, the only thing that either of those women could do would be to file a missing persons report," Grant said, speaking more to himself than to Branch. "No one pays any attention to missing persons reports. Thousands get logged and ignored every year."

"The PI, Truax, could be a problem, though. If Ames turns up missing, he might decide to go looking. He'd know how to do it."

"Russell's report says that the crazy woman, the one called Zoe, is married to him."

"Yes, sir."

"That's damn strange. What kind of an investigator would be dumb enough to marry an escapee from a lunatic asylum?"

"I'm sorry, sir," Branch said somberly. "I don't have the answer to that."

Grant wanted to bang the receiver against the wall a few times in frustration. Branch was useful, but he had his limitations. The guy was very tightly wound. Privately Grant was starting to call him Weird John.

"Truax is an unknown and I don't like unknowns," he said.

"Russell offered to do a more complete background check on him. I can give her a call and have her proceed."

Grant considered that briefly. "No, let's not involve her again in this thing. She already knows more than she should. If Truax is legitimate, it won't be too hard to get a fix on him. I'll handle it personally."

"Yes, sir."

"Where are you now?"

"In my apartment," Branch said. "I was planning to work out this afternoon. Want me to stay close to the phone?"

The guy was obsessed with his workouts, Grant thought. Or something. Definitely weird.

"Not necessary," Grant said. "This will take a while. I'll call you at five-thirty. I should know by then whether or not Truax is going to be an issue."

"Yes, sir."

Grant hung up the phone and headed for the nearest mall exit.

Just what he did not need. Another delay.

But he had to be sure of what he was doing. He could not afford any mistakes. Truax raised some questions that had to be answered before the plan could be safely executed.

Outside the mall he got into a cab. Branch assumed that he was the head of a government agency that was so secret it didn't officially exist. He was right about one thing, Grant mused. The agency did *not* exist. He had invented it and dug out the fake government ID he had saved from the old days to prop up the story for Weird John.

He had been warned that, although Branch was willing to kill, the man had his own bizarre code. He considered himself a patriotic warrior. He would only commit murder in the name of truth, justice and the American Way.

Getting some basic background on Truax would not take long, Grant surmised. All he needed was an anonymous computer. He knew right where to find one: the nearest branch of the Scottsdale public library.

The answers came up quickly enough and he did not like any of them. He redrafted the plan.

At five-thirty that afternoon he was in another mall standing in front of another pay phone.

Branch was right where he was supposed to be. Grant pictured him sitting in his seedy little by-the-week apartment. Got to give him credit. The man took orders well. In fact, obeying orders seemed to be something of a religion to Branch. Grant had the uneasy feeling that it was one of the ways he kept himself semi-sane.

"Truax is definitely a problem," Grant said. "A big one. In fact, what I found out this afternoon puts this entire operation in a whole new light."

"Yes, sir?"

"My contacts in LA tell me that Ethan Truax was involved in the money laundering business there. They were never able to prove it, but they're sure that he ran errands for his brother, Drew Truax, who headed up a very big operation. Ethan did all the dirty go-between work. He's the one who met with the drug runners and the terrorists and arranged for the cash to be transferred across the border and deposited in various banks."

"What happened?"

"LA thinks there was some kind of internal power struggle," Grant said, following the script he had mentally prepared. "When it was over, Drew Truax was dead. The hit was evidently ordered by a man named Simon Wendover. After Truax's death everything started to come apart. Looks like Ethan Truax decided to cut his losses and get the hell out of Dodge. But apparently he got rid of Wendover first."

"He did Wendover?"

"Offically Simon Wendover drowned in a boating accident. There were no witnesses so there was no case against Truax. He was never charged."

"What's Truax doing in Whispering Springs?"

"I think it's safe to say that he's gone back into the family business."

"Money laundering?"

"Right. New location, but still within easy driving distance of the border." Grant paused before delivering the zinger. "Given those photos, we can assume that he's also found himself a new partner."

"Arcadia Ames?"

"Yes. This thing is a lot more complicated than it appeared at first. Truax is definitely a problem. But I've come up with a way to kill a couple of birds with one stone."

He outlined his revised plan, keeping it

very simple out of respect for Weird John's mental limitations.

"Can you handle the, uh, revised mission?" he asked when he was finished. Weird John was very big on the word "mission." It seemed to be some sort of Holy Grail for him.

"Yes, sir. No problem at all with the mission, sir."

"It's got to look like an accident," Grant emphasized. "Is that clear?"

"Yes, sir."

Grant hung up and went to buy himself an espresso. What he really needed was a martini. Talking to Branch always left him feeling tense and jumpy.

He'd had to call in an old favor to get the professional muscle for this job, and as a result, he had not been in a position to be choosy. He'd been forced to take what was offered because he could not afford to miss this window of opportunity.

The Bitch had unknowingly tripped the one and only tripwire that he had been lucky enough to have on her, a bank account that she had established under a different name and ID. For nearly two years he had kept an eye on that account, watching for any hint of activity. When a year and several months had passed with no sign that she had accessed the account, he had begun to wonder if she really had died that night in the lake.

But on the second of November, eight thousand dollars had been transferred out of the hidden account, and he had been forced to deal with his worst nightmare. She was alive and she had the damned file.

He had done what he did best. He had followed the money, all the way to Whispering Springs, Arizona.

7

She started Ethan on the new cereal the next morning.

He did not notice until after he had obligingly swallowed the calcium tablet and the super-fortified vitamin pill with minerals and antioxidants that she had placed beside his glass of fresh-squeezed orange juice.

He picked up his spoon and studied the cereal. "What's this?" he asked mildly.

"Muesli. I thought it would make a change." She poured tea into her cup. "It's got three different kinds of whole grains, several types of dried fruit and a variety of nuts. I mixed it up with some live-culture yogurt and added a little milk."

"Live-culture yogurt, huh? I don't know about this. I usually like my food to be real dead before I eat it. Seems safer that way, you know?"

"You're a PI. You live for danger, remember?"

"Oh, yeah, right. Almost forgot." He dug into the cereal.

She held her breath.

Ethan chewed, swallowed and scooped up another spoonful of the muesli, all without further comment. He opened the morning edition of the *Whispering Springs Herald* and scanned the headlines.

She relaxed. He was taking the switch in breakfast cereals the same way he had dealt with the addition of the antioxidant vitamins to his menu—in stride. She was learning that was the way he handled most things.

The start of a new marriage was probably not the best time to introduce healthy lifestyle changes into a man's routine but she could not seem to help herself. Lately she had found herself spending more and more time in the organic foods aisle at the supermarket and browsing through the vitamin and high-SPF-sunscreen selections at the drug store.

Her new obsession was getting worse.

Three days before, she had bought Ethan a special key chain at a high-tech gadget shop in Fountain Square. It had a tiny flashlight and an emergency whistle attached. The next day she had gone back to the store to purchase an emergency weather radio that could be cranked by hand in the event that a tornado struck Whispering Springs and they lost all electricity.

After breakfast, Ethan kissed her goodbye, taking his time about it. Then he left for the office, new key chain in hand.

She reminded herself that a man like Ethan probably did not want a woman fussing over him. But lately she seemed unable to resist any advertisement that contained words such as "safety," "emergency," "healthy," "fortified" or "protective antioxidants."

The door of the manager's office opened just as Zoe walked past it on her way to the parking lot. Robyn Duncan stuck her head out of the opening.

"Good morning, Mrs. Truax. I thought I heard you on the stairs. Got a minute?"

Robyn's tone was perky. Everything about Robyn Duncan was perky. Zoe tried not to grit her teeth. The new resident manager of the Casa de Oro Apartments reminded her of an anal retentive pixie.

Robyn was somewhere in her late twenties, small and daintily made with sharp features. Her light brown hair was streaked with a wealth of golden highlights and cut in a very short, artfully ragged style that emphasized her bright eyes and elfin ears.

As Zoe and the other residents of Casa de Oro were rapidly discovering, the perkiness was merely a veil for what was proving to be an extremely rigid approach to apartment house management. Robyn Duncan was very keen on rules. Some of the tenants, led by Hooper in 1B, had begun to call her Sergeant Duncan behind her back.

"I'm on my way to an appointment, Robyn." Zoe made herself smile. "Can it wait?"

"Not really." Robyn looked regretful but resolved to do her duty. "I'm afraid it's quite important." She cast a quick, searching glance around the lobby and the stairs, apparently making certain that no one else was in the vicinity. “Would you mind stepping into my office for just a second?”

Damn. She did not need this. She had enough on her plate these days. She glanced pointedly at her watch. “I’d rather not. Is this about the new parking lot assignments?”

“I’m afraid so.” Robyn drew herself up. “The problem, Mrs. Truax, is that I can’t assign a parking stall to Mr. Truax because he is not on the lease.”

“I beg your pardon?”

“The lease is in your name, Mrs. Truax. To be precise, it is in your former name, Zoe Luce. I’m afraid the agreement is very specific. It states that only one resident shall occupy the apartment on a full-time basis. The occasional overnight guest is allowed, of course, but it appears that Mr. Truax has moved into your unit on a full-time basis.”

“He moved in because we got married,” Zoe said evenly. “Believe it or not, people often share a living space after they get married.”

Robyn’s bow-like mouth tightened. “I’m aware of that.”

“In any event, this is a temporary situation. Ethan and I have a house. It’s being repainted inside. We'll be moving into it when the work is done."

"I see." Robyn was evidently taken aback by that news, but she recovered quickly. "I hadn't realized that you were planning to terminate your lease. When do you intend to give notice?"

"It depends." On how long it takes Treacher, the painting contractor, to start work, she added silently. She had been nagging him for two weeks but so far the only sign that anything might be about to happen was the fact that the interior of Nightwinds was covered in drop cloths.

"We require a month's notice," Robyn reminded her.

"I'm aware of that."

"Yes, well, the thing is your personal circumstances and the change in your marital status do not alter the terms and conditions of the lease."

"What do you want me to do?" Zoe asked, exasperated. "Sign a new lease?"

"Modifying the lease is certainly an option."

"Fine. Draw up the paperwork and Ethan and I will sign it this evening." She turned to go.

"You do realize that there will be an increase in your monthly rent?"

That did it. Zoe swung around again, outraged. "You can't arbitrarily increase my rent."

"It's not an arbitrary decision at all, Mrs. Truax." Robyn smiled. "May I call you Zoe?"

"Call me Mrs. Truax," Zoe said between her teeth.

"Very well." Robyn looked hurt. "It's all right there in your lease, Mrs. Truax. If you will take the trouble to read paragraph nine A, you'll see that adding an additional tenant will mean a one-hundred-and-fifty-dollar-a-month increase in the rent."

"Over my dead body. Ethan and I will camp out in Fountain Square before I pay you one hundred and fifty dollars more a month. This place isn't worth what I'm paying now."

"It's not me you're paying," Robyn said primly. "I just collect the rent. The money goes to the owners of the Casa de Oro."

With a supreme effort of will Zoe managed to resist the urge to pick Robyn up by her pointy little ears and toss her into the trash bin out back.

"I am not an idiot," she said, instead. "I am well aware that a couple by the name of Shipley owns this place. But in the entire time that I have been here they have never once, as far as I know, paid a visit. They have invested nothing in the property. There have been no improvements, whatsoever. The Shipleys do not deserve a hundred and fifty bucks more a month and you can tell them that I said so."

"The Shipleys have a number of rental properties in the Phoenix area. They are far too busy to oversee each one personally. But I have had several conversations with them regarding our needs here at Casa de Oro, and I assure you that they are very receptive to my plans for this apartment complex."

"I insist that you contact the Shipleys, wherever they are—"

"They live in Scottsdale," Robyn said, ever helpful.

"Fine. Contact them in Scottsdale and make it clear to them that Ethan and I are a married couple, not roommates. Remind them that I have been an excellent tenant for more than a year."

Robyn cleared her throat. "Well, not exactly."

"*What?* How dare you imply that I have been anything less than an ideal tenant."

"I was going through the files the other day and I noticed that there was an incident in your apartment last month that resulted in police being summoned to Casa de Oro."

"That was not my fault. I was the innocent victim of an attempted kidnapping."

Robyn tut-tutted sympathetically. "Yes, I read about it in the *Whispering Springs Herald*. It must have been a terrible experience for you."

"It was."

"When I discussed it with Mr. and Mrs. Shipley, they felt that it was something of a red flag, however."

An ominous feeling descended on Zoe. "Red flag?" she repeated very carefully.

"The Shipleys expressed some concerns regarding Mr. Truax's profession."

"Concerns."

"They are worried that the nature of his profession might tend to encourage other such incidents, if you see what I mean."

"No, I do not see what you mean." Zoe struggled to keep her voice under control. "My husband's business had nothing to do with that *incident*, as you call it. It was a personal matter involving me. Explain that to Mr. and Mrs. Shipley."

Robyn stiffened. "Are you saying that there is something about you that might attract more criminal activity to this property?"

"No, I am not saying that. The earlier issue was resolved. There won't be any more problems. Make sure the Shipleys understand that. Make certain they also understand that I refuse to pay extra rent simply because I got married."

"I'll talk to them."

"You do that."

"Really, there is no need to lose your temper with me, Mrs. Truax. It is my duty to enforce the rules."

"Yeah, right." Zoe dug her keys out of her purse and, for the second time that morning, started toward the lobby door. "All I know is that the former resident manager was a lot more flexible."

"His excessive flexibility is the reason he is the *former* resident manager." Robyn lowered her voice to a confidential tone. "The Shipleys implied that he had a drinking problem."

That probably explained a few things, Zoe

thought, such as why the Casa de Oro had always looked so down at the heels. Maybe there was something to be said for the rules-are-rules type.

But she was in no mood to admit that to Pixie Ears.

She went outside and got into her car.

She was still fuming an hour later when Tabitha Pine, flamboyantly ethereal in a dress that looked as if it had been fashioned from a lot of expensive silk scarves, floated into her office. The tiny bells stitched to the bottom of her skirts tinkled.

"Zoe, dear, I hope you don't mind me dropping in on you without an appointment." Tabitha smiled, serenely sure of her welcome. "I would have called but I had to come into town this morning to do some shopping so I thought I'd see if I could catch you. I only need a moment."

"Of course I don't mind." Zoe immediately switched into client mode. "I don't have another appointment until eleven. Please sit down."

"Thank you." Tabitha settled into one of the two chairs on the other side of the desk. The scarves fluttered for a few seconds and then obediently went still. "I will come right out with it. I had one of my psychic visions last night while I was traveling on the astral plane. I felt that I had to get in touch with you and Lindsey Voyle as soon as possible so that I could tell you both about it."

"I see."

Zoe reminded herself that she was in no position to doubt Tabitha's psychic visions. Nevertheless, it was difficult to take seriously a woman of some sixty years who dressed like a hippie from the latter half of the last century.

Tabitha's hair was her most arresting feature. It was silver and gray and it fell down her back and around her shoulders in long, flowing waves. Zoe had heard that there was a fashion rule that dictated that the older a woman got, the shorter her hair was supposed to be cut. Obviously, Tabitha did not believe in following that law of nature.

"I've been thinking about the best way to convey a sense of my personal style and energy-flow requirements to you and Lindsey Voyle. I want you both to have all the vital information you'll need to draw up your proposals."

"Oh." Zoe tried to think of something more

to say but nothing sparkling came to mind. She was suddenly feeling very wary.

"In my vision I saw you and Lindsey attending a few of my meditation seminars," Tabitha said. "As soon as the picture flashed into my mind I realized that is the only way that the two of you can possibly come to a full and complete understanding of my unique interior design needs."

"Ah." Zoe swallowed her dismay. She had a hunch that Tabitha's seminars were not cheap.

"Do you have any problem with that, dear?"

Zoe managed a weak smile. "No, not at all. Sounds like a terrific idea."

"Wonderful. I'll look for you at one of my sessions sometime in the next couple of weeks." Tabitha rose from her chair and dropped a sheet of paper on the desk. "Here's a time and fee schedule for you." She wafted toward the door. "Peace to you, dear."

"Peace."

Zoe glanced down at the meditation schedule. She had guessed right. The seminars were pricey. She drummed her fingers on the desk for a while. Then she picked up the phone and punched in Ethan's number.

"Truax Investigations."

"Tabitha Pine just left. She made it clear that I don't stand a chance at her project unless I attend some of her meditation seminars. They're expensive but I've got a feeling that Lindsey Voyle will probably sign up for a full course as soon as she finds out it's the ticket to the job."

"The cost of doing business," Ethan said philosophically. "Don't expect any sympathy from me. Bonnie just called. She wants Truax Investigations to give the Whispering Springs Historical Society a freebie."

"What kind of freebie?"

"I don't know yet. I have an appointment with the mayor in the morning. Guess I'll find out then."

"Not to change the subject, but I had another confrontation with Pixie Ears this morning. She's threatening to increase our rent on the grounds that there are now two of us living in the apartment."

"You can handle her."

"Easy for you to say."

8

The searcher stood in middle of the small office and tried to fight off the brainstorm. *Not another one. Not so soon.*

Got to stay in control. Can't lose it. Not here. The guard might notice the unlocked door. He'll check to see if there are signs of an intruder. Can't get caught.

But the familiar aura of impending night closed in with the fury of a thunderstorm. A split second later everything went dark. The searcher collapsed to the floor, brain filling up with static.

When it ended, the searcher was exhausted. It was always this way after the storms.

A glance at the small clock on the desk showed that only a couple of minutes had passed. There was still time.

The searcher rose and moved toward the filing cabinet. Something crunched underfoot.

Alarmed by the loud sound in the too-quiet space, the searcher aimed the small flashlight down toward the floor and saw a broken pen. It was a silly-looking object decorated with a tiny figure of Elvis. Cheap and tacky. Not an expensive fountain pen that would be missed.

Relieved, the searcher scooped up the broken pen and shoved the pieces into a pocket.

Got to stay focused. Came here for a reason. Got to concentrate.

9

Ethan folded his hands on the top of his desk and gave the mayor what he hoped was a regretful but firm smile. "It's true that solving historical murder cases is a hobby of mine, Mrs. Santana. But I'm afraid I can only do that kind of work when I'm between cases. At the moment I'm a little busy."

Paloma Santana's elegant dark brows rose slightly. "Bonnie explained that to me but she implied that you would make an exception in this situation."

Ethan gave his sister-in-law, sitting in the second client chair, a brief glance. "She did, huh?"

He was pretty sure he knew what Bonnie was thinking. Most of the time they communicated fairly well.

He had liked Bonnie from the moment his brother had introduced her as his fiancée. She had seemed perfect for him and it was clear that she loved Drew with all her heart.

But in the wake of Drew's death, Ethan and Bonnie had forged an even stronger bond. United by the mutual goal of looking after Drew's young sons, they had fashioned an unshakable alliance that resembled a brother-sister relationship. As was the case in such relationships, Ethan occasionally got annoyed with his "sister."

Bonnie leaned forward, her attractive features fixed in a cajoling expression. "Ethan, solving this old murder would make a huge contribution to the festivities that are planned for the opening of the Kirwan House. The Historical Society has been working on the project for over two years. It's going to be a great tourist attraction."

He could see that it was important to her that he take on the project. Maybe it wasn't such a bad idea. After all, they were both trying to put down roots in Whispering Springs.

He turned back to Paloma. The mayor was in her early forties. She was a striking woman with dark brown eyes and an elegant profile. Her camel-colored trousers and cream silk blouse looked sophisticated and expensive.

Bonnie had given him a little background the day before when she had phoned, bubbling with enthusiasm, to tell him that she wanted him to meet with the mayor. The editorial staff at the *Whispering Springs Herald* considered Paloma Santana to be the most effective mayor in recent years. Her family had a long history in the Whispering Springs area. Paloma was married to the successful developer of the Desert View Country Club, and the couple moved in the community's highest social circles.

In short, Paloma Santana was an excellent business contact.

"Tell me about the Kirwan case," he said.

Paloma sat back in her chair and crossed her legs. "Walter Kirwan was a brilliant, eccentric, highly respected author who lived and wrote here in Whispering Springs some sixty years ago. Does the title *A Long, Cold Summer* ring any bells?"

He rummaged around among the handful of memories he retained from his short and extremely limited experience with higher education and found one that was relevant.

"College," he said. "Freshman English. We're talking about *that* Walter Kirwan?"

"Yes. As Bonnie told you, the Historical Society has just finished restoring his house. Kirwan's death was big news in literary circles at the time and has since become something of a legend among Kirwan scholars."

"You say he was murdered?"

"That's part of the mystery. No one is quite sure what happened. According to the newspaper accounts, Kirwan and his housekeeper, a woman named Maria Torres, were alone together on the night of his death. Maria later told the authorities that everything was normal and routine that evening. After dinner, Kirwan retired to his study to work on a manuscript. Maria went to bed. She found his body in the study the next morning. He was slumped in his chair."

"Cause of death?"

"It was ruled a heart attack. But the rumors that the housekeeper had poisoned Kirwan started almost immediately. They have persisted to this day. Most history buffs and Kirwan scholars assume that she was the killer."

The familiar curiosity started to uncoil

deep in his gut. Reluctantly he reached for a notepad and picked up a pen. "Why was she a suspect?"

"Kirwan had made a will." Paloma's elegant jaw tensed slightly. "In it he left the house to Maria."

"So getting her hands on the house was supposedly the motive?"

"Yes. She was a poor woman from a hard-working family that was barely getting by. There is no doubt but that the house would have been a godsend to the Torres family."

Something in her voice made Ethan look up from his notes. "Let me guess. She didn't get it, right?"

"Right," Paloma replied. "Kirwan's Boston relatives had no intention of allowing his housekeeper to inherit the property. They brought their lawyers out to Arizona and had no problem breaking the will."

Ethan contemplated that for a few seconds. "How is Maria supposed to have murdered Kirwan?" he asked.

"They say she poisoned him with some substance that made it appear that he'd suffered a heart attack."

"Huh." Slowly he put down his pen. "I have to tell you that, unless you want to go to the trouble and expense of exhuming the body and running some tests, I doubt that it will be possible to discover the truth. Even if you did dig up the body, there's only a very slim chance that you could identify the poison at this late date."

"Exhumation is not an option," Paloma said. "Kirwan's relatives took the body back to Boston. Their descendants have no reason to cooperate with us."

"I've got to be honest with you. I don't think there's anything I can do that will give you the decisive answer you want," Ethan said.

"There's more to this than the question of whether or not Kirwan was murdered," Bonnie put in quickly. "There's a missing manuscript. It disappeared the same night that Kirwan died, and everyone involved at the time was sure that there was a connection."

Ethan propped his elbows on the arms of his chair and steepled his fingers. "This would be the manuscript that Kirwan evidently took into his study to read that night?"

"Yes." Paloma was very intent. "The same people who say that Maria Torres poisoned Walter Kirwan also insist that she stole the manuscript."

"Why would she do that?"

"Walter Kirwan was already a celebrated author at the time of his death. It had been five years since he'd published a book. His last manuscript would have been worth a great deal to the Kirwan estate. Maria Torres had to know that."

"Any theories on what happened to the manuscript?" Ethan asked.

"The assumption is that it disappeared into the collectors' market, but no trace of it has ever been found."

Ethan tapped his fingers together twice. "Anyone ever ask Maria about the murder and the missing manuscript?"

"Of course." Paloma shrugged. "She died two years ago at the age of eighty-nine, and right up until the end collectors and academics routinely contacted her to ask her about the last Walter Kirwan manuscript."

"What did she tell them?"

"The same thing she told her family and everyone else who asked about it. That Kirwan had been very dissatisfied with the manuscript, just as he had been with an earlier project. She said that he was morose and grim that evening. She claimed that the last thing he said to her before he closed the door of his study was that he intended to feed the manuscript to the fireplace, just as he had the other one."

Ethan frowned. "He told her that he was going to burn it?"

"Yes."

"Well, that would explain the missing manuscript," he pointed out gently.

"Not quite," Paloma said. "It was midsummer, a very warm night. Maria told her family later that the hearth was clean the next morning. There was no evidence that Kirwan had lit a fire."

"Huh."

Bonnie nodded knowingly. "There are a couple of other details about this case that you might find interesting. I did a little preliminary research in the library's collection of the back issues of the *Whispering Springs Herald*. Turns out that according to Maria, the door to Kirwan's study was still locked from the inside the next morning. She had to get the key to open it."

"What's the other detail?"

"Walter Kirwan had a visitor on the day of his death. His name was George Exford. According to Maria, the two men quarreled violently over whether or not the manuscript was ready for publication. Exford left in a furious temper because Kirwan had refused to let him take the book with him."

"Who was Exford?"

"Kirwan's literary agent. He had a vested interest in seeing to it that the manuscript was handed over to the publisher. There was a fair amount of money at stake."

"Huh," Ethan said again.

Paloma glanced at Bonnie.

"Don't worry," Bonnie said. "He always says that when he's getting interested in an old case."

Ethan ignored her. He met Paloma's eyes. "I get the feeling there's something personal here, Mrs. Santana. What makes you think Maria Torres was telling the truth?"

"She was my grandmother," Paloma said coolly. "On behalf of the entire family, I would like to see her name cleared."

10

They sat together at one of the outdoor cafes in Fountain Square. Arcadia ordered espresso. Zoe chose hot tea. It was midafternoon and the day had warmed up nicely. That morning it had been chilly, but Zoe had lathered on the sunscreen as usual. She had lived in Whispering Springs long enough to have developed a good deal of respect for the intensity of the desert light.

Zoe had always been intrigued and attracted by contrasts and intense colors, but she had never expected to find so many of both here in this starkly etched land. The Sonoran desert was a study in opposites and ever-changing hues. A landscape that at first glance looked as if it could not possibly sustain life had proved to be stunningly rich in both flora and fauna.

And the light was incredible. It dazzled the eye and created seductive shadows. The glorious yellows, purples and golds of a morning sunrise gave way to the unrelenting glare of the sun at high noon and then dissolved into the softest shades of twilight. The transition from the heat of late afternoon to the cool, silken air of the evening never ceased to fascinate her photographer's eye.

She took a sip of her tea, put down the cup and looked at Arcadia. "You want to tell me what's wrong?"

"Nothing's wrong."

"Arcadia, this is me, Zoe, remember? I'm the one who busted out of Xanadu with you." Xanadu was the private code word they shared for Candle Lake Manor. Somehow the name seemed to describe the bizarre reality of the place.

"It's okay, Zoe, really."

Zoe put up a hand. "Stop right there. I'm your best friend, with the possible exception of Harry, and he's not here right now. I'm telling you that I know there's something wrong."

Arcadia did a delicate grimace. "I was having a little trouble sleeping earlier this week. I felt sort of edgy and restless. But I'm all right now."

What was it about November this year? Zoe wondered. It seemed like most of the gang were having problems this month. Bonnie and the boys and Ethan were dealing with the anniversary of Drew Truax's death, she was brooding about the future of her marriage and worrying about Ethan's mood swings and now her best friend was on edge for some reason.

Arcadia picked up her tiny espresso cup with both hands. Her long nails, tinted to match her short, platinum hair, glinted a little in the light. Only someone who had known her for a while would have detected the signs of strain, Zoe thought. Arcadia was very good at concealing her emotions.

Zoe assumed that Arcadia was in her early forties, but she possessed the timeless elegance of a 1930s film star. What's more, she radiated the air of aloof, world-weary sophistication that went with the image. Today she was dressed in her signature icy pastels. Tall and willowy, she wore aqua silk trousers and a white silk tunic with languid, Greta Garbo-style grace.

Zoe had a napkin on her lap but Arcadia had not bothered with one. She drank her espresso and nibbled on a croissant with a breathtaking lack of concern for drips or crumbs. Food did not accidentally spill or splash onto Arcadia's expensive clothes.

"Do you want to tell me what's keeping you awake?" Zoe said. "I know it isn't because you're having great sex. Harry is still out of town."

"I'm starting to think that may be the problem," Arcadia said very seriously.

"Lack of hot sex?"

"No, Harry being out of town."

Zoe tore off a bit of croissant and slathered some butter on it. "I'm not following you."

"I think I'm getting used to having him around."

"So? He seems to like being around you. I don't see a problem here."

Arcadia's fingers tightened around the small cup. "The problem is that I may be developing a certain . . . dependency on him."

Zoe swallowed the bite of croissant. "You want to run that by me again?"

"I started having trouble sleeping shortly after he left on this latest job." Arcadia's silvery-blue eyes narrowed. "It was as if I'd become afraid of the dark. Three nights ago it was really bad."

"Tell me about it."

"I had been a little jumpy all day. It took me a long time to get to sleep. And then I woke up very suddenly. For a few seconds I was disoriented. I thought I was back in Xanadu."

"Your reaction was perfectly understandable, if you ask me," Zoe said briskly. "Whenever I dream of that place I wake up in a cold sweat."

Arcadia shook her head. "That's just it, I don't think that I was dreaming about it. I just woke up abruptly and felt afraid. As if someone had gotten through the locks on my front door."

Zoe went still. "But there was no sign of a break-in, right?"

"Of course not. I'd have yelled for Ethan if there was even a hint that someone had tripped Harry's new security system. But I felt very strange until . . ."

"Until what?"

Arcadia's mouth curved wryly. "Until Harry called."

Zoe relaxed a little. "And then you felt a whole lot better?"

"Yes."

"You're thinking that this weird feeling you get at night when Harry isn't there means that you've allowed him to get too close, aren't you?"

"All I know is that I wasn't having these feelings before I met him last month." Arcadia hesitated. "I think Harry sensed that I was nervous. He's started calling me twice a day instead of just at night."

Zoe smiled. "And suddenly you're sleeping better?"

"Much better."

"So you're worried that you might be getting addicted to Harry Stagg."

"It's been a very long time since I've trusted a man," Arcadia said. "I find the thought a little scary."

"For obvious reasons." Zoe patted her hand lightly. "But Harry Stagg is no Grant Loring."

"I know."

Arcadia relaxed visibly and drank the rest of her espresso.

11

Ethan took a bite of olive-and-jalapeño-dotted pizza and let his attentive audience wait while he chewed and swallowed. He caught Zoe's eye. It had been her idea to invite what she called "the gang" out for dinner that night.

He was not sure exactly when or how the gang had come into being, but at some point during the past few weeks, he and the others had formed a closely knit company. All but one of them was there.

In addition to Zoe and himself, the group included Bonnie and his nephews, Jeff and Theo. Arcadia and Singleton Cobb were also part of the odd mix. Harry Stagg, the most unexpected member of the gang, was the only one not present. He was still in LA.

Ethan finished the slice of pizza and surveyed his waiting audience.

"It's a classic locked-room mystery," he said.

"What's a classic locked-room mystery, Uncle Ethan?" Theo demanded, kicking the rung of his chair with his sneaker-shod feet.

Jeff gave a condescending snort. He was eight, two years older than Theo, and he never hesitated to take on the superior air of the all-knowing older brother.

"It means the room where they found Kirwan's body was locked, dummy," Jeff said.

"Don't call me a dummy, smart-ass," Theo shot back.

Bonnie glowered at both of them. "I do not want to hear any more language like that from either of you. Is that understood?"

"Dummy's not a bad word," Jeff said. "It just means that he's not very bright."

"Smart-ass just means an intelligent donkey," Theo proclaimed, defending himself with an expression of angelic innocence. "There's nothing wrong with donkey."

"Do I look like a copy of the *OED* to you?" Bonnie raised her brows. "I'm not discussing definitions of bad words here. I'm giving an order."

"What's an OED?" Jeff asked around a mouthful of pizza.

"The *Oxford English Dictionary,*" Singleton replied.

"A dictionary, huh?" Jeff was clearly intrigued. "Does it have the bad words in it? Our dictionary at school doesn't have any of those."

Ethan looked at him. "You checked?"

"Sure."

Bonnie rolled her eyes.

"Inquiring minds," Arcadia murmured.

"The *OED* is pretty much the final authority on the English language," Singleton said, "so it contains all the words, good and bad. As a matter of fact, I've got a full set in my shop if you want to—" He broke off when Bonnie gave him a warning scowl. "Uh, it's really big and heavy. Lots of volumes. Not what you'd call a light read. I don't think either of you would enjoy it."

Jeff and Theo brightened instantly. Ethan knew they were about to assure Singleton that they were fully capable of some heavy reading if the goal was worthwhile, but Bonnie spoke up swiftly.

"You were telling us about the Kirwan murder case, Ethan," she said. "What have you found out so far?"

"Not much," he admitted. "But it's sort of intriguing, even though the only book I ever read of Kirwan's was *The Long, Cold Summer.*"

"What was it about?" Theo asked.

Jeff heaved a theatrical sigh. "It was probably about a long, cold summer, dummy."

Bonnie frowned. "Jeff, I mean it. If you don't behave, we're going to leave."

Jeff opened his mouth to argue. Ethan caught his eye, saying nothing. Jeff subsided without a word and went back to his pizza.

Bonnie looked at Ethan. He saw the anxiety in her expression and understood her concerns. Jeff had been acting out for the past couple of weeks and it was getting worse. Unlike Theo, who seemed to have gotten past the anniversary of his father's death without too much angst this year, Jeff was not faring well.

Neither am I, kid, Ethan thought. But

sometimes you had to suck it up and act normal.

"How are you going to approach the research?" Zoe asked.

"In my customary brilliant fashion," Ethan said. "Gather all the facts and then hope like heck that inspiration strikes."

Singleton finished his slice of pizza. "Let me get this straight. The goal here is to prove that Maria Torres was innocent, right?"

"That's certainly the result that Paloma Santana would like to get," Bonnie said. "There's going to be a lot of media present on the day the Kirwan House is opened to the public. The mayor would love nothing more than to be able to announce that the mystery of the missing manuscript has been solved. She thinks that locating it would go a long way toward focusing the blame for Kirwan's death on someone other than her grandmother."

"Because it would prove that Maria Torres didn't steal it?" Arcadia asked.

"Right." Ethan looked down the table at Singleton. "You're the expert on locating rare books. Got time for some consulting work on this thing?"

"Sure." Singleton nodded. "Sounds interesting. But what happens if you don't come up with the answers Paloma Santana wants? What if you actually find convincing proof that Maria did kill Kirwan and steal the manuscript?"

Ethan shrugged. "If Paloma Santana insists on the answers, I'll give them to her privately and she can decide what to do with them. There's no reason to make them public. Everyone who was directly involved in the case is now dead, including Maria Torres. Proving that she actually did murder Kirwan wouldn't accomplish anything useful at this late date."

"But, Uncle Ethan," Jeff said, "don't you want the truth to come out on TV and in the newspaper? Mom said it would be really good publicity for your business."

"Yeah," Theo added. "Besides, you and Mom always say that you're supposed to tell the truth."

"I will tell the truth to Paloma Santana because she's the client. But there's no rule that says the truth has to be broadcast on the six-o'clock news."

"In fact," Arcadia said to the boys with the grave air of a wise aunt imparting important knowledge, "the newspapers and the media are the *last* places you should expect to find the truth."

Singleton chuckled. "Your cynical side is showing, Arcadia."

"It's one of my best features," she assured him.

"What does 'cynical' mean?" Theo asked.

Singleton launched into a detailed but carefully worded explanation. Bonnie offered some refinements and warnings about the risks of becoming too cynical. Arcadia defended the wisdom of cynicism. There were more questions from Jeff and Theo.

In the midst of the lively conversation bubbling around the table, Zoe smiled at Ethan. The silent, intimate acknowledgment of the bond between them did something to him deep inside. He heard the now-familiar click and felt the rush of awareness.

He saw the understanding in her eyes. She alone of all the people in his life knew why he spent his spare hours investigating the oldest and coldest of cold cases. The others assumed that it was merely a hobby, but Zoe knew that it was far more than that. She had realized right from the start that it was something he needed to do.

He had never put the compulsion into

words for himself, but Zoe had. *When you do get the answers, you create a little justice. You balance some invisible scales somewhere.*

The connection between them was growing stronger by the day. It sent a bone-deep chill of wonder through him. It also worried him like hell. Although they had been together for only a few weeks and married for even less time, she had somehow gotten closer than anyone else ever had. Maybe too close. She saw parts of his soul that had escaped detection by three ex-wives and the members of his own family. If she looked too deeply with those mysterious eyes of hers, she might see the parts that did not look good in the light of day.

The sense of impending doom closed in around him again. He had never before been involved this deeply. This was not a match made in heaven, he reminded himself. There were issues. But with each passing day he was more and more certain that if Zoe walked away from him, he would fall straight into hell.

After dinner Ethan and Singleton took Jeff and Theo and adjourned to the video arcade on the other side of Fountain Square. Zoe sat on a green wrought-iron bench together with Arcadia and Bonnie. The evening had turned cool, as evenings often did in the desert, but the area around the benches was warmed with large outdoor patio heaters that glowed a bright orange-red.

A profusion of small white lights outlined every tree and storefront. There were a number of signs heralding the upcoming Fall Festival Night. The annual event was the official Fountain Square kickoff to the holiday shopping season.

Arcadia watched the men and boys disappear into the video arcade. "Has Singleton asked you out yet, Bonnie?"

Bonnie did not move or take her attention away from the entrance to the arcade. "No."

"Hmm," Arcadia said. "Wonder why not?"

"What makes you think he might be interested in anything more than a causal friendship?" Bonnie asked quietly.

Zoe turned her head at that. "Are you kidding? Have you even noticed the way he looks at you?"

"He's biding his time," Arcadia said. "Doesn't want you to feel rushed. Making sure he'll be welcome in your life."

Zoe nodded. "I get the feeling he's the slow, cautious type."

Bonnie made a sputtering sound that was somewhere between exasperation and laughter. "What is this? Have you two suddenly decided to become matchmakers just because you're both getting some good sex yourselves?"

"Probably," Zoe said.

Arcadia gave a small, eloquent shrug. "Just making an observation."

Bonnie clasped her hands together in her lap. "Singleton is so very different from Drew."

There was a short silence.

"Maybe that's a good thing," Zoe offered at last. "You won't be tempted to make comparisons. You can let him be himself."

"Is that how it is with you and Ethan?" Bonnie asked.

"Yes." Zoe studied the play of the fountain waters. "Ethan is nothing like Preston. My relationship with my first husband was—" She broke off, searching for the right word. "Uncomplicated."

"And Ethan *is* complicated," Bonnie said. It was a statement of fact.

"Very." Zoe crossed her legs and swung

one foot lightly, thinking about her marriage. "I don't mind complicated. I'm a little complicated myself. But I'm starting to wonder if Ethan really wants me to know that side of him. He isn't big on communicating."

Arcadia was amused. "What man is?"

"Give Ethan some time," Bonnie urged. "He isn't accustomed to having anyone take an interest in his complicated side. Lord knows, none of his ex-wives wanted to experience that part of him. All they wanted was what they saw on the surface."

Arcadia nodded. "A man who looks like he can take care of himself and them, too."

"Yes," Bonnie said. "But none of them wanted to take care of him, at least none of them wanted to do it badly enough to work at it."

"Something tells me that's the way Ethan liked it," Zoe muttered.

Bonnie thought about that. "Maybe you're right. Less of an emotional risk that way, I guess. Whatever his communication issues were in his first three marriages, I can tell you that they got a whole lot worse after Drew was kidnapped and killed."

"He's carrying around a lot of guilt," Zoe said. "He was the older brother. A part of him will always feel that he failed to do what he was supposed to do—protect Drew."

She knew exactly how Ethan felt, she thought. She would never be entirely free of a similar sense of failure. She and Preston had promised to take care of each other. But in the end she had been unable to save him.

"Ethan is definitely going to be a lot of hard work for any woman who takes him on." Bonnie shook her head, smiling wryly. "I love him like a brother and I will always be eternally grateful to him for the way he took care of Jeff and Theo and me after Drew was gone. But I'll tell you the truth, I could never imagine myself married to him. Not in a million years."

"Which brings us back to Singleton," Arcadia said. "I do believe that the man is smitten."

Zoe cocked a brow. "'Smitten'?"

"I've always wanted to use that word," Arcadia said.

Bonnie exhaled slowly. "Smitten or not, I don't know him well enough to even think about marrying him."

"But?" Zoe prompted.

"But the boys like him a lot. They've turned him into a sort of second uncle, I think."

"And?"

Bonnie smiled. "And I think I would like to get to know him better. Much better."

"Good," Zoe declared. "I'm glad."

Bonnie laughed. "Enough about you and me, Zoe. What about your personal life, Arcadia? I assume that Harry Stagg is also a very complicated man?"

Zoe waited with great curiosity for Arcadia's response. Few people dared to ask her such directly personal questions. There was something about her friend that made most folks hesitate to intrude into the zone of privacy that she had erected around herself.

"Harry is not complicated," Arcadia said. "He is what he is."

Zoe shook her head. It was a very Arcadia sort of answer.

"Different from your late husband, I take it?" Bonnie pressed.

"Unfortunately, I don't think Grant Loring is all that late," Arcadia said. "I've got a hunch he's still alive, and if he is, we're still legally married. But, to answer your question, yes, Harry is very different from my husband. For starters, Grant tried to murder me."

Bonnie's jaw dropped visibly. "Good God."

Zoe was equally stunned but for a different reason. Arcadia had told her the truth about Grant Loring shortly after they escaped from Candle Lake Manor. But to her knowledge, Arcadia had not confided in anyone else with the possible exception of Harry Stagg.

Bonnie recovered from her initial shock. "I knew that you never discussed your life before Candle Lake Manor, and I was aware that there was some mystery about it, but I hadn't realized—"

"I faked my own death, hoping Grant would believe that his attempt to kill me had been successful," Arcadia said quietly. "I then checked myself into Candle Lake under a different name with the intention of lying low for a while. I figured that a psychiatric hospital would be the last place that Grant would look for me, assuming he was actively searching. After Zoe and I escaped, I bought a second new identity, hoping to muddy the waters even more."

"Where is Loring now?" Bonnie asked.

"I have no idea. Officially he died in an avalanche at a European ski resort. But I have a feeling that he's out there somewhere, living under a new identity, just as I am."

Bonnie shivered a little in the cool night air. "Scary thought."

"Sometimes," Arcadia agreed.

On the other side of the square, Ethan, Singleton and the boys emerged from the video hall. Jeff and Theo bounced around the men, talking animatedly about whatever had happened inside. The hero worship in their eyes made Zoe's heart turn over. Young males needed their role models so desperately, she thought.

For their part, Ethan and Singleton exuded the indulgent patience of alpha pack leaders. You knew just by the way they moved that even though they laughed and traded wisecracks with the boys, they were aware and on guard. These were the kind of men you could rely on in a crisis.

"I can certainly understand why you said that Harry Stagg was very different from Grant Loring," Bonnie whispered. She still sounded rather stunned.

"Oh, he is," Arcadia said calmly. "If Harry had tried to kill me, he would have succeeded."

12

A brief flash of light at the edge of the searcher's field of vision was the only warning this time. The familiar aura heralded the approaching storm and the temporary darkness that would follow.

Panic struck first.

No. Got to stay in control.

The brainstorm descended, turning everything, including the fear, into mindless static.

The searcher came out of it a short time later, weakened and very shaky. Dread and fear were the first emotions to return. The storms were coming with increasing frequency these days.

The searcher sat up slowly and looked around quickly. *Fell across the footstool. Could have been worse. Could have cut my head on the corner of the table and knocked myself unconscious or left traces of blood for someone to find in the morning.*

That would have been a disaster.

The flashlight had fallen to the carpet beside the reading chair. Its beam lanced aimlessly across the library, illuminating a red mug on a low table.

The searcher reached down for the flashlight and encountered a small, sharp object on the carpet next to the table. A shard of broken glass.

Alarmed, the searcher aimed the flashlight at the table and saw that the vase that had been there a short time earlier was gone. The fragile object was now in a dozen little pieces on the floor.

Must have knocked it off when I fell. It's okay. Just a little bud vase. She'll assume one of the workers broke it.

The hands on the whimsical wall clock showed that only three minutes had passed.

The security guard wasn't due to drive back down the street in front of the Designers' Dream Home for another fifteen minutes.

There was time to find a souvenir. Couldn't leave without one.

13

Zoe was thinking about how Ethan had seemed more energized and less moody at breakfast and about how that was probably because he was involved in the Kirwan murder case, when she parked in front of the Designers' Dream Home the next morning. Maybe solving the old mystery was just the kind of intellectual distraction he needed to help him get through the bad time this November.

A sleek silver Jaguar pulled into the drive and stopped directly behind her. In her rearview mirror she watched Lindsey Voyle climb out from behind the wheel in all her stylish, minimalist glory.

She was an attractive, assertive woman in her late thirties or maybe very early forties. Her expensively cut dark hair was discreetly tinted and showed no trace of gray. Zoe found Lindsey's hazel gaze disconcerting. It seemed to follow her the way the eyes of the figures in an old master's painting did. It was as if Lindsey were tracking her on some inner radar screen.

Lindsey wore so much black that it would have been easy to assume she was from New York, but it turned out that she was a recent arrival from Los Angeles. Today she had on a black knit pullover of very fine cotton, black pants and black sandals. She carried a black leather satchel in one hand. The only pop of color was the unusual turquoise-and-silver necklace around her throat. Zoe recognized the piece. It was a one-of-a-kind creation that Lindsey had purchased at Arcadia's boutique, Gallery Euphoria.

Zoe was suddenly very much aware of her own attire, which consisted of a long, sleeveless dress in brilliant violet topped with a gauzy green duster that floated around her ankles. In the mirror that morning the outfit had looked good, vivid and cheerful. Now, compared to Lindsey's slick, dramatic black, she had a nasty suspicion that she bore a strong resemblance to a circus clown.

Their tastes in clothes pretty much echoed their personal design styles, she decided. The bedroom that Lindsey was doing inside the Designers' Dream Home was a study in minimalist white accented with the palest of woods.

Zoe was doing the library in a look that was the polar opposite: an eclectic mix of rich, saturated colors and textures.

She got out of the car and reached into the backseat to hoist the large, red tote. It was one of a half dozen that she owned, each in a different color. The bag contained several of the necessities of her profession, including a camera, measuring tape, appointment calendar, sketchbook, small tool kit and a box of colored pencils and felt markers. It also held several heavy tile samples and some fabric swatches she intended to take to another project later in the day. And then there was the antique brass doorknob that served as her key ring.

The interior design business was not a career for weaklings, she mused.

She summoned up what she hoped would pass for a friendly smile. “Good morning, Lindsey.” She slung the tote over her shoulder, slammed the car door shut and started toward the front steps. “Beautiful day, isn’t it?”

“Yes, it is,” Lindsey said neutrally. She paused. “I had a visit from Tabitha Pine.”

“So did I. She seems to feel that we need to experience some of her meditation sessions before we can draw up our proposals.”

“I think she’s right,” Lindsey said. “I signed up for a full course of twenty sessions.”

Zoe did a silent *aaaargh*. She had been considering dropping in on one or two of the classes. A full course of sessions probably cost somewhere in the neighborhood of two thousand dollars.

The front door of the show house was locked.

“Looks like we’re the first to arrive today,” Zoe said. Each of the designers had been assigned a key. She reached into the red tote to find hers.

“I’ll get it.” Lindsey already had her key in hand. She fitted it into the lock and opened the door.

“Thanks.”

Zoe found Lindsey's efficiency one of her more irritating characteristics.

Zoe went briskly across the threshold, not hesitating as she usually did before entering a structure because she had already been inside the Designers' Dream Home on several occasions during the past few weeks. There was no need to brace herself for the unknown.

When she was younger she had assumed that everyone picked up on the invisible miasma of strong psychic energy that sometimes clung to the places where people had lived, loved, laughed or died. It was only when she was older that she had come to understand that, while a lot of folks did get occasional twinges of sensation or experience an inexplicable sense of déjà vu when they walked into a strange house or room, what she felt was quite different.

It had not taken her long to figure out that, as far as most people were concerned, "different" usually translated into "crazy." As a result, she had gotten very good at hiding her sensitivity to the psychic energy that was sometimes trapped in the walls of a house or building.

She had gotten so good at concealing the

truth about her psychic side that she had been able to keep it from her first husband. She had loved Preston dearly and she knew that he had loved her. But deep down she had always known that if she told him her secrets he would have worried desperately about the state of her mental health. He never would have been able to look at her the same way again.

She would not have blamed him. There were times in the past when she herself had feared for her sanity, especially during those ghastly months at Candle Lake Manor.

The most unsettling aspect of her relationship with Ethan was that, although she had told him about her sixth sense, he had been relatively unfazed. That was the good news.

The bad news was that she was pretty sure the reason he had taken her revelation so calmly was because he did not really believe that she was psychic. In his opinion, she was merely extremely intuitive. As a private investigator who relied heavily on his own intuition, Ethan could accept and deal with that explanation.

Lindsey went ahead of her down the hall, heading for the wide staircase that led to the second level of the big house.

"I took a look at your library yesterday on my way out," Lindsey said over her shoulder. "I see you decided to go with those dark red bookshelves. Don't you think that color will be too strong in that space? You've already got a lot going on in there."

Take deep breaths, Zoe told herself. *Whatever you do, don't get defensive.*

"The effect will be much different once the books are on the shelves," she said.

"Well, it's your space." Lindsey started up the stairs, clutching her satchel. "But you've already got so many colors in there. All that ocher and terra-cotta is a bit much. The room seems very warm, especially for such a hot climate."

Zoe ground her teeth but managed to keep her mouth shut.

Lindsey did not wait for a response. At the top of the stairs she turned and disappeared in the direction of the master bedroom suite.

Promising herself that she would not swear, not even under her breath, Zoe continued down the hall to her library.

Lindsey was wrong, she thought. The deep red squares of the floor-to-ceiling shelves would act as punchy frames for the books and objets d'art displayed against the blue-trimmed ocher walls. They would also accent the terra-cotta tiles and the colorful rugs.

She told herself that Lindsey was also mistaken when she said that the colors in the library were too hot for a desert climate. The hues did not look warm; on the contrary, they made a cool contrast to the heat. The long-standing success of the Spanish Colonial and Mediterranean styles was proof that rich jewel-toned colors worked in a bright environment. They provided the illusion of shade and helped cut the glare of an intense sun.

In her opinion, *white* was the wrong choice for the desert, Zoe thought as she rounded the corner into her library. Especially when it was used as starkly and extensively as Lindsey had used it in that bedroom upstairs. The last thing you wanted to do in this brightly lit landscape was reflect the light. White could easily act like a mirror when it came to glare.

There were exceptions to every rule, of course. Arcadia could get away with white in her apartment because Arcadia was Arcadia. Pales suited her personality and created the right kind of energy in her living space.

But the energy flow upstairs in Lindsey's bedroom was going to be less than optimal, Zoe concluded.

She stopped on the threshold and surveyed her library. She had designed it with a family in mind. She was not sure why, but for some reason she'd had a picture of a mom and a dad and two little kids in her head from the very start of the project. Both children had Ethan's dark hair and amber eyes.

She had told herself that it was just a useful mental image constructed by her imagination to help her give the space a focus. She was accustomed to working with the needs of an actual client, but in this instance there wasn't a real homeowner with unique requirements and a personality. So she had invented her little family and tried not to think too much about why the kids looked a lot like Ethan.

She was pleased with the way the room had turned out. It was comfortable and inviting. There was something interesting or intriguing going on in every corner.

She walked slowly through the space, opening her senses to the energy flows, making certain that things felt right. It was an old-fashioned space in many ways, imbued with the atmosphere of an early-nineteenth-century library. There was no big-screen television or state-of-the-art sound system. Fortunately, another designer had been assigned the media room down the hall.

This was a room designed for contemplation, study and personal time. She wanted this space to be a refuge for every member of the household, a place where dreams could take shape.

She paused beside the miniature chairs and table she had arranged for the imaginary children and adjusted the position of the globe. Then she crossed to the large writing desk and stood behind it, making certain that whoever sat there would have a view of the fountain in the garden outside.

She liked to incorporate water or a view of it into her rooms. It provided its own special kind of energy. So did plants, which was why she had placed a large cluster of them on the other side of this space. They not only purified the air in a room, they cleansed the energy that flowed through it.

She tweaked the frame of the picture over the fireplace. It was a photograph of Nightwinds Canyon at dawn. She had taken it herself late last month. Ethan had risen with her every morning in the dark for four days in a row to keep her company at the edge of the canyon while she went through roll after roll of film, waiting for the one right shot.

Turning away from the photo, she moved toward the first of the two adult reading chairs, probing for the feel of the energy flow.

She was only a couple of steps away from the first chair when the whispers of darkness snagged on her fully engaged psychic senses.

She nearly screamed in shock. It was as if she had blundered into the sticky strands of an invisible spiderweb. Flinching, she hurriedly stepped back out of range. A shiver went through her as her pulse jumped into high gear. She struggled to close down her wide-open senses.

What on earth?

An old memory from an especially bad night at Candle Lake rose like a monster from the depths. She squelched it swiftly. This was her show house library, for heaven's sake, not H Ward.

Okay, let's try this again. Maybe she had overreacted. It was true that her imagination coupled with her psychic senses could produce some unnerving moments on occasion.

But her psychic senses had never betrayed her, she reminded herself. Cautiously she opened them wide once more and took a step forward.

The cobwebs drifted across her senses, making her shudder. There *was* something there near the chair. She had experienced a similar sensation once before in her life, and the recollection of it still had the power to chill her blood.

This is not H Ward.

She repeated the mantra to herself several times but her throat remained clenched against nausea and she was getting lightheaded. She refused to allow herself to retreat. She had to know what this ghastly stuff was.

The invisible threads drifted around her, so faint she could barely sense them, but unmistakably there.

Impossible. Just two days before she had come here to add some final touches. She had picked up nothing out of the ordinary that day.

What is going on here?

Calm down and think. You've been to

enough murder scenes to know what they feel like, and this room isn't giving off those kinds of vibes. The walls aren't screaming the way they do when blood has been spilled in a room.

The energy was quite faint but extremely murky. That was not typical of most of the psychic sensations she encountered. Her sixth sense responded keenly to traces of the stronger passions, and those tended to be primitive and raw in nature. Rage, fear, panic, hatred, lust and obsessive need were elemental energies. The taints they left behind were usually sharp and clear.

This was . . . something else, something very frightening.

The psychic web seemed to be emanating from an area around the footstool. She examined the space closely. Everything looked exactly as it had the last time she had been in that room. There was no sign of recent violence or destruction.

No, that wasn't quite true.

Light glinted on a shard of glass near the footstool. She reached down and picked it up. The color of the glass was familiar.

She glanced at the small table beside the chair. The bud vase was gone; smashed.

There was something else that was not right about the space, but she could not immediately identify it.

She turned slowly on her heel, examining every inch of the library. When she came to the table in the children's corner she stopped.

She had arranged a handful of colorful, everyday objects on the low table. Jeff had supplied a small dinosaur for the informal collection and Theo had given her a tiny model motorcycle. She had added one of her new chili-pepper red mugs because it picked up the color of the bookcase shelves.

The red mug was gone.

14

That night she dreamed of Xanadu.

She rose from the narrow bed and put on the hospital-issue robe. The garment hung loosely around her. It had fit when she was admitted to Candle Lake Manor, but she had lost a lot of weight during the past few months. The drugs that Dr. McAlister tried to force down her in hopes of inducing her cooperation in therapy had effectively smothered her appetite.

She had eventually learned how to dispose of some of the pills without anyone realizing that she was not swallowing them, but she could not evade all of the meds. And even on those rare days when her mind was relatively clear, she had no appetite. The enormous willpower required to contain the alternating tides of rage, fear and desperation that regularly swept over her left her so exhausted that the task of eating seemed overwhelming.

That had to change, she thought. She had to start consuming the calories she needed to rebuild her strength. She would never escape if she did not eat right.

She went to the small, barred window. Her room was on the third floor of the asylum, providing her with a view over the high fence that surrounded the Manor. From there she could see the lake.

Cold moonlight gleamed on the surface of the evil waters. Sometimes the only possible escape that she could envisage involved swimming out to the middle of the lake and letting herself sink into the depths.

But she had avoided McAlister's poison that morning, and tonight her mind was clearer than it had been in some time. She did not want to think about sinking forever into the depths of the lake.

She needed an objective; she had to start planning her escape. She had to give herself some hope. It was a certainty that no one else around this place would provide it.

She turned away from the window and went to the door, trying the knob the way she always did, in the hope that someone had forgotten to lock it.

The door opened. One of the orderlies had been careless again. It wasn't the first time. The staff at Candle Lake was not composed of what anyone would term dedicated medical professionals.

Dr. Harper, the head of this very expensive, very private loony bin, wasn't paid to cure his patients. He got the big bucks from his clients because he was willing to house their crazy relatives out of sight and out of mind.

Moving from the cell-like room, she drifted along the hall. It was as if she were a ghost separated from reality by a thin veil. Everything felt slightly unreal. She reminded herself that she still had the residue of some of McAlister's drugs in her system.

The lights had been turned down in the

corridors as they always were at night, but they were never switched off. The halls of Xanadu were lit with an eerie fluorescent glow.

She had to learn her way around this place. She wanted to create a map in her head so that when the time came, she would be able to move quickly and confidently.

She passed a series of closed and locked doors and paused when she reached the corner. She had a blurry memory of turning left when the orderlies escorted her to Dr. McAlister's office, so tonight she would turn right.

This was uncharted territory.

She floated through a series of hallways, turned another corner and found herself confronting a pair of swinging doors that blocked the entrance to another corridor of locked rooms. She read the black-and-white sign on the wall: H WARD.

She moved through the swinging doors. This ward looked much the same as the one in which she was housed but there was a different psychic feel to this space.

She sensed the faint, disturbing currents shifting around her but did not recognize them. These sensations were unlike the other strong emotions that saturated the hospital.

Instinct warned her that if she got tangled up in these sticky strands she would be trapped forever.

The spiderwebs of energy seemed to emanate from behind the door of one of the rooms. She went cautiously forward. The invisible strands grew darker, denser, more intense.

She halted, unable to take another step closer to the door of the room.

Fear shot through her. She had gone too far.

The invisible stuff enveloped her, sticking to all of her senses: sight, touch, hearing, taste, even her sense of smell. But it clung most tenaciously to her sixth sense, the one that made her different.

A cloudy darkness closed in around her. She realized that she was about to faint.

She had to get out of there.

She managed to take a step back. The dizziness made it difficult to keep her balance. She grabbed the rail on the wall.

Wispy threads tugged at her, refusing to release her.

Panic gave her strength. Using the rail for leverage, she hauled herself back another step. Some of the threads fell away. She retreated again and this time was able to pull free.

She whirled and fled back to the limited safety of her room.

She had been through a lot at Candle Lake Manor, but whatever it was that seethed behind that door in H Ward scared her more than anything else she had yet experienced.

A last, trailing wisp of silky darkness touched the nape of her neck. She could feel the faint tremors in the gossamer threads that warned of the approach of the spider. . . .

She awoke with the scream still locked in her throat.

"Zoe." Ethan leaned over her, anchoring her to the bed by her wrists, one bare leg trapping hers. "Wake up. You're okay. Wake up."

The comforting reality of her bedroom, together with the reassuring heat and strength of Ethan's body gradually replaced the fragments of the nightmare. A shudder of relief went through her.

"Sorry about that." Her voice was oddly hoarse in her own ears. "Didn't mean to wake you."

"I was awake."

She looked up at him, fresh anxiety replacing the fear left behind by her dream. "Another bout of insomnia?"

"I was doing some thinking," he said.

Yeah, right. He was lying, she knew. He had been unable to sleep. Again.

"Are you okay?" he asked.

"Yes." She tried to breathe deeply. "I haven't had any of the really bad dreams for a while. I was beginning to think that I was free of them. Should have known better."

Ethan sat up against the pillows, wrapped one arm around her and hauled her tightly against him. He stroked her shoulder and arm gently, soothing her the way he would have soothed any startled creature.

"Look on the bright side," he said. "The fact that you're going for longer periods of time between nightmares is probably a good sign."

"Probably." She tried to force herself to relax against him but her heart was still beating too fast and the sticky strands of the dark dream clung to her. "Give me a minute. I'll be fine."

"I know. You can deal with it. You always

do." He continued to move his big hand up and down her arm, holding her snugly against him. "Bad one this time?"

"Yes."

"Want to talk about it?"

A fresh wave of panic shot through her. Tell him about this dream? Try to explain exactly why it frightened her so badly? No. Not a good idea. Definitely not.

She had told Ethan about many of the frightening things she had encountered at Candle Lake Manor; about how the corrupt head of the sanatorium, Dr. Ian Harper, had conspired with her in-laws to drug her and commit her against her will.

She had told him about Venetia McAlister, the doctor who operated a lucrative side business consulting at crime scenes. McAlister had been obsessed with the possibility that Zoe really was psychic and had tried to force her to report her paranormal responses at grisly crime scenes where murder and worse had been done.

She had told Ethan about the ordeal of the escape from Xanadu.

She had told him more of her secrets than she had told anyone else, including Arcadia, but she dared not confide her deepest, bleakest fear, the one she had discovered that night when she wandered the halls of Candle Lake Manor and blundered into a psychic spiderweb.

"The dream was about something that happened one night when I managed to get out of my room and have a look around," she said, choosing her words carefully. "My head was not completely clear of the drugs, but I could finally string a couple of coherent thoughts together. One of the orderlies accidentally left the door of my room unlocked."

"What happened?" Ethan asked quietly.

"I . . . walked around the halls for a while, trying to get a feel for the layout of the building."

"Mapping an escape route?"

"Yes."

He moved his hand rhythmically along her arm, offering silent comfort. "Okay, I can see why that memory would have provoked an anxiety dream."

"That night the place seemed to be a maze. Probably because my brain was still half mush. I was afraid that I would never be able to find my way when the time came."

"But you and Arcadia did find your way out."

"Yes."

"And now you're free." He kissed the top of her head. "Just keep reminding yourself of that fact."

"Okay."

"I know." His mouth curved in humorless understanding. "Some things are easier said than done, right?"

"Uh-huh."

His leg moved under the covers, brushing her thigh. She flinched. His hand stilled on her arm. "This must have been a really bad one. You're so tense you feel like you might snap in my hands."

She closed her eyes briefly, unable to tell him what a poor choice of words "you might snap" actually was under the circumstances.

"Want to do the warm milk thing?" he asked. "That seems to work for you."

"It works." She grimaced. "But I really don't like warm milk."

"In that case, perhaps we should try some exotic massage techniques." He closed his hand around the curve of her hip and squeezed suggestively.

She knew that he was teasing her a little, trying to lighten the mood with hints of playful sex. She knew he was right. She desperately needed the distraction of his lovemaking right now, this very minute. She could not recall ever needing anything so much in her entire life.

"You actually know some exotic massage techniques?" she asked, trying for the same lighthearted, suggestive tone.

"As it happens, I have made an in-depth study of the subject, so to speak." His hand moved under the edge of her thigh-length nightgown. "Would you care for a hands-on demonstration?"

She turned a little in his arms and found one of his bare feet with her toes. "Depends what you intend to put your hands on."

"I thought I'd start here."

He slid his palm between her thighs and moved his thumb very deliberately across the sensitive place he found there.

The searing rush of her own response startled her. Maybe it was the adrenaline left behind by the dream. Whatever the reason, she was suddenly wet.

"I take it that particular technique works for you?" Ethan asked against her mouth.

She drew a deep breath, shivering with

the intensity of her need. "Yes. Yes, it definitely works for me. Got any others you'd like to demonstrate?"

"There's this one."

He eased his way down her body, hands gliding warmly along her waist and hips. She realized that he was already fully aroused.

He raised her knees and did something quite incredible with his tongue.

"Ethan."

Without taking his lips away from her aching, swollen core, he probed her with his fingers, finding the special place just inside the entrance.

Her body reacted as if he had pulled a trigger.

She locked her fists in his hair as her climax rolled through her. She convulsed so tightly and with such force that she could not catch her breath. The sweeping rush of sexual satisfaction swamped all else, including the tendrils of the nightmare.

He was inside her before the small contractions had stopped, filling and stretching her over-sensitized body until she wondered that she did not shatter.

When his climax pounded through both of them she held him with all the strength she possessed, needing the hard, sure feel of him to keep her tethered to the earth.

When it was over they lay in a damp, tangled heap.

"For what it's worth," Ethan mumbled into the pillow, "I believe that we have just proved unequivocally that the exotic massage technique beats the hell out of warm milk."

She smiled. "You mean for dealing with nightmares?"

"Hell, I think it will handle just about anything."

She turned on her side. "Will you be able to get to sleep now?"

"Don't know about sleep," he muttered, in a heavy, drowsy voice. "But if you will excuse me, I believe that I will pass out for a while."

She held him while he fell asleep, listening to his even breathing, thankful for the passion that flared so easily between them. It provided a temporary release for both of them.

But she knew that the source of the anxiety that had animated the nightmare was probably not going to be banished for long now that it had been resurrected. She had faced most of her fears of Candle Lake Manor head-on, but there was one that she could not confront directly. She had tried to bury it in a deep, forgotten corner of her mind. Tonight it had risen from the grave.

She had to find a way to slay the psychic spider or it would stalk her for the rest of her life.

She could talk to Ethan about almost anything but she dared not talk to him about this. He did not even believe that she possessed a sixth sense. How could she possibly explain to him that her greatest fear was that the psychic aspect of her nature might ultimately destroy her sanity?

She could not bring herself to tell him that her in-laws and everyone at Candle Lake Manor who had claimed that she was crazy might someday be proved right.

15

She came awake the next morning with the realization that she needed to concoct a strategy for dealing with the psychic spider-webs that she had encountered in the library at the Designers' Dream Home. Today she would make plans. The decision to take action energized her and renewed her spirits. Ethan noticed her improved mood at breakfast.

"Feeling better, I take it?" he said, pouring coffee for himself.

"Much better."

"No hangover from the nightmare?"

"Your incredible exotic massage techniques made a new woman of me," she assured him.

"And here I was just getting used to the other woman."

"Variety is the spice of life."

"I like variety in my work but I'm not so keen on it in other areas of my life," he said, oddly serious.

She did not comment that three previous marriages argued otherwise. That would not have been fair. Bonnie had told her that none of Ethan's three divorces had been his idea. When Ethan makes a promise, Bonnie explained, he keeps it. The problem was that none of the other three women he had married had kept the promises they had made to him.

"Okay, maybe I'm not a totally new woman," she admitted. "Just a refreshed and rejuvenated woman."

"Sounds good to me." He smiled, got to his feet and pulled her up out of the chair to kiss her. "Glad I could be of assistance."

"I am, of course, deeply grateful," she said when she could speak again.

"Gratitude is good." He flashed her his most wicked grin, the one that never failed to send little shots of lightning through her. "I want you to know that I stand ready to give you my special massage therapy anytime you need it."

"Your generosity leaves me speechless."

"Yeah? Well, turns out generosity also has its own rewards." His mouth curved wryly as he headed for the front door. "I got some sleep myself last night."

She trailed after him, pleased. "I'm glad."

"We've got one of our stimulating little design meetings scheduled today, don't we?"

"Now, Ethan, you know we have to make some decisions about Nightwinds."

"Yeah, sure."

"You said yourself you don't want to live with all that pink around you."

"I'm all for getting rid of the pink. But I'm still not convinced that yellow is an improvement."

"I'm not suggesting taxicab yellow, for heaven's sake. I'm thinking of a warm, faded, ocher-gold sort of color. The shade you see on old Mediterranean palazzi."

"I've never seen an old Mediterranean palazzo. And what's ocher, anyway?"

"Never mind. I'll show you some paint chips today when we go out to Nightwinds."

"Okay. So long as we get to eat first. I can't handle a design meeting unless I've had lunch." He paused at the tiny hall table and looked curiously at the objects lying next to his keys. "What the hell are these doing here?"

She cleared her throat. "They're uh, emergency flares."

"I know what they are." He picked up his new key chain and the flares. "Just wondered why they happen to be sitting here."

"I thought you might like to keep them in your car." She knew she was turning red. "In case of an emergency or something."

She was pretty sure she saw the corner of his mouth twitch, but he merely nodded agreeably.

"Good idea," he said. "You never know when you might need emergency flares."

To her surprise, he actually whistled on his way out the door.

She was definitely not whistling when she left for work a short time later. Outside in the parking lot, she walked briskly to her newly assigned parking space, her mind on her slowly evolving anti-spiderweb plan.

So focused was she on how to approach the matter of the psychic cobwebs, she did not notice Hooper from apartment 1B until he collided with her. The stack of large cardboard cartons he had been carrying in his arms tumbled to the pavement.

"Oops, sorry, Zoe," he muttered. "Didn't see you."

Hooper was short and wide. Male pattern baldness had struck him early in life. He favored polyester pants that had been designed for the full-figured male and a rumpled, short-sleeved sport shirt that looked as if it had been pulled out of the dirty laundry hamper.

Hooper was addicted to high-tech gadgets. His belt was festooned with what had to be at least ten pounds of hardware. Zoe recognized a phone and a small computer, but the rest of the objects that dangled around his waist mystified her.

"No harm done." She glanced at the big boxes and recognized a familiar brand name. "New computer?"

"Yep." Hooper bent down to retrieve one of the oversized cartons. "Arrived yesterday. This baby's loaded. I unpacked it last night and was cruising the 'net by ten. Thought I'd get these cartons out of the way this morning." He straightened. "Hey, you're planning to move soon, aren't you? Need a nice, sturdy box?"

"No, thanks."

Hooper shrugged and surveyed the large metal garbage bin that sat against the wall of the apartment building. The container was filled nearly to the brim with trash, newspapers and bulging plastic sacks.

There was a new, large, neatly lettered sign tacked on the wall above the bin. FLATTEN ALL BOXES.

Hooper's eyes narrowed. "Well, well, well. Looks like Sergeant Duncan has been brewing up some more rules for us. Flatten all boxes, huh? You know something? I've had it with Ms. Anal-Retentive. If she wants these boxes flattened, she can damn well do it herself."

One by one he hurled the empty computer cartons up onto the top of the garbage heap, where they effectively concealed the new sign.

When he was finished with his show of defiance, he raised both arms high over his head, fists clenched in victory.

"Screw you, Sergeant," he chortled.

Zoe was not unsympathetic. Nevertheless, she could not help but notice that with the large boxes sitting atop the garbage bin there was no more room for trash. The bin was not due to be emptied by the garbage pickup company until tomorrow.

Reminding herself that she had other problems, she got into her car, started the engine and drove out of the parking lot.

A short time later she opened the offices of Enhanced Interiors and went straight to the bookshelf. Singleton was helping her locate and acquire books in the field of interior design philosophy. Thanks to him, her collection was growing rapidly.

The concept of designing living spaces so that they promoted harmony and increased the flow of positive energy was not a product of contemporary New Age thinking. Rather, it was thousands of years old.

Throughout the ages, a lot of very intelligent people had spent a great deal of time and effort studying the psychic effects of interior arrangements. Some of the theories were based on ancient religious principles. Others grew out of attempts to create mathematical and astrological approaches to the problems of design. Her growing personal library contained several volumes devoted to the study of theories set forth by the sages of a number of long-dead civilizations.

Research in the field continued, although

modern sensibilities demanded a scientific gloss. She possessed numerous reports of controlled psychological studies that detailed how various colors of paint applied to the walls of prisons, schoolrooms and hospitals dramatically affected the moods of those housed inside. She had reams of data on the therapeutic uses of plants and aquariums in homes and doctors' offices.

On some deep, intuitive level, people had understood for a very long time that they were impacted either positively or negatively by the designs of the rooms in which they lived and worked.

She carried a stack of books to her desk and sat down. There were no appointments on her calendar that morning. With any luck she would be able to spend the next few hours searching for information on psychic spiderwebs.

Several hours later she looked up from an old medieval religious text that detailed a technique for cleansing a room of ghosts and evil spirits and was startled to see that it was already noon. She was supposed to meet Ethan at twelve-thirty for lunch and a discussion of paint chips.

She made one last note on the pad of paper that sat on the desk and wearily got to her feet. She was stiff from the hours of intense study. Worse, she was depressed by the lack of results.

She needed some fresh air.

Grabbing her acid-green tote, she closed and locked Enhanced Interiors and set off for the offices of Truax Investigations.

Although the address was only a few blocks away on Cobalt Street, the neighborhood was very different from the trendy, upscale district where her business was located.

Ethan's office was in one of the older sections of Whispering Springs. Zoe liked the area. True, there was a dated, slightly seedy air about the low, Spanish Colonial-style buildings with their faded stucco walls, red-tile roofs and arched doorways. But they had character, just like Ethan.

At number 49 Cobalt Street, she went up the walk, across a small brick entrance patio and entered the cool, shadowy hall. The staircase that led to Truax Investigations loomed. She glanced at it and then turned and opened the door of the only other business on the premises, Single-Minded Books.

At the rear of the shop she saw Singleton's shaved head gleaming in the alien light of his computer screen.

"Be with you in a minute," Singleton called.

"Take your time."

"Zoe?" Singleton emerged from the grotto that he called an office. "What's up?"

"I'm on my way to meet Ethan for lunch. We have a design meeting at Nightwinds this afternoon."

Singleton chuckled. "No need to look like you're going to a funeral. I'm sure you've had clients who were more difficult than Ethan."

"Maybe, but for some reason I can't recall their names."

"Well, there was that guy who killed his wife a few months back."

"A different matter entirely," she assured him loftily. "David Mason may have been a murderer, but he was not a difficult client. I had no problem at all working with him on design issues."

Singleton folded his arms and leaned on the counter. "So what's the trouble with Truax? Is it the recliner thing?"

"His obsession with recliners is only one minor issue, as far as I'm concerned. The real problem is that he appears to have absolutely no sense of color."

"Not fair. He knows he doesn't like pink."

"I'm not so sure about that. I've got a sneaking suspicion that if you and Harry hadn't told him that long-term exposure to the extensive amount of pink used at Nightwinds would rot a man's brain, he probably would have gone on living there quite happily and never agreed to have the place repainted."

"But he did agree," Singleton pointed out. "So it sounds like you owe Harry and me big-time."

"Ethan went along with the idea of repainting," she admitted, "but he's fighting me every inch of the way, room by room, when it comes to color. We managed to agree on the kitchen but now we're bickering over the great room. I really believe that if he had his way, the entire house would be plain off-white inside and out."

"He says that if you get your way, every room will be a different color."

"Talk about overexaggerating. I'm merely suggesting that we go for some drama. It's not like I've got alternatives here. Ethan insists on sticking to a very tight budget, and paint is the least expensive way to achieve a lot of impact."

Singleton looked thoughtful. "Guys aren't always real big on dramatic impact, at least not in the places where they live."

"I don't know about guys in general, but I have certainly discovered that guys like Ethan are highly resistant to change in their personal space. Probably a control thing."

"Or simple fear." Singleton shrugged. "Don't forget he had a bad experience with the decorator who did his offices in LA."

"That poor designer, whoever she was, had nothing to do with the fact that he was forced into bankruptcy."

"I know, but I think in some weird way, Ethan associates all that expensive furniture she made him buy with the financial disaster that he went through. He told me that he only got pennies on the dollar at the auction."

She swept out one hand in an exasperated arc. "Well, it certainly wasn't the designer's fault."

"Apparently she told him that those high-end desks and the reception-lobby sofas and tables were good investments."

She frowned. "I'm sure she meant that they were excellent investments in the sense that they projected the right image for his business."

"Guess Ethan thought she meant they would appreciate in value."

"Furniture rarely appreciates in value."

"Yeah, well, maybe she didn't explain that clearly to Ethan."

Zoe groaned. "All I know is that every design meeting with him turns into a skirmish."

"Like I said, simple male fear."

"Uh-huh." She paused. "Speaking of fear."

"Yeah?"

She pretended to examine the nineteenth-century diary displayed under the counter's glass top. "I know this is none of my business, but I was wondering if you plan to ask Bonnie out one of these days."

Singleton did not move. "I'm thinking about it."

"Oh." She waited a beat but Singleton did not offer to enlighten her further. "I'm glad. I was worried that you might be hesitating because you thought she wouldn't be receptive to the idea and I am pretty sure she would be. Receptive, that is."

"I'm sure as hell not going to ask her out until we're way past the anniversary of the day her husband was kidnapped and murdered."

She was struck, not only by the comment but by the insight behind it. "You're right. I hadn't considered that aspect of the situation. This might not be the best time to make your move. But I'm happy to hear that you do plan to make one eventually."

"You really think she'll be okay with the idea of going out with me? I'm not exactly what you'd call her type."

"Who can predict when it comes to types?" she said very earnestly. "Take Ethan and me, for example. I'll bet that no one would have guessed that we'd wind up together."

"Good point. Talk about opposites. You with your artsy, feng shui stuff and Ethan with his hard-boiled view of the world. Nope, I don't think any self-respecting matchmaker would have put the two of you together, that's for sure."

The observation did nothing to improve her mood. She abruptly regretted using the opposites-attract argument.

But Singleton's spirits appeared to lift. He

beamed at her. "Thanks, Zoe. You give me hope."

"I'm glad," she said, meaning it.

Ethan heard her footsteps on the creaky stairs. About time.

He had spotted her coming up the street a few minutes before and watched her enter the building, but she had gotten delayed by her conversation with Singleton. He wondered what the two of them had talked about down there.

He sat behind his desk, studying the mirror that was positioned on the wall in such a way that, when his office door was open, it provided a view of whoever entered the outer room. Zoe did not approve of the placement of the mirror. Something about the way it destabilized the harmonic energy flow in the office. She also did not like his client chairs, claiming that they were too large and overwhelming. But the energy flow felt fine to him and he liked his clients to feel a little overwhelmed. It gave him a subtle edge that he often found useful.

Zoe materialized in the mirror. Her dark, red-brown hair was drawn back into a sleek knot at the nape of her neck. She had been in her robe when he left her after breakfast. But now she had on a light turquoise pullover with sleeves that ended just below her elbows and a skirt in a darker shade of the same color. The gauzy fabric drifted gracefully around her calves. He felt his insides tighten with anticipation. She looked terrific. Then again, everything looked good on her. She looked even better when everything came off.

Memories of the previous night's lovemaking made him hungry all over again. He had come to crave those moments in her arms because their shared passion was a drug that gave him a blissful, if temporary, amnesia. When they were locked together in the damp sheets, he could forget the uncertainties of the future; he could also pretend that he did not have a past.

"Ethan?"

"In here." He rose and walked around the corner of his desk.

She arrived in the doorway. "Ready for lunch?"

She was smiling but there were shadows in her eyes. It bothered him that the nightmare that had awakened her in the dark hours after midnight was still haunting her today. Anger heated his blood. He controlled it with an effort of will because there was not a damn thing he could do. He would give anything to be able to go back in time and save her from those months at Candle Lake Manor. But some things could not be changed. He knew that better than most.

"Yeah, I'm ready to eat," he said. He went forward, took her into his arms and kissed her hard, trying to drive the ghosts out of her eyes. When he felt her start to melt against him and put her arms around his neck, he raised his head. "And I'm not feeling too particular at the moment."

"I'm thinking Montoya's," she said.

He drew his thumb along the line of her jaw, enjoying the feel of her soft skin. "I'm thinking you. On my desk."

She stepped back quickly. "Forget it, Truax. We have to make a decision about the color in the master bedroom. We can't put it off any longer."

"How can you think about paint when I've just suggested hot, sweaty sex on a desk?"

"I'm a professional. I know how to stay focused."

* * *

Following lunch at Montoya's, they got back into the SUV and drove out to Nightwinds Canyon. A short time later he pulled into the drive of the old mansion.

Zoe tensed a little in the seat. She flashed him what he had come to recognize as her most dazzling professional smile. "We don't have to argue about this, you know. You could try trusting your interior designer."

"Honey, I would trust you with my life."

"But not with a can of paint?"

"Paint is dangerous stuff."

The flamingo-pink front door of the big house stood wide open. There was a white van parked near the door. The sign on the side of the vehicle read HULL PAINTING CO., ERNEST HULL, PROP.

Zoe brightened immediately.

"A painter," she said. "At last. Treacher must have changed his mind about sending someone out here this week to work on the kitchen. Come on, let's go see what's happening. I want to make sure he's got the right instructions for the crown molding on the north wall."

She shoved open the door and leaped out of the SUV before Ethan could get the key out of the ignition. He watched her fly up the steps and disappear inside the front door.

Your intrepid interior designer swings into action, he thought. It was amazing how fast she could move when there was a painter in the vicinity.

He climbed out of the SUV and went toward the door at a more leisurely pace. A painter on the premises meant that decisions had to be made, decisions that he was strangely reluctant to make.

But hell. The remodeling of Nightwinds had become some sort of crazy metaphor for the marriage. As long as no decision was made, he could pretend that nothing would change, that everything would stay just as it was. He would not have to confront the future.

When he passed the van, he glanced through the driver's-side window. The console held a can of some substance guaranteed to build muscle, improve energy levels and enhance physical performance. There were five more unopened cans of the stuff in a six-pack on the floor. A large paper bag emblazoned with the logo of a nutrition shop sat on the passenger seat.

You had to respect a painter who took care of his health and nutrition, Ethan figured. He wondered if he should feel guilty about the extra-large Montoya's Special Enchilada he had consumed a short time ago.

He took a closer look at the sign on the side of the van. It was one of the magnetic types that could be easily peeled off and stuck on another vehicle if the need arose.

He went up the front steps, past the pink stone pillars that framed the entrance. The interior of Nightwinds no longer looked quite so overwhelmingly pink these days because the pink marble floors and the pink carpets with their huge pink orchids were covered with drop cloths. Ditto for the pink-and-gilt furnishings. Unfortunately, that still left a lot of pink walls and the high pink ceilings exposed to view.

He saw that Zoe had the hapless painter cornered near the coat closet. She no longer looked thrilled. She was pissed.

The painter appeared desperate. He wore pristine white overalls. Blond hair cut with military precision showed beneath the bottom edge of a brand-new peaked cap. The protein shakes appeared to have worked, Ethan noticed. The guy was big, well over six feet. The thick neck and broad chest indicated some serious bodybuilding. He loomed over Zoe, although she did not seem to notice. She was too busy berating him.

"What do you mean, you only came by to drop off some equipment?" she demanded, blocking the escape route to the front door. "Treacher must have sent you here to start work on the kitchen."

"Sorry, ma'am."

The painter looked at Ethan over the top of Zoe's head, silently pleading for some masculine understanding and a little assistance. Ethan folded his arms, propped one shoulder against a pink wall and shook his head slightly. He felt sorry for the guy but not sorry enough to step into the middle of this scene.

The painter's expression hardened when he realized that there was no help coming from Ethan's direction. He scowled at Zoe, who stood planted firmly in front of him.

"Look, ma'am, all I know is that my boss told me to swing past this house on my way back from lunch break and drop off the sprayer and the ladder." He pointed toward the two pieces of equipment on the floor in the great room. "That's it. I can't hang around to work today. I'm supposed to be at another job site this afternoon."

"Which job site?" Zoe asked, suspicion sparkling in her eyes. "The house in Desert View or the one out on Arroyo Grande?"

"Uh, the one in Desert View."

"Hah. I knew it. Treacher lied to me. He told me that the only reason he couldn't start work here this week was because he had to finish my other project out on Arroyo Grande. Instead, he's sneaking his crew off to the Desert View job site. That would be Lindsey Voyle's project, wouldn't it?"

"I wouldn't know, ma'am." The painter made to slip around her.

Zoe stepped squarely back into his path, hands on her hips. "We'll see about this. I've got a contract."

"I don't know anything about the job scheduling, ma'am. All I know is that I'm running late. Hull will fire my ass if I don't get out to that other site real quick."

"Well, you can tell Hull to tell Treacher that I meant what I said on the phone. I swear, if he's giving me the runaround, I'll bring in painting contractors from Phoenix before I ever use his company on any of my projects in the future."

"Sure, ma'am." The painter finally managed to dodge past her. He strode swiftly toward the door. "I'll tell him."

"Did Lindsey Voyle offer Treacher a bonus to finish her project early?" Zoe called after him. "I'll bet that's what's going on here. That's not legal. I'll get a lawyer if need be."

The painter ignored her. He paused briefly in front of Ethan. "You the owner of this place?"

"I am," Ethan said.

"I can see why you want to repaint. Lot of pink in here."

"You noticed that?"

"Yeah. Maybe my boss will send me back here later on in the week."

"Probably be a good idea. As you can see, my decorator is not happy."

The painter reached up, grabbed the peak of his cap and tugged it down a little more securely over his blond hair. "Yes, sir, I can tell that much."

"Never pays to piss off a professional," Ethan said.

The painter went through the door, crossed the entryway, got into the white van and drove off very quickly.

Ethan looked at Zoe, trying to gauge her

mood. She was seething. It occurred to him that she was getting a little obsessive about remodeling Nightwinds. He wondered if that was a good thing or a bad thing.

"So," he said, going for neutral.

"Double-crossing, two-faced, conniving idiot."

So much for neutral. "Are you referring to Treacher, Hull, the painter who just left or me?"

"Treacher."

"Right." He unfolded his arms and straightened away from the wall. "Now that we've got that settled, let's go talk about paint chips."

16

Singleton looked up when Bonnie walked through the door just after one o'clock. Everything suddenly seemed a little brighter inside Single-Minded Books.

Usually he was content with the general gloom that pervaded his shop. The atmosphere suited him and his collection of old and rare tomes. Lately, however, he had become more aware of the shadows because when Bonnie came calling they seemed to lighten. It was as if she brought some of the intense desert sunlight indoors with her.

"I got your message," she said, plunking her purse and a plastic container on the counter. "I can't believe that you actually managed to turn up a copy of that privately published history of Whispering Springs."

"Found it on-line." He hauled the little leather-bound book out from behind the counter and opened it to the title page. "*A History of the Founding of the Town of Whispering Springs in the Arizona Territory*, by J. L. Creek."

"This is wonderful, Singleton." Bonnie bent excitedly over the small book, turning pages with great care. "I was told that the Friends of the Library have been trying to locate an original of Creek's *History* for years. Everyone is going to be thrilled. It will be a terrific addition to the rare books and manuscripts collection."

"You're welcome."

"How much did it cost?"

He shrugged. "Forget it."

She looked up quickly, brows tightening. "I certainly never intended for you to donate this to the library. I realize that it must have been expensive. The Friends of the Library will reimburse you for it."

He folded his arms on the counter. "Consider it my contribution to the community."

She smiled. "That's very generous of you, Singleton."

"Hey, I can do the civic-minded thing occasionally."

"Well, I hope you will accept this slice of homemade lemon meringue pie as a symbol of the gratitude of a grateful public library." She pushed the plastic container toward him.

"Lemon meringue? That's one of my favorites." He popped the lid off the plastic container and inhaled the scent of freshly squeezed lemons. "Oh, man. This is one of the most beautiful sights in the known universe. Consider me repaid in full."

She seemed pleased by his response. "Keep it in the refrigerator until you're ready to eat it."

"Got news for you. This sucker isn't going to last long enough to get into a refrigerator."

He reached under the counter again, found the stash of plastic forks that he had accumulated from past take-out meals and used one to take a large bite of pie.

He chewed slowly, making the experience last as long as possible.

"Ambrosia on the tongue," he announced after swallowing.

"Thanks. You know, I never get remarks like that from Jeff and Theo. They usually just scrape the meringue off the top and try to lob gobs of it at each other before they eat the yellow part."

"Give 'em a few years. Their palates will develop."

"You mean there's hope that with time they will actually learn to eat like civilized human beings?"

"Don't know about eating like civilized human beings, but I've got a hunch that eventually they'll figure out the meringue is a nice culinary complement to the tang of the lemon."

"I don't think I'll hold my breath waiting for them to figure that out but I'm glad you like the pie." She glanced at her watch. "Is Ethan upstairs?"

"You just missed him." He forked up another bite of pie. "He went out to Nightwinds with his interior designer."

"Uh-oh." Bonnie made a face. "Maybe it's just as well I got here too late to catch him. He's always a little testy before and after one of those design meetings with Zoe."

"Zoe gets pretty edgy herself whenever they've got a meeting planned. Says Ethan is stubborn and inflexible, not to mention, cheap."

"I know Ethan is concerned about sticking to the budget they established, but Zoe's had a lot of experience. I'm sure she'll keep the costs down."

He cut another bite of pie. "Don't think it's the budget thing that's really bothering Ethan, although he may be using that as an excuse."

"What is it?"

"I told Zoe that I've got a hunch that he associates major interior design projects with his business disaster in LA."

"And his memories of the bankruptcy are, of course, forever linked to his memories of Drew's death." She sighed. "Add to that the fact that we recently passed the third anniversary of the day he found the place where the killer buried my husband's body, and you've got a very high-stress scenario. Maybe November was not the best month for Ethan and Zoe to start remodeling Nightwinds."

"Probably should have waited until after the first of the year. But I think they both figured the project would be good for them. Something they could work on together. Instead, all they seem to do is argue about it."

Understanding widened Bonnie's eyes. "Do you think maybe they're both projecting? Focusing all of their anxieties and concerns about the marriage onto the remodel project?"

"I'm no shrink, but it sounds like a possibility."

Morosely he studied the bits of pastry that were left in the bottom of the container. Too small to get with a fork, he decided. He wondered how Bonnie would react if he licked his finger and used it to snag the last crumbs. She would probably think it was really gross.

"Ever since Drew's death, November has been a tough month for all of us," Bonnie said reflectively. "But I honestly thought things would be better this year. I know they were for me and for Theo. But Ethan is going through his usual mood swings and Jeff seems to be having a much worse time of it than he did last year."

Singleton put the lid back on the plastic container with a pang of regret. "Jeff does seem to be brooding a bit."

She nodded. "At the beginning of the month he asked me to let him look at one of the albums that contains pictures of his father. He took it into his bedroom. The other day I walked into the room and he was sitting on the bed, staring at a photo of Drew. I asked him if he wanted to talk about his dad."

"What did he say?"

"He said no and closed the album." She shook her head. "I don't know. Maybe the move to Whispering Springs unsettled him more than I realized."

"They say a move puts a lot of stress on a person."

"I know." She paused. "But I still feel that the decision to start a new life here was the right one for all of us. We all had to get out of LA, Ethan included."

"When you think about it, everyone in the gang came here for a new start. You, the boys, Ethan, Zoe and Arcadia. Even Harry and me."

Her brows rose. "You too?"

"Sure. Me too."

"What did you leave behind?"

"My wife decided that she didn't want to have children. She left me to marry another guy who understood her needs better than I did. About that time, the folks who ran the think tank where I worked decided to increase profits by selling my services to the highest bidder, even if I wasn't interested in doing the kind of research the client wanted done." He shrugged. "Figured that between the divorce and the bad job, it was time to leave."

"So you ended up in Whispering Springs. That's part of what the West has always been about, isn't it? A place to start over."

"Yep. And that's what we're all doing. We're gonna make it, too. " He handed her Creek's *History*. "Don't worry about Jeff. One of these days, he'll be ready to start over, too."

Her fingers brushed his when she took the book from him. "Thank you."

He nodded and watched her walk out of the shop. When the door closed behind her the shadows settled around him once more.

17

The creaky staircase that functioned as an early-warning system for Truax Investigations sounded its squeaky alarm shortly before ten the next morning. Ethan listened intently, playing the game he had devised of analyzing a newcomer's footsteps before the person reached the outer office. He told himself that it was good practice for a man in his line of work.

Modern ace detectives were inclined to rely too heavily on flashy gadgets and the Internet in his opinion. The old-fashioned Sherlock Holmes-style skills and methods were in danger of being lost forever.

Someone had to uphold tradition.

These footsteps were not firm, quick and light, so it wasn't Zoe. He did not hear the soft, rapid thud of sneakers that signaled the arrival of Jeff or Theo. Not Bonnie's smooth, brisk tread, either.

A man, he decided. Steady. Decisive. The kind of guy who knew where he was going and made a habit of getting things done. Either the UPS man or a prospective client.

He wasn't expecting a delivery.

He put the yellow pad he had been using to make notes on the Kirwan case aside and took his heels down off the corner of his desk. It was not a good idea to let a potential client think that you had nothing better to do than sit around at ten o'clock on a weekday morning doodling.

His second-stage warning device, the strategically placed mirror, kicked in a moment later when a slender man walked into the outer office. He had thick gray hair cut very short. His trousers and sport shirt looked expensive. The attire was not brown so that pretty much ruled out the UPS man.

Was he an ace detective, or what?

Ethan got to his feet and went to the door of his office. The man had his back to him.

He was contemplating the large secretarial desk near the window. Probably noticing that there was no secretary behind it, Ethan figured.

"I'd tell you that the receptionist just stepped out to get coffee," Ethan said, "but the truth is I haven't hired one yet. Can I help you?"

The man swung around to face him, dark eyes cool and assessing. "You're Truax, I take it?"

"Ethan Truax." He put out his hand.

"Doug Valdez." Doug shook Ethan's hand with the same decisive manner he had applied to climbing the stairs.

"Would that be Valdez as in D. J. Valdez, president and CEO of Valdez Electronics?"

"Yes."

Ethan did a silent whistle in his head. Doug Valdez was a high-profile figure in the local business establishment and this year's chair of the annual Whispering Springs Community Fund Drive.

In other words, a dream client.

D. J. Valdez was, in fact, the kind of client he had once possessed in abundance back in the old days in LA. But these weren't the old days and this wasn't LA and he no longer operated a large corporate security business that attracted clients like this.

Here in Whispering Springs this kind of client usually took his business to Radnor.

So what was Valdez doing here?

"Katherine Compton recommended you," Doug said.

An actual, real-life referral. Life didn't get any better in this business.

"Come in and have a seat." Ethan stood back from the door.

Doug walked into the inner room and lowered himself into one of the client chairs. He was not a large man, but contrary to Zoe's warning, the oversized chair did not overwhelm him.

Doug looked around, smiling faintly. "Just like something out of a hard-boiled detective novel. Except for the computer, maybe."

"I inherited this office from my uncle, who opened the business several decades ago in another century. I'm afraid Uncle Victor had what you might call a highly romanticized view of the profession."

Doug raised a brow. "You don't share that view, I take it?"

"Can't afford it. I'm trying to make a living. Such an approach to the business doesn't allow for a lot of romantic sentiment." He went around behind his desk and sat down. "What can I do for you?"

"I've got a problem in my shipping-and-receiving room. Inventory losses have been higher than usual for the past three months. No big spikes but there is a consistent trend. My security people haven't been able to figure out what's going on. I'd like you to come in, have a look around and see if you can spot a way to close the gap in my current system."

"I can do that," Ethan said. "Before we talk about this any more, though, I've got a question."

"You want to know why I didn't go to Radnor?"

"I was under the impression that Radnor designed your current security program."

"Your impression is correct. Radnor did design it. A detailed analysis of my company's operations was carried out by a team of Radnor experts. When they were through with the analysis, they generated a very thick document that contained their findings, together with a long list of expensive recommendations that were all duly implemented."

"I see." Ethan waited. Sometimes if you let

the silence get a little heavy, people started talking.

But Doug was not the kind of client who responded to that particular tactic. It was obvious that he was deliberating, deciding what and how much he wanted to say.

"I want to use someone from outside my organization."

"I see." Ethan opened a drawer, pulled out a fresh notepad and picked up his pen. "In other words, you think someone on your security staff is involved in the shipping-room losses."

"That's what it feels like to me. And given the fact that Radnor consulted for us when we hired our new security personnel staff, and given that they conducted all the background checks, I am not inclined to go back there to get the problem fixed."

"What you're asking for is an audit of your security system."

"An audit." Doug nodded, pleased with the word. "Yes, that's exactly what I want. Maybe one lone outsider can see something that an organized team might miss, especially if that team has a vested interest in not finding any problems that would reflect badly on Radnor."

Forty minutes later Doug wrote a check, shook Ethan's hand a second time and left the office.

Ethan saw him to the door and then went back to his desk. He sat there for a while, looking at the check. There was a very satisfying amount written on it. The Valdez job was the biggest project that had come his way since he had opened up for business.

He picked up the phone. Zoe answered on the first ring.

"Enhanced Interiors." She was polite and professional but somewhat distracted. "This is Zoe Truax."

Zoe Truax. He liked the sound of that.

"Doug Valdez of Valdez Electronics just walked into my office and gave me a big, fat retainer to investigate some problems in his shipping department."

"Ethan, that's wonderful." The distracted quality vanished from her voice. Zoe was suddenly bubbling with enthusiasm. "Congratulations. What a coup for you."

"I owe it to Katherine Compton. She referred him to me."

"As well she should have," Zoe said with heartwarming loyalty. "You did a terrific job for her, and what's more, you handled it very quietly. There hasn't been a single blip of bad publicity in the papers to embarrass her. Given that she was sleeping with that dreadful Dexter Morrow, it could have been a humiliating experience. I'm sure she is very grateful to you."

"To tell you the truth, I did wonder if she would want to shoot the messenger," he admitted.

"Obviously she isn't blaming you for her bad judgment. Probably why she's a successful executive. Hey, how about we celebrate? Let's go out to dinner. Not the whole gang this time. Just you and me."

He suddenly felt even better than he had a few minutes before when Valdez had written the check. Celebrating small personal accomplishments like the Valdez deal was something real married people did.

"Sounds good," he said. "Just one problem."

"What's that?"

"I haven't solved the case yet." He tapped the edge of the check on his desk. "Haven't even started my investigation. A celebratory dinner may be a trifle premature."

"Nonsense. You'll solve the case. That's what you do, remember? So I say we go out tonight. Your treat, of course, because you're the one who just got the big retainer check."

He smiled a little. "All right. But that means that I get to pick the restaurant."

"Sure. As long as it isn't a pizza parlor. We eat enough pizza whenever we go out with the gang."

"That's because Jeff and Theo are addicted to pizza. According to them it contains all the essential nutrients required to sustain life."

"I wouldn't dream of quarreling with such expert nutritional advice, but once in a while you have to live dangerously. Let's go someplace where they give you real napkins."

"What a concept. Okay, let me contemplate this for a while. It's a big decision."

"Surprise me."

He hung up the phone and looked at the check again. It felt good to be able to call his wife in the middle of the day to tell her he had just picked up an important client.

It was good to hear the enthusiasm and the certainty in her voice when she said things like, *You'll solve the case. That's what you do, remember?*

Good to know that Zoe believed in him; or

at least that she believed in his professional competence.

He pulled out the slender Whispering Springs phone book and turned to restaurants. It was a small community when all was said and done. The list of places where they gave you real napkins was a short one.

It occurred to him that what he was really looking for was the kind of place where you took a woman on a date when you wanted to impress her.

18

He chose the restaurant at Las Estrellas resort. Some might quibble about whether or not it featured the best food in town, but when it came to the category of *fine dining with classy atmosphere* it was at the top of the list. What's more it had the prices to prove it. But what the hell, he thought, Doug Valdez was paying for it.

The plush interior of the establishment was a sea of snowy white tablecloths, sparkling crystal and gleaming silver. The linen napkins were folded into the shapes of exotic flowers. There was muted mood music playing softly in the background. The lights were subdued and the waiters wore black and white.

He requested a booth near the curved wall of glass that looked out over the night-shrouded golf course and the mountains beyond. Not that you could see much of the long sweep of green or the jagged peaks after dark. It was the principle of the thing. Everyone knew the golf course and the mountains were out there somewhere and that the view cost big bucks.

This was the kind of thing you did on a real date, the kind of thing he and Zoe hadn't had a chance to do before that midnight wedding in Vegas. The hasty marriage of convenience had virtually wiped out the customary courtship phase that was part of the traditional mating ritual.

Zoe closed her menu and looked at him across the table. "I'm going to have the pasta niçoise and the romaine salad. What about you?"

He did not want to look away from her. She was glamorous and mysterious and seductive in the candlelight. The little red dress left her shoulders and arms bare. Her hair was swept up into an elegant chignon. Gold earrings sparkled in her ears.

He forced himself to study the menu. "Well, I don't think I can have the pasta niçoise. It doesn't sound like something an ace detective would eat."

"Better than quiche."

"Yeah, but still a sissy dish."

"Probably." She took a small sip of her chardonnay and lowered the glass. "I trust you are not looking at the steak."

"Why not? This is Arizona, not California. I can actually eat red meat here without the risk of horrifying everyone else in the restaurant."

"You'll horrify me. Didn't you read that article on the dangers of eating too much red meat that I clipped and underlined for you?"

He thought about the newspaper clipping that he had discovered slipped under the edge of his desk blotter a few days before. "Sure. I even filed it for future reference."

Amusement danced in her eyes. "Remind me not to inspect your office trash can."

He let that go without comment and closed his menu. "Relax, I'm not going to order the steak. The grilled swordfish sounds good."

"Excellent choice."

The waiter materialized and took the orders without writing anything down. Waiters with good memories were another sign of a classy joint, Ethan told himself.

Zoe raised her glass and touched it to his. "Here's to your new client."

"I'll drink to that."

They each took a sip and put down their glasses. A flicker of concern crossed Zoe's face.

"Think Nelson Radnor will get mad when he finds out that you've been hired to do an audit on the security program he designed?"

"He won't like it, but Radnor's a pro and business is business."

"This is the kind of work you used to do back in LA, isn't it?" she asked. "Corporate security stuff."

"Yeah." He helped himself to some of the dense, crusty bread the waiter had placed in the center of the table. "To tell you the truth, I don't miss it all that much and I'm not planning to give Radnor serious competition. This town can't support two large corporate security firms competing for the same business. But an occasional client like Katherine Compton or Doug Valdez who wants a situation handled quietly is good."

"Good for the reputation of Truax Investigations and good for the bottom line."

"Uh-huh." He wondered if maybe he wasn't coming across as sufficiently success-oriented. He had made money for a while in LA but eventually the business, like his three previous marriages, had collapsed.

He was well aware that Zoe's first husband had been connected to a wealthy, influential business family. Although she was not on good terms with any of her ex–in-laws, she did possess a controlling interest in Cleland Cage, Inc. If the company righted itself in the next few years, she stood to make a tidy fortune.

He, on the other hand, might be able to make a decent income with Truax Investigations but that was about all you could say. His prospects of coming into a fortune were somewhere in the minus-zero range.

When the salads arrived, Zoe picked up her fork and attacked the romaine with enthusiasm.

"You know," she said, "one of the things I admire about you is that you've decided what's important to you and what isn't."

The word "admire" made him uneasy. It

implied respect but also a certain distance. You admired dedicated doctors and teachers and ballplayers from afar.

"Yeah, well, some of the decisions got made for me," he said.

She shook her head. "Not really. You could take on Radnor and go after the same business here in Whispering Springs if that was what you really wanted to do. But you'd have to go back into full executive CEO mode to do it and that would mean giving up the hands-on approach to your work."

He shrugged. She was right.

"You've got other goals and priorities these days," she said.

He winced. "I hate to admit this because it sort of ruins the man-of-vision image, but the truth is that I don't usually think in terms of goals and priorities."

"I know. You just keeping going, doing what needs to be done."

He wondered if that was another way of saying that he was unimaginative. "Okay, I'll concede that I'm the kind of guy who usually takes the one-foot-in-front-of-the-other approach until I get to the end, but hey, we can't all be flashy interior designers."

She ignored the weak joke and turned the

wineglass in her hand, watching the play of the candlelight on the crystal. "You make commitments and you keep them. Regardless of the price you have to pay to do it."

He was not sure where she was going with this and he was pretty certain he did not want to find out. This was supposed to be a date. The last thing he wanted to do was get mired in a conversation that highlighted his lack of long-range business objectives. Time to change direction.

He hunted for a safe topic.

"How's the library project going?" he asked.

Without warning, a veil descended between them. He looked into her eyes and knew that she was keeping secrets. He felt his stomach clench. If she were any other woman, he probably would have begun to suspect that she was having an affair. But this was Zoe.

"Good," she said a little too lightly. "It's going very well."

Something was definitely wrong. Maybe it had to do with her past.

"You ever miss your old job?" he asked, trying for the subtle approach.

"At the art museum?" She shook her

head. "No. But a lot of what I learned in that job about displaying art and antiques is very useful in my new line. Many of my clients collect. A big part of designing interiors for them involves incorporating the items in their private collections into their living spaces."

So much for the subtlety. She wasn't going to give up her secrets easily. Maybe he did not want to learn them.

But he knew that, in the end, he would be compelled to solve the mysteries in her eyes, even if it meant disaster for him. He couldn't do anything else. *One foot in front of the other until you get to the end.*

They lingered over coffee. It was a little after ten before Ethan reached for his wallet and pulled out his credit card.

They walked out of the restaurant, past the shadowy entrance to the hotel cocktail lounge, and crossed the spacious lobby.

Outside, the cool, clean desert night enveloped them. As soon as they left the brightly lit entranceway and started through the parking lot, the night sky bloomed with stars.

Zoe wrapped her light shawl around her bare shoulders. "This was a lovely evening.

You know, we really ought to do this more often."

"Funny you should say that." Ethan got his keys out of his pocket. "I was just thinking the same thing. We never really had a chance to date . . ."

He heard the heavy, rushing footsteps coming up behind them even before Dexter Morrow called his name.

"*Truax*. You son of a bitch."

So much for a lovely evening. He swung around to confront the looming figure bearing down on them.

"Stay out of the way." He did not look at Zoe, his attention on Morrow. "Whatever you do, don't try to interfere. Head for the lobby if this gets out of hand."

"You know this man?" Zoe whispered.

"Meet Dexter Morrow."

Morrow must have spent the better part of the evening in the cocktail lounge. The fumes were detectable across a distance of several paces. Unfortunately he was not dead drunk, Ethan thought. More like stupid drunk.

"So much for my theory that you would leave town," he said to Morrow.

Dexter pulled up about a yard away, hands knotted in fists, mouth drawn back in a grimace of rage. He was probably red in the face, too, but there wasn't enough light to be certain of that detail.

"I'm not going anywhere until I feel like it," Dexter rasped. "I sure as hell don't intend to let you run me out of town. Who do you think you are, you bastard? Who gave you the right to mess with my life?"

"The only thing I messed up was your scheme to rip off Katherine Compton," Ethan said evenly. "We both know that. It's over. This is where you cut your losses and find another target in another town, remember? Things are finished for you here in Whispering Springs."

"It isn't over until I say it's over." Morrow's voice climbed to a loud, harsh place. "You hear me? It's not finished."

"You're drunk, Morrow. Go back inside and call a cab."

"Don't give me orders, you interfering s.o.b."

"If you want to talk about this, you can come to my office tomorrow."

"Don't tell me what I can and can't do. You screwed up everything. You had no right."

"Look, Morrow—"

"I loved her and you screwed up everything. You turned her against me. She trusted me and you turned her against me. I told you you'd pay."

Morrow lunged forward, swinging wildly.

Ethan sidestepped the blow. Morrow was so unsteady on his feet that he was thrown off balance when his punch failed to connect.

He fetched up hard against the fender of a Mercedes and shook his head as if trying to clear it.

"This is not a good idea," Ethan said. He caught movement out of the corner of his eye and realized that Zoe was preparing to dash back into the lobby to get help. "No, Zoe. Not yet."

She hesitated. "Ethan, he's out of control."

"Bastard." Morrow shoved himself away from the Mercedes and lumbered forward a second time, right arm drawn back in preparation for another punch.

This time Ethan let him get closer before ducking the clumsy blow. He grabbed Morrow's right arm and used the man's own momentum to pull him forward and off balance.

Morrow stumbled awkwardly and went down hard on the pavement.

"Ethan?" Zoe's voice was taut.

"No," he said again.

She subsided, trusting in his judgment, but he could tell that she was not happy about it.

Morrow pushed himself to a sitting position and tried to get one leg under him so that he could stand. The effort was unsuccessful. After a couple of attempts, he managed to make it to his hands and knees.

"When did you come to the conclusion that you loved her?" Ethan asked quietly.

"Shut up," Morrow said through clenched teeth.

"Got a hunch it was that day in the hotel room when you realized everything had fallen apart. Was that when it hit you that your scam had cost a hell of a lot more than you realized?"

"I do love her," Morrow muttered hoarsely.

"Maybe," Ethan said. "Maybe not. But I'll tell you something, Morrow. She really cared about you. You had something good and you blew it because you couldn't resist the shot at a big score. Guess some habits are just too hard to break, aren't they?"

Morrow started to weep. "I wasn't going to go through with it. I was going to call it off.

Then you came around, offering to buy the projections. I figured I'd expose you and make myself look like a hero to Katherine."

"It's a nice story, and maybe, looking back, you wish it was the truth. Maybe you've even managed to convince yourself that was the way it was. But you're rewriting history here, Morrow. You know it and I know it."

"No."

"You want to do something to make it up to Katherine? Leave town so she doesn't have to worry about running into you in places like the cocktail lounge here at Las Estrellas. The best thing you can do for her is get out of her life."

Morrow lurched to his feet and stood, swaying for a few seconds. When he regained his balance, he walked away without another word. The slump of his shoulders spoke volumes.

Zoe gripped her shawl very tightly around her shoulders. "Think he'll call a cab? He's in no shape to be on the road."

"No, I don't think he'll call a cab." Resigned, he took her hand and started back toward the lobby. "I'd better go talk to someone inside who will do it for him. Damn. I really hate cases that end the way that one did."

Zoe tightened her fingers around his. "I can see why. Ethan, I think he's dangerous. Maybe you should report this incident to the police."

He just looked at her, not speaking.

"Okay, okay," she said. "So it's against the PI code to go sniveling to the cops when some drunken idiot throws a punch at you."

"The code is certainly a major consideration," he said. "But there's another, larger issue. Katherine Compton hired me because she wanted her problem handled quietly."

"And filing a complaint against Dexter Morrow would certainly draw the attention of the local press, which, in turn, would probably mean that the entire sordid affair would make headlines in the business pages tomorrow morning."

"Honey, you were born to be the wife of a PI. You understand the situation perfectly."

"What if he tries something else?"

"I don't think he will. This was one of those wrong-place, wrong-time things. Morrow spent the evening in the bar and it was just bad luck that we happened to have dinner here tonight. He probably saw me when we walked through the lobby on the way out the door and everything just boiled over. He lost it. Tomorrow morning he'll start thinking like the smart scam artist he is and realize that he had a close call. He won't try anything else."

He could tell that she was not convinced, but she did not argue the point.

"Think he really loved her?" she asked.

"No. I think he's feeling sorry for himself so he's convinced himself that he never intended to go through with the scam and that what he felt for Katherine was real."

"That way he gets to blame you for everything that went wrong."

"Yeah."

Zoe continued to look troubled. "Promise me you'll be careful."

"I'll take an extra all-purpose vitamin in the morning."

Singleton stuck his gleaming head out the door of Single-Minded Books just as Ethan was taking the Truax Investigations mail out of the box in the narrow hall.

"How'd the big date go?" Singleton asked.

"Things went fine right up to the moment when we left the restaurant and Dexter Morrow followed us outside with the expressed intent of pounding me into the pavement."

"Oh, man, see that's what I hate about the modern dating scene. You put on a tie, you take out a loan to cover the dinner tab and then some jerk comes along and wrecks the romantic ambience by trying to beat you up in front of your date."

"Got to admit that Morrow did somewhat negatively impact the mood of the evening." Ethan flipped through the assortment of catalogs and advertising circulars. "Lucky I was married to my date or I might have ended up going home alone."

Singleton surveyed him. "Doesn't look like Morrow did any serious damage."

"He was so drunk he could barely stand. The resort management sent him home in a cab."

"He probably isn't feeling any more sweet-tempered this morning than he did last night." A couple of deep furrows appeared in Singleton's brow. "Watch yourself."

Ethan tossed everything except a catalog featuring pool and garden accessories into the trash can and started up the stairs. "Guys like Morrow are opportunists. They don't like to take physical risks. I doubt that he'll make another run at me, but if he does, I'm prepared."

"How so?"

He jiggled the new key chain Zoe had given him. "I'll blow my whistle and shine the little light right into his eyes."

"Yeah, that should work," Singleton said. "You know, I may have to get myself one of those."

19

The following afternoon Zoe extended her arms along the edge of the spa pool and sank deep into the bubbling water. “I think I may be losing it.”

“What now?” Bonnie asked. “Did you buy another safety gadget for Ethan? One of those fold-up ladders that you can drop out of a window in an emergency, maybe?”

Arcadia’s eyes twinkled with amusement. “Or maybe one of those nifty hidden wallets that a man can wear under his shirt when he travels abroad?”

Humiliated, Zoe sank to her chin in the frothy waters.

Arcadia was the one with the membership at the expensive athletic club but she seemed to have an unlimited number of guest passes. She used them frequently to invite Zoe and Bonnie to join her in the club's elegant spa room.

"No hidden wallets," Zoe said. "I took a break this morning and went to the drugstore."

"Ah." Arcadia assumed a knowing expression. "You upgraded his sunscreen again, didn't you? The one you bought last week was thirty-something, as I recall. What did you get this time?"

"SPF forty-eight-plus," Zoe admitted. "Full spectrum protection, guaranteed waterproof and sweat proof."

Arcadia raised her eyes to the spa room ceiling. "Most authorities agree that SPF fifteen or thirty is fine for routine daily use."

"Especially in November," Bonnie said dryly. "It's not as though Ethan is into serious sunbathing."

"I know," Zoe mumbled. "He must think I'm obsessing. And it's true, isn't it?"

"Maybe," Arcadia replied. "But I think that's entirely understandable under the circumstances."

Zoe frowned. "What circumstances?"

“You’re married to a man who occasionally takes chances for a living.” Arcadia moved her hand through the water in a lazy, sweeping motion. “You worry about him so you try to compensate by giving him a little extra protection where you can. Sounds perfectly natural to me.”

“She’s right,” Bonnie said. “I’m like that with Jeff and Theo. I fuss. Sometimes a little too much.”

“That’s exactly what I’m doing, isn’t it?” Zoe sighed. “I’m fussing. When Ethan finally realizes what’s happening, he won’t be able to stand it.”

Bonnie looked thoughtful. “I wouldn’t be too sure of that. Ethan hasn’t had much experience with being fussed over. None of his previous wives ever fussed, I can tell you that. Wouldn’t surprise me if he’s secretly enjoying the experience.”

“He might feel that he has to draw the line if the sunscreen gums up his gun, though,” Arcadia said.

20

Stupid game." Jeff punched a button on the video game player, silencing the machine. "Dumb, stupid game. I hate this game."

He hurled the game player aside, jumped up from the chair and stormed along the aisle of old books. He halted in the doorway of Singleton's tiny office and glowered. "Don't you have anything else to play with?"

"Afraid not." Singleton looked up from the on-line antiquarian book catalog he had been studying in hopes of finding a lead on the missing Kirwan manuscript. "I guess if you're really bored, you could always do your homework."

"I don't want to do it. I hate homework. I want to go home."

"It's almost four. Your mom will be leaving the spa soon to pick you up here."

"I wish I'd gone with Theo and Uncle Ethan to watch the mechanics change the oil in the car."

"It was your choice to stay here."

"That's because it sounded boring." Jeff's face scrunched up a little more. "But so is this place."

This was the third or fourth time that week that Jeff had opted to spend the afternoon at the shop while Bonnie ran errands or took Theo to various appointments. Usually when the kid hung around the place he divided his time between pestering Ethan upstairs and playing computer games down here. But on these last few visits he had shown little interest in rushing back and forth between the two offices, choosing instead to spend most of his time down here. It was almost as if he was avoiding Ethan, Singleton thought.

He got to his feet. "Let's go for a walk."

"I don't wanna go for a walk."

"Well, I do and you're coming with me because I'm going to lock up the shop."

Jeff scowled, mutinous, but he understood an order when he heard one.

He raised both shoulders in one of those elaborate shrugs that conveyed a bottomless well of youthful ennui.

"Whatever," he muttered.

"Get your hat."

"I don't wanna wear a hat."

"Your mom says you're supposed to wear a hat whenever you go out in the sun."

"Mom's not here."

"Doesn't matter. A rule's a rule."

Singleton snagged a floppy-brimmed canvas hat off a wall hook and planted it on his own head. He was not just trying to set a good example, he told himself. A man who shaved off what little hair he still possessed had to take a few precautions when dealing with the desert sun, even in November.

Jeff snatched up his own canvas hat and stomped out the front door. He waited, doing the eye-rolling thing, while Singleton locked up and pocketed his keys.

Outside they turned left and walked toward the neglected little park at the far end of Cobalt Street. Jeff said nothing for half a block.

"Race you to the park," Singleton said.

"Huh?"

"You heard me. I'll race you to the old fountain in the park. Loser buys sodas."

"Okay."

It was as if a spring that had been wound too tightly had suddenly been released. Jeff exploded into action, pelting off full-speed toward the small patch of greenery at the far end of the street. There was a furious energy in his pounding legs and pumping arms.

Singleton ambled after him, not altering his leisurely stride, trying to think of what to do next. The kid needed a father-son talk but he didn't have a father. He had an uncle who had done a better than passable job of filling in for the missing dad but for some reason Jeff wasn't taking his current problems to Ethan.

That leaves me, Singleton thought. Unfortunately, he didn't know much about father-son talks.

When he arrived at the fountain, Jeff was waiting for him, breathless and slightly red in the face from his exertion. He still looked angry.

"You didn't even try," he said. Accusation dripped from every word.

Singleton sat down on the edge of the stone fountain. The water had been turned off years before. The cracked basin was filled with several seasons' worth of dead leaves and desert sand.

"You're the one who needed to run today," he said. "Not me."

Jeff's face screwed up into a baffled expression. "Why did I have to run?"

"Because that's the kind of thing a smart guy does when he gets mad," he explained, hunting for the right words. "He goes outside and runs or maybe he goes to the gym and works out."

Jeff tilted his head a little and squinted up at him from beneath the brim of his hat. "How come he does that?"

"Because when a guy gets mad it's like a circuit breaker gets tripped in his brain. He suddenly goes from being real smart to being real stupid. If he doesn't get that breaker reset fast, it's for sure he'll do something dumb."

"Like what?"

"He might say stuff that he doesn't really mean to someone or he might bust up a perfectly good game player. Maybe he picks a fight with someone."

"What's so dumb about any of those things?"

"When he does stuff like that, people look at him like he's weird on account of they know he's not in control of himself. They lose respect. When a guy is in stupid mode it's for sure he's going to embarrass himself sooner or later."

"So he resets the circuit breaker by running or something?"

"The smart ones do that. The dumb ones just stay locked in stupid mode and generally end up making fools out of themselves."

"What if a guy wants to be mad?" Jeff demanded sullenly. "What if he just happens to feel like being mad?"

"Being mad is okay. Everybody gets mad sometimes. The difference between smart guys and stupid guys is that the smart ones reset the switch right away. That way they can start thinking logically again. They can still be mad but they're cool about it, see? They're less likely to do stupid things and look like idiots."

"What if a guy resets the switch and he's still mad? What does he do then?"

"He figures out why he's mad and he fixes the problem."

Jeff picked up a rock and thew it into the dry fountain. "What if he can't fix anything? What's he supposed to do?"

"Depends. He could try talking it over with his mom."

"No." Jeff picked up another rock and hurled it into the basin. "What if that won't work?"

"Guess he could try talking to another guy. His uncle, maybe."

Jeff shook his head adamantly, swallowing so hard that Singleton could see the movement of his throat.

"Well," Singleton said slowly, feeling his way. "He could talk to a friend."

"What good would that do?"

"I don't know. But sometimes other people can give you some ideas about how to fix things."

"But it wouldn't do any good to talk about something if there was nothing anyone could do to fix it, right?"

Enough with the subtle approach, Singleton decided. *I don't know what the hell I'm doing here. Might as well get to the point.*

"Look, Jeff, I know that you and your family have been having a tough time of it for the past couple of weeks. I know that you lost your dad at this time of year and sometimes you feel bad all over again when November rolls around. Maybe you're mad because he's not here anymore. That's okay. You've got a right to get mad. Maybe some of that mad is aimed at your mom and your uncle."

"I'm not mad at Mom or Uncle Ethan," Jeff said, voice rising to a raw, sharp edge.

Progress of a sort.

"Okay, so who are you mad at?"

"Me."

Singleton did not move. He did not speak.

"I'm mad at me." Jeff's voice cracked on a sob. "I can't remember him. He was my dad but I can't remember him anymore. How could a kid forget his own dad?"

He started to cry. His small shoulders shook with the force of racking sobs. Tears leaked down his face. He tried to dash them away with the back of his hand but he could not stanch the flood.

Singleton wondered what he was supposed to do now. Unable to think of anything helpful, he just sat there and waited.

After a while Jeff ran dry.

Silence descended.

"You won't ever forget him," Singleton said eventually. "Not deep down where it counts."

"I already have." Jeff used the hem of his shirt to dry his eyes. "I can't remember what he looked like. Mom has some pictures of him. I keep looking at them but it's like I'm looking at a picture of a person I never even met."

"There are a lot of different ways of remembering. What your dad looked like isn't important."

"Yes, it is."

"No." Singleton looked out across the park. "It's *interesting,* but it's not real important. What matters is that he's a part of you. You couldn't change that, even if you tried."

"Then why can't I remember him?"

"Some parts of you do remember him. There are bits and pieces of him in your genes, for instance. Have you studied genes yet in school? About how you inherit stuff from your folks?"

"I know about how I'm supposed to look like my dad, if that's what you mean. Mom says that all the time. So does Uncle Ethan. But when I look in the mirror, I can't see him."

"It's not just the superficial stuff like the color of your eyes and your hair that you inherit in your genes. You get other things that way, too, things like your intelligence. Ethan says you're just as smart as your dad was and that you'll probably be just as successful. The next time you ace a test in school you can think about how one of the reasons you were able to do it is because your dad gave you some good, smart genes."

Jeff thought about that. "What if I flunk the test?"

Singleton smiled. "Good question. A very, very smart question. The kind of question your dad probably would have asked when he was your age. The answer is a little complicated."

"Why?"

"Here's how this gene thing works. Nobody gets a perfect set. You get a few good ones and you get a few bad ones. What matters is what you do with them. All the smart genes in the world won't do you a lick of good if you don't put them to work by studying for the test."

Jeff made a face. "So if I flunk, it's my fault."

"Yep. But it works both ways. If you get an A, you get all the credit on account of the only reason you passed is because you studied hard."

"Huh."

"There's other things you remember deep down about your dad, things that have nothing to do with genes. Things that are even more important."

"Like what?"

"Like the fact that he was a good man and that he loved you a lot."

"But I just told you I don't remember that."

"Don't worry, it's hardwired into you. It's part of what makes you the great kid that you are today."

"What happens if a kid gets a dad who doesn't love him?"

"Someone else has to teach the kid how to be a great kid. A mom, maybe." Singleton sorted through some of the faded images that he kept stored in a quiet corner of his mind and came up with a couple of familiar faces. "Or the kid's grandparents."

Jeff sat down on the side of the fountain. "I don't understand."

"That's the beauty of it, see? You don't have to understand. You just need to know that no matter what happens, you won't ever forget your dad. You'll think about him lots of times as you grow up. Heck, you'll think about him years from now when you have a son of your own."

"Yeah?" Jeff frowned. "What kind of stuff will I think about him?"

"There will be questions that you'll wish you could have asked him and you'll feel kind of sad sometimes because you never got the chance. Mostly you'll wonder if he would have been proud of you. But that's the way it is for everyone. None of us ever gets all the answers we want from our dads."

There was a long silence.

"Do you think my dad would be proud of me?" Jeff asked after a while.

"Oh, yeah. No doubt about it."

"Do you have some questions you wish you could ask your dad?" Jeff asked.

"Sure."

"Why don't you ask him?"

"Same reason you won't be able to ask your dad. He's dead."

"Oh." Jeff nudged some pebbles with the toe of his sneaker. "What did he do?"

Singleton gripped the edge of the fountain on either side. "He was a Marine Corps officer. Everyone said he was real smart and very brave."

"What happened to him?"

"He was killed in a military action a month before I was born."

Jeff was stricken. "He never ever *saw* you? Not once?"

"No."

"And you never saw him," Jeff whispered.

"All I've got are some pictures."

"But you still remember him?"

"I can't ever forget him," Singleton said simply. "He was my dad."

Jeff thought for a while. "You're a lot like him, aren't you?"

Singleton felt as if he had just slammed headfirst into a stone wall. All of his life he had been painfully aware of the fact that he had not turned out anything like his father. He was no dashing military hero, just the opposite. He had chosen the life of a contemplative loner, content with his computer and his rare books.

"I don't think so," he said.

"Yeah, you are," Jeff insisted. "You're real smart and you're brave, just like your dad. You saved Zoe that time when those two guys attacked her, and you're so brainy that Mom says you once worked at some kind of special place where they invent secret codes for computers."

"A think tank," Singleton said absently, still struggling to deal with the shattering concept that had been introduced into the conversation.

"Yeah, a think tank." Jeff seemed oddly satisfied now. "Your dad would have been real proud of you if he could see you now."

And to think that he'd come out here to try to figure out what was bugging the kid and maybe make him feel better. That was one of the really interesting things about life. You never knew what you were going to learn next.

"Thanks." He got to his feet. "You wanna go get those sodas now?"

"Sure."

21

Gallery Euphoria was located in an exclusive corner of Fountain Square. The entrance was accented with an array of artistically arranged pots filled with lush, green plants. The front windows of the shop displayed a variety of handcrafted jewelry and objets d'art created by local and regional artists. There was an unmistakably sophisticated air about the place, Zoe thought, just as there was about the owner.

A tiny bell chimed discreetly when she pushed open the glass door. Arcadia, cool and elegant-looking in a blouse and trousers the color of lime sorbet, was busy with a customer. The woman on the other side of the counter just had to be a tourist, Zoe decided. The big clue was the red knit polo shirt embroidered with the words *Las Estrellas Resort and Spa*.

Arcadia caught Zoe's attention, nodded slightly in acknowledgment of her arrival and went back to showing the vacationer a selection of silver bracelets.

Zoe idly examined a new series of small bronzes crafted in the shapes of various desert creatures. There was a tortoise, a roadrunner and a coyote. She started to reach for the whimsical-looking roadrunner, thinking that it might appeal to Ethan. Her hand paused in midair when she noticed the turquoise necklace in the next case.

Turning her back on the bronzes, she went to stand looking down at the display of jewelry arranged on black velvet. The designs were familiar. The artist was the same one who had created the distinctive necklace that Lindsey Voyle had worn the other day.

The bell over the door chimed again when Arcadia's customer left a short time later.

Arcadia closed and locked the case. "See something you like over there?"

Zoe hesitated. "Lindsey Voyle has a necklace made by this artist."

"I know. She was in here again yesterday looking at some more of his work. She's already got a bracelet on order. It's due in any day now."

"How well do you know her?"

"Lindsey? All I can tell you is that she has very good taste in jewelry. If you're in the market for background information on her you'd better try Ethan. He's the expert when it comes to that kind of thing."

"I know. I was just curious about her, that's all." Asking Ethan was actually a very good idea. The problem was that Ethan would ask her why she wanted him to run the background check on Lindsey and she did not want to try to explain those ghastly spiderwebs in the library. He was remarkably indulgent about her claim to a sixth sense, but if she tried to describe whatever it was she had encountered in the Designers' Dream Home, he might start to wonder.

Why not? She had a few uneasy questions about the source of those vibes herself, questions she did not want to confront too closely. Her research had not yet turned up any reassuring answers.

Arcadia studied her with a considering expression.

"Is there anything wrong, Zoe?"

Act normal. She did not want her best friend probing too deeply, either.

"No." She managed a rueful smile. "I'm just a little stressed out, that's all. I have been for the past couple of weeks. I came by to see if by any chance I left a packet of photos in your office last week. I remember having them in my green tote when I showed them to you but now I can't find them."

'They're here. You left them on top of the file cabinet. I meant to tell you."

"Good. Honestly, what with the show house project and trying to come up with a dazzling proposal for the Tabitha Pine project, I'm getting a little fractured."

"You're not the only one who is misplacing things lately." Arcadia ducked into her small office. "I can't find that little Elvis pen that Harry gave me," she called from the other room. "I've looked everywhere for it."

The glass door opened. A living skeleton ambled into the gallery.

"Hi, Harry," Zoe greeted him. "You're back early. What happened?"

"The client decided that his daughter had

done enough shopping," Harry said. "Sent one of his regular security people to pick her up and take her back to Texas. She was not a happy camper but I sure was glad to see her go. I don't care if I ever see the inside of another shoe store as long as I live."

"Harry." Arcadia appeared in the doorway of her office. "You're home."

Harry smiled his jack-o'-lantern smile. "Yeah. How about that?"

Arcadia was practically glowing. Zoe was amazed. Who would have thought that the aloof Arcadia Ames would ever fall in love like this?

Arcadia dropped her purse beside the cash register, walked quickly around the end of the counter and went straight into Harry's arms. He wrapped her close in his bony grip.

The aura of intimacy that surrounded the pair made Zoe feel very good. She and Arcadia had been through a lot together, but she had never seen her friend genuinely happy until Harry Stagg had come into her life a few weeks ago.

The phone rang in the small office. Arcadia reluctantly raised her head from Harry's shoulder.

"I'll get it," Zoe said quickly. "I'll grab my photos while I'm at it."

"Thanks," Arcadia replied. "Tell whoever it is that I'll be out for the rest of the day. My assistant, Molly, will be back from lunch soon. She'll take over."

Harry chuckled.

"Got it," Zoe said.

She slipped around the counter, stepped into the small, neat office and blundered straight into the sticky strands of an invisible spiderweb.

The shock robbed her of breath. Something deep inside her screamed silently.

No, not here. It isn't possible.

She grabbed the back of the desk chair to keep from falling to her knees. If she'd been able to inhale she probably would have called out. But in that moment of horrified awareness, she could not even breathe.

One coherent thought surfaced. This was the same kind of psychic energy she had encountered in the library.

The gossamer threads clung lightly to her sixth sense, not just clouding her perceptions but subtly twisting and warping them. The memory of her most recent nightmare crashed through her, electrifying every nerve in her body. Panic rose in her throat. What was happening to her?

The phone rang again. The demanding warble sliced through the murky atmosphere. She focused on the sound as though it were a lifeline, concentrating her attention on it while frantically trying to tune out the disturbing psychic energy drifting through the small office.

She succeeded, at least to a point, and started to breathe again. The light-headed sensation receded.

The phone rang a third time and she managed to grab the receiver.

"Gallery Euphoria." She realized she sounded breathless.

"Zoe? Is that you?"

She went limp with relief. Ethan's strong, resonant voice was an anchor in the storm. She seized it and hung on for dear life.

"I'm answering Arcadia's phone for her." Okay, that was better. Her voice was back under control. "She's out in the showroom with Harry."

"I thought Stagg wasn't due back until tomorrow or the next day."

"Evidently the young lady he was supposed to be guarding spent too much time on Rodeo Drive and not enough touring college campuses. Daddy lost his patience." She paused as a thought struck her. "Why are you calling here?"

"Looking for you. You didn't answer your phone."

"I didn't hear it." Baffled, she swung her tote off her shoulder, plopped it on the desk and opened it with her free hand. She peered into the depth. The little phone was right where it was supposed to be, sitting in the special pocket on the inside of the bag. The screen was blank. "Uh-oh."

"Leave it at the apartment?"

"No, it's here." She reached into the tote and picked up the phone. "I forgot to turn it on this morning. Guess I got distracted by the stupid notice that Pixie Ears left under my windshield wiper."

"Duncan struck again?"

"I guess I parked in the wrong place last night. You were parked right next to me. Did she leave a note on your windshield?"

"Now why would she do that? I'm a guest and I was properly parked in a guest slot."

She knew he was grinning. "I don't think that was why she didn't tag you. I think she leaves you alone because you intimidate her."

"Nah. The thing is, see, you're the one whose name is on the lease so she's focusing her attention on you."

"That woman is going to drive me crazy."

Drive me crazy. Cold fingers touched her spine. Her control started to slip. She felt the spiderweb drift past her senses once more.

She sucked in a deep breath and forced herself to refocus. The ghostly threads floated back to the edge of her awareness. She concentrated hard on the curtain-veiled opening that led to Arcadia's back room, steadying herself.

"You can handle Pixie Ears," Ethan said easily. "I've got complete confidence in you. Look, I'm calling to tell you that I'm going to drive out to the Kirwan House to take a look around. I thought that if you didn't have a client appointment this afternoon, you might want to come with me."

"Yes." Anything would be better than sitting alone in her office for the rest of the day, worrying. "I'd like that. I'm going back to my office now."

"I'll pick you up there."

She put down the phone, seized the red tote and fled the cobwebs of dark energy.

"Got to meet Ethan," she said to Arcadia and Harry as she hurried toward the front door. "See you later."

Neither of them paid any attention to her. They were too busy looking at each other.

Outside in the warmth of the desert sun it was easier to think.

Halfway back to her office she finally calmed down sufficiently to contemplate the similarities between her two encounters with the spiderwebs.

There was one undeniable fact that both incidents had in common, she thought. At some point in the past few days, Lindsey Voyle had been in the vicinity of both places where the nasty stuff now lingered.

22

A short time later she climbed out of the passenger seat of the SUV. Ethan came around the front of the vehicle to join her. Together they walked across the newly paved parking lot toward the front entrance of the restored hacienda-style house. There were only a half dozen vehicles in the parking lot because the house was not yet open to the public.

"Bonnie said the Historical Society spared no expense on the hacienda and it looks like she was right." Zoe gestured with one hand. "It's stunning, isn't it?"

"Yeah," Ethan said. "And it's not even pink."

"No, it certainly isn't," she said softly. "It's beautiful."

There was no doubt that the hacienda Kirwan had built was worth the cost of the loving restoration it had received. It was an elegant, graceful structure painted in a rich, warm shade of golden brown. A long shaded and colonnaded patio ran the entire length of the front of the structure and had probably once functioned as an extension of the living room on warm evenings. The wall was studded with intricately worked iron sconces.

"You know," Zoe said, "the paint on the outside of this place is close to the color I'm trying to convince you to go with for the exterior of Nightwinds. You said you've been having a problem visualizing how the house would look if it were any other color than pink." She swept out a hand. "This should give you a good idea. What do you think?"

Ethan removed his dark glasses with slow deliberation. He contemplated the hacienda for a long moment. "Not bad."

She folded her arms and looked long and hard at the walls of the big house. "It's better than not bad. Admit it."

Ethan said nothing for a long moment.

She was aware that he was studying her now, not the house.

"Okay," he said finally.

Startled by the abrupt capitulation, she dropped her arms and spun around to face him. "Are you sure? I see Nightwinds a couple of shades more toward ocher."

He shrugged. "I can't do 'a couple of shades more toward ocher' in my head. But if you like it, let's go with it. Hell, anything is better than peppermint pink."

She smiled tremulously. "Thank you, Ethan. It will work, I promise."

His mouth curved slightly. "Sooner or later, you gotta have a little faith in your decorator, I always say."

"Actually, I'm quite positive that is the very first time that you ever said it in your entire life, but that's okay, I'll take it." She took a step forward and went up on her toes.

She'd intended to brush her mouth lightly across his, but before she could step back, he wrapped his hand around the nape of her neck and pinned her against his chest.

"You didn't tell me there would be a reward for going along with the decorator's choice," he said.

He kissed her slowly and deliberately.

When he was finished she discovered that her knees were a little wobbly.

"Let's get one thing clear," she said breathlessly. "I am not bribing you with sex."

"It's okay. Sex works. I see entire new areas of compromise opening up before us."

"Hmm."

He laced her fingers through his own and they walked toward the wide, arched doorway.

She hesitated, as she always did at the entrance to a new building. Ethan did not comment, nor did he use his grip on her hand to urge her into the shadowy interior. Instead, he waited patiently.

Having been taken off guard twice in recent days, she opened her senses with more caution than usual. But she encountered nothing more than the low-level psychic hum that was typical of older buildings. Layers of human emotions had built up over the years, but it was just the normal stuff, she thought, easy to tune out.

She stepped through the doorway with Ethan, ignoring the gentle, faded psychic energies in the atmosphere the same way she routinely ignored the background noise of a busy city street.

Inside the hacienda, tall, well-proportioned windows illuminated high, dark-beamed ceilings. The paintings and artifacts of the Kirwan Collection were artfully arranged in what had obviously been originally designed as the main reception room.

At one end of the long salon, Paloma Santana stood talking to two men who were dressed in work clothes and tool belts.

The mayor glanced toward the entrance and inclined her head in greeting. She said something else to the workmen and then walked down the length of the room toward Zoe and Ethan. The heels of her designer-label sandals rang on the floor tiles.

"Ethan, I'm so glad you could come take a look at the house."

"It's not often that I actually get to visit the scene of the crime in one of these old cases. I'd like you to meet my wife, Zoe."

The possessiveness in his voice was unmistakable. Zoe felt her cheeks warm.

"It's an honor, Mayor Santana," she said, politely extending her hand.

"Call me Paloma. I understand you're an interior designer, Zoe. What do you think of the restoration job?"

"It's wonderful," Zoe said with real feeling.

"It's going to be a terrific addition to the community and also a fine tourist attraction."

"I agree. We're all quite pleased with it." Paloma looked at Ethan. "I assume you're here to see Kirwan's study?"

"If that's possible," Ethan said.

"Of course. Follow me."

Paloma led the way through the long reception area, past the restored dining room and kitchen and into a long, book-lined room. A massive stone fireplace covered most of the wall at the far end.

Zoe hesitated once again at the arched entrance to the study, bracing herself for whatever awaited her inside. She experienced a profound relief when nothing out of the ordinary brushed across her psychic senses. She did not need any more traumatic encounters that day.

"One of our goals was to re-create Kirwan's library," Paloma said, moving into the study. "Fortunately, there was a complete catalog of the original collection. We were able to duplicate it almost entirely."

Zoe watched Ethan walk into the study. She could feel the predatory curiosity of the born hunter awaken in him.

He prowled the room, examining the

bookshelves, the large desk and the massive stone fireplace. Eventually he came to a halt in the middle of the room and looked at her.

Belatedly she realized that he was waiting to see if she would enter. She probed once more and stepped into the room. Traces of old, low-level emotions whispered around her but nothing strong, violent or worrisome.

"How is your investigation going?" Paloma asked Ethan.

"At this stage I'm still gathering information," Ethan said easily. "I went through several newspaper accounts of Kirwan's death. Singleton Cobb helped me locate some letters that were written by Kirwan's biographer, his agent, Exford, and a few of his friends. From all accounts Kirwan was a difficult, temperamental man."

Paloma nodded seriously. "My grandmother confirmed that. But she always said that she knew how to deal with him. What about Exford? Were you able to locate him?"

"Dead in a car crash a few years after Kirwan died. He had a serious drinking problem."

"I don't suppose you found any indication that he was the one who took Kirwan's last manuscript?"

"I'm still pursuing that line of inquiry," Ethan said.

His professional aplomb made Zoe struggle to conceal a grin.

Outside in the parking lot, she got into the passenger's seat and buckled her belt. "'Pursuing that line of inquiry'?"

"That's what you say to the client when you're not sure what the hell is going on. I'll bet you decorators have a few similar client-handling phrases."

"I've always been partial to 'I thought you understood that special orders from Italy required up to four months' additional delivery time,' myself."

"Remind me not to special-order any furniture from Italy." He twisted the key in the ignition. "Well? Feel anything in that room?"

She glanced at him, startled that he would ask the question. "Hey, you don't believe that I'm psychic, remember?"

"I have great respect for your intuition, you know that." He put the SUV in gear and drove toward the exit. "What did it tell you?"

"Nothing useful," she admitted. "But I've explained to you that I only pick up on very strong, dark emotions, remember? Rage, fear, panic, lust."

"All the fun stuff."

"Yeah. In any event, I've been thinking about it and it occurs to me that I'm not sure I'd pick up anything at all in a case of death by poison."

"Why not?"

She groped to explain something she did not entirely comprehend herself. "There might not be any violent energy released in that sort of situation. Kirwan might never have realized that he had been poisoned. Perhaps he simply felt ill, passed out and died very quietly. Unless the killer stood over him, gloating and generating a lot of intense emotion, I've got a hunch that there would be very few vibes left behind for me to feel years later."

"In other words, you can't tell me diddly-squat."

"Look on the positive side, you're getting the advantage of my psychic consulting services for free."

"Yeah, well, you get what you pay for, I guess."

"Okay, Mr. Hotshot PI, what do you think happened in that room?"

"Well, to begin with, I'm pretty sure that Maria did not steal the manuscript."

That caught her attention. "You didn't say that to the mayor."

"Because I can't prove anything one way or the other yet."

"What made you decide the housekeeper didn't take the book?"

"If she killed him and stole the manuscript, it would have turned up sooner or later. It was too valuable to stay hidden all these years."

"Unless she burned it that night."

He shook his head. "Why would she do that? She had worked for Kirwan for years. Long enough to know that the manuscript was worth a good deal of money. She probably overheard the argument between Kirwan and his agent and knew that there was at least one potential buyer."

"The publisher?"

"Uh-huh."

"What about the agent? Think Exford killed Kirwan and stole the manuscript that night?"

"No. Same reason I don't think Maria took it. The agent had financial problems. If he took the manuscript, he would have sold it or seen to it that it got published."

Zoe contemplated that for a while. "You

know, you're pretty darn good when it comes to this kind of logical thinking."

"Thanks. It sure would be a lot more exciting to be psychic, but I've learned to muddle through using logic and common sense."

"We all have our little gifts."

Ethan laughed.

It was the first time in several days that he had done so. For some reason she found his amusement reassuring.

23

That night they went to Last Exit to celebrate Harry's early return from LA. Arcadia sat close to him, letting her shoulder touch his, stealing a little of his warmth. The slow, soft strains of Billy Strayhorn's "Lush Life" drifted through the lightly crowded nightclub.

It was well after midnight. The jazz was good. Arcadia had a martini in front of her. Harry was home, safe and sound. This was as near to perfect as her life had been in a long, long time. So why couldn't she relax?

"You came back early because of me, didn't you?" she said.

"Nah." Harry munched peanuts from the

bowl in front of them. "I told you, the client pulled the plug on the kid's shopping expedition."

"Liar." She sucked the olive off the little red spear, chewed and swallowed. "You quit the job early on my account. Admit it."

Harry took a sip of his beer. "Hey, I was glad when the gig ended. The kid was driving me crazy."

"I knew it. You're home early because of me."

"So," Harry said, lounging against the padded wall of the booth, "you going to tell me what's wrong?"

She hesitated. "As far as I can tell, nothing's wrong. I got a little jumpy for a few days after you left, that's all." She took a sip of the martini. "I'm okay now. But . . ."

"But, what?"

"But I missed you, Harry."

Harry said nothing. He just waited, as patient as the grave.

She exhaled slowly. "Okay, I'll tell you what I told Zoe. Shortly after you left there were a couple of occasions when I got a creepy feeling. As if someone was watching me or something."

Harry did not move so much as an eyelash. "Yeah?"

"But the feeling went away after two or three days," she added quickly.

"Anything else?"

She made a triangle around the base of the martini glass with her fingers. "I lost the Elvis pen you gave me. I searched everywhere and couldn't find it."

"No big deal. It's just a pen."

"I liked it. It was my favorite."

Harry thought about that for a long time. "Anything else in your office disturbed?"

Having him put her own secret fears into words chilled her to the bone. "No. Nothing. Believe me, I checked. Given my history, I consider paranoia a healthy state of mind. I went through every drawer. Nothing looked out of order."

"A pro wouldn't have left any tracks in your files," he mused. "You don't have the kind of security at the office that we have at home. It wouldn't have been difficult for someone who knew what he was doing to get inside."

She frowned. "You really think that an intruder might have broken into my office just to steal an Elvis pen? It doesn't make any sense."

"The pen could have been an accident or a mistake." He moved one hand dismissively. "Hell, it might have nothing to do with anything. The cleaning crew could have broken that damn pen and tossed it into the trash."

"True." She tried a smile. "In which case I've got no reason at all to think that anyone was inside my office after hours. Just another example of a vivid imagination run amok, Harry. I'm sure of it now."

He did not return her smile. "Earlier this week when you felt that someone was watching you, did you check out the faces of the people around you?"

"Of course. But I didn't see anyone who looked even remotely like . . . him."

She did not have to explain who she meant. Harry knew she was referring to Grant.

"See anyone you didn't know more than once?"

That question gave her pause. An image of an elderly woman with a shopping bag and a camera flickered through her mind. "It was a busy week at Fountain Square. Lots of tourists coming and going. I saw several of them more than once but no one who was suspicious."

"Cars?"

"Who looks at cars?"

"I do," Harry said. "Think about it, honey. You got that creepy feeling from something you noticed, even if you don't remember what it was. That's how it works."

"How what works?"

"The creeps. You get them because you see something or someone out of the corner of your eye and it looks wrong. Maybe you don't think about it much, but something inside goes on alert."

Harry would know, she assured herself as she settled back against the seat and tried to summon up memories of some of the cars she had noticed in recent days. After a couple of minutes, she gave up in frustration.

"I just don't have much of a memory for cars," she said apologetically.

"Try people."

The image of the woman in the shop window popped into her head again.

"There was one," she said slowly. "I saw her two, maybe three times."

"Describe her."

"That's just it. I don't know why she stuck in my mind. She didn't exactly stand out as a dangerous character. She must have been at least eighty years old. She had a large sun hat and those oversized sunglasses that people wear over their regular glasses. She was just a tourist, Harry."

"What else?"

The man would have made a good interrogator, she thought ruefully. He just kept pushing.

She took a sip of her martini and tried to still her mind. In the old days she had made her living in the adrenaline-driven financial world. It was a world where millions of dollars were placed at risk every time she made a decision. In that world, she had been very good at seeing patterns and trends. She had trained herself to notice the tiny signals that appeared before a company went into a death spiral. She had learned to watch for disturbances in the flow that warned of trouble brewing among the members of a company's board of directors. She could spot insider trading before the SEC even woke up in the morning.

It was her talent for catching the small anomalies in the constantly shifting streams of data that had given her advance warning of Grant's intentions. Maybe she should apply those old skills now.

"I saw her at least twice, both times as a reflection in a store window. I remember thinking that the camera was very fancy, not one of those disposable gadgets. And she carried the same shopping bag both times, a blue-and-white one from a dress shop in Fountain Square."

Harry was silent for a while. "Okay."

She raised her brows. "Okay, what?"

"Okay, now we go talk to Truax."

"It's one-thirty A.M. He and Zoe will be sound asleep."

"Not our fault those two keep weird hours."

Ethan managed to fall into a restless sleep but he dreamed the Nightwinds dream.

> He walked through the vast house, opening each door he came to, searching every room. But Zoe was not in any of them. She had to be there. The possibility that he might not find her made despair claw at his insides.
>
> He called out to her, wanting to explain, to plead, to make her understand. But the

words echoed forever in the endless corridors of pink-tinged night.

At last he came to the small, private theater, the room where the old murder had occurred, the one place in the house that seemed to disturb her.

He opened the doors slowly, bracing himself for what awaited him in the darkness.

Zoe stood in the shadows near the small marble bar. Simon Wendover reclined in one of the plush velvet seats facing the screen. He looked at Ethan over his shoulder and grinned.

"You're dead," Ethan said.

Wendover laughed. "That's your problem, not mine. We both know you're going to see me in your dreams now and again for the rest of your life."

Ethan turned away from him and looked at Zoe. "Come with me."

She shook her head. "No."

"She's going to leave you just like all the others did," Wendover said cheerfully. "That's how it works where you're concerned. Been that way all your life. You rescue them and then they wave goodbye."

Ethan kept his gaze on Zoe. "You're different."

"Am I?" she said.

Wendover chuckled. "How could she love a man with your track record? You're a loser, Truax. You couldn't save your brother. You couldn't hold any of your three marriages together. You couldn't hang on to the corporation you built from scratch. You spent months investigating me but in the end you couldn't even put together a case that held up in court."

Ethan knew he had to get Zoe out of the room where Wendover sat gloating. He tried to walk through the doorway of the theater but something stopped him. It was as though he confronted an invisible wall.

Zoe watched him with her mysterious eyes. "I'm sorry, Ethan. You can't come in here. There's a psychic barrier. You can't get past it because you don't believe in the woo-woo thing."

Wendover's laugh echoed in the shadows.

"Ethan. *Ethan,* wake up."

Her voice. So close. So near.

He opened his eyes. Zoe leaned over him. Anxiety radiated from her in waves.

"It's okay." She gripped his shoulder. "It's all right. Just a bad dream."

"You can say that again." He scrubbed his face with one hand and made himself breathe slowly. When he was fairly certain that he had himself under control, he sat up and swung his legs over the side of the bed.

She knelt behind him and massaged his shoulders. "I sure hope you're not catching the nightmare habit from me. Do you suppose bad dreams are contagious?"

"I doubt it." Her hands felt good on his shoulders. He wanted nothing more than to relax under the soothing pressure of her fingers and palms, but the tension hummed through him like electricity.

"Do you want to tell me about your dream?" Zoe asked quietly.

He thought he heard Wendover's laughter somewhere in the distance.

"It was complicated," he said carefully.

Her hands stilled on his shoulders. He sensed her withdrawing. For a couple of seconds he thought she was going to stop the comforting massage.

"I do complicated, remember?" she said. Her hands moved on him once more.

A shudder of relief went through him.

"Ethan?"

"We were both at Nightwinds but the house seemed way too large," he said tonelessly. "There was an endless series of rooms."

"It was probably the thought of redecorating all those rooms that gave you the nightmare."

"Probably." He knew that she was trying to lighten the atmosphere but it wasn't working. He was too cold and too drained. He should stop now, he told himself. There was no point telling her the rest. But it was as if some powerful magnet dragged the words out of him. "You were there somewhere but I couldn't find you."

"Ah, yes, the elusive designer who never returns the client's phone calls," she murmured.

"I eventually tracked you down in the theater." He hesitated and then raised one shoulder in a shrug. "That's when you woke me up."

"You were thrashing around. I got the impression that you were trying to claw your way through something."

He froze. "Did I hurt you?"

"No. You just woke me up." She continued to work his shoulders. "Are you sure there wasn't something else about the dream that bothered you?"

Somewhere in the shadows, Wendover chuckled.

The phone rang. Zoe's hands stilled once more on Ethan's shoulders. He glanced at the clock. It was one thirty-five in the morning. Phone calls at that hour rarely brought good news.

"I'll get it." He picked up the phone. "Truax."

"This is Stagg," Harry said. "We have a problem. We're standing outside the front door of the lobby of Casa de Oro. You want to buzz us in?"

24

Ethan sat on the sofa and watched Zoe serve the tea she had made for the four of them. She had clipped her hair into a loose knot and put on a pair of black slippers that looked like the kind of shoes ballet dancers wore. Her midnight-blue dressing gown was tied snugly around her waist.

He had pulled on a pair of trousers and a tee shirt. Because he could see that his new habit of shaving before bed was starting to worry Zoe, he hadn't bothered to do so that night. The result was that he knew he probably looked more than a little rough around the edges.

Arcadia and Harry, however, were both creatures of the night. They managed to appear oddly stylish at one-thirty in the morning. Arcadia was her customary ice-queen self in a narrow column of a dress that was the color of a pale desert dawn. Harry was surprisingly natty in a short-sleeved sport shirt decorated with surfboards and palm trees.

"Let me get this straight." Ethan sat forward on the sofa, elbows resting on his thighs, fingers loosely linked between his spread knees. "You noticed the same senior citizen in a hat and sunglasses twice over the course of two days and you lost the pen that Harry gave you? That's it?"

"Doesn't sound like much to get freaked out about, does it?" Arcadia said apologetically. "Sorry about this. It was Harry's idea to come here tonight."

"And a very good idea it was," Zoe said forcefully. "When you add this bit with the little old lady to that edgy feeling you mentioned to me earlier this week, it raises some questions."

Ethan frowned. "No one told me anything about Arcadia feeling edgy this past week."

"I thought maybe I was just a bit jumpy because Harry was gone and . . ." Arcadia's platinum-tipped fingernails glinted when she picked up her cup. "Well, the feeling went away so I didn't want to mention it."

"As far as I'm concerned, it's the camera that bothers me the most," Zoe said. "From your description, it was not only expensive, it sounds like something a professional photographer would use. Not the kind of equipment an elderly tourist would favor."

"The lost pen may or may not mean anything," Harry said. "But if someone is watching Arcadia, it would be logical to assume that he searched her office. Maybe he used the pen to pry open a drawer or poke around inside a file cabinet and it snapped. He figured it would be better to get rid of the pieces rather than leave them behind."

"It was an inexpensive pen," Zoe added. "He would have assumed that no one would even notice it was missing."

Ethan looked at Arcadia. "Notice anything else missing or rearranged in your office? Anything seem different in there?"

Beside him, Zoe abruptly stiffened. She offered no comment, but out of the corner of his eye he saw that the teacup wobbled ever so slightly in her fingers. *What the hell was that all about?*

"No," Arcadia said in response to his question. "And I checked, believe me."

Ethan switched his attention to Harry. "What about the condo?"

"Everything is fine there," Harry assured him. "I'd know if someone had got past the new system."

"All right." Ethan picked up the notebook and pen that he had placed on the coffee table. "Here's what we've got. Someone *may* be watching Arcadia. If that is true, there *may* be a connection to Grant Loring."

"Who is supposed to be dead, but I don't believe that for a moment," Arcadia said evenly. "He is definitely my worst-case scenario. But it's also possible that the Feds have tracked me down."

Harry looked at her. "How badly do the Feds want you?"

Arcadia exhaled slowly. "I honestly didn't think that I was that important to them. But I suppose they might have convinced themselves that if Grant is still alive I might be able to lead them to him."

"Except that you can't," Zoe said. "You

than saw the concern mingled with curios-
/ on Zoe's face and realized that Arcadia
ad not told her all of her secrets.

"When I realized that the safest thing to do
as vanish," Arcadia said quietly, "I made
ome arrangements. I stashed money in
everal different accounts under a variety of
lentities, and I tried to muddy my trail by
hecking myself into Candle Lake Manor. Af-
er Zoe and I escaped, I changed my identity
second time."

"Go on," Harry said quietly.

"I took one more precaution. Grant kept
verything that was important to him on a
ecret computer that he didn't realize that I
new he had. A lot of it was the sort of de-
ailed financial information that could have
ent him to jail for a very long time. But as I
ound out later, there was some other, more
langerous stuff on it, too. In any event, I fig-
ured out his password and downloaded the
ntire file. Then I hid my copy."

"Tell me about this dangerous stuff," Ethan
said.

"It consists of the details of some scams
hat Grant pulled on a few folks who are not
as easygoing as the Feds when it comes to
hings like embezzlement." Arcadia's shoul-

don't have any idea where he is. Besides, that scenario implies that they no longer believe that you're dead."

Arcadia shrugged and said nothing.

"Okay, let's stop there for a minute." Ethan made a note. "Best case is that it's the Feds. Problem is, it doesn't feel like a Fed kind of operation."

Harry raised his brows. "The senior citizen with the camera?"

"Yeah. Not Fed style. When it comes to equipment, they're a lot more high-tech. Also, they're big on putting wires on people and sending them into situations to record conversations." He glanced at Arcadia. "I assume no one has tried to get you to open up about your past lately?"

"No." She frowned. "You're right. Probably not the Feds. That leaves Grant or one of his former associates."

"Lucky for you, you've got a real good friend who is also an ace bodyguard," Ethan said. "And you've got another friend who is a hotshot PI. Harry and I will split up the job. He'll keep an eye on you while I start asking some questions. We'll need Singleton's assistance for the on-line work."

Zoe looked at him. "Do you think Harry

should take Arcadia out of town while you conduct your investigation?"

"It's an option," he said neutrally.

"No." Arcadia was suddenly, fiercely, resolute. "If Grant has found me under this new identity, he can find me anywhere. Disappearing again for a while will only delay matters. I'd rather deal with him now and finish it."

Harry nodded in agreement. "Something to be said for staying here in Whispering Springs. It's a relatively small community and it's our turf, not Loring's. We know a lot more about it than he does."

"Also, things have changed considerably in the past few weeks," Arcadia pointed out. "You've got some connections with the local police now, Ethan. You know people around town and at Radnor."

"None of those contacts will do you much good if he tries to take you out with a bullet," Ethan said flatly. "Harry's good, but no one is perfect."

Arcadia held her cup in both hands and studied the depths of her tea as if it were an oracle glass. "I can't be absolutely positive," she said carefully, "but I don't think that he will try to shoot me dead from a distance."

They all watched her.

"Why not?" Ethan asked.

"Two reasons. First, Grant is a s
thinker. It was his forte when he was
his investment empire, and he's not t
to change his stripes. In fact he's alm
sessive when it comes to planning.
mind that he has a reason to be care
last thing he'll want to do is give the
his disgruntled former business assoc
reason to think that he's still alive."

"Good point," Zoe said.

"Running me down with a car or arr
for me to die in a mysterious hou
would be more his style," Arcadia said

Ethan saw Harry's hand flex once.
the only evidence of what he must have
thinking but it was a chilling little move

"What's the second reason he would
to gun you down from a safe dista
Ethan asked.

"I took out a small insurance policy b
I disappeared."

"What kind of policy?" Ethan asked.

"I have something that Grant wants."
dia lowered her cup to the saucer. "An
only way to get it from me is to make m
him where it is."

No one spoke. They all sat there, wa

ders were rigid. "I discovered rather late in our marriage that my husband had ripped off some extremely unsavory people. If they ever find out that he's alive and if they learn that he stole a great deal of money from them, they will surely want revenge."

Harry whistled tunelessly. "If Loring's out there, he won't rest easy until he destroys the copy you made of that file."

"As I said," Arcadia continued, "I hid the file. But I didn't tell Grant that I had done so. I thought I had some time, you see. I was trying to decide what my next move should be. But then he attempted to murder me."

"How?" Ethan asked.

"It was supposed to be an accident. I told you, Grant favors that approach. I had a late evening appointment with a client who lived in a home just outside a resort town in the mountains. Grant knew that my route followed the shoreline of a large lake. He lay in wait for me. Forced my car off the road at a high point above the water."

"Dear God." Zoe reached out and put one hand over Arcadia's.

Harry looked like death made flesh.

Ethan kept his mouth shut and made more notes.

"It was night and it was raining hard," Arcadia went on after a while. "Fortunately, the car landed in a relatively shallow section of the lake. I made it out through the driver's window and surfaced beneath some overhanging tree branches. That was probably what saved my life."

Ethan paused in his writing. "Loring couldn't find you in the water?"

"No. I realized it was him when he got out of the car and walked in front of the headlights. He had a flashlight. He used it to search the surface of the lake. But he never spotted me because of the trees. I honestly thought I would die of hypothermia before he finally left the scene."

Harry rested his palm on her knee. Ethan saw his fingers tighten gently.

"After he drove away, I climbed out of the water. I spent the night in an empty cabin. By morning I decided that the safest thing for me to do was disappear until the authorities caught up with Grant."

"But they never did catch up with him," Harry concluded.

"No, because Grant fled the country early the next morning. He was reported dead in a skiing accident in Europe two weeks later."

"Why didn't you go to the Feds?" Ethan asked.

"Frankly, I didn't think they would be able to protect me from Grant. But I did get the word out about that file I had hidden."

"How did you do that?" Harry asked.

"I used a computer to plant the story in the financial press. It was just a short piece about how, before she died, Grant Loring's wife had confided to an unnamed source that she had copied Loring's private files. I implied that the tragically deceased Mrs. Loring had stashed said files in a secret location. Sadly, she took the secret with her to a watery grave."

Harry tipped his head to one side about an inch. "'Watery grave'?"

Arcadia raised her brows. "You think that was a little over-the-top for the financial press?"

"Nah. It's perfect for the financial press." He nodded. "Watery grave. Yeah, I like it a lot. I'll bet they went for it."

"They did," Arcadia assured him. "And so did a lot of the rest of the media. That was all I cared about. I knew that, wherever he was, Grant would be watching the papers, networks and the on-line news sources to find out if my body was recovered and to see how his own disappearing act was going down. I knew the threat wouldn't provide me with complete protection, but I thought it might give me a little bargaining power if Grant ever came looking for me."

Ethan studied his notes. "All right, here's what we're going to do. We'll proceed on the assumption that Grant Loring is alive and well and has become a problem for Arcadia because it is a reasonable possibility. But we need to keep in mind that we might be wrong."

"Do you think we're jumping at shadows?" Zoe asked.

Ethan shrugged. "Maybe."

Zoe cleared her throat.

Ethan groaned silently. He knew that little sound she made when she was getting ready to tell him something that he did not want to hear.

He eyed her warily. "Now what?"

"I'm not sure what it means," she said, enunciating each word with great care. "But I think there's something you should know."

"Don't drag it out," he muttered. "I can't take the suspense."

Instead of answering immediately, Zoe exchanged glances with Arcadia. He could not read the private message that passed between them, but there was no mistaking that one had been transmitted and received.

Zoe wrapped her arms around her midsection and looked at him with shadowed, somber eyes. "I felt something in Arcadia's office this afternoon."

"Zoe." Arcadia turned toward her with a startled movement. "Why didn't you tell me?"

"It's a little hard to explain," Zoe admitted.

Harry looked interested.

"Okay," Ethan said. "You've got our attention. What did your *intuition* tell you?"

"That's just it," Zoe whispered. "I'm not sure what it told me. That's why I didn't say anything to you, Arcadia. But I know this much: I felt the same thing in my library at the show house yesterday."

"Keep talking," Ethan said evenly.

"It was very faint." She moved her shoulders in a tight shrug. "Just wispy little traces. But it . . . it really freaked me out for a while because I've only experienced that kind of energy on one other occasion."

"When was that?" Harry asked.

"One night when I was out wandering the halls at Candle Lake Manor." She looked directly at Arcadia. "It was coming from a room in H Ward."

"Oh, shit," Arcadia said very softly.

Ethan glanced at Harry, who silently shook his head. Evidently this wasn't making any sense to him, either.

He switched his attention back to Zoe and Arcadia. "One of you want to tell us what was so freaky about H Ward?"

"Yeah, we've got inquiring minds," Harry added.

Zoe drew a deep breath. Ethan could see that she was preparing to take some sort of big plunge.

"You know that Candle Lake Manor is an upscale private sanatorium," she said. "It was established as a place where, for a price, rich folks could institutionalize their more awkward relatives, the ones with mental health issues and psychological problems."

Ethan nodded. "We've got that much. Go on."

"Well," Zoe continued. "Hard as it may be to comprehend, it turns out that the very wealthy have their fair share of seriously disturbed family members, too, just like everyone else. H Ward was the wing at Xanadu where those patients were warehoused."

"'Seriously disturbed,'" Ethan repeated without inflection. "That doesn't sound good."

"She's talking about the potentially dangerous patients," Arcadia explained. "The real crazies, the ones who scared the daylights out of the staff and everyone else."

"Well, well, what do you know," Harry muttered. "The rich are not so different, after all. But what about this weird sensation you got in Arcadia's office and your library, Zoe?"

"I'm starting to think that the crazy psychic energy may have been left behind by Lindsey Voyle," Zoe said.

"Great," Ethan said. "Just what I needed in this case. The interior designer from hell."

25

Singleton was in his tiny office, staring into the depths of his computer when the door of the shop opened. Bonnie walked in, bringing a few megawatts of the late morning sunshine with her.

"Singleton?"

"Back here." He tried to ignore the little surge of pleasure that pulsed through him. *Keep cool, man. She sees you as a friend, not a lover. You don't want to screw this up.*

He pushed himself back from the computer, took off his glasses and got to his feet.

"You must be exhausted." Bonnie came to stand in the narrow doorway. "I understand that Ethan woke you up around three this morning to ask you to start working on this situation involving Arcadia." She held up a large paper cup bearing the logo of a Fountain Square espresso bar. "I thought that by now you could use some caffeine."

"You thought right." He took the coffee from her, peeled off the lid and took a long swallow. When he was finished, he lowered the cup with a sigh of satisfaction. "Thanks. I needed that. You were right about that three A.M. call from your brother-in-law. Lucky for him he's a friend as well as an occasional client."

No point telling her that when he'd picked up the phone and heard Ethan's somber, coolly urgent voice on the other end of the connection, panic had hit him with the force of a hammer in the gut. For a few dazed seconds he'd been afraid that the late night call signaled bad news about Bonnie or one of the boys. In that short space of time his world had started to shatter and collapse around him.

When he'd learned that the threat had nothing to do with Bonnie, Jeff or Theo, he'd been so relieved that he immediately felt a pang of guilt. After all, he liked Arcadia a lot.

She was a friend, and the knowledge that she was in danger worried him. But the concern he felt for her was not the same kind of bone-deep fear he knew he would experience if Bonnie or one of the boys was in harm's way.

Face it, Cobb, you've got it bad.

Bonnie removed a plastic container from another paper sack.

He studied it with interest. "What have we here?"

"Tuna fish."

He took the container from her and opened it with a sense of anticipation. "On rye. My favorite."

Bonnie chuckled. "You always say that. No matter what I feed you, you always tell me it's your favorite."

He removed one half of the plump, neatly sliced sandwich and took a bite. "That's because it's the truth."

She smiled, looking quietly satisfied, and watched him demolish the first half of the sandwich.

"I understand that you and Jeff had a talk," she said when he paused to drink more coffee.

"Jeff told you about it?"

"He said that you explained to him that he didn't have to worry about remembering exactly what Drew looked like. That no matter what happened he would never forget his father."

He got a bad feeling in the pit of his stomach and knew that it had nothing to do with the tuna fish. It was Bonnie's very serious expression and tone that was making him lose his appetite. He wondered if she thought he had overstepped the bounds of friendship when he'd taken it upon himself to have that chat with Jeff.

"Maybe I shouldn't have said anything." He put down the unfinished portion of the sandwich. "Look, Bonnie, I apologize if I intruded too much into your family's private life."

"No, please, don't apologize. That's not what I meant at all." She took a step forward and touched his arm. "What I'm trying to say is that I'm very grateful that you spoke with Jeff. I hadn't realized what was really bothering him this year. I thought maybe he was acting out because he had somehow regressed to the very bad time the first November after we lost Drew. The therapist warned me that could happen."

He looked down at her hand. Her fingertips rested lightly on his bare skin just below the rolled-up edge of his denim sleeve. He was intensely aware of her standing so close; had to remind himself to breathe.

"It's hard for a boy that age to explain what he's going through," he said. "Hell, it's hard for a guy to explain himself at any age."

"I know. You think you know your own children, but like everyone else, they have their private places deep inside. They have thoughts and worries that they feel they can't talk about. It never occurred to me that Jeff was terrified that he would forget his father."

Alarmed, he closed his big hand over hers without stopping to consider the intimacy of the small gesture. "For God's sake, Bonnie, don't blame yourself because you didn't immediately figure out what was bothering Jeff. I know you think you're supposed to solve all his problems for him, but the truth is, he's starting to grow up and he needs to work some things through in his own way."

"He's only eight years old."

"Yeah, but he's on his way to becoming a man, and deep down he knows that. He also knows that he's got some very high standards to meet."

"Standards?"

"The ones set first by his father and now, by Ethan."

She closed her eyes briefly. When she opened them, there was clear understanding in her gaze. "Yes, I see what you mean."

"Jeff's got a lot to live up to and he's trying. He's starting to wrestle with the important stuff."

"Dealing with the loss of his father? Yes, I know, but—"

"No," he interrupted quietly, trying once again to find the right words. "Not just that. See, what Jeff went through this month wasn't just about the loss of his dad. The real struggle he faced was the fear that if he forgot his father, he would somehow betray you and Ethan, the two adults he loves most in this world."

She stood very still. "Betrayal is a very big concept for an eight-year-old boy."

"I know. But the thing is, he's starting to formulate his own private code, the one he'll live by for the rest of his life. Betraying the people he loves is a bad thing and he knows that. So he was scared when he realized that he might be doing exactly that and he didn't know how to stop the process."

"But he wasn't betraying us."

"Yeah, but he didn't understand that. He needed to talk to someone who could explain it to him, but that someone had to be a person he couldn't hurt."

"You." Bonnie blinked back tears. "I don't know how to thank you, Singleton."

An uncomfortable tide of heat rose in his face. He realized that he was probably turning red.

"Hey, no big deal," he said gruffly. "We're friends, remember?"

To his surprise, her expression clouded.

"Right. Friends." She took her hand out from beneath his fingers and moved back toward the door. "I'd better be on my way. Good luck with the investigation."

She walked out of the bookshop. When the door closed behind her, the gloomy shadows returned.

Ethan listened to the footsteps on the stairs. The heavy tread reverberated down the narrow hall outside his office. A man, he thought. One who was not in a good mood.

He put aside the notes he had made after his discussion with Singleton a half hour before, folded his arms on top of his desk and waited.

The footsteps stopped briefly outside the entrance of Truax Investigations. He got the feeling that whoever stood there was hesitating, maybe having second thoughts about the wisdom of hiring a private investigator.

A smart businessman would get up at this point, open the door and try to look sympathetic and encouraging. But he had his hands full at the moment so he stayed where he was. With luck the prospective client would talk himself out of the meeting.

The door opened.

That figured. Never rains but it pours.

The new arrival walked into the outer office. He was clearly visible in the carefully positioned mirror. Athletically built, square-jawed, clean-cut, sandy-haired. His attire was Arizona resort casual: expensively tailored trousers, polo shirt and loafers. He had the look of a guy who had been captain of the football team in high school. He had probably taken the homecoming queen to the senior prom and talked her out of her panties afterward. In college he would have joined the right fraternity, got himself elected president and dated a lot of busty, blond sorority girls.

Nelson Radnor, president and CEO of the competition, Radnor Security Systems.

Ethan cranked back in his chair and stacked his feet on the corner of his desk. "What can I do for you, Radnor?"

Nelson came to the door of the inner office and looked around with an expression of sardonic amusement. "Thought your new wife was an interior designer."

"She is. But I won't let her touch my office."

"Yeah, I can see that."

"A man's got to draw the line somewhere when it comes to decorating. Have a seat."

Nelson walked into the room. He glanced at the nearest of the two client chairs but made no move to lower himself into it. He went to stand at the window instead.

"I hear you've stolen one of my major accounts." Nelson watched the street as if he was expecting something interesting to happen down there.

Nope, that's not it, Ethan thought. Nelson did not sound sufficiently pissed.

"For the record," he said, "I didn't steal the Valdez account. I'm not set up to take over a full-time security management job that big and he knows it. He came to me for a one-time independent audit."

"Sure. So you're going to complete your independent audit and write up an impressive report that says my people missed something on a background check, right?"

"Is that what happened?"

"Maybe. Or maybe someone we hired who was as pure as the driven snow discovered that he couldn't resist temptation when it came his way in Valdez's shipping room." Nelson glanced back over his shoulder. His face was oddly drawn and grim. "Whatever, it's going to make Radnor Security look bad."

"Not for long. The corporate security market is all yours here in Whispering Springs. Everyone knows that. I'm what you call a niche player."

"You weren't a niche player in LA." Nelson's face was unreadable. "You were in the big leagues there. Maybe you've got aspirations here in Whispering Springs."

"Got a few." Ethan sank deeper into his chair and eyed the toes of his running shoes propped on the desk. "But they don't involve going head to head with Radnor. I'm after the small stuff, the one-man jobs that need the personal touch. You know as well as I do that you don't even want that end of the market. You're not set up to handle it."

Radnor turned back to the window. He did

not speak for a while. Then he moved his shoulders as if trying to loosen tight muscles.

"Funny you should mention the small jobs that need the personal touch." He sounded morose but determined. "As it happens, I've got one for you."

Whatever this was all about, Ethan knew it was not good. He was dealing with enough oncoming trains. The last thing he needed was another one bearing down on him. Train wrecks were messy.

"Thanks for thinking of me," he said, "but I'm a little busy at the moment."

"Not like I've got a lot of choice," Nelson muttered. "I need a niche player. And you're the only one in town."

"There must be somebody on your staff who can handle it."

"I don't want anyone on my staff to even know about this job," Nelson said roughly. "That's why I'm here."

"Like I said, I appreciate the opportunity, but—"

"I think my wife is having an affair," Nelson said flatly.

Oh, shit. Out of all the PI offices in this burg, why did you have to walk into mine?

But that was the problem, of course, Ethan thought. There were only two private investigation firms in Whispering Springs.

With great precision, moving as slowly as possible in order to give himself time. He took his feet down off his desk and straightened in his chair.

He hesitated, trying to come up with something appropriate to say. Unfortunately there weren't any good platitudes for this particular situation. He knew that from personal experience.

"For what it's worth, I know the feeling," he said evenly.

Nelson swung around, looking genuinely shocked. "You do? Jesus, man, you've only been married, what? Six weeks?"

It dawned on him that Nelson assumed he had implied that Zoe was having an affair. For an instant, the world around him vanished. A terrible red haze took its place.

A stark vision of Zoe leaving him for another man seared his synapses. The floor dissolved beneath his chair and he felt himself falling down a bottomless pit.

With an effort of raw willpower, he pulled himself back to reality.

"I'm not talking about Zoe," he said. "I was referring to a, uh, previous relationship."

"Oh, yeah, that's right." Nelson nodded. "I read somewhere that you've been married three or four times."

Something clicked in Ethan's head. "You read it somewhere?"

"Did a little background research on you before I came here today." Nelson started to wander aimlessly around the office, pausing here and there to study various artifacts. He stopped in front of the framed crayon drawing that Theo had made of a house. "Came across the references to three former wives but I didn't see any mention of kids."

"Probably because I don't have any," Ethan said without inflection. "My nephew did that drawing."

Nelson moved on to the bookcase and plucked a volume at random. Ethan recognized the red-and-black cover. It was a scholarly history of early-nineteenth-century murder cases in San Francisco.

Nelson flipped through the pages, not paying any real attention. "So which wife cheated on you?"

In point of fact, it had been two out of

three for sure and he still had his suspicions about Wife Number One. The leader of the religious cult she ran off to join hadn't looked like the monkish type. But Ethan saw no reason to go into detail. He was not in a mood to do the male bonding thing with Nelson Radnor.

"I said I understood some of what you're going through." He picked up his mug and examined the cold coffee. "Didn't say I was going to tell you my life story." He decided the coffee wasn't worth drinking and lowered the mug. "Why don't you get to the point and save us both some time?"

"All right." Nelson closed the book and shoved it back on the shelf. "I came here to hire you to find out who she's seeing."

"No."

Nelson turned around to face him again, irritated. "Hell, I'm not asking for any professional favors. I'll pay you your usual hourly rate."

"No."

"Okay, I'll pay you *my* usual hourly rate. What is that? Two? Three times higher? Name your price. Whatever it is, you got it."

"Forget it."

"There's a pattern," Nelson said through

his teeth. "I tumbled into it a few days ago. Tuesday and Thursday afternoons. I checked our bank account. There have been regular withdrawals of cash every week for the past month."

"I said no. I meant it."

Nelson took three strides across the room and planted his hands on the desk, face working now. "I can't use one of my own people on this. The gossip would spread through the company in about thirty seconds. I don't need that kind of aggravation."

"I am not going to take the job. I hate divorce work. It's always bad and it's a thousand times worse when the client is a friend or professional associate."

"This isn't personal. It's business."

"Divorce work is never *just business,*" Ethan said. "You know as well as I do that regardless of how much he claims to want the truth, the client is never real happy to hear it."

"I'm not exactly your average Joe Client. I'm a pro. If you come back with the name of the jerk my wife is seeing, I won't blame you."

"Sure you will. What's more, you won't ever forget the fact that I took pictures of your wife going into a motel room with another man."

Nelson looked stricken. His mouth opened and closed convulsively.

He recovered his composure with visible effort and straightened. "You don't have to go all dramatic on me," he muttered.

Ethan could tell the guy was cracking up inside. Radnor loved his wife.

"Did you try asking her where she goes on Tuesdays and Thursdays?" Ethan said cautiously.

"No." Nelson shook his head emphatically. "She'll make up some story about going to the gym or the hairstyling salon. I don't want to hear it. I need to know the truth."

He was afraid to ask her, Ethan realized.

"Look," he said as gently as possible, "I plan to work here in Whispering Springs for a long, long time. That means that you and I will be running into each other on a frequent basis. There will be more business conflicts like the one we've got now with the Valdez job. We'll see each other at various restaurants around town. Find ourselves at the same gas station some days."

"So?"

"So none of that will be a real problem for either of us if we go on as we are now. Like you said, we're both pros. We can handle the competition. But it will turn real nasty and real personal if I confirm your worst fears about your wife for you."

Nelson looked at him for a long moment.

"You're serious, aren't you?" he said at last. "You're going to turn down the job."

"Yeah."

Nelson gave the office another dismissive survey. "From the looks of this place, you could use the business."

"Maybe." Ethan shrugged. "But I won't starve without it."

"No, you won't, will you? Got a hunch you can take care of yourself just fine," he said tightly. "Is Zoe okay with the idea of you being a small-time operator?"

The question caught Ethan by surprise.

"Thought I explained that I prefer the term 'niche player,'" he said.

"Right," Nelson agreed. "Niche player. She doesn't mind that you are no longer the high roller that you were in LA?"

"Zoe tells me that I'm pursuing a calling."

"Got a romantic view of the profession, does she?"

"Guess so."

"I used to have a romantic view of it myself." Nelson went to the door and paused, taking another look around. "Back when I was just starting out, I thought it would be great to have an office like this. Maybe have a cute, smart-mouthed receptionist out front. Get mysterious lady clients walking through the door. Maybe sleep with some of them."

"Sleeping with the client is usually a mistake."

"Tell me about it. How do you think I met my wife? But then, I guess you know all about what happens when you get involved with a client, don't you? Rumor has it that's how you met Zoe."

Ethan said nothing.

Nelson did not seem to expect an answer. He went through the doorway, crossed the outer office and let himself out into the hall.

Ethan sat listening to Radnor's heavy tread on the stairs and thought about how they had both violated the most basic rule of the profession.

If he had it to do all over again, would he still sleep with Zoe while she was technically a client? Would he still come up with an excuse to rush her into marriage? Knowing the risks involved, would he have worked so hard to convince her to give what was supposed to have been a sham marriage a real chance?

In a heartbeat.

26

At five-thirty that afternoon he got to his feet, stretched, picked up his notebook and went downstairs to consult again with his consultant.

He walked into the gloom of Single-Minded Books and found Singleton in his tiny office, hunched over his computer.

"Are you dozing or are you actually working?" Ethan propped one shoulder against the door frame. "I'm not paying you for sleeping on the job."

"Long-standing tradition for a consultant to sleep on the job." Singleton removed his glasses and massaged his temples. "Thought you knew that. Hell, half the time I walk into your office, you've got your feet on your desk."

"That's a sign that I'm doing some deep thinking."

"Deep thinking, huh? I'll have to remember that." Singleton pried himself away from the computer and swiveled his chair around so that he could squint at Ethan. "Your deep thinking produce anything useful?"

Ethan flipped open his notebook. "Lindsey Voyle appears to be exactly who she claims to be. Thirty-nine years old. Married to a big-time studio exec who divorced her last year to marry an aspiring actress half his age."

"Gee, what a surprise."

Ethan ignored that. "Lindsey and her husband lived the glitzy life. Parties, film premieres, political fund-raisers."

"Whispering Springs must be something of a comedown for her. She do any actual decorating?"

"Uh-huh." Ethan flipped another page in his notebook. "Must have been the designer of the moment for a while back in LA. She decorated several homes and offices for some major stars. Looks like the divorce was nasty, even by Hollywood standards. But she came out of it with enough cash to buy a house in Desert View and start up a new business. No history of financial or legal problems. No mysterious gaps in the record."

"Well, you got the easy one, didn't you?" Singleton drummed his fingers on the edge of his keyboard. "Mine was a little trickier."

"You got the tricky one because you are an expensive consultant who gets the big bucks for handling tricky stuff. Any luck?"

"Made contact with our old buddy the Merchant."

A tingle of anticipation shot through Ethan. The Merchant was the mysterious on-line broker who had sold Arcadia and Zoe their new identities when they escaped from the asylum.

"And?" he prompted.

"And he swears that no one has hacked into his system. Says that if someone has found Arcadia, he didn't get the info from his files." Singleton paused.

"I hear a but."

Singleton exhaled slowly. "The Merchant is good but there is always someone else who is better, and there is no such thing as a perfect false ID. Just ask some of the folks who didn't survive the government's witness protection program."

"True." Anticipation stopped tingling. Of course it wasn't going to be that easy. What had he been thinking? "And there are other ways to find people besides hacking the files of the guy who sold the target a fake ID."

"You ought to know. You do it all the time."

"Grant Loring made a living running various sophisticated financial scams," Ethan said slowly. "Guys like that always do a lot of research. I think we can assume that, if he's alive, he knows more about Arcadia's personal financial secrets than she thinks he does."

"Well, we've got one thing going for us," Singleton said. "The Merchant feels he owes me a favor because of what happened when Zoe's files were stolen a few weeks ago. He says he'll make some inquiries on his end. Chances are good, given his line of work, that he has access to some sources that I don't even know about."

Ethan tapped the notebook absently against the door frame. "It's not like we haven't got a clue here. Thanks to Arcadia, we know a hell of a lot about Loring. If he is on the move in our neck of the woods, he'll leave some tracks."

"She said he was the careful, cautious type."

"He's definitely not staying in a hotel or motel here in town. I spent the morning checking out that possibility."

"That just leaves all of metropolitan Phoenix." Singleton grimaced and stretched his arms over his head. "The good news, like you said, is that we've got a lot to work with, thanks to Arcadia. When I talked to her this morning, she gave me a complete list of Loring's personal eccentricities as well as his business habits. I know what he likes to eat, his favorite wines, his taste in clothes, cars, sports, the works."

"A woman who has lived with a man knows a hell of a lot more about him than he realizes."

"Probably because women pay attention to those pesky little things in life that us guys prefer to ignore. It's your wife who worries about your cholesterol levels and reminds you to get your prostate checked."

"Huh." Ethan thought about that. "None of my ex-wives ever worried about my cholesterol or my prostate. You think maybe that was an indication that they weren't committed to a long-term relationship?"

"Could be. Has Zoe mentioned your prostate yet?"

"No. But I noticed this week that she moved me up to an SPF forty-eight-plus-strength sunscreen."

Singleton whistled. "That explains that new, youthful glow."

"Any more sarcastic remarks and I won't let you play with my new emergency flares." Ethan straightened away from the door frame, turned to leave and then hesitated. "By the way, Jeff told me that he had a long talk with you. He's obviously feeling a heck of a lot better. Thanks."

"That conversation went both ways." Singleton looked at his computer screen as if he saw something of great interest there. "I got as much out of it as he did."

"Glad to hear it. So when are you going to ask Bonnie for a date?"

"Aren't you supposed to be somewhere doing some detecting?"

"As a matter of fact, I got to go home." He glanced at his watch and headed toward the door. "Zoe will be waiting."

"Lucky you," Singleton said.

He said it so softly that Ethan could barely hear him.

Zoe was in the small Casa de Oro parking lot when he arrived. She was struggling with her large black tote and two hefty grocery bags that she was trying to pry from the trunk of her car. Her position, bent at the waist and leaning forward, gave him a nice view of her excellently shaped rear. He admired the sight as he got out of the SUV.

Zoe had managed to get one sack stabilized in the crook of her arm and was groping for the other when he reached her.

"I'll get those," he said.

"Ethan." Startled, she nearly banged her head on the trunk lid. "Didn't hear you."

"Probably because I have trained myself to move in a very stealthy way."

"Is that so?" She glanced down at his shoes. "I figured it was because you were wearing sneakers."

"These are not sneakers." He scooped the sack out of her arm. "They are high-tech, state-of-the-art running shoes."

"Ah. That explains it."

He snagged the second bag out of the trunk and waited while she closed the lid.

Together they walked to the green, wrought-iron gate.

"Well?" She dug her doorknob key chain out of her tote and opened the gate. "How did it go today? Did you dig up any information on Lindsey Voyle?"

"I know you don't want to hear it, but she appears to be exactly who and what she claims to be—a recently divorced decorator from LA who just opened up a business here in Whispering Springs."

"Doesn't it strike you as strange that someone from LA would choose a town like this to start over in?"

He just looked at her.

Her brows snapped together. "Okay, so you're from LA and you came here to start over. See? That proves my point. Your background isn't exactly normal."

"And I try so hard."

"You're not taking Lindsey Voyle seriously, are you?"

"Honey, I swear, I looked at every possible angle. Up until she moved here her entire life was dedicated to decorating the homes of movie stars and drinking very expensive champagne with the rich and famous. There is no mystery there."

"But—"

"I don't claim to be psychic but you've said yourself that my intuition isn't too bad when it comes to this kind of thing."

Her surrender, when it came, was distinctly reluctant. "I suppose."

He caught her chin on the edge of his hand and brushed his mouth against hers. When he felt her mouth soften a little under his, he raised his head.

"Have a little faith in your personal private investigator, okay?" he said.

She gave him a wan smile. "Okay."

He followed her through the gate. "I didn't come up with anything real exciting on your decorator nemesis, but I did have an interesting visit from my competition today."

"Nelson Radnor?" She glanced at him, brows knitting in fresh concern. "About the Valdez job? I was afraid he would be upset."

"Not too upset to offer me gainful employment."

She made a face. "He made you another offer of a position at Radnor? I'm not surprised. You would be a huge asset to his company. I trust you turned him down?"

"Actually, he wanted to hire me to trail his wife. He thinks she's having an affair."

"Oh, no." She halted in the middle of the path, appalled. "You refused, didn't you?"

"Give me a break. Just because I'm from Southern California, it doesn't automatically follow that I've got the brain of a surfer. I told him I don't do much divorce work and that I sure as hell wouldn't do it for a business associate."

Zoe shuddered and resumed walking quickly along the path. "It would put you in an absolutely terrible position. That situation involving Katherine Compton and Dexter Morrow was bad enough. Just imagine what it would be like if you took Nelson Radnor on as a client and discovered that his wife really is having an affair. He would hardly thank you for the news."

"I explained that to him. He wasn't happy but I think he understood."

They stopped again, this time in front of the door of the main entrance to the apartment building. Zoe let them inside with her key.

The door of the manager's office opened as if on cue. Robyn Duncan popped out. Some of her perkiness faded when she saw him, Ethan noticed. Determinedly, she zeroed in on Zoe.

Ethan did not pause. He headed straight

for the stairs. *Keep your head down here, Truax, you don't have a dog in this fight.*

"I've been waiting for you, Zoe," Robyn said brightly. "There's a problem with the lock on your door."

Ethan went cold. He stopped and turned.

"There's no problem with my lock." Zoe did not stop. She went briskly toward the stairs. "It works fine."

"No, it doesn't," Robyn said. "I can't open it with the master key."

"That's because I changed the lock." Zoe started up the staircase to the second floor.

She went past Ethan, who stayed right where he was.

"It is clearly stated in the building rules that the manager shall have access to every apartment," Robyn said. "It's a health and safety issue."

"The previous manager didn't have a problem with me changing the lock."

"The previous manager is no longer in charge." Robyn cleared her throat. "Given his lack of attention to details, he probably didn't even know that you had changed your lock."

True, Ethan thought. But he wisely kept his mouth shut.

"I rented this place from the former manager, and as far as I'm concerned the arrangements that I made with him stand."

Zoe paused halfway up the stairs and glared down at Robyn. "I would consider any attempt to alter my original verbal agreement a violation of my rights as a tenant. If you insist on pushing this matter, I will consult a lawyer."

"There's no need to get a lawyer involved," Robyn said quickly. "I'm sure we can work this out. You can keep your personal lock, if you like, but I'll need a key."

"Absolutely not."

The last thing Ethan wanted to do was get between these two, but he no longer had a choice.

He looked at Robyn. "Mind if I ask why you happened to notice today that Zoe's lock had been changed?"

Robyn tensed, her body language both defensive and virtuous. "I noticed it when I attempted to give the repair person access to your apartment. Although, I should tell you that in the future I would appreciate it if you would inform me whenever you schedule a repair or delivery to your apartment. That way I can make certain that there is no conflict with repairs and deliveries in other units."

Ethan saw Zoe's hand tighten abruptly around the grip of her tote. Her knuckles went white. She glanced at him, alarm flaring in her eyes.

He kept his attention on Robyn Duncan. "Are you telling us that someone asked you to let him into Zoe's apartment today?"

"That's exactly what I'm telling you. As I said, even though it was an unscheduled repair, I thought I would do you a favor and let him in for you. That's when I discovered that my master key didn't open your lock."

"Who was it?" Ethan asked.

Robyn frowned. "The TV repairman, of course. He showed up around noon. I have to tell you that it was pure luck that he even found me in my office. My hours are clearly posted on the door. I usually close from twelve to one for lunch. But I was delayed by a phone call and—"

"We didn't schedule a repairman today," Ethan said.

Robyn halted in mid-sentence. She blinked a couple of times and then gathered herself. "You must have scheduled him. He had a properly filled out form and everything."

"You were going to let a complete stranger

into my apartment?" Zoe was seething now. "What kind of manager are you?"

Robyn looked deeply offended. "I would never let anyone into a tenant's apartment unaccompanied. I have established a very strict policy regarding repairs and deliveries. If the tenant is not at home, I remain in the unit with the repair or delivery person at all times. That is why it is imperative that such appointments be properly scheduled."

"Describe this TV repairman for me," Ethan said, trying to keep his tone mild and unthreatening. It was not easy.

Robyn blinked several times. He could see that it had finally occurred to her that there was something very wrong.

"Well, he looked like a . . . a *repairman,*" she said. "He wore a uniform and carried a case full of tools and he had paperwork."

"What color was his hair?" Zoe asked sharply. "Was he tall or short?"

"How old do you think he was?" Ethan asked.

"His hair?" Robyn took a nervous step back toward the sanctuary of her office. "I didn't notice."

"Long or short?" Ethan asked.

"Short." Robyn retreated another step. Her

face started to crumple. “I guess. I’m not sure. It was covered by his hat.”

“Did he give you a name?” Ethan asked.

“No.” Robyn swallowed. “I think there was one embroidered on his uniform but I don’t remember what it was. Something long.”

“What about the name of his company?” Zoe prodded.

“I can’t remember,” Robyn whispered. Her eyes glistened.

Hell, she was going to cry, Ethan thought. That would not be helpful. “Take it easy. We’re just trying to get a handle on this guy. Sounds like he may have been a burglar who knew we were away for the day and tried to con you into letting him into the apartment so that he could rip off the TV or the computer.”

Robyn blanched. “I would never have allowed anything like that to happen.”

“Did you get a look at his truck?” Ethan asked without much hope.

“No,” Robyn whispered.

“Now you see why I prefer not to leave a spare key in the manager’s office.” Zoe swung around and continued up the stairs. “Let’s go, Ethan. I need a drink.”

“If you think of anything that stood out

about the repairman, would you please make a note for me, Robyn?"

"Why?" she asked somewhat blankly.

"Because I'd like to find him," Ethan explained. "I want to ask him what the hell he was doing trying to get into our apartment."

"Maybe he wasn't a phony," Robyn said. "Maybe he just made a mistake about the address."

"You never know." Ethan followed Zoe up the stairs. "If he was a burglar, he might try the same trick again with one of the other apartments tomorrow or next week. After all, now he knows that you're willing to open the door for him."

Robyn burst into tears, turned on her heel and fled into her office. The door slammed shut behind her.

Zoe reached the landing. She paused and turned to look at the closed door of the office. Guilt shadowed her face.

"We were kind of hard on her, weren't we? Maybe I should go talk to her."

"Forget it." Ethan reached the top of the stairs and went down the hall. "She deserves to feel bad."

"I suppose so." She trailed after him. "Ethan?"

"Yeah?"

"You're thinking what I'm thinking, aren't you? That maybe that TV repairman wasn't an ordinary, garden-variety burglar? That he was involved in this thing going on with Arcadia?"

"The possibility did occur to me, yeah." He waited while she unlocked the door. "I'll call Harry and Arcadia and let them know what happened."

Inside the apartment, he set the groceries down on the kitchen counter and pulled out his phone.

"If this is connected to Arcadia," Zoe said, "why would the man try to get into *our* apartment?"

"Maybe because he knows that you and Arcadia are close. Maybe he wanted more information about her and figured he could get it from her best friend."

She reached into the first sack and took out what appeared to be a carton of milk. A thoughtful expression crossed her face. "A man this time. Not a woman in a hat with a camera. If Grant Loring is behind this, he seems to have a number of assistants. Two, at least, so far."

"Unless the TV repairman was Loring in disguise."

"Oh, jeez, I never thought of that. If only Pixie Ears had gotten a better description."

"Typical witness. She wasn't paying attention." Ethan put the phone to his ear. "Why would she?"

Zoe made a derisive sound. "All she cared about was the fact that I hadn't followed her precious rules."

He watched her open the refrigerator door and place the carton on the top shelf. The label did not look familiar.

"What the hell is that stuff?" he asked, waiting for Harry to pick up.

"Soy milk." She turned to pluck a plastic bag full of broccoli out of the grocery sack. "It's supposed to be good for your cholesterol and your prostate."

"Is that right?" He suddenly felt a little more positive about the future. She was worrying about his cholesterol and his prostate. That had to be a good sign.

He was still smiling to himself when Harry finally answered the phone.

27

Later, after the table was cleared and the dinner dishes had been stacked in the aging dishwasher, Zoe poured two small snifters of brandy and carried them into the living room.

Ethan was on the phone again, talking to Singleton this time. It was his fifth or sixth call of the evening.

She set the brandies down on the table and studied his hard, intelligent face. He was intensely focused, speaking to Singleton in that very even, very neutral tone that he used when he was on the hunt. There was a sense of fierce, contained energy humming through him but it was under complete control.

She was amazed by his powers of endurance. He should have been exhausted by now. She certainly was. Neither of them had gotten any sleep after Harry and Arcadia had arrived on the doorstep early that morning. But while she had spent most of the day worrying about Arcadia and trying to figure out how Lindsey Voyle fit into the equation, Ethan had been working nonstop.

It dawned on her that maybe this all-consuming task was just the tonic he needed to distract him from the memories of November.

"Right. I agree. Call me if you get anything else." Ethan cut the connection and made a note on the pad of paper. When he put down the pen he noticed the brandy. "Thanks."

"You're welcome." She sat down on the small sofa across from him and curled her legs on the cushion beside her. "What did Singleton have for you?"

"The Merchant made contact again." Ethan picked up the brandy, settled back in his chair and stretched out his legs. "He says he found a competitor who may have been the one who sold Loring his new identity."

"That's wonderful news. If we know Loring's new identity, it will be much easier to find him."

"Not necessarily. He may have adopted another phony ID when he set out to find Arcadia." Ethan took a sip of brandy and lowered the glass. "But the information can't hurt, that's for sure."

"What are you thinking?"

He leaned his head against the back of the chair. "I'm thinking that we're going on the assumption that this is all about Loring being out there somewhere, waiting to grab Arcadia. But what if that's not what's happening?"

"You said yourself it was the most logical possibility."

"It is, so we have to guard against it." He met her eyes. "But there are others." He turned the brandy glass between his palms. "About this feeling you said you experienced at the show house and in Arcadia's office . . ."

Her stomach knotted. The snifter in her hand trembled a little. Very carefully she put the glass down on the coffee table. "What do you want me to say, Ethan? That I imagined whatever it was I felt in those places?"

"No." He swallowed some brandy and lowered the glass. "Not unless you think you really did imagine it."

"I didn't," she said tightly.

"I believe you. I don't know what it was that bothered you in the library or at the gallery, but I am not discounting your, uh, intuition."

She said nothing. She was too tired to quarrel about the issue of whether or not she was really psychic. An argument was the last thing either of them needed that night.

For a time neither of them spoke. They drank their brandies, letting the silence settle around them. Zoe groped for a change of subject and came up with the one that Robyn Duncan had interrupted with the tale of the phony repairman.

"I still can't believe that Nelson Radnor tried to hire you to follow his wife," she said. "He's got an office full of investigators."

"He didn't want to hire anyone on his own staff because it would fire up a lot of in-house gossip."

"Yes, I can see that it would be a little embarrassing to have his staff chatting about his wife's affair." She sighed. "When you think about it, isn't it a little weird that he would want to hire anyone at all to tail her? I mean, this is his wife and he's a trained investigator. Why doesn't he do his own detective work? Why bring someone else into such a personal situation?"

Ethan contemplated his brandy.

"He wants the answer," he said eventually. "But it doesn't necessarily follow that he wants to watch his wife come out of a hotel room with another man. That would be . . ." He hesitated. "A very hard thing for any man to do."

She sensed the undercurrents shifting through him and thought about his three previous marriages. The odds were good that one or two of those spectacularly failed relationships had involved someone fooling around. But it wouldn't have been Ethan. She was very sure of that.

For a man who had been married four times, Ethan was surprisingly old-fashioned when it came to matters of honor, commitment and fidelity.

"If the circumstances were reversed," she said quietly, "it would be just as hard for a woman to watch her husband walk out of a hotel room with someone else."

"But some people need the answers." Ethan put down his empty brandy snifter. "So they go to private investigators to get them."

"I don't think you would go to another investigator. If you had to know the truth, you'd find it yourself. You wouldn't hire someone else to do the dirty work for you."

"No," he agreed. "I wouldn't hire anyone else."

There was something edgy and bleak in his simple response. She could not identify the emotion, but whatever it was, it worried her. What was this all about?

A few seconds of heavy silence ticked away and then a possible answer struck her with such force that she sputtered on a swallow of brandy.

"Ethan?"

"Yeah?"

"You're not hinting what I think you're hinting, are you? You don't really—" She broke off, her tongue unwilling to wrap itself around the unbelievable words. With an effort she pushed forward, determined to get this out into the open. "You're not implying that you think I'm involved with someone else, are you?"

The question seemed to baffle him at first, as if she had just asked him to explain the origin of the universe in one easy sentence. When his expression cleared, however, his gaze was cool and steady.

"No," he said.

It was a very flat, very unequivocal no, she decided.

"Well, that's a relief." She picked up the snifter and took a fortifying sip of brandy. "For a minute there, I thought maybe Radnor's visit to you today had put some ideas into your head."

"You wouldn't cheat on me."

She was touched by the deep certainty in his voice. "And you wouldn't cheat on me. Something in common, hmm?"

"Yeah, we've definitely got that much in common."

Her heart sank for the second time in five minutes. What was wrong now? She felt as if she were on some sort of invisible roller coaster.

She cleared her throat. "Similar standards of morality are vital to the long-term success of a relationship." Sheesh. She sounded like a page from a pop-psych relationship book. *Dr. Zoe's Ten Simple Rules for a Terrific Marriage.*

Dark amusement gleamed briefly in

Ethan's eyes. "Believe it or not, I sort of figured that out for myself."

She'd had enough. "Ethan, what's going on here? You're acting weird."

"Sorry." He rubbed the back of his neck. "It's been a long day."

She uncurled her legs and put her feet on the floor. "We've established that you don't think I'm cheating on you. So what *are* you worried about? I can tell that this has something to do with us, not with what happened to your brother or what's going on with Arcadia. Talk to me."

He looked at her very steadily. "Sometimes a man doesn't want to hear the answers to his questions."

"Ask me, Ethan. Please. I can't deal with the unknown, not when it involves us."

For a moment she thought that he would refuse.

"All right," he said finally. "I'm wondering if you're regretting our marriage."

"What?"

"I'm thinking maybe you feel you have to stick to it because I talked you into promising that you would give it a try. You're one of those people who stands by her promises."

Stunned, she could only stare at him. This

was the very last thing she had expected to hear from him.

"Where did you get the idea that I was having second thoughts?" she whispered.

"From the way you seem to pull into yourself and away from me at times." He looked at her, stone-faced. "You're doing it more and more lately. Especially when we talk about whatever it is you feel when you walk into certain rooms."

"Ethan." She stopped. She did not have the foggiest idea of where to go with this issue. He was right, she was getting increasingly frustrated with his refusal to accept that she was psychic.

But what right did she have to force him to acknowledge a claim that the vast majority of rational, intelligent people would treat as a case of serious self-delusion at best and deliberately fraudulent at worst?

"I get the sense that if I don't buy into your theory that you've got some sort of sixth sense, you won't be able to tolerate me as a husband," Ethan said evenly. "Am I right?"

A strange panic swept through her. This was not the time or the place for this conversation. They had other problems at the moment.

Okay, so I've been hoping to postpone it for a while. Like indefinitely. So sue me. I don't want to lose this man. I love him.

But Ethan was not the kind of guy who went through life postponing the inevitable.

She drew herself up and clasped her hands around her knees. She had to swallow twice before she could speak.

"I'm afraid that if you can't eventually learn to accept that part of my nature," she said quietly, "you won't be able to live with me. Not as a husband, at any rate. Maybe we could be lovers and get by. But marriage is different."

"Different?"

She was aware of a dull ache in the region of her heart. When she looked down she saw that she had her fingers so tightly laced together that her knuckles had turned white.

"Ethan, I have already been involved in one marriage in which I had to hide the truth about myself. I loved Preston very much, but I knew that he could never have handled the idea that I might actually be psychic. He would have feared for my sanity. Probably tried to get me to see countless doctors. The stress on our marriage would have been intolerable."

"So you never told him?"

She shook her head once. "I did not want to put that burden on him because I knew what it would do to him. To us. But it cost me a great deal to pretend that I was . . . normal. Later, after he was gone, I'd wake up in those really dark hours between midnight and dawn and I'd wonder if . . . if . . ." She closed her eyes against the welling tears.

"You wondered, if Preston had lived, whether your marriage would have survived what you think is the truth about yourself?"

She nodded. The tears leaked out from under her lids. *Damn, damn, damn,* she thought. *Not now.* The last thing she wanted to do was dissolve into a puddle. This was not the time for a big emotional scene.

Irritated, she unclasped her fingers and swiped at the moisture on her cheeks with the back of her hand. *Breathe. Act normal. You can do this. You've been faking it all your life.*

But she didn't want to have to fake anything with Ethan.

When she had herself under some semblance of control, she opened her eyes and saw Ethan watching her with enigmatic intensity.

"And you felt guilty," he finished for her.

"Sooner or later I think I would have had to tell Preston the truth," she admitted. "I don't think it's the kind of secret you can keep forever. Not in a marriage."

Ethan got to his feet, crossed to the sofa in one stride, reached down and closed his hands around her shoulders.

"In case you haven't noticed, there's a really major difference between this marriage and the one you had with Preston." He hauled her up to stand in front of him. "The fact that you think that you're psychic is not a secret here, remember?"

"I know, but it amounts to the same thing because you don't believe me."

"No, it isn't the same thing at all. I realize that you're convinced that you're psychic. I think you just happen to be a hell of a lot more intuitive than the average person. But regardless of how we each interpret your abilities, let's get one thing clear. I do *not* think that you need to see a doctor. You're not crazy."

"Ethan—"

He kissed her, quick and hard, sweeping away her arguments. When he raised his head she was breathless.

"You've had some extremely unpleasant experiences because of your intuition," he said steadily. "So you think you're not normal."

She clenched her hands at her sides. "It's true. I'm *not* normal."

"Well, hell, neither am I. I told you once that I was the exact opposite of my brother Drew. He did everything right. Met and exceeded all expectations. Followed a straight upward trajectory from kindergarten to president and CEO of a major corporation. Along the way he found time for a good marriage and a couple of terrific sons."

But it was Drew who had been murdered in cold blood, she recalled, leaving Ethan to pick up the pieces of his brother's life and seek cold justice in an uncaring universe.

"I understand what you're trying to do here," she whispered. "But it isn't necessary."

"Me, I did it all wrong," he continued roughly. "I'm a college dropout with three failed marriages and a multimillion-dollar bankruptcy behind me. And those are just a few of the highlights. The truth is, my life is a history of screwups."

"Stop it." Incensed, she grabbed his wrists. "Don't say that. You are not a screwup."

"And I don't think you're crazy just because you're into the woo-woo thing." He moved his hands from her shoulders to cup her face.

"Ethan?"

"I want you more than I have ever wanted anything or anyone else in my whole life."

Before she could respond, he was kissing her again. This time he wasn't trying to keep her silent. This kiss was all about a driving, elemental need. The starkly powerful hunger radiated from him in dizzying waves that enveloped her.

The desperation and despair she had been feeling a moment before vaporized in the all-consuming fire of passion. The desire that sparked between them would not solve all of their problems, she realized, but it was a potent drug. They could use it to push aside the uncertainties and the unknowns for a time.

Ethan deepened the kiss, seeking the response she knew he needed from her. She was shatteringly aware of his erection. The knowledge that she had this effect on him excited her, made her feel powerful.

She put her arms around his neck, fighting him for the kiss.

He cradled her head in one hand and explored her throat with his mouth, letting her feel the edge of his teeth. Playing the dangerous lover, she mused. No, not playing the part. There was a hint of the real predator under the surface.

It was an incredibly erotic sensation because she knew that, although he was a hunter at heart, he was her hunter. She could trust him in ways that she had never trusted anyone else in her life.

She pushed her hands up under his black tee shirt and sank her nails into the contoured muscles of his chest. He sucked in his breath and then released it in the wake of a heated groan, making no secret of his desire.

The room spun around her. When the world steadied again she discovered that she was flat on her back on the carpet. Ethan loomed above her, anchoring her with one hand and his leg. He used his free hand to unfasten her blouse and bra. Then he went to work on her trousers, pulling them off together with her panties. The garments fluttered and disappeared in the shadows.

He settled one leg between hers and moved it deliberately upward, easing her thighs apart until his knee was pressed firmly against her. She knew she was already wet; knew he could feel the dampness through the fabric of his pants.

She slipped her palms along his ribs beneath his tee shirt. He leaned over her and took one nipple into his mouth. Then he found her with his fingers.

The delicious movement of his hand, together with the increasing suction on her breast was almost too much to bear. She moved her hips, trying to assuage the tight, swollen sensation, but it only got more intense.

A restless energy moved through her, filling her with a luscious, decadent sense of abandon. Ethan freed her in more ways than one. Not only could she argue with him about whether or not she was psychic; with him she could revel in this daring, outrageously sexy side of her nature. It was an aspect of herself that she had not even suspected existed until she met him.

She realized that she thought of her sex life as divided into two parts: Before Ethan and After Ethan.

Before Ethan sex had been a pleasant, usually cheerful experience but not a particularly compelling one. The *After Ethan* sexual experience, however, had altered all of her long-standing definitions of what constituted great sex. *After Ethan* sex was hot and intense and exhilarating.

It was the experience of After Ethan sex that had taught her that she actually possessed a surprisingly passionate nature. That discovery had struck her as far more amazing and infinitely more strange and wondrous than her psychic side, which she had taken for granted all her life.

Ethan eased two fingers inside her. She shuddered, her body clenching. He covered her mouth with his own. She reached down, unzipped his pants and encircled his heavily engorged erection.

"I want you inside me." She tried to guide him with her hand. "Right. Now."

His laugh was like the rasping tongue of a great cat against her skin.

"Not yet," he said against her throat. "First I want you to show me how hard and how fast you like it."

She smiled slowly up at him, feeling infinitely mysterious and seductive in his arms. "Ah, but that's just it. Sometimes I like it slow and easy."

His eyes gleamed in the night. "I'm adaptable."

She arched herself against his invading fingers, determined to have what she craved. Again and again she moved, arching and contracting, creating a thrusting sensation that stoked the hot tension in her lower body. And through it all, the pressure of his thumb on her clitoris never lessened.

When she could stand it no longer, she encircled him with her legs and tightened her thighs around him. She felt his control slip the leash.

He whispered to her, wicked, sexy, provocative words that drove her to the brink.

She'd had enough.

She pushed against his shoulder, absolutely determined now. He went willingly over onto his back, eyes gleaming with anticipation and dark pleasure. She lowered herself slowly down onto him.

Ethan wrapped his palms around her buttocks and thrust upward, deep and hard. She shattered at the first stroke. Her release rolled through her in waves.

"Zoe."

His fingers tightened around her. His whole body went rigid. He pumped himself into her until oblivion overcame both of them.

* * *

A long time later they made their way into the bedroom. She did not have the energy to put on a nightgown. She crawled under the covers. Ethan fell into bed beside her and gathered her close.

She felt him slide into sleep almost immediately, his favorite cure for insomnia once again working its magic.

But the tonic did not prove equally effective for her. Exhausted though she was, she lay awake for a long time, thinking about the past and the present.

Nothing had been resolved that night. Ethan still did not believe that she was psychic. But on the plus side, he did not think that she was crazy just because she happened to think that she possessed a sixth sense. She was not sure where to go with that.

It wasn't just sex that was different with Ethan. Everything was different with him.

She nestled closer to him, savoring the comfort she took from the strength and heat of his body.

After a while she slept.

It was a good night. She did not dream.

[illegible]

[illegible] had best been—[illegible]

[illegible]

[illegible]

[illegible] did not move quickly [illegible]

[illegible]

[illegible] did not believe that [illegible]

[illegible]

[illegible]

28

At six-thirty the next morning, she poured the soy milk over an extra large serving of muesli and set the bowl in front of Ethan. He did not take his attention off the notebook he had open on the table.

She sat down across from him and doled out his morning vitamins. "What's Plan A today?"

"Same as it was yesterday. Keep digging."

She unscrewed the cap of the large bottle of calcium tablets. "I've got an idea."

"Yeah?" He picked up his spoon, still focused on his notes.

"Lindsey Voyle is still a bit of a question mark in this case, right?"

His spoon stilled above the bowl of muesli. He raised his head, wary now. "I told you, I checked her out six ways from Sunday, honey. She's clean. There's absolutely nothing to connect her to Grant Loring or any of the people on Arcadia's list of Loring's enemies and known associates."

His calm, reasonable tone irritated her. If this marriage was going to work, he had to realize that a night of great sex was not enough to make her back off from her own theories.

"My *psychic intuition* picked up something in two different places where Lindsey has been recently. I don't think that's a coincidence." She knew she sounded stubborn, probably downright mulish, but she was not about to let it go.

"Psychic intuition, huh?" His mouth curved up. "Is that what you've decided to call it?"

"It occurred to me while I was fixing breakfast a few minutes ago that the phrase covers all the bases. It's a compromise."

"Uh-huh. Well, whatever it is, I don't think it's going to be real helpful on this case. I couldn't find a damn thing linking Voyle to this thing going on with Arcadia."

"I know. But maybe I can uncover something."

"I had a feeling you were going to say that."

She smiled very sweetly. "Hey, maybe you're a little bit psychic, after all."

"No."

"No, you're not psychic?"

He did his Wyatt Earp squint. Looking dangerous. "No, you are not going to do whatever it is you're thinking of doing at Lindsey Voyle's house."

"I'm just planning to take a look around."

"No."

"It would be easy to get inside legally. She's one of Arcadia's regular customers. I'll bet that Arcadia could help me come up with an excuse to visit Lindsey at her home. I'll just sort of feel my way around. I won't take any chances."

"I don't believe that for a second."

She ate some cereal.

"I'm dead serious, Zoe. I'm running this investigation. That means we do things my way. Got it?"

"You ever worry that you might have control issues?" she asked.

"I've got 'em, but they don't worry me at all. I like being in control." He stuck his spoon into his cereal and put a healthy-sized amount into his mouth. He started to chew and then stopped abruptly. He stared at the muesli with an incredulous expression.

"What the hell?" he said.

"Probably the soy milk," she said. "I think it may be an acquired taste."

He finished chewing very quickly, swallowed and grabbed his glass of orange juice. He downed half the contents in a single gulp.

When he eventually lowered the glass he examined the liquid in his cereal bowl as though it were some alien life form.

"Good for my cholesterol and my prostate, you said?"

"I read it in a newspaper article."

He poked at the cereal with his spoon. "You can't believe everything you read in the papers, you know."

"Just give it a try for a few days," she urged. "If you don't develop a taste for it, we can switch back to regular milk."

He scooped up another spoonful. "I'm not

real concerned about my cholesterol, but, hell, anything for my prostate."

Robyn Duncan was lying in wait for her when she went downstairs shortly after eight.

"Good morning, Zoe," she said, chirpy once more. "Mind stepping into my office?"

"Sorry." Zoe clutched her chartreuse tote very tightly and kept going toward the door. "Got an appointment."

"This will only take a minute," Robyn said quickly behind her. "It's very important."

"I really don't have time."

Robyn's tone turned ominous. "I'm afraid I've had some complaints."

Zoe stopped short of the door. She turned slowly. "What sort of complaints?"

Robyn cleared her throat. "Mr. Hooper phoned me late last night to tell me that he had been awakened by some thumping noises overhead. He lives in one-B, the apartment right under yours, you know."

"I am well aware of where Hooper lives."

"He said that at first he thought there was an intruder. Then he decided that you and Mr. Truax were moving the furniture around. Eventually he concluded that the sounds indicated that, uh, activities of an intimate nature were taking place."

"I see. Hooper could tell that, could he?"

"He was quite shocked," Robyn said. "He wanted me to do something about it immediately so that he could get some sleep. But I did not want to disturb you at that hour so I told him I would talk to you this morning."

That did it. So much for loyalty to one's neighbors.

"Hooper's got a lot of nerve turning me in for a few thumps in the middle of the night."

"As a tenant in good standing, he has every right to a noise-free environment."

"Screw Hooper's rights. In case you haven't figured it out yet, he's the one who doesn't break down his cardboard boxes before he puts them in the trash bin out back."

Robyn's mouth dropped open in stunned amazement.

"Are you certain?" she demanded. "The address labels had been removed from the unflattened cartons so I was unable to identify the person who tossed them into the bin. But it is hard to believe that it was Mr. Hooper. He is such a neat and orderly tenant. He always pays his rent on time. I've never had any complaints about him."

Zoe was already feeling guilty. You weren't supposed to turn in your neighbors, she reminded herself. There were rules about that sort of thing.

"Uh, well, maybe it wasn't him," she mumbled. "I mean, I thought those were his computer cartons but I suppose they could have belonged to someone else."

Robyn drew herself up and squared her shoulders. "I shall speak to Mr. Hooper immediately and get to the bottom of this."

What the heck, the damage was done, Zoe thought.

"You do that." She swung around on her heel and yanked open the door. "And you can tell him that I wouldn't have ratted him out if he hadn't turned me in first."

"For goodness sake, you make this place sound like a prison."

"Complete with our very own warden."

"I've explained time and again that I'm just trying—"

"To do your job. Yes, you've mentioned that on several occasions."

"The rules exist to help make Casa de Oro a more pleasant place for all the tenants—"

Zoe went outside and made sure that the door closed as loudly as possible behind her.

There would probably be a new rule against door slamming tomorrow.

Ethan's phone rang shortly before nine. He picked it up.

"Truax Investigations."

"I'm trying to get in touch with Ethan Truax. It's important."

"I'm Truax."

"Right. My name is Branch. I work for Hull Painting. My boss has been doing some subcontract work for Treacher. Met up with you the other day when you and your wife stopped by your place. I was leaving off some equipment?"

Ethan thought about the bodybuilder painter he and Zoe had encountered. "I remember."

"Well, I hate to tell you this, but it looks like you got a situation out here at your house."

Interior design issues were at the very bottom of his to-do list today, Ethan decided. A man had to prioritize.

"My wife is in charge of the decorating," he said. "If you've got questions, you can call her."

"Not exactly a question," Branch said. "More like a problem."

"What kind of problem?"

"I swung by to pick up that sprayer I left the other day. Treacher told my boss that he wanted our crew to use it on another job site."

Zoe would not be happy to hear that Treacher was going to retrieve the sprayer before it had even been used.

"What about it?" Ethan prompted.

"Went to put my key in the construction lock and realized your front door was wide open. Thought at first maybe my boss had sent someone else to pick up that sprayer and maybe the guy had forgotten to lock up when he left."

Ethan got slowly to his feet, stomach chilling. "Get to the point, Branch."

"Well, I'm not sure about this on account of everything's pretty well covered in drop cloths and I can't tell if any of your stuff is missing, but I think maybe someone might have broken in here."

"Where are you, Branch?"

"Sitting in my van outside your front door."

"Don't go back inside."

"I've already been in and had a look around. Like I said, I didn't realize that there was anything wrong at first. But there's nothing to worry about. Whoever was here is long gone."

"Stay out and don't touch anything."

"I won't. Look, I'm not positive that there's been a break-in. Maybe someone just forgot to lock up."

"I'll be there in fifteen minutes."

"Sure. I'll stick around until you get here."

"Thanks. Appreciate it."

Ethan cut the connection and headed for the door. At the foot of the stairs, he paused at Single-Minded Books.

"I'm going out to Nightwinds," he said to Singleton. "One of the painters called. He thinks maybe someone broke into the place, but he's not sure."

Singleton peered at him through his spectacles. "You want company?"

"No, I'll handle it. Probably nothing, but I'd better check it out. Keep working on Loring. If you get anything new, call me."

"Got it."

Ethan went outside, loped across the brick patio to the curb where the SUV was parked and got behind the wheel. Probably kids, he told himself. Thank God he'd covered the pool.

* * *

He made it to the front door of Nightwinds in less than fifteen minutes and parked behind the van. There was no sign of Branch.

The front door stood wide open. He went up the steps and looked into the hall. Branch was right, there were no obvious signs of a burglary. The drop cloths appeared undisturbed.

"Branch?"

"Out back near the pool," Branch shouted from somewhere in the distance beyond the great room. "Found a couple of empty beer cans."

Swell. Everyone was an amateur detective.

Ethan walked through the hall and crossed the great room. One set of French doors was open. Branch was outside, standing near the edge of the pool.

What's wrong with this picture?

The crystal-blue waters of the pool sparkled and flashed in the sunlight.

Okay, that was problem number one, Ethan thought. He had covered the pool as a safety precaution before turning the house over to the painters. But now the heavy plastic tarp lay in a careless heap on the patio.

Branch was near the deep end of the pool.

He was dressed in crisply laundered white overalls and the peaked cap he had worn the other day. His big, muscled shoulders were slightly hunched. There was a long-handled roller brush in his beefy right fist.

Not a single paint stain on those white overalls, Ethan thought. Ice formed in his gut.

He took another look at the scene.

The pink loungers and chairs were in their usual positions in the shade of the broad, overhanging roof. The door of the small structure that housed the pool machinery and equipment was closed.

Branch looked at him across the restless water, his mouth twisted into a rueful grimace.

"Thought you were going to wait in the van," Ethan said.

"Figured it wouldn't do any harm to check around out here. Looks like it was just kids sneaking a swim."

The pink concrete coping that edged the pool was dry except for one spot. Ethan studied the damp area as he walked slowly toward Branch.

He stopped a few feet away. "Don't think it was kids."

He thought about the gun he had left

locked in his office. Maybe not one of his brighter moves. He watched Branch's hands. The good news was that he could see both of them.

At Ethan's feet, the pool waters shifted and pulsed. The atmosphere had a sharp, crystalline clarity that was almost painful. This wasn't the first time he'd experienced this kind of hyper reality; this feeling that if someone spoke too loudly or moved too quickly the invisible bubble would shatter.

Branch's fingers tightened around the handle of the long roller brush. "Sorry about the false alarm."

"Where do you fit into this, Branch?"

Every muscle in the man's big body rippled and went taut. Ethan was surprised that the snaps on the coveralls did not pop open.

Branch scowled, baffled by the question. "What are you talking about?"

"You working for Loring?"

There was no flicker of recognition at the name.

"I don't know anyone named Loring. I told you, I'm with Hull, one of Treacher's subs."

"What do you say we call Hull and confirm that?"

Branch lunged forward without warning. The transition from absolute stillness to violent motion was so fast that Ethan knew it implied hand-to-hand combat training.

Branch swung the long brush in a sweeping arc designed to connect with Ethan's midsection.

But Ethan had caught the telltale thickening of the muscles in Branch's wrist a split second before the brush handle moved. He dove for the ground, coming down hard on the pink concrete. An instant later the wooden handle sliced through the air where he had been standing.

If the handle had connected, Ethan thought, it would have swept him into the pool.

Braced for the impact against Ethan's ribs, Branch was caught off balance when the handle failed to connect with anything solid. He staggered briefly and recovered almost at once, sliding across the concrete with the agility of a ballet dancer.

Ethan did not even attempt to get to his feet. He rolled twice, hoping to collide with Branch's legs.

Branch leaped over him, coming down

hard on the other side. Spinning, he raised the roller brush for another blow.

Ethan put up his hands and twisted once more. The roller caught him on the forearms and back, but missed his throat.

Branch jerked the handle upward again and lashed at Ethan's exposed rib cage.

The impact sent a thunderclap of pain through Ethan, stealing the air from his lungs. Blindly he rolled again, trying to escape the next lash of the handle, buying himself a few seconds while he fought for his breath.

He came to a halt on the coping at the edge of the pool. The blue waters seethed and flashed.

Branch evidently decided that the brush handle was more trouble than it was worth. He hurled it aside and moved in on his target.

Ethan made it to his knees just as Branch readied himself for a kick.

Ethan threw himself to the side. Branch's heavy boot grazed his shoulder. The jolt spun him onto his back on the concrete.

His fingers brushed against the fabric of Branch's trouser leg.

Branch tried to turn, preparing for another kick. Ethan yanked hard on the trouser leg.

Branch stumbled back, arms flailing as he lost his balance.

Ethan kicked out with every scrap of strength he could muster and connected with Branch's knee.

Branch staggered back another step, trying to find his balance. For an instant his foot and leg hovered in space over the water.

He screamed and tumbled backward, flailing and twisting wildly in midair in a futile attempt to save himself.

The shriek of raw terror stopped the instant he hit the water. He convulsed once and went limp, facedown.

Ethan scrambled to his feet and ran for the pool equipment locker, relying on the torrent of adrenaline rushing through him to stave off the waves of pain emanating from his ribs and shoulder.

The pool house door was unlocked. That didn't surprise him. He jerked open the door and saw that the panel of the circuit breaker cabinet was unfastened.

That figured, too.

He hit the master breaker, shutting off all the electrical equipment connected to the pumps, heater and underwater lights.

He was vaguely amazed to discover that

his phone was still in his shirt pocket. He pulled it out and called 911 while he limped heavily back to the pool.

"Drowning accident," he said to the operator, knowing that would elicit fewer questions and bring help a lot more quickly than a long discussion of attempted murder.

He looked down and saw Branch floating facedown, unmoving, near the steps.

He put the phone back in his pocket, ignoring the operator's urgent chatter, reached down and gingerly grabbed Branch by the back of his coveralls. Although he knew for a fact that the electricity had been shut off because he had just taken care of it, he nevertheless breathed a small sigh of relief when he didn't get a jolt.

You never thought much about electricity until you had a nasty brush with the stuff, he thought. When this was all over, he'd probably drive everyone nuts obsessing on electrical-safety issues.

Branch was heavy, maybe already a dead weight. He put one foot on the top step to gain some leverage and hauled the big man out of the pool.

There probably wasn't much point, he

thought, but he started mouth-to-mouth anyway.

He noticed the tiny tattoo right below Branch's collarbone just as an emergency vehicle pulled into the drive.

Branch is alive but the doctors say he's in a deep coma." Ethan settled into the cushions and pillows that Zoe had arranged on her dainty sofa. "Which means we don't get any answers."

Zoe, Arcadia and Harry were arranged in various poses around the small living room. Zoe's eyes were shadowed. Arcadia dripped with even more ennui than usual, a little too blasé. Ethan knew that she was as tense and anxious as Zoe.

Harry looked the way he always did, like a man who dug graves for a living.

"So what d'ya think?" Harry asked. "This was all about you? Not Arcadia?"

"I can't be absolutely certain, but I sure as hell can't come up with any other really good reason why Branch would try to murder me in my own swimming pool."

"But why would anyone try to murder you?" Arcadia asked.

"Dexter Morrow," Zoe announced in grim accents. "Maybe he decided to get his revenge after all."

"Nah." Ethan wasn't certain of much about this situation, but all his instincts pointed away from Morrow. "I'm sure he's still pissed at me, but I can't see him risking a murder rap just because I derailed his plan to rip off Katherine Compton."

Zoe waved her hands. "You keep saying he's not dangerous, but he tried to clobber you the other night. He's obviously violent."

"What happened at Las Estrellas was just one of those wrong-place, wrong-time things," Ethan said patiently. "Morrow was drunk, saw me and saw red. The setup at the pool was different. It was well planned and carefully staged."

“Ethan’s right,” Harry said rather casually. “This deal with the pool looks more like a contract hit.”

Zoe froze. “Are you saying that someone hired Branch to murder Ethan?”

“Take it easy, honey,” Ethan soothed. He shot Harry a warning look. “Just a figure of speech. You misunderstood.”

“I most certainly did not misunderstand.” She was on her feet, hands on her hips, glowering at Harry. “What do you think is going on here?”

Harry looked at Ethan for guidance. Ethan shrugged. There was no point trying to soften the conclusion now. The damage had been done.

“Got to consider the possibility that this is something left over from Ethan’s investigation into his brother’s death,” Harry said with surprising gentleness.

Zoe swallowed. “That doesn’t make sense. Ethan, you told me that Simon Wendover was dead and so is the killer he hired to murder your brother.”

“All true,” Ethan agreed.

Harry leaned back in his chair and stretched out his thin legs. “Thing is, Ethan here managed to irritate quite a few people in the course of that investigation."

"Do you think that one of those people might be seeking revenge?" Zoe asked tightly.

Harry spread his skeletal fingers. "It's a possibility. Although, knowing what I do about my former employers, I wouldn't have figured any of them for a revenge killing."

Arcadia gave him an inquiring look. "Why not?"

"They're businessmen," Harry said. "They figured that they made their point when they drove Truax Investigations into bankruptcy, and it didn't cost them a dime to do it. Why risk murder?"

"And why come after me now, especially when there's no money in it?" Ethan said.

Arcadia crossed her legs. "I hate to ruin the drama here, but I think we should all bear in mind that the police aren't sure yet just what happened today. They're still investigating. It's possible that Branch is simply some kind of psycho stalker who targeted Ethan for reasons that we might never know."

Zoe perked up visibly at that suggestion. "You're right. Maybe Branch is just flat-out nutso. That would explain those bad vibes I picked up in your office and at the Designers' Dream Home."

"Yeah?" Harry was dubious. "So what was he doing in either of those places if he was stalking Ethan?"

"Good question." Zoe sunk back into gloom.

"Stalkers are, by definition, crazy," Arcadia pointed out. "They don't think the way the rest of us do. They're obsessed. Maybe Branch wanted to know more about you, Zoe, because you're close to Ethan."

Ethan got the cold feeling in his gut again. "This kind of speculation won't get us anywhere." He sat up cautiously, trying to ignore the throbbing pain in his ribs. "Let's stick with what we know."

"What we know," Harry said, "is that Branch tried to kill you. We also know that he figured out how to bypass the GFI circuit breaker. He was trying to make it look like an accident. That doesn't seem like something a true loony would worry about."

Arcadia shrugged. "Who knows what kind of logic would make sense to a crazy person."

"You know, Ramirez made a couple of interesting observations," Ethan said. "After he calmed down and stopped chewing on me, that is."

"As if you were to blame for what happened," Zoe said, seriously annoyed. "From the sound of it, Detective Ramirez acted as if you deliberately set the whole thing up just to make his life miserable."

"Well, to be fair, you've got to look at the situation from Ramirez's point of view," Ethan said. "After all, this thing at my pool today happened only a few weeks after those incidents that you and I were involved in last month. I think he's still a little stressed out."

"*He's* stressed out? What about us? We're the ones who almost got killed, not him."

She definitely had a point. It struck him that he should have considered that angle sooner. Talk about a blinding flash of the obvious. He ought to have understood that the stress of what she had gone through the previous month had probably had more of an impact on her than either of them had realized.

She was a gutsy lady but everyone had limits. Zoe had nearly been killed a few weeks before. That sort of thing took a lot out of a person.

Maybe her conviction that she had sensed something weird in Arcadia's office and at the show house was some sort of delayed reaction to the trauma she had endured. It made sense that, given her conviction that she was truly psychic, her imagination might have translated her anxiety and stress into a metaphysical experience involving strange vibes.

He tucked that possibility away for further consideration and returned to the subject at hand.

"What Ramirez pointed out that was important," he continued, "was that just tampering with the circuit breaker wouldn't guarantee a shock, let alone a lethal one. But I think Branch may have put a little more planning into his backyard electrical experiment."

"What do you mean?" Zoe asked.

"I'm going to have an electrician take a close look at the wiring in the underwater light fixtures tomorrow morning. Got a hunch we'll find out that Branch did some surgery on it."

"That would make it look even more like a professional hit," Harry mumbled.

Ethan nodded reluctantly. Zoe squeezed her eyes closed for a couple of seconds, but when she opened them, her gaze was clear and determined.

Arcadia swung one leg. "Do you think that the elderly woman I saw, the one with the camera, really was just an innocent tourist?"

"Maybe," Ethan said. "Maybe not. If this was a contract arrangement, it's possible that Branch hired her to gather some background information on me before he made his move. The research might have included a rundown of my known friends and associates."

Zoe shuddered. "In which case that woman probably took photos of all of us."

"Except maybe Harry," Ethan said, thinking it over. "He was out of town for most of the last two weeks."

There was a short silence. Everyone looked at him.

Harry cocked a brow. "So?"

"So, it occurs to me," Ethan said slowly, "that if Branch was relying on that woman with the camera to supply his background data, and if she missed you because you were out of town, whoever is behind this might not know about you, Harry. Not yet, at any rate."

Harry smiled his grave-digger's smile. "Think maybe that makes me your ace in the hole?"

"Could be."

"Want me to talk to some folks in LA? See if any of my former business associates can come up with the name of someone who might be really, really pissed at you because of what happened after Drew was killed?"

"All right. Thanks." The ache in his ribs was getting worse. He stretched out an arm, groping for the bottle of pills on the coffee table.

"Don't move." Zoe leaped to her feet. "I'll get those for you."

She unscrewed the cap and spilled two of the tablets into his palm. Obediently he put them in his mouth and took the glass of water she handed to him. She rearranged the pillows while he swallowed the anti-inflammatories.

It was strange having a wife hover like this, he thought. On one level he had to admit that he was sort of enjoying himself. Furthermore, chances were excellent that the situation would only get better. Zoe hadn't even seen the bruises at their worst yet. By tomorrow morning they would be downright colorful.

He tried to imagine what new level of protection she would institute following the close call at the pool. Maybe he would find a crash helmet or some knee pads waiting for him on the hall table the next time he left the apartment.

But beneath the satisfaction of knowing that she cared enough to fuss, the cold, gray feeling lingered. It hadn't gone away. It was just temporarily obscured by the adrenaline and the distractions of this case. When things got back to normal, he knew that he would wake up one morning and discover that nothing had changed. The sword of Damocles was still hanging over his head.

Arcadia leaned back in her chair. "I appreciate your concern about me, Ethan, but I think it's clear now that you're the target. You're the one who needs protection. Harry should be guarding you, not me."

"That's an excellent idea." Enthusiasm sparked in Zoe's voice.

She probably figured Harry was even better than soy milk and SPF 48-plus sunscreen, Ethan thought. She was right.

Harry nodded somberly. "The ladies have a point."

"Maybe," Ethan conceded, "but you can't guard me and be my secret weapon at the same time. We need to keep you in the shadows until we know what's going on here."

"Seems pretty clear to me," Harry said. "Someone tried to kill you. Got to expect he'll try again."

"But probably not right away. With Branch in a coma, whoever sent him after me is going to have to reassess his options."

Harry nodded. "Okay, I'll go along with that. We may have a little time."

"How can you be sure of that?" Zoe demanded, plumping up the pillow behind Ethan's shoulders.

Harry shrugged. "Well, for one thing, it's gonna take some time to find another hit man."

Zoe paused in mid-plump, looking a little ill.

Arcadia frowned. "Are you sure about that, Harry?"

"In spite of how they make it look in the movies," Harry said mildly, "guys like Branch don't grow on trees."

There was a short, acute silence.

"What?" Harry said. "You didn't think I had a sense of humor?"

Arcadia patted his hand affectionately. “You never cease to amaze me.”

“That’s actually a really interesting point,” Ethan said.

“You mean about people like Branch not being that easy to hire?” Zoe asked.

“Hell, no. There are probably several hundred thousand sociopaths out there who would be happy to kill someone for a few bucks,” Ethan said. “But finding one who knows how to make the result look like an accident, a guy who has had some professional hand-to-hand combat training, a guy who’s a pro, that’s not going to be so easy.”

“What are you thinking?” Harry queried.

“I’m thinking it might be a good idea to find out more about Branch.” Ethan reached for his notebook on the coffee table and immediately regretted the action when his ribs protested. He realized Zoe was watching him closely so he tried to do the John Wayne thing. “I’m also thinking it might be a good idea not to sit around and wait for the cops to get the answers.”

Harry was intrigued. “How do you plan to research Branch? You said all he had on him was a phony driver's license with a no-good address in Phoenix."

"He also had an unusual tattoo. I drew a picture of it for Singleton, who is checking it out on-line. And I saw some more of those protein shakes in his van. The address of the nutrition shop in Phoenix was on the sack. Thought I'd start there."

30

He walked through Nightwinds, searching for her. He opened the door of the theater but she was not there.

He went outside into the night. She was standing at the edge of the pool looking down into the water. When she saw him she smiled sadly and shook her head.

"You can't come out here," she said. "There's a psychic barrier."

He would not let it stop him this time. He kept walking until he stood on the coping beside her.

"The barrier doesn't matter," he said.

"Yes, it does. You can't feel it because you don't believe in it but it matters to me."

The underwater lights were on. He could see Simon Wendover floating, faceup, just beneath the surface of the gently slapping water. Wendover laughed his silent dead man's laugh.

"She may stay with you for a while but eventually you'll lose her, just like all the others," Wendover promised.

"I don't care about the others," he said. "I just need Zoe."

Wendover grinned. "Don't worry, you won't be lonely. I'll drop in now and again to keep you company. You'll never be rid of me."

He awoke in the sudden, fully alert way that he did when his sleeping brain registered an unnatural sound somewhere in the household. He lay still for a moment, listening intently. But he knew that it was the dream that had awakened him, not the sound of someone moving stealthily through the apartment.

Zoe stirred beside him, shifting a little in her sleep. Her bare foot brushed against his leg. He wanted to put his arm around her and pull her close but he was afraid he would wake her. If she knew he'd had another nightmare she would ask questions.

After a moment, he realized that the adrenaline produced by the dream images was not going to evaporate quickly. The stuff coursed through his veins, making him edgy and restless. He had to move, had to get out of the bed.

He eased aside the covers and got to his feet, trying not to jostle Zoe.

He found his trousers in the darkness and made it to the bedroom door before she spoke.

"Ethan?"

He paused. "I'm going to get a glass of water. Go to sleep. I'll come back to bed in a while."

But true to form, she did not follow orders. He heard the brush of her legs under the sheets as she rose from the bed. Then he heard her bare feet padding on the carpet behind him.

"What is it?" she asked, snagging her robe off the hook and trailing after him down the hall. "Another dream?"

"Yeah."

He went into the kitchen and halted long

enough to step into his pants. He pulled up the zipper and went to the counter, not bothering with the lights. The moon shone through the window, etching the small space in a ghostly silver glow.

He opened a cupboard, took down a glass and turned on the faucet.

"Maybe we should talk about your dreams," Zoe said.

Her voice was gentle but it was imbued with the determined, stubborn quality that he had come to know so well. She wasn't going to let go this time. He was probably doomed. Somewhere in the shadows he thought he heard Wendover laugh again.

He sat down at the table and thought about his options. They were limited. He could try feeding her a comforting lie that she might buy for a while, or he could tell her the truth.

He had never been much good with the comforting lies.

"The dream was about you and Simon Wendover."

She sat down slowly across from him, her face unreadable in the ghost light.

"Both of us? Together in your dream? What was the connection?"

"I'm not sure." He wrapped both hands around the glass. "Wendover shows up now and again, especially in November. He comes back to remind me that I crossed a line because of him."

She said nothing; just waited.

"Once that happens, you can never cross back to the other side. Things are never the same."

She took one of his hands away from the glass and wrapped her warm fingers around his cold ones.

"I was obsessed. My wife said I was crazy and she was right. I swear to you that I truly believe that I required vengeance to stay sane. But looking back I realize that what I really wanted was absolution for the sin of having failed to protect my little brother. Goes without saying that I never got it."

Her fingers tightened on his.

"I knew even then that revenge can't buy that kind of peace of mind," he said after a while.

"If you could go back in time, would you turn aside from your vengeance?"

He thought about how he had felt that day when Simon Wendover had walked, smiling in triumph, out of the courtroom.

"No," he said finally. "But I have to deal with the fact that the reason he went free was because I didn't keep his hit man alive long enough to testify. I screwed up and the whole damn case fell apart."

"The police were supposed to keep the hit man alive, not you."

"Doesn't matter. Wendover got to him and that was the end of it." He was acutely aware of the warmth of her hands. "Hell, I shouldn't have dumped this on you. I never meant to burden you with it."

"I already guessed most of it," she said simply. "From the first time that Bonnie told me about Wendover's death in a mysterious boating accident, I knew."

He gripped her fingers convulsively, so tight that he almost crushed them. "You never said anything."

"Ethan, please understand. It hurts me to know what it must have cost you to do what you did. I also know that you could not have stopped until you got justice for your brother. You would do the same thing for Theo or Jeff or Bonnie or me. It's part of who you are. I think I've known that almost from the beginning. I'm only sorry that you have to live with the bad dreams and the memories."

"I can live with them," he said, opting for stark honesty. "That's not what's scaring the hell out of me."

A tremor went through her but she did not try to pull her hand away from him. "What does scare the hell out of you?"

"That I can't be the kind of innocent, gentle man you once loved. I'll never be another Preston Cleland. I'll never be free of my past."

"I don't care." She leaned forward a little, hanging on to his hand now as tightly as he was hanging on to hers. "You're not the only one who has been changed by the past. I'm different. I'm weird. Heck, I believe that I'm psychic, remember? You think you went a little crazy once? Well, I've got a bulging file of medical records that *proves* that I'm downright crazy."

"Zoe—"

"Trust me, after what I went through at Candle Lake Manor, I'm not the same woman who married Preston. The woman I am today loves you, Ethan."

The night sighed around him. He let her words and the promises in her eyes sink deep. He felt them settle into his soul. After a while he could no longer hear Wendover's laughter.

31

The electrician's name was Jim. He was a strong, solidly built man with the easygoing self-assurance of a person who knew his craft.

He stood beside the pool, opposite Ethan. Together they studied the sealed, waterproof light fixture that Jim had removed from the underwater socket. A length of cord dangled from it.

"What tipped you off?" Jim asked with an expression of great interest.

"It was a couple of those JDLR things," Ethan said.

Jim raised his brows. "Something just didn't look right?"

Ethan nodded. "I had secured the pool cover with a lock. Got a couple of young nephews so I take extra precautions when it comes to attractive nuisances. When I noticed that the cover had been removed, I started wondering just what the hell was going on. The fact that the same painter was here again with no one else around worried me a little, too."

"How did you figure out he'd tampered with the lights?"

"When I walked toward him across the patio I noticed a damp spot on the concrete near this fixture." Ethan glanced down at the light. "Didn't see any other signs of recent splashing, though. Couldn't figure out why it would be damp in just that one particular place and nowhere else. When kids jump into a pool they get everything in the vicinity wet."

Jim chuckled. "So it was what guys in your line of work probably like to call a clue, huh?"

"Right. The suckers don't come along often, so when one shows up, I try to pay attention."

"Good thing you noticed this one." Jim picked up the cord and displayed the clean slice in the heavy insulation. "This is a brand-new cut mark. It left the wire exposed to the water and created a short. Once that GFI circuit breaker was bypassed, this whole pool was an accident waiting to happen."

Ethan examined the sliced cord more closely. "How can I prove to the cops that this slice was done recently?"

"Copper wire under the insulation isn't corroded at all." Jim bent the cord to show him more of the gleaming wire inside. "It would have turned green real quick in this chlorinated water."

"Oh, yeah, right," Ethan said, impressed with the pure logic. "Good thinking."

"It's an electrician thing," Jim said.

Singleton came to the door of his bookshop when he heard Ethan on the stairs.

"You're on your way to Phoenix?" he asked.

"Yeah." Ethan checked his watch. "Zoe's going with me. I don't want to leave her here alone, and you and Harry both have your hands full right now."

"This thing is getting more complicated by the minute."

"I've noticed that."

32

Zoe waited in the front seat of the SUV, drumming her fingers on the seat, while Ethan went inside the nutrition shop to make inquiries. Through the window she could see him talking to a young clerk who looked like he probably did steroids for breakfast, lunch and dinner.

They had left Whispering Springs shortly after Ethan confirmed his suspicions with the electrician. The drive to Phoenix had taken a good hour. It had required another half hour of stop-and-go driving to reach the strip mall where the shop was located.

She had the unpleasant feeling that time

was running out. She was pretty sure Ethan had the same sensation.

Inside the store, Ethan fished out his wallet. A good sign, she thought. The clerk must have come up with some useful information.

A moment later Ethan walked swiftly outside and got into the SUV.

"What did he tell you?" she asked. "Did he have an address?"

"No." Ethan put the vehicle in gear and drove toward the exit. "That would have been too easy. What he did know was that Branch paid cash and never gave his name, but the clerk recognized him right off when I described him."

"That doesn't give us anything new."

Ethan's mouth twisted a little with cold satisfaction. "Got one thing that may help."

"What?"

"The clerk gave me the names of the local gyms. There aren't that many of them in this part of town."

"How does it follow that Branch would use a gym in this neighborhood?"

"It's not a sure bet but it seems reasonable that he'd pick one that was convenient. He's a stranger in town. Why drive miles every day through Phoenix traffic if he can avoid it?"

"Good grief, do you think that Branch was concerned with his daily workouts while he was plotting to kill you?"

"Guys like him go a little crazy if they don't get their daily workouts."

Crazy. Yes, that certainly fit her new theory. It made sense that John Branch might be the source of the scary psychic energy she had encountered on two occasions recently.

The nagging *ping-ping-ping* of the alarm on her digital watch finally pierced Shelley Russell's concentration. Reluctantly she pulled herself away from the computer.

Time for lunch and her midday pills.

"Yeah, yeah, I hear you." She hit *save* on her laptop, took off her glasses and got to her feet.

She winced when her shoulders and knees protested. The arthritis was really kicking in today. Served her right. She should know better than to spend such a long stretch of time hunched over the computer. One of these days she was going to have to look into getting some ergonomically correct furniture for the office.

She went into the small combination washroom and storage closet and gave herself a critical survey in the mirror above the sink. Her hair was practically flat. No perm left in it at all. She would make that appointment at the beauty shop this afternoon, right after she finished reviewing her notes on the Whispering Springs case.

She opened the drawer and removed the plastic container that held her ration of pills for the entire week. She shook out the batch in the small bin marked *Noon* for that day and filled a glass of water.

She swallowed the pills, found the cheese-and-tomato sandwich in the miniature refrigerator and wandered back toward her desk.

There was something strange about the Whispering Springs situation. It had turned into one of those cases that kept her awake most of the night.

Hell, it seemed she hadn't had a good night's sleep in years. Still, what she had been experiencing for the past couple of nights wasn't her usual brand of senior insomnia. She only got these particular early morning wake-up calls when her unconscious mind was trying to signal her that she was overlooking something important.

She went back into the office and started a fresh pot of coffee. It was going to be a long day and possibly an even longer evening. Wouldn't be the first time she had spent the night in her office.

She sat down at her desk and ate her sandwich. She studied what she had written on the computer screen while she waited for the coffee to finish brewing. What hadn't she done that she would have done if Branch hadn't been with the Feds?

A lot, was her answer. More thorough background checks on all the players, for starters.

It was downright scary to realize how quickly you stopped asking the usual questions when folks claiming to be government agents waved their credentials in your face. Patriotism was a great thing but it worked best when it was tempered by common sense.

The newspaper article from the on-line edition of the *Whispering Springs Herald* popped up on her screen a short time later, right after she'd read the old news stories about Ethan Truax in the LA papers.

> . . . A man identified as John Branch was the victim of a swimming pool electrocution accident yesterday afternoon at the home of Ethan Truax. Branch is reported to be in a coma at Whispering Springs

Medical Center. Police are investigating. His condition is listed as critical.

Authorities stated that Branch was saved from near-certain death because of the timely actions of the home owner, who pulled him from the water and started CPR.

The circumstances surrounding the incident remain unclear. . . .

Branch in a coma? Nearly electrocuted at Truax's house? What the hell was going on here? She stared at the screen, trying to focus. It was hard work because she seemed to be sinking beneath a tide of exhaustion. She really had to get more sleep.

She remembered the coffee. She hadn't even had a cup yet. She needed some caffeine.

But when she looked across the room at the full pot it seemed to be a mile away from her desk. Gripping the arms of her chair with both hands, she shoved herself to her feet.

The wave of nausea hit her halfway across the room. She didn't lose the sandwich but it was close.

This isn't good. Wasn't nausea one of the symptoms of a heart attack?

The queasy feeling receded. She breathed

a sigh of relief. Maybe the mayonnaise she had used on the sandwich was bad. She couldn't recall when she had bought the jar. Months ago, at least.

She managed to pour herself a mug of coffee but it took almost every ounce of energy she had to carry it back to her desk. Her hand was shaking so badly she could barely set the cup down without spilling the liquid.

Something's wrong with me. Just like there's something wrong with the Whispering Springs case. A connection?

No. Impossible.

A new kind of fear flashed through her. Her notes. She needed to take another look at those notes.

Forget the notes. She needed help. She swayed on her feet, trying to think through the fog that was rolling across her brain. *Probably ought to call 911.* But that seemed too complicated. Maybe she just needed a good long nap.

She picked up the small spiral-bound notepad that contained her original notes and tried to concentrate. There was another PI involved in this thing. According to everything she had read about Truax, he was the kind of man who was willing to let a marriage and a multimillion-dollar business go down the tubes in an effort to get some justice for his murdered brother. Reading between the lines of the Simon Wendover obit, she had a hunch that Truax had gone even further in the pursuit of vengeance.

She could relate to a man like Truax.

Her feet went numb. Was she dying? She thought about all the pills she had recently swallowed. Had they messed up at the pharmacy? Given her the wrong meds? She'd heard that sort of thing happened more often that anyone wanted to admit.

Call 911

But first figure out where to put the notebook. Because if this wasn't a screwup on the part of the pharmacist, there were two other possibilities, neither of which was especially encouraging. The first was that it was her time to go and no pill on earth was going to save her.

The second was that someone wanted her dead.

If Truax came in search of answers, where would he look?

Think like the old-fashioned PI you are. Maybe he'll think like that, too.

She found the right hiding place, tucked

the notebook into it and then turned to struggle back toward the phone. But she knew now that she would never make it.

Should have listened to my daughter when she told me to get myself one of those damn emergency alarm buttons to wear around my neck. But I didn't want to admit that I needed it. Not yet.

Maybe her son was right. Maybe she should have retired last year.

She crumpled to her knees. The phone might as well have been on another planet.

The door of the office opened. A figure drifted toward her. She was so groggy now she could not be certain if it was a man or a woman.

"Need help," she whispered.

"Yes, I know. But I'm not here to help you. I just came for the computer and the file. You did an excellent job, Mrs. Russell. It's too bad you're going to be dead soon. I would have been delighted to recommend your services to others."

The last thing she saw before she lost consciousness was a hand reaching out to shut down her laptop.

Day turned into night and she plummeted into the deepest sleep she had ever known.

* * *

Shortly after one o'clock, Zoe and Ethan walked out of the fifth fitness club on the list. Zoe was losing hope. They had struck out again. No one at the front desk had ever seen anyone answering Branch's description.

"Damn, damn, damn," she said on the way back across the parking lot. "This isn't getting us anywhere."

"Can't say I'm surprised that he wasn't a regular at this club." Ethan sounded remarkably philosophical. "Not exactly the kind of place you'd expect to find a really buff guy like Branch."

"Really?" Zoe followed his gaze and saw an attractive young woman dressed in an outfit that brought new meaning to the definition of short shorts. Her bouncy blond ponytail was the last thing to disappear behind the heavily tinted windows. "What was your first clue?"

"I think it was that nonstop schedule of aerobics classes on the wall." Ethan unlocked the SUV. "Can't see Branch working out with a bunch of people who use a gym primarily to lose weight."

"Good point." She thought about Branch's carefully molded physique while she climbed into the SUV and fastened her seat belt. "He was obviously obsessive about his body-building."

"Is." Ethan fired up the engine with a quick snapping motion.

She glanced at him, confused. "Is what?"

"Branch *is* obsessed. Present tense. He's not dead. At least not yet."

"Thanks to you," she said softly.

Ethan did not respond. He concentrated on easing the SUV out into the flow of traffic.

"You didn't have to pull him out of the water," she said after a moment. "And you certainly didn't have to do CPR. After all, the man had just tried to murder you."

"Branch is no use to me dead. If he lives, I may get some answers out of him."

"You don't have to talk that tough PI talk around me. I'm your wife, remember? You pulled him out of the pool because saving people is one of the things you do."

His hands tightened on the wheel. He looked straight ahead through the windshield. "Not always. Not every time."

"No, not always," she agreed. "But most of the time, and that's what counts."

The next stop was Bernard's Gym. The instant she walked through the door, Zoe saw that they were in an entirely different world, one that bore only a passing resemblance to the other athletic clubs on Ethan's list.

Bernard's Gym was filled with seriously bulked-up men and women dressed in workout clothes that appeared to be several sizes too small for their elaborately contoured bodies. The ranks of heavy, gleaming exercise machines looked like so much alien battle armor.

Zoe tried to remain unobtrusive while Ethan talked quietly to a large man dressed in a gray tank top and sweatpants at the front desk.

A few minutes later money changed hands. When Ethan turned around he had the hard look of the hunter closing in on its prey.

He pushed open the door for her and followed her back out into the parking lot.

"Can't say that I like this business of being my own client," he muttered, shoving his wallet into his back pocket.

"Gets expensive when you can't put the bribes down as expenses on someone else's tab, does it? Well, don't look for sympathy from me. I haven't forgotten how much you charged me for those little *incidental* items on my bill last month."

"You can't let it go, can you? I told you,

good information costs money. You get what you pay for."

"Yeah, right." She climbed back into the SUV and slammed the door. "Well? Did we get some good information here?"

"Maybe." Ethan cranked up the engine.

"What does that mean?"

"It means that the guy at the front desk recognized the description I gave him. He said Branch has been coming in on a regular basis for about two weeks, although he didn't see him yesterday or today. He paid for each visit with cash. Told the manager that he didn't want to buy a quarterly or full-year membership because he didn't plan on staying long in the area."

"So you think he's renting short-term somewhere in this neighborhood?"

"I'm counting on it." Ethan unfolded the map of Phoenix and studied the circle he had drawn in red. "Now comes the hard part."

"Don't tell me, let me guess. We're going to have to talk to the manager of every motel, hotel and apartment building inside that circle, aren't we?"

"Not quite. We got a break. The clerk said that Branch forgot some of his personal workout equipment one day last week. When he offered to rent Branch whatever he needed for the session, Branch refused, saying he'd rather use his own stuff. He went back to his place, picked up the equipment and returned to the club in less than fifteen minutes. That was early morning, before rush hour."

"So Branch's motel or apartment can't be too far away."

"That's my theory at the moment," Ethan said.

"Now what?"

"Now we get on our phones and start calling every motel and apartment complex with an address on one of these streets."

"This is why I got to come with you today, right?" She pulled her phone out of her tote. "So that I can cut down the time it takes to make all these calls."

"Brilliant deduction, my sweet." He opened the phone book he had brought along. "You may have an aptitude for the profession."

She got lucky forty-five minutes later. Within the hour she stood, together with Ethan, in the small office of the manager of the Tropical Paradise Apartments.

The aging complex was a three-sided, single-story structure built around a postage-stamp-sized pool. Rusted air conditioners projected out of the walls beneath the windows. The weedy concrete walk was badly cracked. A few straggly paloverde trees and a couple of barrel cactuses planted inside a brick border constituted the extent of the landscaping.

The Tropical Paradise looked as if it had started out as a budget motel and had gone downhill from that point.

"Yeah, Branch lives here." The manager, who had identified himself only as Joe, absently poked through his thinning, artificially black hair to scratch his scalp. "Said he planned to stay a month. Haven't seen him since yesterday morning. You say he's been in some kind of accident?"

"He's in a hospital in Whispering Springs," Ethan said, voice drenched in somber concern. "I have the number if you want to get in touch, but he won't be able to talk to you. He's still in a coma."

"Coma, huh?"

"The accident happened on my property, and since I'm the only person he knew there in town, I felt obligated to pick up some of his things and take them to him."

"But he didn't give you his key?"

"The key got lost in the process of transferring him to the hospital," Ethan said very smoothly. He pulled his wallet from his back pocket. "Naturally, I'd like to cover his rent. Wouldn't want him to lose the apartment just because he's in a coma."

The manager smiled for the first time.

Five minutes later, Ethan stopped in front of the door of number twenty-seven. He tugged two sets of medical gloves out of his pocket and handed one set to Zoe.

He pulled on his own gloves, fit the key the manager had given him into the lock and opened the door.

Stale air wafted out from the darkened interior.

Ethan moved across the threshold and disappeared.

A shiver went through Zoe, part unease, part anticipation. She hesitated just outside the door and peered into the shadowed room. All she could see was part of a bed and a wedge of worn, green carpet.

She probed cautiously but from her position on the step she could not pick up anything unusual in the way of psychic energy. Nevertheless, she had been rudely surprised on at least two occasions in recent days, she reminded herself. If her latest theory was right and John Branch was the source of the spiderwebs, there were bound to be some drifting in the room where he had spent so much time lately.

"Well, hell," Ethan said, very softly.

"What's wrong?" she asked. "Please tell me there aren't any dead bodies in there."

"No dead bodies. But I think we can now say with great certainty that this really is all about me."

She put one foot into the cramped, drab room, feeling her way. Nothing screamed at her from the walls. No cobwebs cloaked her senses. She picked up the accumulated psychic residue of the years, an old, dank, vaguely depressing vapor, but that was all.

Under any other circumstances, she would have been enormously relieved. But this time things were different. She suddenly realized just how badly she had hoped to find traces of the murky stuff in that room. Such a discovery would have answered so many disturbing questions.

She was about to tune out the old, low-level vibrations when she felt a tendril of something dark and powerful snaking through the atmosphere. Not a spiderweb. It was something else—a desperate, unwholesome desire flickered like a broken neon light in the room.

"He wanted something badly," she whispered. "He needed it like a drug."

"Me, dead, apparently."

She spun around and saw that Ethan was standing at the one table in the space, leafing through a stack of photocopies.

"What are those?" she asked.

"Take a look."

She walked across the room and stopped in front of the table. The photocopies were reproductions of newspaper articles. Some were dated three years earlier. Others were more recent. All came from Los Angeles–area newspapers. She glanced at the nearest one and immediately went cold inside.

SIMON WENDOVER DEAD
IN BOATING ACCIDENT

The body of Simon Wendover, former CEO of a privately held investment firm, was found floating in the water off Santa Barbara early this morning. Authorities believe that he fell overboard from his yacht at some time during the past three days.

Officials at the marina where Wendover kept his vessel said that he had a long-standing practice of taking the yacht out by himself, especially on moonlit nights.

Wendover made headlines a month ago when he was acquitted of all charges stemming from a plot to murder Drew Truax, the head of Trace & Stone Industries.

The trial was closely watched by the entire Southern California business community because it involved a series of revelations concerning Wendover's recent financial transactions. The resulting scandal negatively impacted the portfolios of several prominent investors and shook stockholder confidence. . . .

She picked up another photocopy, scanned the story quickly and stopped at the last paragraph.

. . . authorities noted that an autopsy had revealed the presence of drugs. . . .

She looked up and saw Ethan watching her intently.

"Wendover dabbled in the drug trade," he

said without inflection. "He not only sold, he used."

She nodded. "I see. Well, everyone knows that is an extremely high-risk business."

She glanced at another story.

> . . . authorities stated that the death may have been drug-related. There was no indication of foul play. . . .

Ethan flipped through some of the clippings. "They talked to me but I had an ironclad alibi."

"Of course you did." Ethan was not stupid, she was certain of that.

"The cops were not particularly eager to build a case. They knew as well as I did that Wendover had skated on the murder charges."

She put the article down on the table and picked up another stack of papers. They were all reprints of newspaper photographs of Ethan. Several showed him walking into a courthouse, sometimes accompanied by Bonnie. In others he was pictured exiting the driver's side of a silver BMW. A couple showed him leaving a handsome, modernistic office building. The sign on the wall behind him spelled out TRUAX SECURITY in sophisticated metallic letters.

"The newspapers had photographers hanging around the courthouse throughout the trial," Ethan said. "A couple of them staked out my office and Bonnie's house."

She shook her head. "It must have been a nightmare for all of you."

"It was." He let that go and turned slowly on his heel, studying the room. "But after Wendover died, I figured that at least it was over. Looks like I was wrong."

"If someone is trying to get revenge and if you and Harry are right when you say it's probably not one of the investors who got hurt, then it has to be personal, Ethan."

"I know."

"What about a member of Wendover's family? Someone who blames you for the death of his relative? Or a friend?"

"That's just it, there was no one who was close to him." Ethan crouched down to survey the floor beneath the sagging bedstead. "If you looked up the definition of the word 'loner' in a dictionary, you'd see a picture of Simon Wendover. Trust me, I checked him out all the way back to the day he was born. His mother was a drug addict who died when he was three. He was raised in a series of foster homes. No friends, no pets, no children."

"Wives? Lovers?"

"Wendover always had a good-looking woman on his arm when it suited him, but none of them lasted more than a few months. He never married."

Ethan stood up and crossed the room to open the small desk. He went through the drawers rapidly. Nothing.

He opened the closet door. Zoe saw a handful of shirts and trousers arranged with military precision inside. A khaki duffel bag sat on the floor.

"Looks like Branch is the neat and orderly type," she said.

"Military training, I think."

"How do you know?"

"Something about the way he moved."

Ethan went swiftly through the pockets of the garments in the closet. When he came up empty, he crouched down and unzipped the duffel bag.

Zoe took a few steps toward him and saw that there was nothing inside.

"Huh." Ethan looked thoughtful. "Funny he'd leave clothes behind in the closet but nothing in the duffel."

He got to his feet and went into the small bathroom, where he stood for a moment examining the space.

"Huh."

She knew that particular *huh.* Something didn't look right to him. She went to stand in the doorway of the bathroom. A handful of masculine toiletries were arranged on the counter but they all had a generic quality. The razor, shaving cream and toothpaste could have been purchased in any drugstore in the country.

"Guess he didn't want to leave a trail," she said.

"The place is clean, all right." He glanced into the empty trash container. "Maybe a little too clean."

"Explain."

"There isn't so much as a piece of paper in the trash, not even an empty bottle of one of those protein shakes he's apparently addicted to. Everything in here and in the closet looks like it was arranged by a robot. Nothing is out of place. The desk is empty."

"But?" she prompted when he stopped talking.

He walked past her into the other room.

"But those photocopies of the Wendover case were left scattered carelessly on the table. You'd think an obsessive-compulsive as precise in his ways as Branch would have stowed them more securely."

Zoe thought about the whispers of desperate obsession that drifted through the room. "He might have wanted to immerse himself in the Wendover story one last time before he made his move against you. Perhaps going through those newspaper accounts was a way of getting himself psyched."

"Maybe." Ethan did not sound convinced. "I can't figure out where the woman with the shopping bag and the camera fits into this thing, either. If he sent her to Whispering Springs to get some background on me, where are the photos that she took?"

"Good question. If she's really involved in this, you'd think her pictures would be part of that file of newspaper clippings."

"Unless whoever cleaned up this room after Branch left removed them," Ethan said.

A new trickle of dread tingled through her. "You think somebody got here before we did?"

"I'm not absolutely certain, but, yeah, the place feels like it's been scrubbed and prepared for viewing."

"By whom?"

"Probably whoever paid Branch to hit me."

She winced. "I wish you wouldn't say things like that so casually."

Ethan prowled through the room a second time, shifting the meager furnishings around, checking between the mattress and the box spring and pulling the headboard away from the wall.

She went back to the desk and did a second run-through of the drawers, checking to see if Ethan had missed a vital clue. She was not terribly surprised when she failed to turn up anything but a pencil and a blank pad of paper. There were no helpful indentations on the first page of the pad that had been left by whatever had been written on the sheet above it.

Ethan grabbed the small nightstand and eased it away from the wall.

An envelope that had been trapped behind the nightstand fluttered to the carpet.

They both looked at it.

"Well, what do you know?" Ethan leaned over to pick up the envelope. "I think we just found ourselves a clue."

Excitement stirred through her. "Looks like a photo lab envelope."

"It is. Empty, unfortunately." He glanced at the name of the lab and the address printed on one side. "But we're in luck. It's a local firm."

33

The woman's name tag announced that she was Margaret. She appeared to be in her late sixties, one of the legions of retirees in the area who, driven by either boredom or the inability to make ends meet on Social Security, had taken a low-paying, benefit-free, part-time position behind a counter.

"The pictures of the tall woman with the short silver hair?" Margaret beamed. "Sure, I remember 'em. She looked like one of those actresses you see in those old late-night movies. Thought maybe she was somebody famous. I asked Shelley about her but she said she couldn't tell me anything. Said it was confidential. I figured it was another one of her divorce cases."

"Who is Shelley?" Ethan asked, leaning casually against the counter.

Zoe, standing beside him, managed a weak smile. Privately she was amazed by his easygoing attitude. *Like this is no big deal. Like we have all the time in the world.* Meanwhile, she was so tense she was sure that if someone picked her up and dropped her she would bounce.

"Shelley Russell is one of our regulars," Margaret said proudly. "She's a real private investigator, you know. We've been doing her processing work for as long as I can remember." She paused, frowning. "Say, you look sort of familiar." She switched her gaze to Zoe. "So do you. You two were in that set of photos Shelley took."

"Probably," Ethan said.

Margaret began to look uneasy. "Hey, you're not the husband or anything like that, are you?"

"He's *my* husband," Zoe said in a cool, possessive tone. "Not the husband of the platinum-haired woman."

"Oh, good." Margaret relaxed. "Thought for a minute there . . . Well, never mind."

"Is Shelley Russell's office near here?" Zoe asked before Margaret could have more misgivings.

"Oh, sure, she's in the neighborhood. The address is about three blocks over."

"Thanks." Ethan straightened. "Maybe we'll drive by and have a look."

"Uh, why?" Margaret asked, looking dubious again.

"I read a lot of mysteries," Ethan said. "Always wanted to see what a real PI's office looks like."

Outside it seemed to Zoe that the colors of the cars and buildings around her were sharper. The desert sky was a little bluer. The sun was brighter.

A small shiver coursed through her. Was this cold thrill part of the lure that drew Ethan to his work?

If so, it was not unlike the edgy, adrenaline chill that she got after she'd had a particularly vivid experience in a room laced with seething psychic energy.

Ethan glanced at her, brows raised, as he got behind the wheel. "What?"

"You've always wanted to see what a real private investigator's office looks like?" she asked dryly.

"Who knows?" Ethan gave her a feral grin. "Maybe I'll get some cool decorating ideas."

"Right." She sat back in the seat. "You know, that was very clever of you to ask Margaret about recent photos of a platinum-haired woman who looks like she could have modeled at one time."

"We knew the photographer took pictures of Arcadia. It was a safe bet that some of those pictures were of her, and she is rather unusual-looking."

Five minutes later he wheeled the big SUV into the small parking lot of a shabby, one-story office building. Two of the three storefronts were vacant and looked as though they had been that way a long time. The third had the words RUSSELL INVESTIGATIONS lettered on the front window in faded black-and-gilt paint.

The window shades were pulled down and the sign on the front door had been turned to CLOSED.

"Now what do we do?" Zoe asked.

Ethan took his phone out of his pocket and dialed the number he had copied down from the phone book.

"Automated answering service," he reported a few seconds later. He checked his watch. "It's almost five. Chances are Russell was having a slow day and decided to knock off a little early."

"So?"

He switched the engine back on and put the SUV in gear. "So if I want to see what a real PI's office looks like, I'll have to give myself the tour."

She turned swiftly in the seat. "You're going to break into her office? Ethan, no, it's way too risky. She's a detective, for heaven's sake. She'll have an alarm system."

"Maybe. Maybe not." He drove around the block and parked near the entrance to the alley behind the offices of Russell Investigations.

"Pay attention here," Zoe said, growing more uneasy by the minute. "You cannot afford to get arrested. Not with all the stuff going on back in Whispering Springs."

"I'll be careful." He got out of the car. "If I trip an alarm, there will be plenty of time to get away before the cops show up."

She unbuckled her seat belt. "I'm coming with you."

"Probably be better if you stayed here."

"If you get inside, I might pick up something that you might overlook."

He frowned, contemplating what she had said. For a moment she was afraid that he would make some disparaging remark about phony psychic consultants, but he finally nodded. "All right. I can use all the help I can get."

A few cars cruised past on the street but there was no one on the sidewalk or in the alley. It was the kind of neighborhood where people invested in wrought-iron security grills, and Zoe was not surprised to see that the small rear window of Russell Investigations was protected by one.

"Told you so," she said.

"If you're going to insist on being so negative, I won't let you be my assistant next time." Ethan tried the handle of the door.

It turned easily in his hand.

Zoe stared. "I don't believe it. How could a private investigator forget to lock up her own office?"

"Anyone can have an off day."

The flip words did not fit with his suddenly grim tone, she noticed. Her heart started to beat a little faster and harder. She watched him open the door and move into a small, shadowed hall. She followed cautiously, braced for whatever psychic energy lurked in the walls.

She felt the usual mix of low-level emotions but none was especially troubling. She tuned them out and followed Ethan down a narrow passage, past what looked like a bathroom, and into the office.

Ethan walked around the corner and stopped so quickly Zoe bumped up against him. They both looked at the figure of an elderly woman crumpled on the floor.

"Dear God." Zoe's insides twisted.

"Looks like Shelley Russell had more than an off day," Ethan said, moving to crouch beside the motionless body. He put two fingers on the woman's throat.

Zoe went closer. "Is she . . . ?"

"No. Not yet, at any rate. She's breathing but she's in bad shape. I don't see any wounds or signs of violence. Maybe she had a stroke." He pulled out his phone and punched in 911.

Zoe knelt beside the unconscious woman and picked up one limp hand, aware of how fragile it was. The knuckles and joints were swollen with arthritis. She looked at the strong, heavily lined face while she listened to Ethan give the operator the information.

When he ended the call, she looked at him across Shelley's frail body.

"She's just a little old lady, Ethan."

"Got a feeling she's a pretty tough little old lady."

He rose to his feet, reached into his pocket and pulled out another set of thin, plastic gloves from what appeared to be an inexhaustible supply. Zoe wondered if he bought them in bulk from a medical supply store.

There was nothing she could do for Shelley Russell while they waited for the medics, she knew, except hold her hand. She had read somewhere that people who were unconscious sometimes reacted to voices.

"Stay with me, Shelley," she said, speaking in a firm, authoritative tone. She massaged the knobby fingers, trying to infuse them with some of her own warmth. "Hang on tight. The medics are on the way. You're going to be okay, Shelley."

She kept talking quietly, aware that Ethan was conducting a swift search.

"Any idea what we're looking for?" she asked.

"Anything that will help me figure out who hired her to do surveillance in Whispering Springs." He studied the contents of a drawer. "I don't see a file on Truax. Guess that would have been too easy."

"Probably. Nothing about this situation has been simple. Why should things change now?" She clung to Shelley's hand. "You've got to stay with us, Shelley, so you can help us solve the case. That's what you investigators like to do, isn't it? Solve the case? Just hang in there so you and Ethan can figure out what's going on here."

"Looks like she specialized in low-end divorce and missing persons work," Ethan muttered as he flipped through another file drawer.

"This isn't a sophisticated-looking business. I wonder why someone hired Russell to take those pictures."

"People who make a career of following wandering spouses around are usually good with a camera," Ethan stated. "The client always wants pictures."

"Yes, but you'd think that one of your old LA enemies would have opted for a PI who was a little more cutting edge." She continued to stroke Shelley's fingers. "From what you've told me, those people you managed to annoy were all wealthy, big-time investors. Hard to imagine one of them choosing a small-time investigator like Shelley Russell."

"Maybe whoever hired her figured it would be easier to get rid of her after it was all over. Who's going to question the death of a frail old woman?"

"Oh, God, do you think someone tried to . . ."

He shrugged. "She's a witness." He slammed shut the file drawer that he had just opened and turned to give the room an assessing survey.

"What is it?" she asked.

"There's no computer."

"I think of you as an old-fashioned kind of PI. But it looks like Shelley Russell could give you lessons."

"She isn't that out of date," he said softly.

Something in his voice made her turn her head. She saw that he was holding a sheet of paper in his hand. "What?"

"A report she wrote up recently. The client's husband evidently had a standing appointment with a woman he met in a motel room in Scottsdale."

"So?"

"So, this report is three months old and it was written on a computer." He opened a cupboard. "Here's the printer." He closed the door and stood in the center of the small space, grim-faced. "So where the hell is the damned computer?"

"Maybe she left it at home."

Ethan shook his head. "Don't think so. I think she pretty much lived in this office." He went back to the desk and switched on the lamp. His eyes narrowed as he studied the surface of the faded blotter.

"There was a computer here, all right," he said. "I can see where it sat on the desk. There's a light film of dust everywhere except for one rectangular patch."

He left the desk and disappeared into the short hall. Zoe heard the bathroom door open.

"It's okay, Shelley, you're going to be just fine," she said. "I can hear the sirens. The medics will be here any second."

"Found her purse," Ethan called. There was a muffled rattling. "Also some pills. Looks like she took a lot of them on a regular basis. I'd say that probably explains her current condition, but her collapse at this point in the case is a little too coincidental to suit me."

The sirens were closer now. Flashing lights lit up the tiny parking lot. About time, Zoe thought. Shelley's breathing was noticeably more shallow. Her pulse seemed weaker, too.

"Don't leave us, Shelley. Don't let the bastard who did this to you win."

"Damn," Ethan muttered.

"Now what?"

"Found her recent billing records but there's no invoice for a John Branch. No record of payments from him, either."

"The medics are here, thank heavens."

Ethan emerged from the bathroom, scribbling quickly in his notebook. "Got her address off her driver's license. She's eighty-two years old. Wonder if I'll still be in this business when I'm her age."

"You will still be in the business when you're a hundred and two, Ethan." She gripped Shelley's cold hand more tightly, aware that the woman was slipping away. "Hold on, Shelley, the good guys are here. Everything's going to be okay."

Ethan opened the door for the medics.

An exhausted-looking resident paused in the doorway of the emergency room. "I think

Mrs. Russell will make it, thanks to you two," he said. "She was fading fast. If you hadn't found her when you did, she would have been gone by midnight."

"Where is she?" Zoe asked. She was almost as tired as the doctor. Her shoulders and neck muscles ached from the tension of trying to tune out the chaos of screaming psychic energy that had soaked into the walls of the waiting room.

"They just moved her into ICU. She's stable and her vitals are surprisingly strong, given her age and chronic health problems."

"Is she awake?" Ethan said.

"No, and even if she was, they wouldn't let you talk to her." The resident hesitated. "Are you family?"

"We're friends," Zoe said smoothly. "The clerk at the front desk said she doesn't have any relatives here in Phoenix. They notified her son and daughter, but they both live out of state and can't get here until tomorrow afternoon."

The resident nodded. "Like I said, barring complications, I think she's got a good chance. We see a lot of this kind of thing with older people."

"What kind of thing?" Ethan asked.

"Medication mix-ups. Accidental overdoses. Unpredictable drug interactions. When it comes to seniors, we're dealing with a frail population taking an incredible amount of very powerful, very sophisticated meds. It's no wonder there are problems like this."

"You think that's what happened to her?" Ethan asked neutrally. "She took an accidental overdose?"

The resident shrugged. "Sometimes it's not exactly an accident."

Zoe stilled. She sensed Ethan going on high alert.

"Not an accident?" he repeated very carefully.

"You've probably heard that depression is a huge problem with the elderly," the resident said. "They get tired of all the meds. Life seems like too much trouble. They're alone. Sometimes they just don't want to go on any longer."

"Suicide?" Zoe shook her head. "I really don't think—" She stopped in mid-sentence when Ethan brushed his shoulder lightly against hers in silent warning. She cleared her throat. "Then again, who knows?"

"Right," the resident said. "When she

wakes up, I doubt if she'll remember much about what happened. They'll probably have a psychiatrist examine her, but if she did take too many meds on purpose, don't expect her to admit it. That's another thing about that age group. They usually won't admit that they've got mental health issues. They still feel the old stigma too strongly."

"They aren't the only ones," Zoe said evenly. "I know all about that stigma." She must have spoken rather forcefully because the doctor looked at her with an odd expression.

Should have kept my mouth shut, she chided herself.

A gurney rolled past in the hallway. The orderly pushing it was almost running. A nurse rushed alongside, an IV bag raised high in one hand. Zoe glimpsed a sheet that was saturated in blood. Her stomach lurched. Another layer of screaming psychic energy was already sinking into the walls around her. *How do the folks who work here stand it?* she wondered.

The resident glanced at the gurney and seemed to wake up. "I've got to go," he said. "The staff can tell you how to find ICU."

"Thanks," Ethan said.

But the resident was already in motion, revving up fast on adrenaline.

Zoe looked at Ethan, who was taking his phone out of his pocket. "Now what?"

"It's nearly seven and we haven't eaten since lunch. Let's grab a bite and head back to Shelley Russell's office."

"All right. There's a fast-food place across the street." She turned smartly toward the front doors of the emergency room, trying not to make a fool out of herself by breaking into a gallop.

"Wait up," Ethan said, striding after her. "I was thinking we could get something from the hospital cafeteria."

"No," Zoe said very precisely. "I do not want to eat here in the hospital."

She did not intend to spend one single minute longer there than was absolutely necessary. The years of pain, fear, hope, desperation and rage accumulated in these walls were starting to overwhelm her psychic barriers. It had been a trying day. She could handle only so much.

"You okay?" Ethan asked, voice sharpening in sudden concern as he fell into step beside her.

"I will be in a few seconds." She pushed through the glass doors and sighed in relief. "I don't like hospitals."

"Who does?"

But he did not try again to persuade her to go to the hospital cafeteria. Instead, he busied himself punching in a number on his phone while they crossed the parking lot to the SUV.

He did not believe that she was truly psychic, but he was willing to change his plans because she had told him that she was uncomfortable. This wasn't the first time he had done something like this, she recalled. Looking back over their short marriage, she had to admit that he routinely made allowances for what must seem at best an overly active imagination.

He put up with what other people would consider exceptionally flaky behavior with little more than a shrug, as if her claims to being psychic were nothing more than a minor eccentricity.

Could this man walk and chew gum at the same time or what?

Maybe it was time she learned how to do the same thing.

For the past few weeks she had been increasingly frustrated by Ethan's refusal to accept the psychic side of her nature. She had told herself that unless he bought into the reality of her sixth sense, their relationship would suffer. She was convinced that she needed him to acknowledge the part of her that was different.

Now she wondered if that was absolutely necessary. Ethan accepted her the way she was, no questions asked. That was a rare and wondrous gift in this life.

Her musings were interrupted when Harry answered his phone. Ethan gave him a quick summary of events.

"I agree, things are getting complicated." Ethan unlocked the SUV and got behind the wheel. "But keep working your LA connections. Everything points to me being the target, not Arcadia. Looks like her cover is as solid as it ever was, just as the Merchant claims."

Zoe fought a wave of panic as she fastened her seat belt. Arcadia was safe, but the situation had not improved, because now Ethan was in danger.

"No, we're going to be here in Phoenix for a while." Ethan switched on the engine. "We're headed back to Shelley Russell's office. The doctors think she accidentally took an overdose of meds, but her computer is missing and there's no file on me."

There was a pause while Harry said something on the other end. Zoe's blood chilled another few degrees.

"No, I didn't find one on Arcadia, either," he told Harry. "But Russell has to be the woman with the camera and the shopping bag Arcadia noticed. Yeah, right, stay in touch."

He ended the call and punched in another number. "Come on, Cobb, pick up." He paused. "What the hell were you doing? . . . You did? Shit. Sorry about that. I had the phone turned off for a while. Hospitals don't allow them to be used around the high-tech equipment. . . . No, we're both okay. It's a long story. I'll explain later. What have you got for me?"

Zoe sat tensely, listening to the one-sided conversation. When Ethan severed the connection, she pounced.

"Well?" she demanded.

"He went to some on-line sites that cater to military types and asked some questions about Branch's tattoo. He found out that the design is the emblem of a very elite, very low-profile Special Forces re con group."

"So you were right," Zoe said. "Branch is military."

"Not exactly. Not any longer. Once Singleton identified the re con group, he was able to hack into their database. It's a small organization. He used a physical description of Branch to find his file. Turns out Branch was selected to enter the initial training program but he flunked out the first month."

"Why?"

"Singleton says the records are vague but it looks like Branch had some kind of mental breakdown. He wound up in the psych ward of a military hospital for several months. Eventually he was discharged from the service."

"Crazy," she whispered. She thought about the dominant emotion that had moaned in the walls of Branch's cheap motel room, an obsessive desire that bordered on lust. "He wanted something very badly."

"Singleton said that after Branch was released from the hospital, he left the country and worked as a professional mercenary for a few years. He returned to the States about eight months ago. The trail ends there."

"Maybe we should go to the Phoenix police and talk to them about Shelley Russell."

"What are we going to tell them? All we've got at the moment is a little old lady who, as far as the medics are concerned, probably got her pills mixed up. I don't see anyone getting too excited about it."

"What about the pictures she had developed at the photo lab?"

"Russell didn't break any laws taking those shots. Hell, we can't even prove she took them in the first place."

Shelley Russell's office was shrouded in night. Ethan used a flashlight to do a cursory check of the aging Ford parked in front. When he found nothing of interest in the vehicle, he led the way back into the run-down building.

He stood in the center of the office for a while, not moving, not speaking; just brooding on the surroundings. Zoe waited quietly. She had seen him go through this ritual on other occasions. She wondered if he was unconsciously opening himself up to some of the psychic energy in the space. If so, she was certain he would never in a million years admit it. When she had asked him what he felt when he did this kind of survey, he had said simply that he was looking for whatever didn't look right.

After a while, he started to prowl. He stopped at the desk and looked at the mug full of cold coffee.

"She made herself a fresh pot of coffee," he said. "Doesn't seem like something you'd do if you were getting ready to overdose yourself on your meds."

"No," Zoe said. "And the pot is still almost full. She only poured one cup and she didn't get a chance to drink any of it."

"Must have collapsed right after she poured that mug for herself. The full pot indicates that she was planning to work for a while." He went to the counter and studied the aging coffeemaker. "It's switched off."

"She changed her mind? Decided to go home?"

"Why pour a full mug in that case?" Ethan continued to contemplate the coffeemaker. "Okay, she makes the coffee, pours a mug and carries it to her desk. But we found her collapsed halfway across the room. So for some reason she decides to go back across to switch off the burner beneath the nearly full pot. Why would she do that?"

"What's with the coffee?"

"It's the one thing in this room that doesn't look right." He lifted the pot off the burner and set it aside. Then he picked up the coffeemaker and whistled softly. "Just as I thought, Shelley Russell, you are a lot tougher than you look."

Zoe hurried toward him. "What did you find?"

He scooped up the object that had been hidden under the coffeemaker. "Her notebook."

"Oh, wow. Who says you're not psychic?"

34

The uniform was a lousy fit and the cap smelled of someone else's sweat, but it would do for his purposes.

Grant Loring stood in the shadows of the narrow walkway that separated the bookstore from a clothing boutique and watched the entrance of Gallery Euphoria.

It was just past eight o'clock. The Fall Festival was in full swing. The evening had been a nightmare. He'd been forced to listen to group after group of schoolchildren singing and performing on the outdoor stage. Their shrill, high-pitched voices had given him a headache. The throngs of laughing, chatting people milling around the outdoor mall had driven the decibel level up a few more notches. And if that damned miniature engine pulling the small cars filled with squealing kids went past him one more time, he would be tempted to stage a train wreck.

He watched the window of Gallery Euphoria. The Bitch was showing a necklace to a customer. Her assistant, a large woman with short brown hair, was busy with another potential buyer.

There had been a steady stream of people in and out of the shop all evening. Looked like his wife was turning a nice profit in there. One thing you could say about the Bitch; she was a natural when it came to making money. That talent was what had made her so useful to him in the past.

His plan had finally come together. True, Branch had screwed up by failing to take out Truax, but the desired objective had been achieved, regardless. It would have been better if the PI was dead, but the fact that he was even now chasing his own tail in Phoenix worked just as well. If Truax got lucky and found Branch's apartment, all signs would point back to LA. If he actually got as far as Shelley Russell's office, he would find nothing but a little old lady who had overdosed on her meds.

The time had come to grab the Bitch and be gone, Grant decided. He'd focused the revised plan on tonight, the evening of the Fountain Square event. He wanted the cover of crowds and noise.

All he needed were three or four minutes alone with the Bitch. He had hoped to pick her up half an hour before when she had taken a break to go to the rest room on the other side of the square. But that walking cadaver had accompanied her right to the door of the facility and then waited there to escort her back to the gallery.

Grant was annoyed that Russell hadn't supplied any photos or background on the skeleton in a plaid sport shirt. Sheer incompetence.

The good news was that the guy didn't look like he'd be much of a problem. He was probably an underpaid accountant or maybe a funeral director. Other than that brief trip to the ladies' room with the Bitch, he'd spent the evening on the bench directly in front of the door to Gallery Euphoria, making phone calls. A *lot* of phone calls. Maybe he was a bookie.

The Bitch's taste in men had certainly changed. Either that or she had deliberately chosen a lover who was the exact opposite of the type of man who had once appealed to her, for the same reasons that she had bought a new identity and altered her style of dress. The silly woman had tried to reinvent herself because she knew that he might still be alive and would someday come looking for her.

It was getting late. There weren't going to be any more easy opportunities to get her. He couldn't afford to wait any longer. It was time to make his move.

He was so eager to finish this business and disappear again that he could taste it.

Ethan sat down in Shelley Russell's chair and was not surprised to discover that he felt instantly at home. The squeak was just right. Russell kept a supply of yellow pads and unused notebooks in a drawer and a bunch of pens in a tray. The items on the surface of the desk were well ordered and comfortably arranged.

"I think the two of you may have a few things in common," Zoe said dryly. "Her notes even look a little like yours." She leaned over his shoulder to get a better view. "Hieroglyphs."

"Everyone who takes a lot of notes ends up inventing his or her own form of shorthand," Ethan said absently. "But she was careful to spell out all the names, and she took pains with numbers. See? Here's the number on the plate of that van that Branch was driving."

"Why would she take down a client's license plate?"

"I do the same thing. Standard procedure as far as I'm concerned. You can't have too much information on a client."

"Now that's a heartwarming comment." She perched on the corner of the desk. "If I'd known that when I decided to hire you the first time, I probably would have gone to Radnor, instead."

"Yeah, but just look at all the great sex you would have missed."

"Well, there is that."

After Branch's name and license, the first thing that caught his attention was the word *Fed.* It was underlined twice.

"He told her that he was some kind of secret federal agent," he said. "Probably figured that would keep her from asking too many questions."

She swallowed. "Do you think it's possible you're the target of some kind of federal investigation? Maybe that's why someone wants you dead. So you can't talk to the Feds."

"Relax," Ethan said. "If that was the case, we would have been buried in Feds by now." *I think,* he added silently. He paused to decode a couple more sentences. "Looks like Branch took his time getting around to the reason he wanted to hire her. Feeling her out, making sure he could rely on her to do the job and keep her mouth shut."

"Appreciate the info, Carl." One foot resting on the wrought-iron bench, forearm propped on his thigh, Harry watched Arcadia through the shop window while he finished the conversation with his old associate in LA. "Consider that favor we both agreed did not exist to be repaid in full."

He ended the call, never taking his eyes off Arcadia.

Six weeks ago, before he had come to Whispering Springs to give Truax a hand, he would have laughed at the idea that guys like him could ever get this lucky. A lot of things had changed for him in this town. His life would never be the same.

On the other side of the glass window, Arcadia smiled at a customer. A warmth that was still strange and unfamiliar flowed through him.

He made himself switch his attention to the people milling around the square, scanning for both those who stood out and those who faded into the background a little too easily.

His gaze lingered on a security guard who was about to slip into a narrow passageway between two nearby shops. The back of the man's jacket was emblazoned with the words "Radnor Security Systems." He had a cap pulled down low over his eyes.

This was the third time in the past hour that the guard had ducked into that shadowed space.

Security guards made him nervous. It was easy to overlook them, for one thing. For another, most of them walked around with sets of keys.

He glanced once more into the windows of Gallery Euphoria. Satisfied that Arcadia and her assistant were both busy with a crowd of customers, he took his foot down off the bench and strolled toward the entrance to the lane.

The whistle of the miniature train shrieked on his right.

"Coming through." The conductor was a large man who looked as if he'd been forcibly stuffed into the tiny cab. There was an expression of malignant glee on his broad face. "Make way for the Fountain Square Express."

Harry stepped back quickly, barely managing to get his left foot out of the path of the oncoming train. The conductor smiled maliciously. The children screeched and clapped.

The conductor blew the whistle in a long, satisfied blast of triumph and drove off in the direction of the fountain. The kids waved at Harry.

When the last car full of laughing, giggling children went past, Harry saw that the security guard had disappeared into the darkness of the small passageway.

Something prickled at the back of his neck.

He went swiftly toward the lane and stopped briefly at the entrance, trying to peer into the unlit shadows. The bright lights that illuminated the square did not penetrate far. For a few seconds, he was almost blind.

Then he saw movement at the end of the lane. The guard's hand lifted. Harry could just barely distinguish the outline of an object in the man's hand.

Arcadia heard the phone ring. She glanced at the nearest instrument and saw that it was her private line.

She looked across the room. Molly was involved with a customer. They were discussing the artistic merits of a handcrafted ceramic bowl. Three or four other shoppers were scattered about, waiting their turn.

She smiled at the woman who had just purchased an expensive ring and handed her the distinctive silver-foiled shopping bag.

"Thank you so much," she murmured. "I know you'll enjoy wearing it."

The phone rang again.

"I certainly will," the woman replied. She took the Gallery Euphoria bag from Arcadia's hand and went toward the door.

The phone warbled insistently. Very few people had the number of her private line.

Zoe was at the top of the list, and Zoe was in Phoenix. Maybe there was news.

She did not want to take the call out there where the customers could overhear her.

Hurrying to the end of the counter, she turned into the short hall and opened the door to her office.

A large palm slapped across her mouth. Simultaneously the barrel of a pistol pressed against her throat.

The man tilted his head slightly and she saw the familiar face beneath the oversized cap. Grant had come for her.

Panic slammed through her, stunning in its intensity. She started to shake.

"Try anything, my dear wife, anything at all, and I'll shoot the first person who walks through that door."

She did not doubt him for a moment.

"I know you, Bitch." He sounded coldly satisfied. "You won't let some innocent die if you can help it, will you? We're going out the back." He slapped a strip of duct tape across her mouth. "Make one sound that brings anyone running and you've signed that person's death warrant. There's a silencer on the gun, by the way."

She thought about the pistol she had

bought for just such an occasion as this. It was safely locked up at home, right where it could not do her any good.

He shoved her through the back-room door and outside onto the bricked walkway. The path led to a service lane and the employee parking lot. Thickly planted oleander bushes served as a decorative fence between the walk and the lane.

Hope rushed back into the empty places inside her. The service lane was almost never entirely deserted; even at night shop clerks took smoking breaks back there. Some of the teenagers who worked in the fast-food restaurants occasionally met near the cover of the trash containers for purposes that would no doubt horrify their parents. Transients often came there to mine the piles of garbage in the massive dumpsters and drink cheap wine.

She heard low voices coming from the other side of the oleanders and caught the faint scent of marijuana. How did Grant think he could possibly get her out of there unnoticed?

And then she saw the large janitorial cart looming directly in her path. A rack at the front bristled with a variety of brushes, brooms and mops. A cardboard carton stood on a tray attached to one side.

"You're going to get into the garbage container and you're going to stay down," Grant commanded. "I won't shoot you unless you give me no choice because I'd rather keep you alive so that we can do a deal for that file you hid. But if I run out of options, I'll kill you, I promise you."

She forced herself to walk toward the cart, trying desperately to think.

When she got close he yanked a bucket off the front of the cart and turned it over so that it functioned as a step. "Use that. Hurry, damn you."

She stepped up onto the bucket and looked down. The interior of the trash container was empty. There was just enough room inside to conceal a slender, full-sized adult crouched on her knees.

Despair struck hard. No one would look twice at a janitor and his cart, she thought.

"Get in," Grant rasped.

She looked at the carton that stood on the side tray. The top had been cut off. She could see several rolls of toilet paper inside.

With a nervous awkwardness that was only partially feigned, she put one leg over the rim of the cart. She staggered a little, as though trying to catch her balance, and drew her other leg up and over the edge.

The toe of her silver sandal bumped forcibly against the carton of toilet paper. The box shot off the tray, spilling the contents. The rolls tumbled out onto the bricks. Several landed in the dirt beneath the oleander bushes.

"Stupid bitch. *Get down.*" His voice rose. "Do it now."

He was not as calm as he had seemed, she realized. That shocked her. Grant had always been so sure of himself. But tonight he sounded as if he were teetering on some dangerous psychological precipice.

She lowered herself onto her hands and knees inside the cart. Grant threw a tarp over the top. The darkness closed in around her. The smell of old garbage combined with her fear almost made her gag.

An instant later the cart jolted into motion. A tiny flame of hope burned deep inside. Grant was in a hurry. He could not afford to take the time to retrieve the rolls of toilet paper.

How much longer until Harry came looking?

She heard the voices of two people near the dumpsters in the service lane.

"Better get back to work," one of them said. The words were faint. "You know how Larry gets when we're a minute late coming off break."

The other person answered but she could not make out the response.

The cart jolted onto the service lane pavement.

35

Ethan studied Shelley Russell's cryptic notes. "She got impatient with all the emphasis on the necessity for extreme secrecy. I can almost see her tapping a toe under the desk while she waited for Branch to get around to telling her exactly what he wanted her to do."

He flipped to the next page of notes.

A name jumped out at him, stopping him cold. "Oh, shit."

He yanked his phone out of his pocket and punched in Harry's number.

"What is it?" Zoe jumped to her feet and hurried around the corner of the desk to read over his shoulder. “Did you find out who hired Branch?”

“No. I found the name of the target.”

“Put it down.” Harry gave the order from the mouth of the alley, using the corner of the building for cover. “Now.”

“Hey, look, mister, I was just havin’ a little drink, thash all.”

The guard sounded drunk but it was easy enough to fake the slurred speech and the whining tone of a man who had been nipping at the bottle for a few hours.

“Put it down and walk out with your hands on your head.”

“Fuck. Are you a cop or something?”

“Or something.”

The guard started forward. “Plainclothes? What’s goin’ on here? You gonna report me to my boss? Man, don’t do that. Please. I really need this job.”

“Drop it.”

“Okay, okay, take it easy. I’m comin’ out like you said.” The guard let the object fall from his hand.

Glass smashed on the paving tiles. The odor of a strong, cloying, heavily fortified wine wafted out of the slim passageway.

"Waste of perfectly good hooch, though," the security guard said mournfully.

Harry heard the phone ring in his pocket. The prickly sensation got worse. It felt like someone had applied stinging nettles to the back of his neck.

He yanked the phone out of his pocket. Turning away from the confused guard, he started back toward Gallery Euphoria.

"You got Stagg," he growled into the phone.

"Where are you?"

Harry recognized the flat, too even tone of Ethan's voice. It meant serious trouble.

"I'm still at Fountain Square," he said. "What's up? Get an ID on the guy who sent Branch after you?"

"I'm not sure what that pool scene was all about but it looks like Arcadia is the target. She has been all along."

"Shit. Loring."

"Looks like it."

Harry was already moving, cutting through the crowds. He could see the front windows of Gallery Euphoria clearly now. Molly was at the counter. There were still two or three customers wandering around the shop, looking at the expensive items on display.

Everything appeared normal.

Then he realized that he could not see Arcadia.

Take it easy. She probably just ducked into her office or the back room for a minute.

"I'll call you back when I've got her," he said into the phone.

He disconnected and ran toward the boutique.

Molly and the customers looked up in shock when he slammed through the front door.

He concentrated on Molly. "Where is she?"

"Arcadia?" Molly stared at him as though he had changed into some kind of freakish monster. "Uh, she, uh, just went into her office to take a call a few minutes ago. It was her private line and I guess she . . ."

He was no longer listening. He crossed the shop in a few long strides and went down the short hall to the office.

The small room was empty.

For the first time in years, he knew the taste of real fear.

Stop it, he thought. *You're no good to her if you lose it now. She's only been gone a few minutes, at most.*

He pushed through the curtains that led to the back room and flipped on the light. The door that opened onto the service lane was closed but it was no longer locked.

Molly came to stand in the entrance to the back room.

"Is something wrong?" she asked tentatively.

"Yes. Call square security. Tell them we're looking for a man who has Arcadia with him. Then call the cops."

"Oh, my God."

"Get on the damned phone. Now."

She whirled and dashed into the office.

He went to the back door of the shop, jerked it open and found himself looking at the narrow, empty walk that led to the service lane.

The light coming through the doorway behind him revealed a number of white cylinders on the ground.

Rolls of toilet paper.

No one took much notice of a man in a uniform. If that was true of a shopping mall guard, it was doubly true of a mall janitor.

He raced down the walkway and turned into the service lane. The lighting back there was minimal. A single streetlamp stood guard at the entrance to the employee parking lot.

He heard the distant, muffled rumble of a cart. The rattle of the hard rubber wheels echoed from the parking lot.

He kicked off his loafers, afraid the sound of his footsteps thudding on the pavement would alert Loring.

Barefooted, he ran quietly toward the nearest of the two large garbage bins and halted in the deep shadow it cast.

He could make out a portion of the poorly lit parking lot. A man in a cap pushed a janitorial cart toward a nondescript van.

It had to be Loring. But what if it wasn't? What if he'd figured wrong? What if this was an honest, hardworking janitor going home after a long night? Maybe a guy with a wife and two or three kids.

He held the gun alongside his leg and moved out from the shadow of the dumpster. He started walking silently toward the van, keeping parked cars between himself and the janitor.

"Loring," he shouted.

The janitor jerked violently and started to turn, hand lifting. Not necessarily Loring,

Harry thought. Anyone who found himself alone in a deserted parking lot would be startled by a stranger calling out a name.

Light glinted on the barrel of the gun in the janitor's hand.

A tarp flew off the top of the cart. Arcadia rose like an avenging goddess from the depths of the garbage bin.

She made no sound but Harry could see that she was struggling to hurl the tarp over Loring's gun arm.

Loring reacted swiftly, wrenching himself to one side. He spun back toward Harry and fired.

Harry heard the shots punch through the metal fender of the pickup on his left.

Now, at last, the world went into slow motion, the way it was supposed to when things got dicey. He no longer felt any emotion—not rage or dread or panic.

Just doing his job.

He raised the pistol and pulled the trigger.

Loring staggered once under the impact and collapsed on the pavement. He did not move again.

36

Forty-eight hours later Ethan rested his fore-arms on the side rails of the hospital bed and looked down at Shelley Russell. Zoe stood across from him. Harry and Arcadia occupied positions at the foot of the bed.

Considering what Shelley had been through, she was in good shape, he thought. She had told them that she was due to be released in the morning, but she couldn't wait that long to get the whole story.

Ethan understood. It was a PI thing.

"Loring is dead?" Shelley asked sharply.

"He died in the ambulance on the way to the hospital," Arcadia said quietly. "But he talked to Harry and me in the parking lot while we waited for the medics. He knew he wasn't going to make it so he had nothing left to lose."

"How did he find you?"

Arcadia sighed. "Unfortunately, Grant knew more about my personal financial arrangements than I realized. He had the number of one of several accounts that I thought I had hidden from him. He kept an eye on it. A month ago I accessed it for the first time to move some money into another account."

Shelley nodded. "And Loring pounced."

"Yes, but Arcadia's new ID was very good," Ethan said. "He needed to be certain that he had the right woman before he made his move. He also wanted to get the whole picture of Arcadia's new life. Friends, business associates, that kind of thing. He didn't dare show up in her vicinity until he was positive."

"So he used John Branch to hire me to take the photos."

"His goal was to keep himself in the shadows until the very last possible moment," Zoe explained.

"Grant has a lot of old enemies, you see," Arcadia said. "Including the SEC and the

Feds. He didn't want to risk being seen on U.S. soil if he could avoid it."

"I understand why he sent me to get the photos in Whispering Springs," Shelley said slowly. "He had to be sure you really were his wife. But why send Branch to take you out, Truax?"

"Loring's original plan called for Branch to grab Arcadia," Harry said. "But after you brought back those photos of the gang in Whispering Springs he started to worry that Truax here might be a potential problem."

"Being a problem is one of Ethan's many professional skills," Zoe said proudly.

Ethan shrugged modestly.

Arcadia cleared her throat. "After researching Ethan, Grant decided to redo his plans. He was always very good at making strategic adjustments on the fly. He figured that getting rid of Ethan would resolve two issues. It would not only remove the one person he thought might come looking for him in the event I were to disappear, it would also refocus everyone's attention in another, entirely different direction and thus give him even more cover."

"What's with Branch?" Shelley demanded.

"He came out of his coma this morning,"

Harry said. "At first he would only give his name, rank and serial number. But eventually Detective Ramirez convinced him that he was in serious trouble and Branch started to babble. Seems he really did think he was working for a super-secret government agency. Never got past the fact that he washed out of that elite military unit he tried to join. He was obsessed with proving that he could handle his mission."

"Grant planned to get rid of both you and Branch to cover his tracks, Shelley," Arcadia said.

"Well, he damned near succeeded in my case." Shelley made a face. "The doctors finally concluded that someone emptied one of my pill capsules and refilled it with a hefty dose of some fancy designer drugs. Combined with all my other meds, it would have done me in if Zoe and Truax here hadn't found me when they did."

Zoe patted her hand.

Shelley looked at Zoe's fingers touching hers. She frowned again, thoughtful now. "I have this weird memory of a dream I must have had while I was out of it. Someone kept calling my name, over and over. Telling me that I had to hold on."

"That would be Zoe," Ethan said.

He looked at her across the bed. He could see that the strain of being inside the hospital was starting to take its toll. There was a tightness at the corners of her eyes and mouth. He had to get her out of there soon.

Shelley peered at Arcadia. "What are you going to do with that file you hid? Sounds like it could still be dangerous."

Harry snorted softly. "She turned it over to the Feds first thing this morning."

"Harry thought it would be the best way to neutralize the situation," Arcadia added. "My goal was to use it as insurance to protect myself from Grant in case he was still alive. Now that he's gone, there's no reason to hang on to it. I've got some legal maneuvering to do in order to reclaim some old assets, and the IRS has a few questions for me, but that's about all I have to worry about."

"Nothing we can't make go away with the help of a good lawyer," Harry said easily.

"Glad to hear it." Shelley sighed. "Sorry about my part in this mess. I damn near got you killed, Truax."

"Bottom line is that it was your notes that helped save Arcadia's life," Ethan said.

"Just wish I'd put it all together a little quicker than I did. In the old days I wouldn't have been so easily dazzled by the phony government ID."

"When did you get suspicious?" Zoe asked.

"Branch made me a little uneasy right from the start, to tell you the truth. Sometimes you get a feeling about a client." Shelley appealed to Ethan. "Know what I mean?"

"Sure. Something just didn't look right."

"Yep. Anyhow, when I learned that Branch was in a coma in a Whispering Springs hospital after being electrocuted in your pool, I knew I had a big problem. I was getting ready to contact you when I started feeling real sick."

"Did you realize that you had been poisoned?" Harry asked.

"I wasn't sure what the hell was happening at first, but I figured that was a possibility, yeah."

"So you hid your notebook," Ethan said. "Nice move, Russell."

A man and a woman came through the door at that moment. Both glared at the group gathered around Shelley's bed.

"What are you all doing in here?" the

woman demanded. "Mother is supposed to be resting."

The man scowled at Ethan. "The sign outside says that she is allowed only two visitors at a time."

"Meet my daughter, Julie, and my son, Craig," Shelley rasped. "They think I should retire."

Ethan looked at Julie and Craig. "I sure hope she doesn't get out of the business. I could use a reliable contact here in Phoenix, and your mother is one hell of a pro."

Shelley grinned. "Takes one to know one."

37

The trio on the small, intimate stage consisted of piano, guitar and bass. They were playing "Sweet Lorraine," a signature Nat King Cole piece, and they were doing it the way it was supposed to be done. The sound was upbeat and lovely. But it wasn't having its usual effect on him, Harry thought. It wasn't taking him to that special place.

He swallowed some of his beer and settled deeper into the cushions. Last Exit was only lightly crowded tonight. He and Arcadia were seated in what had become their usual booth.

"You got a lot of regrets about the way things turned out?" he said.

What he really wanted to ask was, *Are you sorry that you're sleeping with a guy like me instead of one of those classy executive types you went with when you were in the big time?* But he was afraid to say the words out loud. He didn't want to corner her. In his experience, you had to take the moment and not look too far ahead.

She met his eyes across the top of her martini glass and he knew immediately that she had understood the question behind the question. Sometimes it seemed like they could almost read each other's minds.

"No," she said. "Not a single one."

She put her glass down, leaned forward and brushed her lips against his. "You are the best thing that ever happened to me, Harry."

A sensation for which he had no words unfurled inside him.

"I love you." The words sounded rusty in his mouth. He couldn't remember the last time he had used them. Maybe never.

She touched his cheek. "I love you, too. You're my soul mate, Harry."

The music finally started to go to work, taking him to that special place.

He knew then that this new feeling did have a name, after all. This was what folks meant when they talked about being happy.

He reached across the table and took Arcadia's hand. Her fingers intertwined tightly with his. They sat close together and let the music sweep them away.

38

Dexter Morrow left Whispering Springs the following day. When he was sure of his facts, Ethan picked up the phone and called Zoe at her office.

"A moving company just finished packing up his household belongings. He gave them an address in Florida. I checked, and he's signed a lease for a condo just outside Miami. He is definitely moving out of our neck of the woods."

"Where is Morrow right now at this very instant?" Zoe asked bluntly.

"Honey, you've got to get past this tendency to be so suspicious of people."

"You're a fine one to talk."

"It's okay for me to be suspicious. I'm in the suspicion business. However, if it will put your mind at ease, rest assured that I checked and Morrow did indeed purchase a one-way ticket to Miami. Trust me, he's gone."

"You're sure?"

"How about a little credit here? I'm a trained detective."

"Well, okay. If you're positive."

"I am. What do you say we try another date now that we know I'm not quite so likely to ruin the ambience by gettting into a brawl in the restaurant parking lot?"

She hesitated for only a fraction of a second but he caught it and the pause made his heart sink a little.

"That sounds great," she said.

The enthusiasm sounded forced. He pretended not to notice.

"Tonight?" he asked.

"Okay. But this is the day I'm scheduled to take in one of the meditation sessions at Tabitha Pine's house. I may be a little late getting home."

"I'll make the reservations for seven."

He hung up the phone and sat there for a

long time asking questions that had no answers.

The street in front of Tabitha Pine's desert estate was lined with expensive cars. Zoe spotted Lindsey Voyle's Jaguar near the front.

A uniformed housekeeper opened the door. Not sure of what kind of psychic vibes to expect inside a meditation guru's home, Zoe entered with more than her usual degree of caution.

Nothing bizarre shouted at her from the walls. The house had the usual, very low-level background hum common to new construction but that was about it.

She was shown into a vast white-on-white great room that looked out toward the mountains. Zoe counted twenty people seated in rows on neatly arranged white pillows. Lindsey Voyle was in the front row. She regarded Zoe with cool eyes.

Zoe saw at once that she had made a serious fashion error. All of the other meditators-in-training wore white yoga-style outfits. In her black leggings and purple tee shirt she stood out like a badly bruised sore thumb.

Tabitha Pine was the only other person in

the room not wearing white. She was draped in flowing silver and gold silks, her long gray hair piled high in a strange hairdo reminiscent of a figure on an ancient Roman coin. She occupied a low, white lacquer-and-gilt chair.

She gave Zoe a radiant smile.

"Welcome to our group of seekers, Zoe. I'm so glad you could make it today."

"Thanks." *Like I had a choice if I want your business.*

Aware that she was the only one standing, Zoe hastily sat down on the nearest available pillow. She found herself next to an attractive woman with stylishly cut blond hair.

The woman leaned over and lowered her voice. "Is this your first session?"

"Yes." Zoe noticed that no one else was wearing shoes. She pried off her sandals and assumed a cross-legged position. "What about you?"

"I've been attending for the past month. Very enlightening."

Tabitha rang a tiny crystal bell. A hush fell on the small crowd.

"We gather here today as seekers, open to truth and new perceptions," Tabitha intoned. "We walk the long road of enlightenment together, learning from each other and from those who have walked this path before us. The skills we study appear to be uncomplicated, but it is the nature of reality that what appears most simple is, in fact, the most difficult to know and comprehend."

Tabitha directed them to rest their hands, palms up, on their knees.

"Close your eyes and allow your senses to open wide. Look at the world from deep inside. Go to the special room in your mind, the place where the light is pure and warm and clean. This is your own private space, a place where there is no stress, no tension, a place where you do not have to think or plan or feel. . . ."

Zoe obediently closed her eyes and tried to get into the spirit of the thing, but after about five minutes acute boredom set in.

"Allow yourself to simply exist in the moment, conscious only of the present. . . ."

Zoe peeked through her lashes and saw that Lindsey Voyle was concentrating furiously. It was evident that the woman couldn't even relax in the middle of a meditation exercise.

Surreptitiously she examined the spacious room, feeling for the natural flow of energy, contemplating various ideas for positioning the furniture.

"Release the past and the future. Float on the crest of the wave that is the present. Understand that you are a part of the great cosmic tide. . . ."

Window treatments were going to be especially tricky in the Pine residence, Zoe decided. The house had been positioned to capture the view, not with regard to heating and cooling issues. The intensity of light that would pour through the windows in the summer would be a major problem. The architect had obviously decided to rely entirely on the air-conditioning system, rather than roof overhangs.

"Let yourself float toward the horizon. This is the astral plane. Our perceptions are so much different here. . . ."

It was a huge house. Tabitha would no doubt want to stick with the white-on-white scheme. But maybe she could be made to see that there were other neutrals that would work as well and would not invite so much glare in the summer.

"We are all one with the universe. . . ."

The forty-five-minute session seemed interminable, but eventually Tabitha urged her audience to return to their bodies and awaken to the present.

"We have used far more psychic energy than you probably realize," Tabitha said, rising gracefully from the ornate chair. "So please refresh yourselves with the herbal tea that has been prepared for you. It is my own special blend."

The woman who had been seated next to Zoe smiled as they both got to their feet.

"Well? How did it go?" she asked with enthusiasm. "Did you get anything out of the experience?"

"I don't think I'm very good at meditating," Zoe admitted, wondering why she felt apologetic.

"It takes practice, just like anything else. I've been attending the sessions for the past month and I feel I've made a great deal of progress. I've been a lifelong worrier but meditation is teaching me to relax and take things as they come."

"That's wonderful."

"I've still got a long way to go." The woman grimaced. "For example, I haven't worked up the nerve to tell my husband that I signed up for the classes because he'd never in a million years approve. He's a good man, but he's a very linear thinker, if you know what I mean."

"Everything is suspect unless he can view the hard evidence for himself?"

"Exactly. And anything that is even remotely connected to metaphysical philosophy is, by definition, a fraud or a scam or the product of a fevered imagination, as far as he's concerned."

"My husband holds a similar enlightened opinion," Zoe said dryly. "But to his credit, he seems to be able to deal with the fact that I'm, uh, sort of into metaphysics."

"Lucky you."

"Not that it's any of my business," Zoe said, "but if you're not telling your husband about these sessions, how are you explaining the cost? This is an expensive course."

"In our household, I handle the finances. It's been that way since the beginning of our marriage because my husband has got his hands full running his business. Don't laugh, but for the past few weeks I've been reduced to writing checks to myself for cash and then giving the money to Tabitha so there's no paper trail for my husband to find. I'll have to come clean one of these days, but I'm dreading it. I know there will be a major scene."

"Paper trail?"

"Hey, I'm not married to a private detective for nothing. You live with one long enough, you pick up the jargon. By the way, I don't believe I've introduced myself. I'm Daria Radnor."

Zoe started to laugh.

"What's so funny?"

"Is this a case of psychic intercept, or what?" Zoe put out her hand. "Zoe Truax. I'm married to Ethan Truax. Truax Investigations?"

"Of course. I'm delighted to meet you. Nelson has mentioned your husband on several occasions. There's a bit of competition there, I'm afraid, but frankly, I think he secretly envies Ethan a little for having gotten out of the corporate rat race."

Before Zoe could respond, Tabitha wafted over to join them.

"Zoe, I'm delighted that you could make it today. I was so anxious for you to participate in one of my sessions before you started to draw up your proposal. It really is the only way you can get a true feel for the sort of energy flow I require in this space."

"The experience was very helpful," Zoe

said politely. She was aware of Lindsey Voyle watching them from the other side of the room.

Tabitha narrowed her eyes, studying Zoe with a peculiar, unsettling intensity. "So often we get locked into the pattern of viewing the world around us from a single, narrow perspective. When we do that, we fail to open ourselves up to other realities and possibilities."

"Very true," Daria agreed.

"I have a theory." Tabitha touched Zoe's arm and then instantly withdrew her fingertips, as if she had been burned. Her eyes widened briefly. Then she swallowed and relaxed into an oddly knowing smile. "I believe that it is fear that makes us avoid those other perspectives. We must get past that fear if we are to find the answers to our questions."

For the first time that afternoon, Zoe picked up a trace of unusual psychic energy in the great room. It flickered a bit and then disappeared.

Tabitha turned away in a cloud of silver-and-gold silks and walked off to join another group.

A light-headed sensation came over Zoe. Her palms tingled. She could hardly breathe.

It is fear that makes us avoid those other perspectives.

"You're kidding." Ethan paused with his fork halfway to his mouth. "Daria Radnor is taking meditation lessons?"

Seated on the other side of the table, Zoe smiled, not bothering to conceal her satisfaction. "Every Tuesday and Thursday afternoon for the past month."

"Damn." He thought about the strain he had seen in Nelson's face. "The poor guy thinks she's having a wild affair."

"I didn't know what to say. I couldn't bear to tell her that her husband was so worried about the possibility that she was cheating on him that he tried to hire you to tail her. So I kept my mouth shut."

"Always a wise decision." He took a bite of his salad. "Can't go too far wrong that way, I always say."

"Well? What are you going to do about it?"

"Me?"

"Yeah, you, Traux. You have to do something."

Absently he listened to the muted background noises around him. The intimate little restaurant was crowded this evening. Singleton had suggested the place when Ethan explained that he was reluctant to take Zoe back to Las Estrellas so soon after the unfortunate incident in the parking lot.

What the hell *was* he going to do? "Probably nothing. Eventually she'll get around to telling him about the sessions."

"*Eventually.* That could be a long time. Weeks, maybe. Daria obviously has no idea that Nelson is suffering. Who knows what impact his growing suspicions will have on their relationship."

"Now, honey, this really isn't—"

"Tabitha Pine said something after the session about how our private fears lock us into certain perspectives. I think she has a point. Nelson is trapped by his own worst-case-scenario perspective. He can't get past it."

"As a general policy, it's never smart to interfere in someone else's private life."

"No offense, Ethan, but you do it all the time. You make a living interfering in other people's private lives."

He exhaled deeply. "There is that." He contemplated the situation for a while longer. "Thinking that his wife is having an affair is eating Radnor alive."

She considered him for a long, somber moment. "If the situation was reversed, what would you want Radnor to do?"

Everything inside him tightened. "I wouldn't have asked someone else to get the truth for me."

"What would you have done?"

He shrugged and reached for another chunk of bread. "I would have asked you."

The answer startled her. "Me?"

"You wouldn't lie to me." He felt the tightness in his gut ease as he followed the path of his own logic. "Which means you wouldn't cheat on me in the first place."

"Of course not."

"Which, in turn, makes the whole question one hundred percent hypothetical. So let's change the subject."

"Okay. You know, I've got to tell you that this detecting business is sort of fun. It felt good to close the Radnor case today."

His mouth twitched. "Once in a while you get a good one."

"Makes it all worthwhile, huh?"

"Yeah."

"That reminds me." She reached under her chair and grabbed her purse. "I got you a little present."

"Oh, boy."

She pulled out a small, neatly wrapped package and handed it to him across the table.

He took his time opening it and grinned when he uncovered the package label. "Just what I've always wanted. Pepper spray."

39

Arcadia lowered herself slowly into the bubbling spa pool and sat down across from Zoe and Bonnie.

"I've got a confession to make," she said. "I will never again make fun of you, Zoe, for buying all that safety gear and health stuff for Ethan. Yesterday afternoon I went out and bought vitamins and an industrial-strength sunblock for Harry."

"That sounds like an eminently reasonable thing to do under the circumstances," Bonnie assured her.

Zoe shuddered. "Every time I think of the

two of you out there in that alley with Grant Loring, I get twitchy."

"You and me both," Arcadia admitted.

"I can't even imagine how awful it must have been for you inside that janitorial cart," Bonnie said.

"That was bad enough. But the worst part was hearing Harry call Grant's name. I realized that he was not certain of the identity of the janitor and was trying to make sure he had the right man before he made his move. I was terrified that Grant would kill him first."

"So you leaped out of the cart to distract Grant and give Harry a shot." Zoe shuddered. "That was very brave of you. Grant might just as easily have tried to kill you first."

"You two would have done the same thing and you know it. Besides, look at the alternative," Arcadia said. "I still can't quite believe that Grant is gone for good. I feel as if I can breathe freely again for the first time in ages."

"What are you going to do now?" Bonnie asked. "Return to your old life?"

"No. I've got a new life now. It feels like my real life. I'm sticking with it."

"I know just what you mean," Zoe said fervently.

Arcadia tilted her head a little, examining her closely. "How's it going with you? Any more encounters with the crazy stuff?"

"No, thank goodness. But I have to say that I'm convinced those spiderwebs weren't left behind by John Branch. I'm sure I would have picked up some trace of them in his apartment if he was the source."

"What next?" Bonnie asked curiously.

She looked at her two friends, steeling herself. "There is one more possibility that I want to check out. Lindsey Voyle."

Bonnie and Arcadia stared at her. They looked worried, she noticed. Very worried.

"Just how do you plan to check her out?" Arcadia asked.

"Well, as it happens, I've been working on a plan."

"I was afraid of that," Bonnie said.

Arcadia looked resigned. "Tell us about it."

Zoe sat forward. The water simmered and bubbled around her. "I've been thinking about the two locations where I picked up the bad energy. In addition to the crazy vibes, there were a couple of other similarities."

"Such as?" Bonnie asked.

"Some items were missing or broken in both locations." She looked at Arcadia. "Did you ever find your Elvis pen?"

Arcadia shook her head. "No."

"Yesterday I went through the photos in the packet that I left on your file cabinet. I had ordered two sets of each. One of the pictures, a shot that Theo took of you and me, is missing."

"Is that all?" Bonnie asked dubiously.

"Not quite. There was a vase broken in my library at the show house and I never found the red mug that I used in a display there."

Arcadia pondered that information for a moment. "Think the missing and broken items are significant?"

"I don't know," Zoe admitted. "But I'm convinced there's a connection. Like I said, I've ruled out John Branch as the source of the spiderwebs but that still leaves Lindsey Voyle. I'm going to need your help, Arcadia."

"Don't you think you should ask Ethan for some advice? He's the expert, remember?"

"No," Zoe said. "I don't want to get Ethan involved. Not yet."

* * *

Ethan stopped at the gleaming front desk and looked at the well-groomed receptionist.

"Hello, Jason."

"Mr. Truax. Are you here to see Mr. Radnor?"

"Yeah. Tell him I'll make it quick."

Jason picked up the phone, spoke briefly and put it down. "This way, please."

Ethan followed him through the handsomely appointed headquarters of Radnor Security Systems, past a series of desks occupied by a number of professional-looking types working hard in front of a lot of very expensive computers. Every time he came here he got a strange feeling of déjà vu. The corporate offices of Truax Security in LA had looked a lot like this place. He sometimes wondered if he and Nelson had been victimized by the same decorator.

Jason knocked once and opened the door of Nelson Radnor's private office.

Nelson looked up from a file. He had aged about a hundred years in the past week, Ethan thought.

"I'm a little busy at the moment, Truax. What's this all about?"

Ethan glanced at the door, making certain

that it was firmly closed. Then he lowered himself into one of the expensive leather client chairs.

"Thought you might like to know that my wife ran into your wife yesterday afternoon."

Nelson did not move but Ethan saw that the significance of yesterday's date had not escaped him. Yesterday was a Thursday.

"Where?" Nelson asked in a hoarse voice.

"They both attended a class on meditation techniques at the home of a woman named Tabitha Pine. It was Zoe's first session, but evidently your wife signed up for the full course. She's been attending classes every Tuesday and Thursday for the past month."

"Every Tuesday and Thursday."

"In the afternoons. Pays in cash because she didn't think you'd approve and didn't want to have to go through a big scene about it."

Nelson closed the file with great care. He rubbed the bridge of his nose. "I don't know what to say. I've been an idiot."

"Yeah, well, don't be too hard on yourself. When it comes to Zoe, it doesn't take much to make me stop thinking rationally, either. Nature of the beast, I guess."

"Probably."

Ethan rose from the chair and went to the door. "My advice is to buy some flowers on the way home tonight."

"I think I'll do that." Nelson leaned back in his chair. "Meditation classes, you say?"

"Yeah."

Nelson made a face. "Daria was right. If she'd told me that she had signed up for a course in meditation techniques with that Tabitha Pine operation, I'd have hit the roof."

"But you won't do that now, will you?" Ethan asked evenly. "I mean, what with your consciousness having recently been expanded and all."

"Tell me the truth, Truax. What would you do if your wife announced that she was going to spend a couple thousand bucks to take a meditation course from a phony like Pine?"

"You're talking to a man who is married to a decorator who specializes in maximizing positive energy flows inside the living spaces of her clients," Ethan said dryly.

"Oh, yeah, right. The feng shui thing. I forgot." Nelson grinned, looking a hundred and ten years younger. "I reckon if you can handle your wife's career, I can deal with Daria's new hobby."

"Beats the hell out of the hobby you assumed she had taken up."

"Oh, yeah," Nelson said in prayerful tones. "It does."

Lindsey Voyle lived in Desert View, an exclusive, gated golf course community that held some unpleasant memories for Zoe. She tried not to think about a former client who committed murder in one of the expensive homes. She had other problems today.

A uniformed guard wearing a patch on his pocket that identified him as a member of the Radnor Security Systems team checked his computer and then waved Zoe and Arcadia through the gate.

Zoe followed the guard's directions and drove along a curving road studded with palm trees, turned right and stopped in front of a large stucco-clad, southwestern-style residence.

She turned off the engine and examined the big house for a moment.

"Lindsey may want the Tabitha Pine project very badly," she said, "but it doesn't look like she needs it, not if she can afford to live here in Desert View."

"There are many reasons why a person

might want something very badly," Arcadia reminded her. "Not all of them involve money."

"True."

They got out of the car and walked along a path that took them through a dramatically designed cactus-and-rock garden. For some reason, Zoe found it surprising that Lindsey had chosen to put in cacti. Then again, the Whispering Springs town council frowned on any landscaping that required a lot of water, unless, of course, you were building a golf course. Here in Arizona restaurants frequently served water only on request and private lawns were almost illegal, but golf courses never went thirsty.

If anyone had asked her what she thought of cacti before she moved to Whispering Springs, Zoe thought, she would have said, *Not much.* But a year in the desert had taught her to see many things differently. She had discovered that the varieties of cacti were never less than fascinating, and many specimens were truly spectacular. Lindsey had invested in a particularly stunning display.

Cactus names were often wonderfully descriptive, Zoe mused. They usually went straight to the point, as it were. She picked out examples of Bigtooth, Fish Hook Barrel and Toothpick cacti on the way to Lindsey's front door. A cluster of Golden Barrels marked the entrance to the house. Their plump, dark green bodies were gilded with a thousand yellow spines. They looked as beautiful and as dangerous as any objet d'art that had ever been created by a Renaissance craftsman.

"Do you usually personally deliver a specially designed piece of jewelry to a customer?" Zoe asked while they waited for Lindsey to respond to the doorbell.

Arcadia glanced at the silver box in her hand. "No, but Lindsey doesn't have to know that."

The door opened. Lindsey looked out at them from a pale, limestone-tiled foyer. Her smile of welcome congealed when she saw Zoe.

"I didn't realize that you were coming out here, too," she said.

"Zoe and I are on our way to a friend's house after we leave here," Arcadia said easily. "We didn't want to take two cars. I hope you don't mind."

"No, of course not." Lindsey recovered

quickly. She stepped back to allow them to enter the house. "Please come in. Do you mind removing your shoes?"

"No problem," Zoe said. She stepped cautiously over the threshold, hoping to feel a trace of the foul energy.

But there were no spiderwebs in the foyer.

Damn. She stepped out of her red slides.

Arcadia gave Lindsey a cool smile while she removed her sandals. "I think you'll be very pleased with the bracelet. In my opinion, it's far and away the finest work that Meyrick has done to date. A real masterpiece."

Some of the tension eased out of Lindsey's shoulders. She looked at the small silver box with undisguised eagerness. "I can't wait to see it. Let's go into the great room. The light is excellent in there at this time of day."

She turned and led the way.

Zoe caught Arcadia's attention and grimly shook her head. Nothing.

But this was a large home, she reminded herself. The spiderwebs, if they existed, might be trapped in one of the other rooms.

Lindsey's residence looked a lot like the bedroom she had designed at the Designers' Dream Home. It was a study of white-on-white carpets and furnishings accented with blond wood and pale stone. The great room windows framed the cool green of the golf course.

Lindsey poured three glasses of iced tea and served them on a white tray. Arcadia put the Gallery Euphoria box on the glass coffee table and removed the lid with an elegant flourish.

Amber and turquoise glowed in a heavily worked silver setting.

"It's fabulous." Lindsey was clearly entranced. She picked up the bracelet and held it to the light. "Absolutely fabulous."

"I'm glad you're pleased with it," Arcadia replied.

Zoe waited until the two were engaged in a discussion of the design of the bracelet before she gently cleared her throat.

"Would you mind if I used your powder room?" she mumbled.

"At the end of the foyer." Lindsey did not look up from her new bracelet. "To the right."

Zoe exchanged another quick glance with Arcadia and rose to her feet.

The powder room was at the front of a hall that led to what looked like a bedroom wing. Zoe ducked into the small room, turned on the fan to provide some background cover in case anyone came to check on her and then stepped back out into the hall and closed the door firmly.

Grateful for Lindsey's no-shoes-inside-the-house policy, she went barefooted down the hall, darting quickly into each room she passed.

Quick forays into a master bedroom suite and a guest room proved disappointing. No spiderwebs drifted in any of the spaces.

A chill of dread went through her. Her hopes were fading fast.

She opened the last door in the wing and found herself in a space that obviously served as Lindsey's home office. The walls were covered with framed photographs of Lindsey and the man who was, no doubt, her former husband. A major player in Hollywood, Ethan had said.

Picture after picture featured Lindsey and her ex in the company of famous stars and glitzy-looking jet-setters. Some of the shots showed the pair hobnobbing with important politicians.

There was no doubt that life had changed for Lindsey Voyle after her divorce. Whispering Springs was not exactly a watering hole for the rich and famous. There were no glittering premieres here. No renowned chefs had opened trendy restaurants in town. Stars and politicians did not hang out in the local resorts.

She was about to close the door when she realized that there was some strong energy swirling through the office. Anger, emotional pain and sadness mingled.

In that moment she realized that Lindsey was mourning not just a lifestyle, but a marriage. She had loved the man in the photos.

Reluctantly she went back to the powder room, opened the door and switched off the fan.

Arcadia took one look at her face when she walked back into the great room and got to her feet.

"I'll let you know when I receive another shipment of Meyrick's work," Arcadia said, slipping the strap of her aqua handbag over her shoulder.

"Thank you." Lindsey's mood had altered appreciably. She actually looked cheerful when she ushered her guests out the door.

The acquisition of the spectacular bracelet had probably fired up a bunch of endorphins, Zoe figured.

She got behind the wheel. Arcadia slipped into the passenger seat and closed the door. They buckled up.

"I get the feeling you did not find what you wanted to find in that house," Arcadia said.

"No trace." Zoe tightened her grip on the wheel. "I was so certain . . ."

She stopped. There was no reason to inflict the gory details of her deepening fears on Arcadia. There was nothing Arcadia could do except panic with her.

But between close friends, some things did not have to be put into words.

"You're not going crazy," Arcadia said calmly.

"Someone sure is."

40

She dreamed of Xanadu that night.

She walked down the endless corridor of H Ward, past one locked door after another, following the trail left by the dark strands of psychic energy.

The sticky web became denser and more terrifying as she drew closer to the room where they originated.

Stop. Turn around. You don't want to do this.

But she had no choice. *It is fear that makes us avoid other perspectives.*

At last she reached the locked door that

concealed the source of the ghastly pulsing energy. She reached out to open it.

Then she noticed the number of the room.

232.

She came awake in a cold sweat, panting for breath, trembling violently. Room 232 in Xanadu had been her room.

Beside her Ethan slept. Evidently she had not cried out this time.

She pushed the covers aside and sat up carefully, trying not to disturb Ethan. The residue of panic washing through her veins made her so shaky she almost lost her balance when she got to her feet.

She took her robe off the hook, put it on and made her way along the hall to the living room. Standing at the window, she looked out at the predawn sky.

How much longer could she pretend that nothing was wrong? It was bad enough that she had managed to fool herself for the past couple of weeks. Now she had to face the fact that she was guilty of concealing what might prove to be the truth from the man she loved.

You wouldn't lie to me.

She had not lied to him. Not exactly. But

he deserved the whole truth, not just the sanitized version she had given him.

She felt tears gather in her eyes. If the truth turned out to be the stuff of her nightmares, she would have to set Ethan free. It was the right thing to do. She knew that.

She also knew that it would break her heart.

In the morning, she decided. She would tell him at breakfast. That would be soon enough. It was nearly dawn, already.

The tears dampened her cheeks. She brushed them away on the sleeve of her robe.

"You going to tell me what's wrong this time?" Ethan asked very evenly. "Or just leave me hanging in limbo?"

Jolted, she turned sharply to see him standing in the shadows. He had pulled on his trousers but nothing else.

Barefooted, he walked toward her and stopped a short distance away.

"Breakfast," she managed.

"I'm not real hungry."

"I meant that I was going to tell you at breakfast."

"Tell me what?"

This was it. Time to walk through the fire. "Oh, Ethan . . ."

"You want out, don't you?" He shoved his

fingers through his hair. "We might as well get it on the table. I appreciate the fact that you don't want to hurt me, but you're not doing me any favors by trying to force yourself to make this marriage work."

Understanding dawned. It shook her to the core.

"Don't say that," she whispered fiercely. "Don't even think it. Not for one moment. I love you more than I have ever loved anyone else. I will love you for the rest of my life. I will never stop loving you."

He went very still. "But?"

She braced herself against the wave of despair. "But I think there is a very good chance that I am going insane, and I love you too much to let you stay married to a crazy woman."

An eerie silence fell.

"Let's try that again," he said very carefully.

She sank down onto the edge of the sofa, wrapped her arms around her waist. "You heard me."

"You actually believe you may be going nuts?"

"Yes." She focused on the gold-and-pink orchids that floated in a low glass bowl on the coffee table. "For a while, I tried to tell myself that the spiderwebs I ran into in Arcadia's office and at the Designers' Dream Home were left by John Branch or Lindsey Voyle. But I'm sure now that neither of them was the source."

"So you figure you're the one who's leaving the psychic junk behind?"

"It's a possibility, Ethan. A strong one. I'm the only other person who was in both of those places."

"This is bullshit."

She tore her gaze off the orchids and looked up at him. "I know you don't believe that I can sense psychic energy. But it's the truth and I have to deal with it, even if you can't."

He reached down and pulled her to her feet. "Let's say for the sake of this particular discussion that you are psychic and that you have begun to give off some kind of weird vibes. There's one real big flaw in your analysis."

"What's that?"

"If you were the source, the crazy energy would be all over this apartment. Think about it. This is where you live, remember?"

She blinked back more tears. "Believe me, I'm hanging on to that possibility because it's my one remaining hope. But it's also possible that whatever is happening to me on the psychic plane is sporadic and intermittent. Like occasional bursts of static interfering with a radio signal at dusk. It starts out slowly and gradually gets worse as night comes on."

"Bullshit," Ethan said again.

"I knew you wouldn't understand."

"Listen up, honey. I understand one thing just fine and that is that you are not going crazy."

"How can you be so sure?" She fought to keep her voice from climbing. The terror of going insane was bound up with the fear of losing Ethan. Both were threatening to crush her. "How can you be so damned sure? You don't even believe that I'm psychic, so how the hell can you know I'm not a crazy psychic?"

"For the same reason that you don't believe that I'm a homicidal maniac even though I told you that I deliberately plotted a man's death."

There was a short, stark silence.

She frowned. "For heaven's sake, Ethan, that was different. You're not a cold-blooded murderer."

"When I look in your eyes, I don't see any craziness."

"It's not something you can see."

"Sure it is. How do you think we diagnose mental illness in the first place? People who are genuinely crazy are usually the last to figure it out. It's the folks around them who notice that something's not right. Trust me, none of your friends thinks you're nuts."

"Ethan, something's wrong." She was shivering now, hope and fear combining in her system to create a terrible tonic. "I can feel it. I think Tabitha Pine had a point. I need to get past my fear and examine reality from a clear perspective."

"Tabitha Pine may have a few nifty, all-occasion guru sayings, but like I told you the other day, we've got some of our own in the detective business. One of which is, don't look for complicated answers if you've got a perfectly good, simple answer right in front of you. And the simplest answer in this case is that you've been under a lot of stress lately and you're reacting to it in your own unique way. You're tough, but you're not invulnerable. No one is. Give yourself a chance to get back to normal before you start worrying about the psychic static."

"But what if it gets worse even after life returns to normal?"

"I'm pretty sure it won't. I've got a hunch your so-called spiderwebs will turn out to have a lot in common with the bad times I go through in November each year. Some kind of post-trauma thing."

"But, Ethan—"

"If it does get worse, we'll deal with it." He tightened his grip on her shoulders. "Together."

Together. The word glowed in the darkness. She had been alone for so much of her life that the condition had come to feel normal. Even during the course of her short marriage to Preston she had known a degree of loneliness because she had never been able to confide the truth about herself to him.

But Ethan could handle anything, even a wife who believed she was psychic.

"I love you." She put her arms around his waist and held him with all of her strength.

He lifted his hands, cradled her face in his palms and kissed her.

"I love you, too," he said. "We're a team

now. Regardless of what comes, we stick together. Agreed?"

"Agreed."

After a while he took her hand and led her back to bed. There, in the light of the new dawn, he made love to her with a consuming passion that effectively blotted out all her fears.

At least for a while.

41

Hooper emerged from the rear door of Casa de Oro just as Zoe pulled into her assigned parking slot. He had an unflattened cardboard box in one hand and a white plastic garbage bag in the other.

Zoe got out of the car and watched him toss first the garbage bag and then the cardboard box into the metal bin. He managed to prop the fully erect carton directly in front of the F LATTEN ALL BOXES sign.

She was not sure why she had come back to the apartment so early in the day. She had spent the past few hours alone in her office, unable to concentrate on any of her design projects because of an uneasy, edgy sensation that grew steadily stronger.

She had tried immersing herself in her research on spiderwebs, but as soon as she opened the first book—a treatise on the ancient system of Vastu—the restlessness had become impossible to ignore.

The need to return to Casa de Oro had become so overpowering that she finally stopped fighting it. Somewhere, somehow, she sensed that she had overlooked something important there.

She looked at the unflattened carton and tut-tutted. "Petty, Hooper, very petty."

"It's my gesture of triumph." Hooper dusted off his hands, admiring his handiwork. "The rest of you may have abandoned the war, but I intend to fight on. What's more, I've got a secret weapon. I can't wait until Sergeant Duncan knocks on my door to give me another lecture about breaking down the boxes. I'm really going to let her have it."

"You're planning to terminate your lease?"

"Hell, no." Hooper tossed his car keys into the air. "I've got the goods on Ms. Anal-Retentive."

"What goods?"

Hooper looked smug. "Get this. Robyn

Duncan was fired from her last job here in Whispering Springs because she lied on her job application. All I have to do is pick up the phone and call the folks who own Casa de Oro and she's history."

"How did you find out that Robyn lost her other position?"

Hooper surveyed the parking lot quickly to make sure no one could overhear, and then he took a step closer to Zoe.

"Last night I had a couple of beers with a friend of mine. I started telling him about the drill sergeant we've got for an apartment house manager and he said it sounded just like a woman who worked for him for a few days at the end of last month. When I mentioned her name, it turned out to be none other than our Robyn."

Zoe tightened her grip on her purse strap. "You're certain that she lied on her job application?"

"That's what my buddy said. She was hired on a provisional basis because they were shorthanded, but after the background check went through they let her go because they found out she'd faked her previous work history for the past two or three years."

"What was wrong? Was she in prison or something?"

"Worse." Hooper uttered a malicious chuckle. "Get this, she was locked up in some kind of private mental hospital."

Zoe went cold. "You're sure?"

"That's what my buddy said." Hooper tossed his keys again and strode off toward his car. "I can't wait until she hits me up about that damned unflattened carton. I'm really looking forward to telling her that I know she's a certified loony."

"Hooper?"

"Yeah?" He unlocked his car.

"Where does your buddy work?"

"He's a supervisor at Radnor Security Services."

She stood there, stunned, while Hooper drove out of the parking lot.

Eventually she pulled her wildly skittering thoughts together and let herself into the lobby. There was a neatly lettered sign on the door of the manager's office informing tenants that the manager was away from her desk due to *personal business.*

Zoe tried the office door and was not surprised to discover that it was locked. She stepped back and checked the small lobby and the stairs that led to the second floor. There was no one in sight. The apartment complex felt empty, as it usually did in the afternoons when most of the tenants were away at work.

She considered her options. She could call Ethan and ask his advice, but she was pretty sure he'd tell her not to do anything.

Doing nothing was no longer an option. The edgy feeling was rapidly metamorphosing into acute anxiety.

It was impossible to wait. She had to know.

Robyn's apartment was the last one at the end of the first-floor hall. It was no doubt locked, too. But she had noticed that Robyn usually left her bedroom window open during the day.

She went outside and followed the sidewalk around to the back of the building. The storage locker that contained gardening and pool equipment partially concealed the open window. She took another quick look over her shoulder. There was no one around to witness her somewhat less than legal entry.

She reached into her bottomless tote and found the small tool kit she always carried with her.

It was no trick at all to pry the screen out of its aluminum frame.

She gathered her nerve and swung first one leg over the window ledge and then the other.

The first touch of the dark energy was no worse than what she had encountered in Arcadia's office and at the show house.

Not too bad. She had been prepared for it. She could deal with it. An exultant sense of relief flashed through her. She wasn't the crazy one, after all.

She stood on the carpet near the window and studied the bedroom.

To describe the space as spartan in design would have been to understate the painful precision with which the minimal furnishings were arranged. The narrow bed, with its crisply folded white spread, was eerily reminiscent of a patient bed at Candle Lake.

She looked across the room at the small chest of drawers. The photo that had gone missing from the envelope she had left in Arcadia's office stood propped against the mirror. The chili-pepper red mug was positioned next to it.

She took a step toward the dresser. There

was no warning. She blundered straight into a tangle of dense, seething energy.

Panic ripped through her. She was caught in the heart of the spider's web.

The ghastly stuff shrouded her senses, blinding all of them, not just the part of her that was psychic. She was plunged into total darkness. The sudden absence of light was disorienting. She reached out to grab hold of some object of furniture to steady herself and realized that she could not feel anything through her fingertips.

Terror arced through her. She had to get out of there. But how could she do that when she could not see, hear, touch or feel? She willed her legs to move but had no way of knowing if they got the message.

She was trapped in a waking nightmare. She would go mad if she did not regain her senses. She opened her mouth to scream for help but could no longer hear so she had no way of knowing if she had even made a sound.

She flailed wildly at nothing for what seemed an eternity, fighting the cloaking static. She knew she had to regain control or she would be lost forever in this terrible darkness.

She remembered how to shut out the low-level stuff. The technique for getting through this mess couldn't be all that much different. It was all about fine-tuning the energy flow and finding harmony in the patterns.

Feng shui of the mind.

Slowly, painfully, exerting every ounce of will and psychic energy she possessed, she forced back some of the static. Gradually some of the dark vibes faded and fell away.

Without warning, the light came back. So did the rest of her senses. She was aware of the rough feel of carpet under her hands and realized that she had fallen to the floor.

She opened her eyes, weak from her internal struggle, and looked toward the doorway of the bedroom.

Robyn Duncan stood in the opening. She had a pistol in her hand.

"You could have knocked," Robyn said.

Ethan stood behind Singleton and looked at the computer screen.

"Nice job getting into those files," Ethan said absently. Most of his attention was focused on the one name that stood out from all the rest.

"No problem," Singleton said. "Radnor's

computer security is an off-the-shelf program. Any halfway decent hacker could get through it in about fifteen minutes."

"Only took you five."

"That is because I'm way better than halfway decent."

"True."

Singleton tilted his head slightly. The light from the screen glinted on his glasses. "What made you think that the person who invaded Arcadia's office and Zoe's library might work for Radnor?"

"Harry mentioned that he got sidetracked by a Radnor guard the other night at Fountain Square. He said security guards make him nervous because they can go anywhere without drawing attention and they've usually got access to keys. It occurred to me this morning that Radnor handles security for the show house neighborhood as well as the square. Someone with a Radnor uniform who knew where the keys were kept and who also knew the security layout could get in and out of both locations without leaving any tracks."

"Okay, I'm impressed."

"It was a long shot," Ethan admitted.

Singleton leaned back in his chair. "So

why didn't you just come right out and ask Radnor for a list of employees?"

"I didn't want to put him into what we in the trade like to call an untenable ethical position."

"Oh, yeah, right. A responsible employer isn't supposed to release that kind of info unless the cops come calling with a warrant."

"Besides, it's a hell of a lot easier this way."

"Sure is," Singleton agreed.

"And, naturally, I've got no qualms at all about invading the Candle Lake Manor files, not after what the folks at that place did to Zoe."

"I'm with you."

Ethan read quickly. "Looks like Robyn Duncan was a patient at Candle Lake for three years."

"Zoe spent a season in hell there. Three years would probably feel like an eternity."

"I'm a little short on sympathy at the moment," Ethan said. "I think Duncan is stalking my wife."

"Got to admit that her presence here in Whispering Springs and her job as the manager of the apartment house where you and Zoe just happen to be living is hard to write off as a coincidence."

Ethan studied the information on the

screen. “When was Duncan discharged from Candle Lake?”

“Looks like she wasn’t.” Singleton scrolled through a couple of pages of data and paused. “Not officially, at any rate. According to this record, she walked out under her own steam last month.”

“Well, hell.”

Singleton squinted at the screen. “Right after you and Zoe went back to Candle Lake and tore the place apart. Things were probably in chaos for a while. My guess is Robyn Duncan just up and left while everyone was running around trying to figure out what was happening.”

“Does Duncan have any family?”

“Let’s see.” Singleton pulled up the admitting sheet. “Nope. Not anymore. But it looks like she inherited a lot of money, and a trustee was appointed to administer the estate. A guy named Ferris. He signed the commitment papers.”

“And then paid Candle Lake Manor to keep Robyn out of sight and out of mind while he went through the assets of the estate, probably.”

“That’s how the system worked there at Candle Lake.”

Ethan scanned the admitting notes and stopped abruptly when he read some very familiar phrases.

. . . Patient suffers from severe auditory hallucinations. . . . Claims to hear voices in walls. . . .

"Oh, shit," he said softly.

Singleton cocked a brow. "Same diagnosis as the one they wrote up when they admitted Zoe, I take it?"

"Almost identical."

42

You never noticed me at Candle Lake, did you?" Robyn said. "Nobody ever noticed me there. Not after the first few months. I stopped trying to tell them that I wasn't crazy. I just shut up and pretended I was invisible. And after a while everyone ignored me. Everyone except for Dr. McAlister, that is."

"That was the trick to surviving at Candle Lake, wasn't it?" Zoe said gently. "Keeping your mouth shut and not making any trouble."

"Three times a week they let me out of H Ward so I could go to the library on the second floor. I passed you in the hall a few times. I could see that the orderlies were taking you to Dr. McAlister's office. That's when I knew that you were probably different the same way I'm different."

"Did McAlister try her tricks on you, too?" Zoe levered herself slowly to a sitting position on the floor. The movement was difficult because so much of her energy and concentration was focused on keeping the clinging spiderwebs at bay. They drifted at the edges of her senses, threatening to envelope her once more.

"Don't move." Robyn's voice rose in panic. The pistol in her hand shook violently.

Zoe held her breath. "It's okay, Robyn. I'm not moving. See?"

After a moment, Robyn regained some semblance of control. "Stay right where you are."

"Tell me about your experience with McAlister."

"I thought she liked me," Robyn whispered. "She was the only one who believed me when I told her that I could sometimes feel things in the walls."

"She convinced you that she wanted to help you, didn't she?"

"Yes."

Zoe sighed. "How long did it take you to

realize that she just wanted to use you for her crime-scene consulting work?"

"I didn't mind helping her. I *wanted* to assist her. Things went okay for a while. I liked the work. It was good to know that I was helping the police catch criminals who deserved to be punished."

"Even though McAlister took all the credit and didn't do anything to get you out of H Ward?"

"She promised me that when I was ready, she would get me released from Candle Lake."

"But you were never quite ready, right?" Zoe asked. "Good old McAlister. She never had any intention of getting either of us out of Candle Lake. She wanted to keep us right where we were so that she could continue to run her experiments and tests on us."

Robyn blinked several times. The hand holding the gun trembled so violently Zoe feared she would pull the trigger by accident.

"The problem was that I started having my little brainstorms," Robyn said.

"Brainstorms? Do you mean the spiderweb stuff?"

"What are you talking about?" Robyn demanded. "There are no spiderwebs."

"There's something here in this room. It feels like a sticky kind of energy. I found it in Arcadia's office and in the library at the show house, too."

"You're lying. I can't sense anything."

"Probably because whatever it is came from your own mind," Zoe said. "Haven't you noticed that, while we can sense emotions left behind by other people, we don't pick up the traces of the energy that we ourselves leave in a room?"

Robyn sighed. "I always wondered why that was. Sometimes when I was alone in my room at Candle Lake I would be so frightened, so angry. But afterward I never sensed any of those things in the walls."

"It's the same for me. I guess it must be some sort of natural defense mechanism." Zoe paused. "Tell me about your brainstorms."

"I can feel them when one is coming on, but then everything gets distorted and I blank out for a couple of minutes."

"Like a seizure?"

"Yes, I guess so. When I come out of one of the storms, I feel okay again but I can't remember what happened during the dark time. When I first started having the brainstorms I thought it was a sign that my psychic sense was growing stronger. Maybe because I was working with McAlister. She often gave me drugs before she ran her tests. I told myself I was responding to them."

"She tried those meds on me, too. I hated the feeling they gave me."

"So did I. But I told myself that if they worked it would be worth it. Then, I had two brainstorms in two different sessions and McAlister freaked."

"What happened?"

Robyn's mouth trembled. "The first one wasn't too bad. At least, I didn't think so. It only lasted a few seconds. But I guess I knocked something off Dr. McAlister's desk and fainted. The next one was a little stronger. She told me later that while I was in the dark period, I smashed a lamp. She had to summon the orderlies. I guess I scared her."

"Good for you. She deserved it."

"She decided that I was going crazy. I saw the notes that she made in my file. She concluded that I wasn't strong enough mentally to handle my psychic sense and that it was driving me mad."

"Why did you come here to Whispering Springs?" Zoe asked.

"I followed you here. Don't you see? When

you escaped from Candle Lake I realized that, unlike me, you were strong. I wanted to be in control like you. At night after you left I used to lie awake wondering where you were and what you were doing. When I heard the orderlies say that you were dead I didn't believe them. I told myself that you had tricked them all and I was glad, *glad.*"

"You are strong, Robyn. You had to be in order to survive Candle Lake."

"I survived, but I couldn't stop the brain-storms. They got worse. But then you and Ethan Truax came to Candle Lake a few weeks ago, and afterward everything changed."

"Is that when you escaped?"

"I just walked out one day," Robyn said simply. "No one tried to stop me."

"And you came looking for me?"

"I thought that if I watched you and studied you, I might be able to figure out how you control your psychic sense so that it doesn't destroy you."

"Why didn't you just tell me who you were and why you wanted to meet me?" Zoe asked.

"Because of the storms," Robyn said sadly. "I didn't want you to know that I was going crazy. I thought that if you found out, you might worry that I would contaminate you or something."

"Why did you go to the show house and to Arcadia's office?"

"One was a place where I knew you had spent some time with your closest friend. I've never had a friend like that. I wanted to know how it felt to have that kind of connection to someone else. I went to the show house because I wanted to feel the influence of your creativity."

"There was no TV repairman, was there?" Zoe said. "That's why you couldn't give us a good description of him. He never existed. You just wanted to get your hands on a key to my apartment so you could go inside and soak up some of my vibes."

"I wanted to know how it felt to live a normal life with a man." Robyn's voice broke on a sob. "I've never dared tell any man the truth about myself. I wanted to experience how it felt to be in love."

Zoe looked at the dresser. "Why did you take the photo and the mug?"

"I thought that if I had some things that belonged to you, I might be able to use them to help me concentrate and focus. I didn't take anything valuable. It wasn't stealing. Not really. I just sort of borrowed them. I didn't think you would miss them very much."

"You broke that pen in Arcadia's office. And the vase in my library."

"Those were accidents." The gun trembled again. "I had one of my . . . my seizures in both of those places. The pen and the vase got broken during the storms."

Zoe could see that Robyn was getting more agitated by the second. The gun could go off at any time.

"It's all right," she said soothingly. "I understand."

"No, you don't understand." Robyn seemed to grow strangely calm. "Because you're strong. You have no clue what the brainstorms are like."

"Yes, I do. I can feel the aftereffects right here in this room. I sensed you once or twice back at Candle Lake Manor, too."

"I came here because I wanted to watch you, to learn from you. But I see now that it's no good. I'll never be strong like you."

"Killing me won't put a stop to the brainstorms."

Robyn seemed puzzled by that observation. "Of course it won't."

"Robyn, put the gun down. I want to talk to you."

"It's too late to talk. There's nothing you can say that will help. You shouldn't have come here today. I was getting ready to do it when I heard you come through the back window. If you hadn't interrupted me, it would have been over by now."

Comprehension descended on Zoe. "Robyn, listen to me."

A shadow shifted in the doorway behind Robyn. Ethan glided silently through the opening, his gun in his hand.

She tried to signal him with a tiny movement of her head. To her relief he appeared to get the message. He stopped a short distance behind Robyn.

"Goodbye, Zoe," Robyn said. "I had hoped that we could be friends someday but I know now that's not possible. Why would a strong person like you want to be friends with a weak one like me?"

Robyn turned the gun toward herself and opened her mouth.

"No," Zoe said, desperate now. "Please don't."

"It's better this way. As long as there was hope that I could learn to control the brainstorms, it was okay. But they're getting worse, Zoe. And I can't bear the thought of going crazy."

"I understand. But I'm asking you not to do it for my sake." Zoe got slowly to her feet, fighting the tendrils of dark energy. "Please don't."

"I told you, I'm not going to hurt you. I never wanted to do that."

"You'll hurt me if you kill yourself. You can't imagine what a relief it is to know that you exist, Robyn. I just wish we had met back at Candle Lake. I'll bet it was McAlister who made certain that we never did. She wouldn't have wanted us to get to know each other because it was easier for her to manipulate us if we each thought that we were alone in the world."

"I can't help you, Zoe. I'm going crazy."

"We don't know that for sure."

"Dr. McAlister said—"

"McAlister was a manipulative liar and a quack who was only out to use you. Did she run any real medical tests on you?"

"She tried lots of drugs."

"If they were the same drugs she used on me, they weren't meant to help you. Please don't kill yourself. Because if you do, I'm going to have to wonder if that's what's waiting for me. Maybe someday I'll want to stick a gun in my mouth, too."

"No," Robyn said tightly. "You'd never do that. You're too strong."

"Nobody is perfectly strong. Look, I'll make a deal with you. Give the doctors a chance to see if they can figure out what's causing your brainstorms."

"When I tell them I sense things in the walls, they'll say I'm crazy. They'll send me back to Candle Lake."

"I won't let anyone send you back to Candle Lake. I promise you that. As for the doctors, we won't tell them you're psychic. We'll just say you're having blackouts. Maybe whatever is going on has nothing at all to do with your sixth sense. You owe it to yourself to find out for sure before you take this final step. You owe it to me, your friend."

Unwilling hope flared in Robyn's eyes. "You'll come with me to talk to the doctors?"

"Yes. I give you my word."

Robyn stood there, frozen.

Ethan reached out and deftly removed the gun from her fingers. She did not even seem to notice. She put her hands over her face and started to weep.

Zoe pulled her close and hugged her until the last of the tears had fallen.

When Robyn finally raised her head there was resignation and a deep sadness in her eyes.

"When they find out that I might be crazy and that I came from Candle Lake Manor, Mr. and Mrs. Shipley will fire me," she whispered. "I'm going to miss this job so much. I feel that I was born to manage Casa de Oro."

43

"Robyn is scheduled to undergo surgery?" Arcadia lowered the tiny espresso cup. "When?"

"Day after tomorrow," Zoe said. "Ethan and I plan to drive into Phoenix so that I can be with her when she wakes up."

It was just after ten. Fountain Square was thronged with enthusiastic shoppers. The morning was sunny and warm.

"I'll bet she's scared to death." Arcadia shuddered. "I certainly would be at the thought of brain surgery."

"She is frightened, but not nearly as scared as she was when she thought she was going insane. I was with her when they went over the results of the CAT scan and the MRI with her. She started to cry. You should have seen the doctor's face when he realized that she was crying in relief, not because of the diagnosis."

"Probably never had a patient shed tears of joy after being told she has a brain tumor," Arcadia said.

"Probably not. Naturally, we didn't try to explain. We just told him that we were both enormously relieved to know that he considered it operable."

"You never mentioned the psychic thing?"

"No. As soon as he did the tests he said he was almost one hundred percent certain that the tumor was causing Robyn's seizures. He said it had probably been there for a long time."

"Benign?"

"He won't commit until he gets the lab results back after surgery, but he told us that it had all the hallmarks of a type of slow-growing tumor that is, technically speaking, fairly simple to remove."

"Personally, I find it mind-boggling to hear the words 'simple' and 'brain surgery' in the same sentence, but I suppose everything is relative."

"Well, there are plenty of surgical risks, of course. But to tell you the truth, now that her worst fears have been put to rest, Robyn's biggest concern is losing her job."

"Born to manage the Casa de Oro." Arcadia shook her head in wonder. "Imagine that."

"You want to know the really scary part? She's actually pretty good at it. The place has never looked better, and every apartment is rented." Zoe drank some tea. "Nevertheless, I'm glad that Ethan and I will be moving out soon."

"Treacher finally promised to send the painters into Nightwinds?"

"They started at seven o'clock this morning. Ethan drove to the house to make sure the men showed up for work."

"What about the color?"

"Ethan says he's not feeling too particular about the exact shade anymore." Zoe grinned. "He just wants the place finished so we can move back into our home."

The hospital walls screamed. But that was par for the course with hospitals, Zoe reminded herself. She wouldn't be there long. Visiting hours were kept to a minimum on this ward.

"You okay?" Ethan asked in a low voice.

They turned the corner into the hall where Robyn's room was located.

"I can handle it," Zoe said. "I just hope Robyn's psychic abilities have returned to normal."

Ethan shrugged. She was amused to see that he was dealing with Robyn's claim to a sixth sense the same way he dealt with hers. He could accept that something out of the ordinary was going on with both of them, but he did not feel the need to delve into metaphysics to explain it.

Maybe he was right, she thought. Who could say for certain where the boundaries between intuition and true psychic sensitivity lay?

It occurred to her that she was getting rather laid back about the issue herself.

The wait for Robyn to come out of surgery the day before had seemed endless. She and Ethan had spent most of the time on the patio outside the surgical waiting room because she couldn't take the bad vibes inside for extended periods.

The surgeon had appeared eventually to tell them that the operation had gone well.

But when they went to visit her a few hours later, it soon became apparent that Robyn wasn't doing well at all.

"I can't feel anything, Zoe." Tears welled up in Robyn's eyes. She clutched Zoe's hand very tightly. "This is a hospital. I should be sensing all kinds of things in these walls. But it's all blank."

"You just went through brain surgery, for heaven's sake. Give yourself a chance to heal."

Zoe had spent most of the night hoping that she was right and that Robyn would eventually regain her psychic senses. But the truth was, they were in uncharted territory.

One thing was for certain; she had no plans to ask the neurosurgeon for his opinion about the effects of post-surgical trauma on psychic senses. Dr. Grange appeared to be a good man and an excellent surgeon, but not everyone had Ethan's ability to balance on the fine edge that separated the highly improbable from the absolutely impossible.

She and Ethan walked through the door to the room. The first thing Zoe noticed was that Robyn, her head swathed in bandages, was smiling as she lay ensconced on the white pillows. Got to hand it to a woman who could look that cheerful after brain surgery, she thought. Robyn definitely had what it took to be a professional apartment house manager.

The second thing she saw was that Robyn was not alone. An elderly, gray-haired couple stood beside the bed. The man was leaning heavily on a wheeled walker. The woman teetered on a cane. Diamonds the size of automobile headlights glittered on her gnarled fingers.

"Zoe, Ethan." Robyn winced a little as she turned her head to greet them but her eyes were bright with pleasure. "Meet Mr. and Mrs. Shipley. They're the owners of Casa de Oro."

"How nice to meet you, dear." Mrs. Shipley bobbed her head graciously.

"We were just telling Robyn that she's not to worry about her position as the manager of the Casa de Oro," Mr. Shipley said. "We're going to hold it open for her."

"We had our driver take us to Whispering Springs yesterday so we could have a look at the property," Mrs. Shipley confided. "Couldn't believe the improvement. We had been on the verge of putting it on the market, you know. But not anymore."

"Robyn is far and away the best manager we've ever had at that complex," Mr. Shipley said. "The last thing we want to do is lose her."

"I'm sure Hooper in one-B will be thrilled to hear that," Ethan said.

There was movement in the doorway. Zoe turned around and saw a bouquet of flowers that was so large it blocked the entrance. The man holding the vase peeked through the stems, looking uncertain of his welcome.

"Speaking of Hooper," Ethan muttered.

"Uh, hi." Hooper moved awkwardly into the small room and found space for the large vase on the windowsill.

"Mr. Hooper." Robyn's smile was radiant. "You came all the way from Whispering Springs just to see me?"

"I, uh, heard you had surgery. Didn't know you were sick." Hooper grimaced. "I went into the hospital for some major surgery a couple of years ago. I know how it feels." He motioned toward the giant flower arrangement. "I, uh, thought you might like those."

"They're beautiful. No one has ever brought me flowers. I don't know what to say. Thank you."

Hooper grinned, pleased with the reception of his gift. "Yeah, sure. You're welcome."

Zoe cleared her throat. "How are you feeling today?" she asked.

Robyn made a face but her relief was obvious. "Everything's back to normal, just like you said." She rolled her eyes at the nearest wall. "I can't wait to get out of here."

Zoe chuckled. "I know what you mean."

44

Singleton leaned on his counter and looked at Jeff and Theo. Both boys wore unusually serious expressions.

"What's wrong?" he asked.

"We think you should ask Mom out on a date," Theo said.

"Yeah." Jeff's face scrunched up with fierce concentration. "You could take her to a movie or something."

He thought about that for a long time. "You're sure?"

"Yeah," Theo chimed in. "You could take us with you, if you want. We could have pizza before the show."

"Don't be so dumb," Jeff said to him. "It won't be a real date if we go with them."

"Why not?" Theo whined.

"We go with them for pizza all the time and it's not a date," Jeff explained.

"Oh." Theo did not appear to be too depressed by that news. He shrugged it off. "We can have pizza with Uncle Ethan and Zoe, instead."

The shadows in the bookshop lifted. Warmth and light spilled into the small space, driving out the gloom.

Singleton realized that he was grinning like a fool, but he didn't care.

"Works for me," he said.

Zoe stood in the center of the gracious, white-on-white master bedroom suite. She had to admit that the finished space was impressive and quite beautiful in its own way.

"Congratulations, Lindsey, you've created a remarkable room. Very harmonious and tranquil."

Lindsey did not move out of the doorway. Her expression was cautious "But not your style, right?"

Zoe turned toward her. "No, but that

doesn't mean I can't admire a work of art when I see one."

"You're serious, aren't you?" Lindsey replied.

"You've got a real talent," Zoe said sincerely. "What's more, I think you're the right designer for Tabitha Pine. She's into this kind of look. I'm not. I've decided that I won't present a proposal to her, after all."

Lindsey shifted uneasily. "We both know that you could give her what she wants. You're a pro. You don't have to love the look to create it for someone else."

"In most instances, I'd say that was true. But Tabitha is different. She needs a finely tuned energy flow in her home, especially in that meditation room. You're more sensitive to her requirements than I am." Zoe shrugged. "Besides, I've suddenly got my hands full. A couple of the architects who came through on the tour yesterday want me to meet with some of their clients."

Lindsey nodded, relaxing a little. "I got a lot of positive feedback from some of the people on that tour yesterday myself."

"Looks like all this work we did here will prove to be worth our while." She glanced at her watch and started toward the door. "If you'll excuse me, I'd better get moving. I promised my husband I'd meet him for lunch."

"Zoe, wait."

She paused. "What is it?"

Lindsey appeared to be having trouble deciding just what she wanted to say.

"I think your library turned out brilliantly," she finally muttered. "I was wrong about all those intense colors. They really work in that room."

Zoe could see that Lindsey was struggling. But she was trying to be nice. That counted for a lot.

"Thanks."

"I'm sorry if we got off on the wrong foot," Lindsey continued slowly. "It's just that this project and the Pine job were very important to me."

"It's all right."

"In the past my interior design work was more or less a social hobby. I was fashionable because I was married to a man who wielded a lot of clout in LA." Lindsey's mouth twisted wryly. "People lined up around the block to kiss his ass."

"I understand."

"I enjoyed designing but I didn't have to make a living at it. It was one of those things women in my world did. Some arranged important dinner parties. I did the homes of stars and entertainers."

"Lindsey—"

"But after my divorce, I lost everything. All of my big-name clients deserted me. I was suddenly nobody because I was no longer married to the man whose ass had to be kissed. It was then that I finally realized that if I wanted something to call my own, I was going to have to create it myself." Her mouth tightened. "I've been obsessed with proving that I could make a new life without my husband and his influence. I wasn't sure I could do it, you see."

"How did you decide to settle here?"

"I wanted to start over in a place that had no connections to my ex or his friends. I love the desert. So I more or less threw a dart at a map and here I am."

"Join the crowd." Zoe smiled. "Just about everyone I know came to Whispering Springs to start over. It's a good place to begin a new life. You'll do fine."

45

Walter Kirwan's beautifully restored study was crammed with Whispering Springs dignitaries, members of the Historical Society and a sprinkling of Kirwan scholars and enthusiasts. The patio doors had been opened to allow access to the reporters, photographers and television cameras.

Zoe stood with Bonnie, Arcadia, Harry and Singleton at the back of the room. Jeff had managed to wriggle his way through the throng to get a front-row position. Theo was perched on Singleton's shoulders.

Zoe could only catch glimpses of Ethan. He was at the other end of the long study, standing next to Mayor Santana in front of the massive stone fireplace.

Dressed in a khaki green shirt and black trousers, he appeared amused by the small media frenzy going on around him. She blew him a kiss over the heads of the crowd. He winked.

"If I may have your attention," Paloma Santana said in authoritative tones.

Everyone immediately hushed and turned toward her. Zoe noticed that Nelson Radnor and his wife had managed to squeeze into the room. She saw that Nelson had his arm around Daria's shoulders. Daria looked very happy.

"Welcome to the Walter Kirwan House," Paloma said, speaking into a microphone. "Thanks to the efforts of a great many people in this community, it has been restored as nearly as possible to the way it looked when Kirwan lived and wrote here. Before we get to the mystery, I'm going to ask Professor Millard Cottington, a noted Kirwan scholar, to give you some background."

Professor Cottington, looking every inch the distinguished academic, took the microphone and rambled on for several extremely boring minutes about the importance of Kirwan's contributions to literature. He finally got to the exciting stuff.

"The exact cause of Kirwan's death has been a matter of conjecture and gossip for years," he intoned. "But it was the disappearance of his last manuscript that has proved the most frustrating aspect of the mystery for those of us who have devoted our careers to the study of his work. The possibility that it was stolen, rather than destroyed, on the night of Kirwan's death has intrigued all of us. Many are watching today to see if Ethan Truax, a private investigator with no expertise in Kirwan's work or in American literature in general, can solve a mystery that has baffled two generations of Kirwan scholars and collectors."

How dare he make Ethan sound like an uneducated gumshoe, Zoe fumed, hissing softly.

"Down girl," Arcadia murmured.

At the front of the room Ethan took center stage, clearly unfazed by the professor's condescending remarks.

"There are really only three possibilities here," he said easily. "The first is that the manuscript was stolen and disappeared into the private collectors' market. I ruled that out after my associate, Singleton Cobb, an authority on antiquarian books, conducted an extensive investigation of the underground collectors' market and found no trace of the missing manuscript."

He nodded at Singleton and everyone turned around to look at the biker dude with the kid on his shoulders at the back of the room. Singleton smiled and turned red. Theo grinned proudly.

Professor Cottington's face clouded in a troubled frown. *Take that, you condescending, elitist twit,* Zoe said to herself. Evidently Cottington had never considered that there might be an expert in rare books in Whispering Springs.

"The second possibility," Ethan said, "is that Kirwan burned the manuscript on the night of his death. His last words to his housekeeper could certainly be interpreted to mean he intended to do just that. Most scholars, including Professor Cottington here, have assumed that is the most probable answer."

Cottington nodded sagely.

"The difficulty with that explanation," Ethan said, "is that the housekeeper, Maria Torres, told her family on several occasions through the years that she saw no trace of what must have been several hundred sheets of typing paper in the ashes the next morning. In fact, she always claimed that there was no indication that any fire had been built that night."

Cottington's white brows snapped together in obvious annoyance. He cleared his throat portentously.

"I would like to remind everyone present that the housekeeper's story was never verified and that there is some question about her veracity," he said loudly.

Paloma's elegant profile went taut but she did not speak.

"Maria Torres happens to be an excellent witness," Ethan told the crowd. "She had a history of stable employment with Kirwan. He evidently trusted her, and those who knew her best maintained that she was an honest, hardworking woman whose word could be taken to the bank."

"She also knew that she was in Kirwan's will," Cottington sputtered. "She stood to inherit this very house."

"As we all know, the will was contested and she got nothing," Ethan said. "But that's beside the point. What matters here is that, even if your assumption was true, you're left with the fact that her only interest would have been the house. She had no particular use for the manuscript. If she had taken it, she would have sold it."

Cottington glowered. "What is your conclusion, Truax?"

"My conclusion is that the manuscript is still here."

There was an appropriately dramatic gasp from the crowd. Cottington's jaw dropped visibly. Zoe heard Bonnie chuckle.

Ethan produced two long-handled screwdrivers. "I could use a little help here. I'd like to ask the other private investigator in town, Nelson Radnor of Radnor Security Systems, for some professional assistance. Nelson? Would you mind? This will go faster with two of us."

Zoe glanced at Nelson and saw a startled expression cross his face. But he recovered quickly.

"My pleasure." He took his arm off Daria's shoulder and made his way through the crowd. "What have you got in mind?"

"After eliminating the other possibilities, it occurred to me that Kirwan really did feed his manuscript to the fireplace, but not to the flames, as everyone assumed." Ethan handed one of the screwdrivers to Nelson. “You take the right side, I’ll take the left. Start tapping.”

Nelson raised a brow as he took the screwdriver, but he merely nodded.

Excitement erupted in the room as Ethan and Nelson began systematically tapping the stones. The cameras moved in closer. Journalists fired questions.

“You think there’s a secret safe somewhere in that fireplace?” the reporter from the *Whispering Springs Herald* asked, holding out a microphone.

“I think it’s the one explanation that fits all the facts in this case,” Ethan said.

He rapped a series of stones. Each gave off the flat sound expected from a solid chunk of rock. On the opposite side of the hearth, Nelson went through the same exercise. He got the same response.

Ethan moved up a row and struck a large gray stone directly to the right of the heavy wooden mantel.

Unlike the others, it produced a distinctly hollow tone.

The entire room fell silent.

Nelson stopped tapping and looked at Ethan. “That sounded interesting.”

“Let’s have a look.” Ethan moved his fingertips around the edge of the stone. "I'm betting there will be a spring mechanism somewhere. What do you think, Radnor?"

"I'd say it's a very, very good bet there's a spring mechanism there somewhere," Nelson said, smiling. His eyes glinted with amusement.

Ethan probed a little more. Then he reached under the mantel.

"Here we go," he said softly.

There was an audible click. The stone that had sounded hollow when it was tapped slowly swung open.

"Uncle Ethan, look," Jeff shouted from the front row. "There's something inside."

The crowd broke into wild applause. Reporters hurled more questions. Professor Cottington stared, dumbfounded.

Very carefully, Ethan reached into the hidden safe and removed a large leather box. He set it down on Kirwan's desk and looked at Paloma.

"Would you care to do the honors, Mayor?"

Her smile illuminated her dark eyes. "I'd be delighted."

She unfastened the latch and raised the lid. For a couple of seconds she just looked into the box. Then, very carefully, she reached inside and removed what appeared to be a ream of paper.

"Canyon Visions," she read aloud.

A murmur of wonder went through the room.

"There are two manuscripts in here," Santana announced. She took out another bundle of paper and glanced at the title. "*Light of a Desert Dawn,* by Walter Kirwan."

"I don't believe it," Cottington roared. "Let me see those manuscripts."

Paloma handed both bundles to him. "Of course, Professor. Be my guest."

Cottington examined the two manuscripts. "These will have to be authenticated. Tests will have to be run on the paper, the ink, the writing style."

"Certainly," Paloma agreed.

Gradually Cottington's outrage and disbelief turned into reverent awe. "If these are real," he whispered, "this is an absolutely extraordinary event in the history of American literature. Extraordinary."

The gang went out for pizza that night. Zoe had watched the evening news with Ethan a short time earlier and she was still fuming.

"I can't believe that the local station went with Professor Cottington's quote about an *extraordinary event* as the lead-in," she said. "They had no business giving him so much airtime. They should have used a quote from you, Ethan. Instead, all we got was about two seconds' worth of you and Nelson Radnor tapping on the fireplace."

"Yeah," Theo said around a mouthful of pizza. "They hardly showed Uncle Ethan at all."

"How come they let that professor do so much talking?" Jeff asked. "He wasn't the one who found the manuscripts."

Ethan helped himself to a wedge of pizza. "Glory is fleeting."

"Who's Glory?" Jeff demanded. "Where did she flee to?"

"Never mind." Ethan munched pizza. "It's complicated."

Bonnie looked at him across the table. "Okay, I've just got to ask. You didn't really leave that big discovery to chance, did you?"

"I'm a PI, not a magician," Ethan said. "Of course I didn't take any chances. I got the key from the mayor the night before last and went over to the hacienda with Zoe to take a look. We did a little tapping and got lucky."

"Ethan's very good at solving old mysteries, so it was no big surprise when he turned up the missing manuscript," Zoe said. "It was finding the second one inside that leather box that really blew me away. Think of the impact on the literary world. Not one but two unpublished Kirwan manuscripts."

Harry contemplated that. "You think they're for real?"

Ethan shrugged. "We'll have to leave that to the experts, but judging from the dust we found inside that fireplace safe, it's safe to say no one had opened it since the night of Kirwan's death."

"So Kirwan did die of natural causes?" Arcadia asked.

Ethan nodded. "That's obvious. If Maria had poisoned him, she would have done something with the manuscript. She knew it had value. At the very least she would have tried to sell it to the agent."

"Unless Kirwan hid it before he collapsed from the effects of the poison," Harry mused. "Obviously Maria didn't know about his secret safe."

Ethan shook his head. "Zoe and I took a look at the manuscript. Kirwan noted his changes in red and dated them that night. It looks like he spent several hours going through the book before he hid it. Maria Torres was a housekeeper, not a professional hit lady. Most of the common poisons that she might have had access to in those days would have been very fast-acting. Furthermore, they would also have produced some fairly obvious and messy results that would have been noticed by the authorities."

"So Maria Torres is cleared on all charges," Harry said.

"Yes, but something tells me Professor Cottington is going to hog all the credit for finding those manuscripts," Zoe grumbled.

Singleton chuckled. "So what? Ethan scored a whole bunch of points with the mayor of Whispering Springs. Got a feeling that's going to be a lot more useful to him in the long run than getting his name into the textbooks."

"Just doing my civic duty," Ethan said.

Zoe looked around the table. "Not to change the subject, but Treacher promised me this morning that his crew would be finished with the kitchen and the great room at Nightwinds by the end of the week. What do you say we all do Thanksgiving there this year?"

There was a chorus of cheerful agreement.

Ethan met Zoe's eyes across the table. He smiled at her. She smiled back and he was almost certain that he could feel the positive energy of happiness in the air.

After dinner, Singleton drove Bonnie, Jeff and Theo home. Arcadia and Harry announced that they were going to spend the evening at Last Exit.

Ethan got into the SUV and looked at Zoe. "What do you say we go out to Nightwinds and see how far the painters got today?"

"Okay."

The big house was cloaked in moonlight. Ethan parked in the drive and got out.

Together he and Zoe went inside and made their way across a sea of drop cloths to the kitchen.

"Look," Zoe said. "They finished in here." She turned to him, eyes alight with pleasure. "What do you think about the color now?"

Ethan stood in the doorway and studied the kitchen with its newly painted walls.

An eerie tingle of awareness stirred the hair on the back of his neck. The sensation lasted only a couple of seconds but during that brief span of time he could have sworn that a scene shimmered in the air in front of him.

He saw himself sharing breakfast with Zoe at the table near the window. Two small children, a boy and a girl, sat with them, laughing at some unheard joke. Their crayon drawings were taped to the refrigerator. An unmistakable aura of love enveloped the kitchen.

The image dissolved in the next instant, but he knew deep inside that even though he wasn't psychic, he'd just had a tiny glimpse of the future.

"The color works just fine," he said. "I knew it would. After all, you're an expert."

"Hah." She put her arms around his neck. "You had your doubts, admit it."

"Okay, maybe I was a little worried about the paint color for a while." He framed her face with his hands. "But I don't have any doubts at all about us."

Her smile was filled with more than enough love to last a lifetime.

"Neither do I," she said.